"Lute, no!"

She pulled back, and he let her go. "Rhetta will be wondering what's taking us so long."

"Okay. I certainly wouldn't want Rhetta to get the idea that I'm out here kissing my ex-wife. It could damage my image of most eligible bachelor." His words were tinged with sarcasm.

"What you're really afraid of is that Miss Home Ec will find out." Her tone matched his.

"You're right. I've got to have someone to fill in when you leave."

She balled her fist, wishing that she had the nerve to hit him.

He reached across her and opened the car door. The interior light came on, and Nelda collected her shoes and purse. Without looking at him, she got out of the car. By the time she reached the porch he was beside her, his hand on her elbow. She wanted to jerk away, but the thoughts rushed in like an ocean wave— last kiss, last touch. . . .

"Garlock, as always, writes a sterling story with characters you want to hear about."
—*Southern Pines Pilot* (NC) on *After the Parade*

Please turn the page for more acclaim for the novels of Dorothy Garlock.

ACCLAIM FOR THE NOVELS OF DOROTHY GARLOCK

❧ *AFTER THE PARADE* ❧

"[A] touching story of two people at cross purposes who struggle to save their marriage and get on with their lives after the Second World War."

—*Romantic Times*

"This story oozes with danger and intrigue. Ms. Garlock keeps the reader rooting for the lovers. . . . A wonderful ending to a terrific series."

—*Rendezvous*

"Fast paced, poignant. . . . No one brings home small-town America in a more picturesque manner than bestselling author Dorothy Garlock."

—**Harriet Klausner,** *Under the Covers Book Reviews*

"A compelling relationship drama. . . . The characters are well crafted. . . . A refreshing tale."

—*Affaire de Coeur*

❧ WITH HEART ❧

"Another winner! . . . Unique touches and continous surprises that keep the reader enthralled and turning the pages . . . *With Heart* is a testament to the human spirit."
　　　　　　　　　　　　　　—Bookbug on the Web

"Four stars! . . . Combines murder and corruption with a sweet, tender love story and compelling secondary characters."
　　　　　　　　　　　　　　—*Romantic Times*

❧ WITH HOPE ❧

"A warm and satisfying love story. . . . Garlock launches a promising trilogy of novels set during the Great Depression. . . . This difficult, dynamic time comes alive in her hands. . . . Always likable characters drive the plot of this vividly depicted romance." **—*Library Journal***

"Garlock tackles Depression-era Oklahoma with wit, freshness, and memorable characterizations."
　　　　　　—*Publishers Weekly* (starred review)

❧ WITH SONG ❧

"This is an excellent book. . . . She writes about the era so well that you really feel you are there."
　　　　　　　　　　　　　　—*Interludes*

DOROTHY GARLOCK

More Than Memory

WARNER BOOKS

A Time Warner Company

WARNER BOOKS EDITION

Copyright © 2001 by Dorothy Garlock
All rights reserved. No part of this book may be reproduced in any form or by any electronic or mechanical means, including information storage and retrieval systems, without permission in writing from the publisher, except by a reviewer who may quote brief passages in a review.

Cover design by Tony Greco
Cover illustration by Franco Accornero
Book design by Milá Ercole

This novel contains portions originally published as *Passion's Song* by Johanna Phillips, published by Jove Publications, Inc.

Warner Books, Inc.
1271 Avenue of the Americas
New York, NY 10020

Visit our Web site at
www.twbookmark.com

W A Time Warner Company

Printed in the United States of America

First Paperback Printing: February 2001

10 9 8 7 6 5 4 3 2 1

To my many friends in Clear Lake, Iowa, my hometown, who helped me remember how it was during the winter of 1958 and 1959.

A special thanks to Nels Larsen, who was the chief of police during that time, and to Iola Cash, who farmed with her husband Bob Cash north of town.

SEASONS OF LOVE

Do you remember the springtime,
When young love was sweet and strong
And we were swept by its promise sublime
Into joy and passion—headlong?

We can never forget the autumn
When anger and venom held sway.
Defaming our love and its outcome
Casting our dreams away.

In sorrow, I felt the winter's breath,
In my arms, my daughter, so cold.
The lonely days passed stark as death
Until my ambition took hold.

It was summer at last when I found you here.
Birds sang when I knew your embrace,
But now you're remote when I am near.
Has a new love taken my place?

That lost spring can come to us once again
Though outside the soft snow falls.
Love stands rapping at the door.
Will you say "yes" when it calls?

—F.S.I.

More Than Memory

❧ Prologue ❧

Clear Lake, Iowa
1949

"I NOW PRONOUNCE YOU MAN AND WIFE."

The young girl, her hand held tightly by the slim blond youth standing beside her, scarcely heard the muttered words of the justice of the peace. Still in a daze, she signed the papers that lay on her grandmother's dining-room table.

"I appreciate your doing this on such short notice." Vaguely, Nelda Hansen (spelled with an *e*) heard her father thank the man he had brought out from town to marry her to Lute Hanson (spelled with an *o*) so that the child she carried would not be born a bastard. His voice reached her as if through a tunnel, but, it pierced her to the heart when he returned to issue a brutal order to Lute.

"Get out of here, you little prick. My lawyer will send you the divorce papers. You'd better sign them damn quick and send them back. Hear me?" Captain Donald P. Hansen was an impressive figure in his Marine Corps uniform emblazoned with a string of medals.

"Nelda, come with me." The boy tugged on her

hand. "Please . . . Nelda," he begged. "We'll get by. I'll take care of you."

"I don't think you heard me!" her father bellowed. "I said get the hell out of here. Take care of her?" he sneered. "You've not got a pot to piss in, nor has your old man. All he knows how to do is scratch in the dirt out on that hardscrabble farm his daddy left him."

"Donald, that's enough," Grandpa Hansen gently admonished, only to be quickly overridden by his son.

"By God I never thought my daughter would stoop so low as to get herself knocked up by a rutting, wet-eared, hog-slopping hayseed!"

"Captain Hansen, Nelda is my wife now. I'll take care of her—" The boy tried vainly to stand his ground against the angry Marine captain hardened by years of experience in intimidation.

"Boy, get this through that dumb head of yours. Don't try to contact my daughter . . . ever. She's not for the likes of you. *You*," he said to the girl in the bobby socks and ponytail who leaned for support against the table, "get upstairs and get your things. We're leaving here in five minutes."

"Nelda, it's now or never. Don't let him do this—"

Through her tears, she saw a big hand clamp down on the boy's shoulder, propel him out the door, and slam it shut behind him. Over the roaring in her ears, she heard Lute's old truck start and, with blurred vision, saw it go past the window. Then her grandma's arm was around her, guiding her up the stairs.

Nelda had always feared her father: his loud voice, his piercing eyes, his forceful manner. All of her life she had lived on or near a Marine base and was used to hearing him issue commands that were immediately carried out. She was programmed to obey him.

Captain Donald P. Hansen had enlisted in the Marines right out of college and had quickly been singled out to attend officer's school. The Marine Manual was his Bible. He lived for the Marine Corps. He had married the daughter of a general, a gentle girl who had given birth to their only child. Three years ago, Nelda's mother had died during a fever outbreak in the Philippines.

When the captain remarried, his second wife understood that a career officer needed to be socially active if he expected to advance in rank. She went with him when he was called on to fulfill a special assignment in the Pacific, and Nelda was sent home to spend the school year with his parents.

Returning to the farm of his youth to introduce his new wife to his parents, he learned that his sixteen-year-old daughter was four months pregnant. He took control of the situation immediately. Twenty-four hours later, the captain, his wife and his daughter were in a car headed for the airport in Des Moines.

1950

On a cold January day, seventeen-year-old Nelda Hanson stood beside her grandparents and Lute's mother at the graveside service for her six-month-old daughter, Rebecca, and wept quietly. She had gained an unwelcome maturity.

Sick for most of her pregnancy, she had given birth to the tiny baby girl who now lay at rest in the black Iowa soil. Her father had insisted that she give the child up for adoption, but for once in her life she had stood firm against him and refused. In the tirade that followed, she learned that Lute's father had been the captain's boyhood enemy. Her father swore he would never forgive her for disgracing and betraying him.

Her stepmother had helped Nelda leave Virginia while her father was away. She had returned with her baby to her grandparents' farm only to discover that Lute had enlisted in the Navy the day after the wedding.

When she learned that Lute had not come by to see her grandparents or to inquire about her and their baby when he'd come home for a brief visit after boot camp, Nelda could not really blame him. He had been treated despicably by her father, and she had been too weak to stand by him. It was plain that he had cut her out of his life and wanted nothing more to do with her. With that knowledge, the dream she'd been harboring that they would meet again someday and renew their love, died a quick death.

Two weeks after Nelda and the baby arrived in Iowa, Becky woke with a high fever and had to be rushed to the hospital. Nelda's grandmother had insisted that Lute's mother be told, and Mrs. Hanson had come to the hospital and at last held her only grandchild. During the hours Nelda sat with her beside the baby's crib, Mrs. Hanson had been careful not to give out any information about Lute.

When the doctor told her that there was little hope her baby would survive, Nelda felt guilty for bringing the baby across country.

"Don't blame yourself," the doctor said. "The infection had long been in the little one's bloodstream and would have run its inevitable course even had she stayed in Virginia."

After the funeral service, Nelda told her grandparents that she was determined to start a new life far from her father and stepmother. Deeply disappointed in their only son for his insensitivity and his harsh treatment of his daughter, the old couple had lavished their affection on Nelda. With their support, she had been able to enroll at the University of Chicago.

The pain of the past could not be erased, but the future held hope and challenge. Nelda was ready to begin her new life.

❦ Chapter One ❦

August 1958

SHE WAS HOME. SHE HAD LIVED IN CHICAGO FOR quite a few years, but she had always considered Iowa as her home.

Over the years since she last had been here, she'd forgotten how hot and sultry it was in summer and how high the country roads were graded to allow the winter's snow to blow off and into the ditches on each side. She'd forgotten the miles and miles of cornfields, though she was once again amazed at how corn could be knee-high by the Fourth—a farmer's standard for a good crop—and be well over six feet tall in time for the county fair in the middle of August.

Nelda drove slowly through Mason City, remembering marching down Federal Avenue with the Clear Lake High School Band on Band Festival Day. Lute had met her, and they had sneaked away to eat a hamburger before she had to board the school bus back to Clear Lake.

She passed the fairgrounds, where acres of cars and stock trailers were parked, and the grandstand, where rodeos were held. A Ferris wheel was spinning, and pennants were fluttering. During her other life, she had been there, holding tightly to Lute's arm as they strolled toward the cattle barns. Lute had loved to hang around the stock pens, looking at the champion stock and talking to the boys who were exhibitors.

Lute. How long had it been? Eight years? She could scarcely think of herself living that other life.

"Want to get out, Kelly?" she said, hearing a whine from the back seat. "I'll find a place for you." Turning off at a crossroads, she drove a short distance and stopped. When she opened the car door, the big Irish setter jumped to the ground, shook himself, then went the few steps necessary to reach the tire, where he hoisted his leg.

"My tires will be rotten by the time we get to the farm," Nelda complained as she stroked the dog's head when he returned to her. "But what the heck! You've come all the way from Chicago in this old car. I know you're tired of being cooped up. It won't be long now. You're going to think you've died and gone to heaven when you see all the space you'll have to run in."

She drove the eight miles into Clear Lake singing Elvis Presley songs to Kelly. When Kelly lifted his nose and howled, Nelda said, "You don't like the hound dog song? How about 'Heartbreak Hotel'?" Kelly howled again. "You don't like that one either? What's the matter with you, dog?"

She reached Clear Lake, turned down Eighth Street, and drove past Central School.

"This is where Grandpa went to school, Kelly," she said to the dog. "It's old. Grandpa said it was built back in 1912. The redbrick building at the end of the block is where I went . . . for only a year. On the steps of that building, Lute asked me to go out for the first time. I was afraid Grandpa wouldn't let me go, but he liked Lute, and he said I could. I just had to be back by ten-thirty."

She turned on Main Street and angle-parked in front of Jensen's, the grocery and meat market where her grandma used to trade. When she had called her grandpa's lawyer, Mr. Hutchinson, and told him that she was coming, he had assured her that the house would be ready for occupancy and that all she had to do was bring her personal belongings and stock the refrigerator.

At the motel the previous night, she had made a list . . . several lists. At times she thought that she lived by lists. She took the grocery list from her notebook and got out of the car.

"Stay here and watch things, Kelly."

"Arrr-woof," was the answer.

Nelda was greeted by one of the clerks when she entered the store, then little attention was paid to her. The merchants were used to strangers in the summer because the lake, one of only a few in Iowa, attracted tourists. She quickly filled the cart with what she needed to get by for a few days, wheeled it up to the counter, and waited to be checked out.

"Here for the big dance?" the clerk asked.

"What big dance?"

"At the Surf Ballroom. The Everly Brothers will be here tonight."

"I didn't know that."

"Are you from around here?"

"Chicago."

"Ah . . . Chicago. I thought you might have been in before, but I guess not."

"I've been here off and on. I used to come in here with my grandma, Mrs. Eli Hansen."

"Ah, Freda Hansen, she was a dear soul."

"Yes, she was."

"Ah, then, you're . . . Donald Hansen's daughter. He was a couple of grades ahead of me in school. Ah, let's see, your bill is six dollars and sixteen cents."

While the woman bagged the groceries, Nelda dug in her purse for some bills, wondering if the woman could talk without saying . . . ah.

"Careful, the eggs are on top," the woman called, as Nelda pushed at the screen door with her backside and went out to the car.

She drove slowly down Main Street, past the Corner Drug, then the two blocks to the lake. During the WPA days a wall had been erected along the lakeshore at the foot of Main Street. People sat on it now, watching the fishermen on the long dock that stretched out from the boat ramp. Children played in the grassy space in front of it and in the square that was City Park.

Turning back from the lake, she headed out of town, eager to see the old farmhouse that was now hers. It had been a long drive from Chicago, and she was exhausted; but the trip had helped her unwind from her last job of creating a totally new decor for one of Chicago's most expensive nightclubs.

The road she traveled ran parallel to the lake, which had fourteen miles of shoreline. Nelda breathed deeply, savoring the cool fresh air blowing off the water. She turned off at a gravel road.

On the crest of a hill she caught her first glimpse of the white frame, two-story house with the glassed-in front porch and the long-paned windows. It was set back from the road on a grassy knoll bordered on the north by a thick grove of cedars and on the west by a cornfield. East of the house she could see the rambling hedge of lilac bushes and, behind it, the big red barn and the tall silo. The most pleasant times of her childhood had been spent on this farm.

The car bumped over the rutted lane. When she reached the house, she pulled around behind it and parked alongside the back porch as Grandpa used to do. The doors of the barn and the other outbuildings were closed. Wheel tracks were visible where someone had driven in through the barnyard to the corncrib—the man who rented the land, no doubt.

She sat in the car and looked out over the yard. It had been neatly mowed and the bushes trimmed. A piece of heavy rope—all that remained of the swing Grandpa had made for her—hung from the big elm tree. She was glad that her friendly giant had survived the Dutch elm disease that had swept this part of the country. It looked as sturdy as ever, but somehow it didn't seem as huge as it had when, as a child, she'd peered up into its branches.

"We're home, Kelly," she said softly. "No Grandma or Grandpa to greet us. I miss them so."

As soon as she opened the door, the dog scrambled out and began dipping his nose to the ground to sniff all the new, exciting smells. Nelda climbed the steps to the door of the back porch, fumbled in her purse, and found the key to the house the lawyer had sent her.

Her eyes misted when she entered the kitchen and looked around the familiar room. Everything was clean, the tile floor shining, the windows sparkling. She smiled when she spotted the big refrigerator/freezer—one of her grandma's concessions to "modern conveniences," the other being the electric stove. On the kitchen table lay a note that said the boxes she had sent ahead were on the front porch.

Nelda went to the door and called Kelly in before she inspected the rest of the house. Enraptured by the natural scents of grass, trees, and warm earth, the dog took his sweet time responding to her whistle.

"You're a city mutt," she scolded, as he trailed into the house. "You'd better stay inside until I can go out with you. This is a different world, fella. No telling what trouble you'd get into out there. You might even scare up a skunk. Now isn't that a frightening thought?"

His tail between his legs, Kelly looked adequately chastened, sulking like a disappointed child.

He definitely was not happy to be called into the house. He pressed his wet nose against the clean windowpane and looked out, something he couldn't do in their high-rise apartment in Chicago.

"Look at it this way, dog. We'll be here for at least six months. You'll have plenty of time to explore the countryside. So come on, wag your tail and let me know you're happy that I'll have time to work on my textile designs."

Kelly wagged his tail halfheartedly, then he turned back to gaze with longing at the grove of thick evergreens and underbrush.

The steady hum told Nelda that the refrigerator, next to the range, was running. On the other side of the room was the wood-burning cookstove that Grandma had refused to give up. Memories of freshly baked bread from that old stove assailed her. It kept the kitchen toasty warm in the winter. Nelda sighed. The best and the worst times of her life had been spent right here in this house.

On her first trip to the car she brought in the groceries. She put away the perishables, then lugged in the two large suitcases that almost filled the trunk of her cream-colored 1954 Ford.

By the time she finished the unloading, her back hurt, two of her long, beautiful nails were broken, and her shirt was glued to her body with sweat. She tried to run her fingers through her hair, but it was a mass of damp curls. Grimacing, she remembered the years when she'd wanted it long and straight so that she could have a beautiful, flowing ponytail like that of her friends. Now it was short and artfully

styled with every second wave cut so that it no longer
resembled a curly metal pad used to scrub pots and
pans.

In her old room, she made her bed, using the
freshly laundered sheets she found in the chest in
the hall. Nelda reminded herself that she must compliment Mr. Hutchinson for the excellent job. Her
grandmother's linens, towels, dishes, everything was
as neat and clean as if her grandmother had done it
herself. Grandpa Hansen's land had been rented, but
the house had been closed and left just as it had
been when her grandparents lived in it.

The bathroom off the kitchen—converted from
a pantry so necessary to the houses of eighty years
ago—was roomy, and it was charming. The old-
fashioned fixtures included an oak commode with a
towel bar across the top. Peeling off her clothes,
Nelda filled the claw-footed bathtub with warm
water and eased her slender frame down into it.

Kelly nosed open the door and padded into the
room. He tilted his head and looked inquiringly at
Nelda.

"It's a far cry from the big tub in the apartment,
isn't it, fella? But we'll get used to it. All that peace
and quiet out there is going to be a blessing for both
of us. I hadn't realized how easy it was to lose sight
of goals in the hustle and bustle of the city. Here
I'll have plenty of time to rest and think and decide
what direction my life should take now."

After her formal education, Nelda had been invited to join an interior-decorating firm, where she
had quickly established herself in the field of com-

mercial decorating. Her last job had cemented her status among her contemporaries, and had left her more than solvent for a while. She had decided that it was an ideal time to take a leave of absence and pursue an unfulfilled dream of trying her hand at textile design. The perfect retreat was the farmhouse her grandparents had left her.

Only by coming here, she had reasoned, could she make a decision about whether or not to sell the farm. She pushed to the back of her mind the fear that unpleasant memories might stifle her creativity and make her unable to work. Here for a short time, she reminded herself, she had been wonderfully happy and free of the burden of being the daughter of the dreaded Captain Hansen.

During the past eight years her thoughts had often returned to little Rebecca and to Lute. How different her life would have been if her father hadn't torn them apart. As far as she knew, Lute was still in the Navy. Did he ever think of her and the child he had never seen? His mother would have told him that his baby had died. Did he grieve just a little bit for that wee life he had helped to create?

Two years after they buried Rebecca, Nelda's grandmother had died, and her grandpa followed her a year later. Nelda had come back for both funerals. Both times she had seen Mrs. Hanson, but had learned nothing of Lute.

Her father, stationed overseas when his parents had died, had not come back for either funeral. Nelda had neither seen nor heard from him since she and her baby had left Virginia, which was all right with her.

She was doing the best she could to forget the damage her father had done to her life.

❧ *Chapter Two* ❧

NELDA WORKED AS IF POSSESSED. AT THE END OF the day, she was pleased that the boxes she had thought would take forever to unpack were empty, folded flat, and stored in the shed. Her books were arranged on the long oak library table in the living room, her record player was set up, and her work-bench and supplies were in place on the glassed-in front porch.

She had even spent an hour in the yard gathering plants, leaves, and wildflowers for possible use as patterns for her designs. Her aching muscles attested to the fact that she alone was responsible for these miracles.

By night she was so tired that she opened a can of soup for herself, then bathed and got ready for bed. She missed seeing the evening news, a program she watched regularly in Chicago.

"Kelly, do you suppose they sell television sets in Clear Lake?" she muttered to the dog at her heels as she headed up the stairs to the haven of the four-poster walnut bed. "I wish I hadn't sold mine. Oh, well, it was too heavy for me to load in the car anyway."

Waking early the next morning out of the deep sleep of the righteously weary, she heard a stock truck rumble past the house before she jumped out of bed to attack the new day. This was a special day, Becky's birthday, and this year she was here in Clear Lake to put fresh flowers on her daughter's grave.

As she ate buttered toast and drank her coffee, she wrote out her list of things to do. Go to florist, cemetery, buy TV, washer, and dryer, go to telephone office, see Mr. Hutchinson.

Since she planned on calling on the lawyer who handled Grandpa's estate, she dressed up a bit in a sleeveless yellow dress with a tight bodice and a full skirt, slid her bare feet in high-heeled sandals, and went to the back steps.

"Kelly. Come." She waited a minute, then called again. After a little while she went around the side of the house and whistled. Kelly came loping toward her from the lilac hedge, his ears flopping and his nose covered with black dirt.

"For goodness sake! What have you been doing? If it was safe to do so, I'd leave you here."

"Arrr . . . woof!"

"Well, get in the car. I swear that this country living has gone to your head."

After rolling down the back windows so that Kelly could poke his head out, she drove down the lane to the road and turned east toward the greenhouse across from the cemetery.

*　　*　　*

This was crazy! It had to be here, right on the far end of the plot. The lush grass was just as smooth as if it had never been disturbed, but there was no marker that read: REBECCA LOUISE HANSON. The marker for Grandpa and Grandma was there, so this had to be the right plot.

Nelda's heels sank into the spongy turf as she walked around the plot where her ancestors were buried. Hansens all—Hansens with an *e*. There were at least ten graves in the plot, surrounded by a low stone divider. A large marker proclaimed the Hansens one of the first families to settle this rich Iowa farmland.

Puzzled, Nelda scanned the names on the row of small headstones set on a concrete base level with the neatly manicured lawn, then read them again to be absolutely certain what she was seeking was not there.

Her heart pounding, Nelda stood clutching a slender parcel of flowers while she fought for control. Unbelieving, she stared at the spot where her daughter should be buried, choked back tears, and blinked against the glare of the sun. A weak breeze ruffled her curly dark hair, and she pushed it back from her forehead.

As she looked across the lawn dotted with markers toward the custodial building, a man came out the door and bent to work on a large power mower. The scolding of a blue jay from its perch in an evergreen tree reached into Nelda's consciousness, its squawk almost surreal in the stillness.

In a daze, she walked toward the workman, trying to push aside the thought that she was losing her mind. Becky had to be there, in that spot! Her grandfather had given her the plot, and he had bought the small stone for the grave.

She reached the man as he stood to wipe his hands on a greasy rag.

"Mornin', ma'am."

"Morning." Nelda was so breathless she could barely speak. "I'm Nelda Hanson. I'm terribly confused. My relatives are the Hansens down there." She lifted her arm to point at the large granite monument. "I haven't been back here for a long while." Tears sprang to her eyes. "She was buried in that plot, but she's gone. My daughter . . . Rebecca Louise Hanson. It would have been her birthday today."

"Well . . ." The man continued to wipe his hands, obviously uncomfortable at witnessing Nelda's distress. "Well . . . now, I've been working here only a couple of years. What's the name again?"

"Rebecca Louise Hanson . . . with an *o*. All the Hansens down there are spelled with an *e*. We put her there . . . she was only six months old."

"Was there a stone on the grave?"

"A small one." Nelda felt as if she were in a hollow tunnel, her own voice echoing distantly in her ears.

"Well . . . maybe if you looked around . . ."

"Where else would I look?" She felt the hysteria rising again.

"Well . . ."

Distraught, she was sure if she had to stand before this blank face another minute, she would scream with exasperation.

"All the records are down at the city office, but— wait a minute—hey, Walter." A man wearing overalls emerged from the utility shed.

Nelda looked at him as if he were a lifeline, her anxious eyes clinging to his weathered face.

"Do ya know anythin' about a Rebecca Hanson . . . with an *o* . . . bein' buried down there with old Eli Hansen and his bunch?"

Sharp blue eyes raked Nelda's face. "You mean Lute Hanson's little girl?"

Nelda's heart plunged wildly. "Yes, yes. Lute's and . . . mine." The voice that erupted from her throat was cracked and breathy.

"Well . . ."

Dammit! Couldn't they say anything, but *well*? She clamped her mouth shut to keep from yelling at them.

"Lute had her moved a long time ago. Right after old Eli died."

"Moved her?" She opened her mouth, closed it, opened it again, and gasped. "Where?"

"Over yonder in the new part." The man in the overalls raised his arm. "It's been a long time. Five or six years . . ." Nelda murmured her thanks and started walking in the direction of his pointed finger.

"It's a long way," the other man called after her. "Clear up against the fence at the far end. Maybe ya ought to drive up there."

His words were soon lost to Nelda as she hobbled quickly in her thin-soled sandals over the bumpy, narrow, cobblestone lane past Sorensons, Andersons, Jacobsons, and Olsons, some with an *e* and some with an *o*. She absently noticed how well the grounds were kept, how quiet and peaceful it was. It was fitting that the only sound was a mourning dove cooing its lonely call.

At this end of the cemetery the walk curled around carefully plotted flower beds of colorful petunias backed with a border of chrysanthemums. The trees were young and vigorous, and the snowball bushes thick with glossy leaves.

Reaching the last section, she walked along until she saw a long, low marker of dark granite with simple straight lines. It had the look of eternity about it, and carved in the stone was the name: HANSON.

Nelda stumbled toward it. Two smaller markers were set in the ground to the side of it. One read: REBECCA LOUISE HANSON, daughter of Lute and Nelda Hanson. The next line was a date span of only six months. A box overflowing with sunny yellow marigolds sat snugly against the small marker.

The words on the other marker hit her like a dash of cold water. LUTE HANSON.

Lute! Nelda felt her strength draining. She swayed closer, then realized that only the date of his birth was carved in the stone; a blank space was left for the other date to be filled in when he was buried here. Relief made her knees weak.

Nelda stood with her head bowed, a strange calm replacing her panic of moments before. After a few minutes she knelt down beside the grave, losing herself in silent reflection.

Becky would have been eight years old today and in the second grade at school. Would her hair have been brown and curly like mine, she wondered, or blond and straight like Lute's? She'd had Lute's blue eyes, and the little fuzz on the top of her head had been blond, but it might not have stayed that color as she grew older. She had been such a sweet, good baby, crying only when she was hungry or wet or tired.

Oh, Lord, it had hurt so when she lost her little one.

Why had Lute moved Becky here? It must have been a blow to his pride to have a grave space and a marker for his child provided by someone else. But what else could she have done?

With her toes and knees cushioned in the soft grass, Nelda placed the gladiolas, still swathed in protective green tissue, on the ground. They were the only pink flowers the florist had. Peeling away the wispy layers of paper, she realized that the stems of the flowers were far too long for the glass vase she had brought for them.

Nelda dug into her shoulder bag to find a nail file. Then, as she sawed away with the crude cutting tool, memories flooded her mind. Her senior year of high school here had been the happiest year of her life, especially after meeting Lute. They had spent every spare minute together, going to the basketball games, riding the roller coaster and roller-skating at Bayside Park. They had sat in his old pickup truck at the Lighthouse drive-in and devoured root beer floats. And on special occasions, when Lute could afford it, they had gone to a dance at the Surf Ballroom.

Nelda-and-Lute. Their names had been linked into a single phrase by their classmates. Of course, they accepted without question, that Nelda and Lute would spend their lives together. How wrong that prediction had been.

Absorbed in her task and her memories, Nelda was completely unaware anyone was nearby until out of the corner of her eye she glimpsed large scuffed boots and the legs of faded work jeans.

She scrambled to her feet to face the man standing silently on the other side of her child's grave. She felt as if every drop of blood in her body had drained to her toes. Speechless, she opened her mouth to draw in a gasp of life-saving air.

Lute?

Could this big, muscular man be the lanky boy she had married when she was sixteen and he was eighteen? It could be no one else. His thick blond hair glistened in the sunlight. It was trimmed close at the sides, the top combed back. He had not adopted the flattop or the ducktail hairstyles so many men were wearing nowadays. His shoulders looked a yard wide in the short-sleeved, faded work shirt. In one hand he clutched a bouquet of flowers. Bright blue eyes were fastened to her face.

"Hello, Lute," she whispered, unable to speak normally.

When he just stood there staring, saying nothing, she had to stifle the wild impulse to reach out and touch him, to verify his physical presence. Finally, he spoke.

"What brought you here?"

She lifted her shoulders, trying to encompass a world of explanations with the silent gesture. She wished he would stop looking at her.

"Why did you move her?" she asked, startled by her own bluntness.

"Why not?" he replied evenly, as if she'd posed the most commonplace question in the world. "She was my daughter. As soon as I had enough money, I bought a plot of ground and buried her in it. I sent your grandpa's estate lawyer the money for the marker."

Even his voice was deeper and stronger than she remembered. This man didn't resemble the soft-spoken boy who had stood valiantly beside her when she told her grandparents that she was four months pregnant.

"You could have notified me."

"You could have notified me when my baby died. Didn't you think I'd be interested?"

"How can you say that? I knew your mother would let you know."

"I say it because you never made any attempt to communicate with me. You shut the door firmly in my face just as if the baby you carried wasn't mine." His face was suddenly harsh and powerful, his jaw jutted in angry determination, the mouth curved downward, reflecting his contempt for her.

Stunned by his outburst and grasping in a flash

of sudden clarity how badly they'd each misread the other's withdrawal, Nelda sprang to the defense.

"I was sixteen, and I was sick—"

"You didn't protest once. If you had come with me when I begged you to, things might have been different. Your daddy considered me white trash and shoved me out of your life not ten minutes after we were married, and you let him."

"It wasn't what I wanted—"

"—Five days later I got the divorce papers."

"You signed them fast enough. Daddy said you were glad to be rid of me." Relived anguish tore at her heart.

"And you believed him. I don't suppose he told you that I had tried to call you. He knew that I was in the Navy and said that if I called again, I would hear from my commanding officer. I was a kid then, too, and his threat scared the hell out of me. He said the only thing I had to give you was a baby in your belly and an *o* in your name."

"Oh, Lute. I'm . . . sorry."

Nelda almost reeled from the force of his bitterness. His words hit her like stones. She knew her face had paled, and she looked away from him. Her gaze fell on the grave of their child, and all the sweet, bitter memories came rushing back. During the dark days of her pregnancy and after Becky was born, she had held out the hope, even after Lute had signed the divorce papers, that he would come to her, that their love was strong enough to overcome her father's objections. Then after a while she'd had to reconcile herself to the fact that their time together was over.

"Are you trying to make me feel guilty, Lute?" Fairly quivering with torment, Nelda looked directly into his eyes. "I've never blamed you for anything. Even at sixteen, I knew the chance we were taking when we made love. I've never regretted it for a second. You and the baby were my life. For the first time I had something of my very own, something that had nothing to do with my father." Tears filled her eyes, and she tried to blink them away.

Not since Becky's death had she felt such crushing anguish. She wanted to hate Lute for being here, for bringing back the heartache she had tried so hard to overcome, but hate wouldn't come. Instead, she remembered his tenderness when she told him she was pregnant, and how he had held her and promised to love her and take care of her and their baby for the rest of his life. A big promise for a skinny boy of eighteen with only his mother and a not-too-reliable father for a family.

Then she remembered their wedding day. How awful it had been! Her father had made what should have been the sweetest, most sacred moment in her life . . . dirty and degrading. He had ranted and raved, calling her a slut and Lute a randy whoreson. He had said that *he* would be disgraced if it became known that his daughter screwed around in a haystack like a common whore.

Nelda put her hands on each side of her head in an attempt to squeeze out the thoughts.

She looked up to see Lute studying her. Looking deeply into his eyes, she tried to read the emotions flashing across his features. For a moment she thought that he was on the verge of tears, but then he was down on his knees, his fingers raking some dead grass away so he could place his bouquet next to the marker.

Through a blur of her own tears Nelda watched his capable movements. She remained standing, the full weight of what was happening holding her in place. She saw the sun glisten off the blond hairs on his forearms, and her gaze traveled down to his hands. The glint of a wedding ring caught her eyes.

Lute had remarried. A wave of sickness surged through her. She should have expected it. Eight years had given him plenty of time to meet someone and fall in love.

Lute! Oh, Lute, with the windblown hair and the sun-browned neck, where did our love go? Do you ever think of that time so long ago, when we couldn't be near each other without touching, and when our eyes would cling to each other, even across a crowded room? We had to be together every possible minute in those days. I remember. Oh, I remember, my love, my only lover—

Lute stood abruptly and looked down at her, his face shuttered once more. She instantly dropped her gaze to the flowers at her feet.

"You'll need water for those. I'll get some." He pried his hand into the pocket of his jeans, brought out a jackknife, and opened it. "Here. You can cut the stems with this," he offered, almost gently.

Nelda took the tool from his hand without looking at him and knelt to work on the flowers still lying spread out on the waxy florist paper. Her fingers were shaking, and she could hardly hold the knife, but she managed to cut the stems. Her mind was still in an eddy of confusion when she finished and bunched the flowers to fit into the vase.

Lute returned and poured a generous amount of water from a coffee can into both the box of blooming marigolds and her vase. Without a word he took the knife from her hand and dug a hole beside the marker for the vase, anchored it securely, then picked up the stem ends she had cut and dropped them in the can.

When he stood, Nelda stood beside him.

"I didn't remember that you were so tall."

"I've done a lot of growing during the past eight years, both in mind and in body. A man grows up fast when his wife is jerked from his arms ten minutes after they are married. And when she has his child, and he never even gets to see it."

During this crisp, clipped speech Nelda stood quietly, only her eyes moved, looking quickly away from him and back again.

"Can't you understand what a strain I was under? I was sixteen and I was sick—"

"You were old enough to have a baby." He paused, a pained expression crossing his face. "Old enough to sue for a divorce," he added, his words as brittle as icicles.

"Stop! I've had to live for eight years with what my father did. He told me that you wanted nothing more to do with me." In her frustration she yelled the words.

"You could have found out for yourself. But it's

over. Over and done with." He flung the last words
over his shoulder and walked rapidly toward the black
pickup truck parked in the lane.

"Over for you maybe," she whispered. "It will
never be over for me."

❧ Chapter Three ❧

NELDA LOOKED DOWN AT THE GRAVE ONE LAST time before she turned and headed back to her car. She felt as if all the strength had been drained out of her, but she stiffened her back, determined to hold her head up . . . at least until she passed Lute.

Lute put the can into the back of the truck and stood waiting for her to reach him.

"How did you get out here?"

"My car is over there . . . where I thought Becky would be."

"Get in. I'll drive you over. You look as if you're about to melt into a puddle."

Nelda hesitated, then said, "Thanks."

By the time she reached the passenger side of the truck, Lute had flung open the door. The step into the cab was high, but she grabbed on to the door handle and pulled herself up. It had been years since she had been in a pickup, and never one as nice as this one, with its red-leather seats and black-rubber floor mats. She thought of the battered old pickup Lute used to drive when they were going together.

They'd driven that old truck to Clausen's Cove, a remote beach on the lakeshore, and made love for the first time.

Nelda rushed into speech, not wanting to remember.

"Is your mother well?"

"Fine."

"My father's married for the third time. He divorced his second wife. She was all right. She's the one who helped me leave Virginia and bring Becky back here to Grandma's."

"I was aboard ship when I got word about your grandparents. I liked them both. They were decent folk."

"They liked you, too."

"Is that your car?"

"Yes. Oh, my goodness. I forgot about Kelly! I bet he's dying for a drink of water."

Disregarding Lute's quizzical glance, Nelda popped out of the truck and hurried to her car.

"I'm sorry, boy. I forgot it would be so hot in there."

Kelly shot out the door the minute it was opened and put his nose to the ground to explore the vicinity.

Nelda heard the truck door slam, then saw Lute getting the coffee can from the back.

"Come on, boy," he called. "Let's get you a drink."

Kelly happily bounded after Lute across the lawn to the water hydrant and waited patiently for the can to fill. He lapped the water greedily.

Nelda watched them, hardly believing that it was Lute who was there with her dog. Lute. In all her dreams she had never imagined that he was anything but an older version of that thin, blue-eyed boy with the shy smile. Discovering that he was now a virile, rugged, terribly handsome man sent her already confused senses into a reeling revolution.

When the pair returned, Lute dropped the can back into the truck and stood staring at her, looking as though he were about to speak.

What could he say to the sophisticated career woman who had barged into his life again? Suddenly he felt uncomfortable at having just taken over— driving her back to her car, tending to her dog. He was angry with himself for rehashing the past. Enough talk! He turned and got into the cab, immediately starting the engine.

"Thanks," Nelda said, just as the truck began to move.

Lute raised his hand in a salute and drove on down the lane toward the gate. He had not expected their first meeting would be at the cemetery. Seeing her had been like a blow to his gut.

Hutchinson had told him about her success in Chicago, that she had not remarried. He had said that she was coming back for a while and would decide then if she was going to sell the farm. Lute had not been prepared for the fact that she was no longer the slender, shy girl whose eyes seemed too large for her face. She had been so timid back then and so starved for affection that it had invoked a protectiveness in him the first time he saw her. Just a kid himself, he had wanted to put her in his pocket and take care of her. Instead, he had let his passion get the better of him and had ended up leading her into trouble they were both too young to handle.

She had the rounded figure of a mature woman now. He remembered the first time he had touched her breasts. They had been the small breasts of a fifteen-year-old, scarcely a handful. Their lovemaking had been so sweet, so all-consuming, so beautiful. But all that had been a lifetime ago. He had just had his twenty-seventh birthday. Nelda would be almost twenty-five. Hard knocks had made her stronger. She was no longer that timid girl.

All the old hurt had come bubbling up when he saw her. He had come down on her pretty hard. In a way he understood why she had acted as she had. A lifetime of being intimidated by that arrogant bastard had beaten her down . . . and she had been just a kid.

That's all water over the dam, he told himself as he turned into the driveway of his farm home. Still, he hadn't been prepared for losing all his brainpower when he looked down on that mop of curly hair and realized it was . . . *her*.

Lord, how he had loved that girl. She had been like food and water to him. When her father had shoved him out the door that day, he had cried all the way to their favorite picnic spot at Clausen's Cove and had sat there in his old pickup for hours. Finally, he had gone home to tell his worried mother that he had decided to join the Navy.

The service had been good for him. He had grown

up, learned that there are all kinds of people in the world: some good, some bad, and some arrogant sons of bitches like Captain Hansen, although Lute had not met one to compare with him.

When his four-year enlistment was up, Lute had come back to bury his father and to farm the land that had been in his family for many years. He sponsored a 4-H chapter, enjoying mentoring kids who would someday be farmers. He had refereed a few basketball games, was active in the Lions Club, had his horses, his bike, and a few close friends. He had been fairly content with his life . . . until now.

Nelda watched until the black truck passed between the stone pillars, then got into her car and called to Kelly. The dog was reluctant to come, and she had to call several times. Finally, he jumped into the car and she closed the door.

Automatically she put the car into gear and drove out of the cemetery. She followed the county black-top to the graveled road leading to the farm and turned in at a rusty tin sign that proclaimed: 4-H MEMBER LIVES HERE.

"We'll have to do something about that sign, Kelly," she observed tiredly, fondling the dog's ears. "We'll have to put up one that says: POOPED INTERIOR DESIGNER AND HOUND DOG LIVE HERE." The setter nuzzled her arm and made a swipe at her face with a wet tongue.

Not until she had parked the car behind the farmhouse and turned off the motor did she remember the list she had made that morning. Kelly's eyes were fixed on the lilac bushes, and he was whining to get out.

"Okay, fella. We'll go into town after lunch."

Nelda stood on the back porch steps and watched the dog, his tail wagging, his nose to the ground. He ran around the side of the house, then back, chasing a squirrel until it ran up the oak tree. He continued to bark at it as it scampered high into the branches. At least her dog was happy, Nelda thought with a touch of self-pity.

She picked up an apple on her way through the kitchen to the front porch. She sank down in the wicker rocking chair and looked out across the lane to the field of tall corn. All her attempts to put Lute from her mind were futile. She kept seeing the ring on his finger. *I never had a wedding ring.* She wondered what type of woman he had chosen for his wife and if he had bought her a plain gold band to match the one he wore?

Why did it hurt after all these years to picture him with someone else? She had thought of him off and on over the years, not continually, because she had become resigned to the break between them. But not a day had passed that she wasn't reminded that she had given birth to his daughter. A child playing in the street, an advertisement in a magazine, or a program on television always pulled that memory sharply into focus.

For a long time the pain of remembering Becky had been powerful enough to double her over, but gradually she was able to recall the pleasures of motherhood as well. She sometimes wondered if she'd ever experience those joys again.

After she was told that Lute was eager to be rid of her, she had tried to close her mind to him, to pick up the threads of her life, and, by keeping busy, to hold thoughts of him at bay. She had managed quite well at first. She had the baby to occupy her thoughts, then school, and finally her career. Now the magic, the inexplicable magnetism of him, was drawing at her. Contentment would be impossible now if she stayed here.

She'd always felt that she would see him again . . . someday. But now, on her second day back, he had come barreling into her life again, blasting all her cool philosophizing.

And he was married.

She didn't understand why she was surprised and why she even cared. Something was terribly wrong with her character if just the thought of him with someone else, making love to another woman as he had made love to her, made her heartbeat escalate, her palms grow moist, and a dull ache settle in the middle of her body.

Disgusted with herself, she went to the door to throw out the apple core. It opened at her push. It was unlocked! She pulled it closed and locked it with a click. She was sure that she had locked it last night before she went to bed, and she hadn't come out to the porch this morning.

Grandma and Grandpa never locked the doors. She doubted they had a key. That was then. Times had changed. Living in Chicago, where break-ins were a common occurrence, had taught her to keep doors locked.

On her way back through the house, she paused at the big oak coffee table and looked down at her picture album. Had she left it there? She must have, she thought, and picked it up to put it back on the shelf under the library table. Oh, well, with so much on her mind, it was a wonder she didn't forget where she had left her head.

After repairing her makeup and combing her hair, she locked the back door and went to the car. Kelly was nowhere in sight, but she could hear excited yelps coming from behind the shed.

"Kelly. Come," she called.

When there was no response, she walked across the yard to the shed to see Kelly digging fiercely in the ground in front of the door.

"Stop that!" The dog looked up at her and whined. "I'm leaving, and if you want to go you'd better get in the car or you'll stay here locked on the porch. Now come on."

She waved her hand and the dog, with his tail between his legs, walked beside her to the car. Before he got in he looked back at the shed.

"Arrr . . . woof!"

"There's nothing in that shed but Grandpa's old harnesses and things like that. Nothing to eat, except maybe a mouse, and you have never eaten a mouse in your life." She opened the car door. Kelly jumped up onto the backseat and sat down on the blanket she kept tucked over the seat cushion.

Nelda drove directly to Mr. Hutchinson's office.

She parked the car, leaving the windows partially open for Kelly.

"Don't let anyone get in the car. That's your job until I get back."

"Arrr . . . woof."

"I'm glad you understand. Be back soon."

Inside the office she was greeted by a pleasant gray-haired woman who smiled at her when she came in.

"May I help you?"

"I'm Nelda Hanson. I'd like to see Mr. Hutchinson."

"Have a seat, and I'll tell him you're here."

The receptionist left the area and Nelda settled in a chair beside the window. Almost immediately the woman was back, followed by a tall man whose face was young and unlined though his hair was iron gray. He wore a dark suit, a white shirt, and dark red tie.

"Mrs. Hanson." He came toward her with an outstretched hand and a smile on his face. "We meet at last."

"I'm glad to meet you, Mr. Hutchinson. After our many phone conversations, I feel that I know you."

"The same here. Come on back to my office."

They walked down the hall to the large office at the back. The lawyer offered her the chair in front of his desk, then went around and sat down.

"Are you settled in? Did you find everything all right?"

"Yes and yes. Thank you for making it so easy.

The house and all in it was in perfect order. I had no idea what condition it would be in after being vacant for so long. I was pleasantly surprised."

"I have good people who checked on it from time to time. When you called to say that you were coming, they cleaned it thoroughly."

"They did that all right. Even lined the drawers with fresh paper before the clean linens were put away. I appreciate it. Will the cost be taken out of the farm account?"

"Yes. The farm has made money the last few years. I invested some of the profit for you, and you have a tidy sum on hand."

"I don't think I'll need to draw on it. I'll be all right money-wise for a while."

"It's available, as are the books anytime you want to look them over or have an accountant do so."

Earl Hutchinson leaned back in his chair and studied the woman seated before him. He had not pictured her as being so pretty. For a woman so young, she was well thought of in her profession. When he had talked with her on the phone she had been all business, quick and firm in what she wanted. He liked that.

"I've heard from your father . . . several times, in fact."

"Oh, dear. Hearing from my father is never good news."

"He wants to buy the farm now that he has given up on breaking Eli's will."

"Why does he want it? He hated the farm. As long as I can remember, he was ashamed that his

father was a farmer. He would refer to him as own-
ing farms . . . plural. At times he would talk about
the Hansen Estates, again plural."

"As your lawyer, I feel I can speak frankly. Major
Hansen—"

"Oh, he's a major now?" Nelda said with a sarcastic tone in her voice. "It took him long enough.
He's been trying for it for years."

"Yes, well, the major was considerably put out
when his father left the farm to you. He did all he
could to break the will, but it was airtight." Mr.
Hutchinson pulled open a drawer on the side of his
desk and brought out a file. "He says that when it
goes on the market, he wants a chance to bid on it."
He placed a letter on the desk in front of Nelda.

"I don't want to read it, Mr. Hutchinson."

"He was foolish enough to ask me not to tell
you he wanted the farm. I'm your lawyer, not his."

"I've not made up my mind about selling. I'll
be here for six or eight months. It depends on how
long my boss in Chicago will hold my job. There
wouldn't be much of a demand for a commercial
decorator around here."

"There's another party here who is interested in
buying the farm if you decide to sell. Eli wanted you
to sell to a local person rather than a conglomerate,
you know. The farm was clear of debt when you in-
herited it. Eli left money to pay the inheritance tax.
You can sell the farm and invest the money, or keep
it and rent out the land. In a few years land may go
up in value. Either way you will have a nice little
income."

"I'll think about it. If you answer my father's letter, tell him that I don't intend to sell, and if I do, it won't be to him." Nelda stood, her face frozen in lines of determination. "If there's nothing else to discuss, I'm off to buy a television set. I miss watching the evening news."

Mr. Hutchinson stood and followed her down the hall.

"You can get a television down the street at Clear Lake Appliance, or go over to Sears in Mason City, where there's a larger selection."

"I'll need an antenna installed."

"You can arrange that with the appliance store. If not, let me know. I've got a handyman who will do the job. By the way, I notified Bob Halford down at the telephone company to hook up your phone and to send out a desk phone. The one on the wall has been there since the Civil War."

Nelda laughed. "Well, not quite, but almost. Thank you. I was going to the telephone office next. You've saved me a trip."

"If there's anything I can do, let me know."

"I will. Thank you. Mr. Hutchinson, who is renting the land?"

"Lute Hanson."

"Lute?"

"When Oscar Olsen sold out and went south, Lute asked to rent it. His land is next to yours, and he's a damn good farmer. The land produced more this past year than it ever has. Lute rotates his crops. Corn one year, soybeans the next. Is that a problem?"

"No problem. I was just curious. Who cleaned up the yard and trimmed the hedge?"

"Lute or his hired man."

Nelda heard Kelly barking as soon as she stepped out the door. She hurried to where she had parked the car. A woman had backed away and stood looking at Kelly.

"Don't put your hand in the car," Nelda warned anxiously.

The young woman turned and smiled, her big brown eyes sparkling and amused. Though a bit plump, she radiated a wholesome charm with her fresh complexion and shining brown hair.

"I know better than to do that. Your dog is beautiful and so protective."

"He thinks the car belongs to him, and he'll not allow anyone in it if I'm not here."

"I thought I knew every Irish setter in the area." Her eyes widened when she looked at Nelda. "Well for goodness sake! I can't believe it. You're Nelda Hansen. Remember me, Linda Sharp?"

"Linda?" Nelda's brows puckered, then she smiled in sudden recognition. "Of course. Linda from my homemaking class."

"I know. I know. I've gained weight."

"It's been such a long time—"

"I'm so glad to see you." Linda suddenly, impulsively, hugged her. "I've thought about you."

"You were my closest friend, Linda. I'll never forget that."

"You didn't have much time for girlfriends, if I

remember right." Linda's brown eyes teased. "You only had eyes for Lute in those days."

"Those days are over, Linda. What about you?"

"I married a fella from Ventura and have a five-year-old boy. I'm Linda Branson now. I'd love to hear about all you've been doing. I saw your picture once in a magazine, and I was so proud that I knew you. Do you have time for a Coke?"

"Sure. Where can we go?"

"Corner Drug okay? I've a weakness for fountain Cokes."

Thirty minutes later, Linda was walking with Nelda back to her car.

"You've seen Lute?"

"Yes, I've seen him."

"Good-looking devil, isn't he?"

"He is that."

"I'm sorry about your little girl. I never even knew that you and Lute had married, or about the baby until after it died and you had left here."

"It was . . . sudden. Lute was in the Navy. We were already divorced."

"Yeah." Linda sighed. "You two were . . . so in love."

"And . . . so young," Nelda said laughingly, although she felt like crying—remembering.

They reached the car and Kelly allowed Linda to stroke his head. "He's a beautiful dog. We have two setters," Linda explained. "One English, one Irish. Kurt likes to hunt."

"I've had Kelly three years. He was a year old when I got him from a coworker who was moving into an apartment that didn't allow pets. He is my best friend. We talk to each other, don't we, boy?"

"Arrr . . . woof!"

Kelly's eyes were on his mistress's face, and his tail was beating a tattoo against the back of the seat.

"Do you need to get out and water the tires?

In answer, Kelly's tail went faster.

"All right. You can get out for just a minute. We're going to see about buying a television set. After that, we'll go to the grocery store and then home. That's what you want, isn't it?" She didn't stop to think that Linda might think she was slightly wacky talking to a dog as if he were a person.

"He's very well trained. Too bad husbands don't train as easily," Linda said with a short laugh. "This has been such fun, but I've got to get on. Eric, my son, goes to afternoon kindergarten, and he'll be home soon."

"It's been fun for me too, Linda. My phone is being connected. Call me sometime, or come out. I'd like to keep in touch."

"I'd like to. I really would." Linda's eyes were focused on a car coming slowly down the street toward them. It stopped and the man in the car spoke to Linda.

"Ain't it 'bout time for Eric to get home?" The man wore a greasy billed cap. The arm that rested on the window ledge was generously sprinkled with dark hair. Dark eyes swept over Nelda then stayed on her face.

"Not for fifteen minutes yet." Linda glanced down at her watch.

"Better get goin' then." The car moved slowly away. Linda's face was flushed when she turned back to Nelda, who was urging Kelly into the car.

"I had better get going. It's been great seeing you."

"Can I give you a ride home?"

"I'll walk down to Lincoln School and walk home with Eric. This is his first week of school. Besides, I need the exercise." She laughed nervously. "Kurt says I'm as broad as a barn door." She waved and walked briskly down the street.

Nelda was pleased that she had met Linda. She had thought about her over the years, hoping that she was happy. Although pretty and smart, Linda had not been one of the "in" group because her mother and her father spent more time in the beer joints than they did at home.

At the appliance store, Nelda bought a television set and an antenna and made arrangements for delivery and installation. It took longer to buy enough groceries to last for a while than it did the television. Mr. Jensen helped her put them in the car.

"I'm ready to go home, Kelly. How about you?"

"Arrr . . . woof."

❧ *Chapter Four* ❧

THE DAY HER PHONE WAS CONNECTED, NELDA called her boss in Chicago and left her phone number—which was a mistake. The very next evening she had a call from the owner of the nightclub she had decorated in Chicago.

"Hey, babe, whatcha doin' out there in the sticks?"

"Hello, Mr. Falerri. How did you get my number?" she asked, although she knew. *Darn you, Della. You know I'm not interested in this man.*

"I got ways, babe. When ya comin' back to the big windy?"

"I've not decided, Mr. Falerri."

"Where ya gettin that 'mister' stuff? I'm Aldus, sweetheart. Ever'body calls me Aldus. Say, folks really like the looks of the place, and I been braggin' ya up."

"I'm sure Elite Decorators appreciate it."

"Not Elite Decorators, puss, you. The broads at Elite didn't have nothin' to do with it. Come on back here and open up your own joint. I'll getcha all the business ya can handle. When Aldus Falerri talks, folks listen."

Nelda closed her eyes and gritted her teeth before she answered, trying hard to remember that he was a client, a valuable client who could steer thousands of dollars worth of business to Elite Decorators.

"I've business to finish up here, Mr.—Aldus. It will be some time before I can get away."

"Hurry it up, babe. I want to show you off and . . . show you the town."

"That's kind of you."

A roar of laughter exploded at the other end. Nelda could picture him laughing with the smelly cigar clenched between his teeth.

"That's rich, sweetheart. Ask anybody. Aldus Falerri ain't kind! Aldus Falerri is business, little puss. It's what made my club the best on Chicago's South Side. When I want somethin', I go for it. Remember that, puss. Aldus Falerri's got strings: I can call in favors."

Was that a threat? Nelda hated it when he called her *puss*.

"I've got to go. This is a six-party line and someone else wants the line. It could be an emergency." She jiggled the dial to add authenticity to her statement.

Forgive me, God, for this lie.

"Six people on your line? Honey, I can fix that!"

"No. No, please. That's the way it is here. I'll get in touch with you as soon as I get back to Chicago."

"That's my babe. 'Bye, honey."

"Good-bye."

Nelda hung up the phone and looked down at Kelly lying on the floor beside her.

"Sheesh! That man is enough to make me want to stay here forever. You wouldn't like him one bit, Kelly. He's fat, he's almost bald, and he smokes smelly cigars. I had to put up with him while I was decorating his nightclub. I never thought that I'd have to put up with him out here."

During the following week, Nelda became absorbed in her work and time passed quickly. She and Kelly roamed the ditches along the roadside looking for specimens to take back to her workbench. For every quarter mile Nelda walked, Kelly ran a mile. At the end of the day they were both tired. On the back steps Nelda brushed the burrs and twigs from Kelly's furry coat before she allowed him in the house. After watching her new television for a while, she was ready for bed.

It was so peaceful, so quiet, except for that motorcycle! It had gone by the house several times, always in the evening. And Kelly detested motorcycles. On the long trip from Chicago he snapped and growled at every motorcycle they passed. Whenever this one sped past he went crazy, racing through the house and barking furiously.

"Hush," Nelda scolded each time. "That bike has a right to be on that road. Calm down."

On Monday morning she washed clothes for the first time. Remembering the fresh, outdoorsy scent of line-dried bedding from her childhood days at Grandma's house, she decided to forgo the convenience of the new electric dryer and hauled the basket of wet laundry to the clothesline. She wiped off the line and pinned up the sheets, towels, and various pieces of clothing: panties, bras, shirts, shorts, and two cotton skirts. Then she stood back and admired her work.

"Pretty neat, huh, Kelly?"

Lying on the back steps, the dog moved his tail in a swipe at the screen door. His eyes were on the shed.

"Still think you're going to get a mouse out of that shed? Well, good luck."

Nelda went back into the house, put a roast in the oven on low heat, then began to work on the project she had started the day before. She spent the rest of the afternoon at her easel painstakingly painting a yellow tiger lily she thought would transfer beautifully to fine cotton fabric.

Sometime in the middle of the afternoon, she felt a prickling on the back of her neck as if someone were staring at her. She stopped painting and looked all around. Surely Kelly, who lay on the back step, would let her know if anyone was around.

In late afternoon, Nelda added a couple of potatoes to the meat roasting in the oven. She liked cooking, but not just for herself. The roast beef would be enough tonight and for sandwiches for a few days. How much more gratifying it would be, she mused, to be preparing this to share with someone else.

Banishing her errant thoughts, she went out to

gather the clean, dry clothes from the line. She had started on the towels when she heard the dreaded roar of the motorcycle. She looked about for Kelly. He was standing beside the house, his head cocked to one side, the fur on the back of his neck standing at attention.

"Kelly! No!" Nelda knew even as she shouted that the dog, fixated on that hated machine, wouldn't hear a word she said. She dropped the towels into the basket and took off in a run after the red streak tearing down the lane toward the road. "Kel—ly! Kel—ly! Come back here."

Kelly reached the road, whirling and barking at the monster coming toward him. He lunged and jumped, his own barks drowning out the voice of his mistress calling to him. For a moment Nelda thought he'd turn tail and come back, but instead he dashed back directly into the path of the machine. When it hit him, he flew into the air, landed hard, and lay still. The rider had done his best to avoid the collision. The back wheel of the cycle spun in the gravel before the machine skidded down the incline into the ditch beside the road.

Nelda slammed to a halt and clapped her hands over her ears, her heart pounding like the beat of a drum.

"Oh, no! Oh God, no!"

She began to run again. Her frightened eyes saw the rider limp up out of the ditch. Thank God, he was all right, but Kelly lay like a rumpled red blanket in the road.

The man reached the dog the same time Nelda did. She threw herself onto her knees.

"Oh, Kelly, don't be—" With relief she saw that he was still breathing. He whined and tried to lift his head. In anguish, she cried, "Do something. Oh, please, do something—"

The man snatched a knit cap off his head and removed a pair of goggles.

"Lute!" Blond hair was plastered with sweat; blue eyes so narrowed she couldn't see them carefully examined the dog. "Lute, are you hurt?"

He looked at her and then back at Kelly, who was weakly emitting pitiful yelps.

"I'm all right. Get your car and a blanket to lay him on and we'll take him to the vet."

"Is it . . . bad?" She hated to ask the question, but she had to know. The dog had been her companion for the past three years, and she couldn't bear to lose him.

"I don't know. He's stunned, and he must have broken or cracked ribs. Get moving. Get the car."

Nelda ran to the house, grabbed a sheet off the line, snatched up her purse, turned the lock on the door, and slammed it. In the car she fumbled for the keys, then whipped the car into gear, backed it up with a jerk, and turned it around. She had run so fast she was gasping for breath and had a pain in her side but refused to acknowledge it.

She saw Lute wheel the cycle up out of the ditch and park it in the yard beside the lilacs. When she stopped the car, he reached for the sheet and spread it over the backseat. Nelda knelt beside the dog, who looked up at her with pleading eyes, bringing tears to her own.

"You'll be all right," she crooned. "You just forgot that you're a city dog and not used to running free." She rubbed the back of her hand over her eyes to rid them of tears before she looked at Lute.

"I'll try not to hurt him when I lift him," he murmured. "Hold the door open. Easy now, fella. This is going to hurt, but we'll do it as fast as we can and get you to the vet. He'll have you fixed up in no time." Kelly let out a yelp and tried to move his back legs when Lute burrowed his hands beneath his body. "Whoa, fella. Easy now."

Lute spoke to the dog in a low, soothing voice, lifting him in his arms and easing him onto the sheet-covered seat.

"You ride back here with him and try to keep him quiet," he said to Nelda.

Cautiously she climbed in and squatted on the floor, careful not to jar Kelly's long body which took up the entire seat.

Lute had to move the seat back in order to get under the wheel of her car. Loose gravel noisily spattered the fenders as he drove the car swiftly down the road. On her knees beside the dog, Nelda stroked his head, praying he was not seriously injured. She thanked God it was Lute who had hit him, not some uncaring stranger who would have simply driven away.

As Nelda looked at the sun-streaked blond head, unbidden thoughts invaded her mind.

Oh, Lute! I remember when my hands knew every inch of your body, and yours knew mine.

As if she had spoken, blue eyes met hers in the rearview mirror, and Lute's intense stare brought color flooding to her face.

"It's just a mile or so now." His words broke the spell. "I hope Gary is home. There's a dog show at the fairgrounds. He could be over there." Seeing Nelda's panic-stricken eyes in the mirror again, he added reassuringly, "If he isn't home, we'll go to the fairgrounds; it's only a fifteen-minute drive."

By the time they turned into a driveway and stopped in front of a brick building set close to a new ranch-style house, Kelly was lying quietly, his eyes closed, his mouth open, and his long tongue hanging limply out the side of it.

"I'll see if Gary is here." Lute spoke softly but moved quickly.

Nelda watched him try the office door. It was locked, and her heart sank to her toes. Lute strode briskly to the house and rang the doorbell. Despite her anguish over Kelly, Nelda couldn't take her eyes off him. His shoulders, hugged by a knit shirt, were broad and muscular, his waist and hips narrow in comparison.

She had loved him for all his tender, caring qualities when he was young. She recalled the harshness of his words and the hardness in his eyes that day at the cemetery. Yet here he was, all gentleness and compassion. Was he still, inside, the Lute of their youth?

Why do I keep wondering about him—and long-

ing for him? Stop it, Nelda! He is beyond your reach now.

Nelda tugged her attention back to the wounded dog, and within minutes Lute was there opening the door. She looked at him hopefully.

"Gary will open the office."

A tall, thin man wearing jeans cut off at the knees, a faded knit shirt, and an old pair of dirty white sneakers came into view behind Lute.

"Gary, this is Nelda." Lute extended a hand to help her out of the car. She clung to it because her legs were numb from squatting on the floor for so long.

"Nelda?" Gary's eyes flew to Lute, then back to her. "Well, hello, dear lady. Let's see what we can do for your beastie here. Lute says he ran him down with that blasted cycle of his."

"It wasn't Lute's fault." Nelda jumped to Lute's defense. Her hand was still tingling from the contact with his. "Kelly hasn't been in the country before. He'd only been outside off a leash a few times in his life until we came here. It's hard for him to cope with all the space and the freedom."

"I'll get a stretcher out of the office and we'll get him onto the table." He fondled Kelly's ears. "That's a good beastie. Just hang in there, old boy, and we'll see what's to be done with you."

"Lute! What did he mean?" Nelda blurted as soon as Gary disappeared in the office. Her lips trembled. She was torn between her anxiety for Kelly and the heady experience of being with Lute.

"He won't put him away. Don't worry."

"Oh, I was afraid that's what he meant."

"Gary's a good vet—the best." His voice was gentle and reassuring. "Even if he is an *Englishman*," he amended in a loud stage whisper.

"I heard that, Lute. One more disparaging remark from you, and I'll bloody well castrate that bull of yours when I come out to vaccinate him tomorrow." Gary positioned a stretcher beside the car. "Get to the other side, Lute, and we'll lift him out on the sheet and slide him onto the board. Righto, out you get, old boy."

Nelda sat in the waiting room, too nervous even to thumb through the magazines there. She had wanted to go into the treatment room with Kelly, but Gary had vetoed the idea. Lute had guided her to a chair.

"Gary knows what's best. If you like, I'll go in with him," he said. "Relax. You look worn-out."

It wasn't until she was seated that she thought about his words. It had been a long time since anyone had been solicitous of her. In Chicago, her job consumed most of her time, and her shy nature prevented her from making many close friends when she did have a spare weekend.

She wondered for the hundredth time if Lute might be the father of a sturdy little blond-haired boy or a dainty little blue-eyed girl. Now that she'd seen him, and still felt about him the way she had so long ago, the thought of meeting his children— Becky's little half brother or sister—tied her stomach in knots.

"Don't look so terrified." Lute was back beside

her, his voice gentle. "Gary says Kelly has a few cracked ribs and some paralysis in his back legs, but that he'll probably fully recover."

"Thank God!" Nelda rose unsteadily. "And thank you, too, Lute. I was so scared. Kelly's really a very smart dog. He understands most of what I say to him, but he gets a little crazy when he hears a motorcycle." She had rushed into breathless speech.

Lute smiled. "He'll not be chasing any more cycles. I can almost guarantee it, but just to make sure, I won't ride by the house anymore."

"It was you all the time?"

"I usually take a spin out that way several times a week to look over the crops. Come on in and talk to Gary."

His hand was beneath her elbow as he ushered her into the treatment room. He didn't remove it, and she was grateful for his support. The stark white room smelled of disinfectant. Her precious Kelly lay still on the table.

"My wife took the kids to the dog show," Gary began conversationally as soon as she entered the room. "She'll want to meet you. She's a great crusader, my Rhetta. She'll try to rope you in on her bloody projects." He was drying his hands on a towel, his dark eyes intent on her and Lute. He was an attractive man, long and lean, with dark hair and eyes. Nelda warmed to him instantly. They reviewed Kelly's condition, then he gave her some medication when she was ready to leave.

With Kelly sedated and ensconced on the sheet

in the backseat once again, Gary completed his instructions.

"When he comes to, he may vomit. If he'll eat, wrap one of these pills in a piece of ground meat or his favorite dog food, and he'll sleep the night. After I go to Lute's tomorrow, I'll stop by, that is, if that blasted bull hasn't gored me to death. Ring me if Kelly has any problems before that."

Gary firmly closed the back door and opened the front for Nelda.

"I'm expecting to be fed well tomorrow at teatime, Lute. Crumpets, biscuits, scones. Oh, yes, and don't forget the cucumber sandwiches."

"It costs darn near as much to feed you, you hollow-legged cow-quack, as it does to pay your bills," Lute retorted, hiding a grin.

"He always says that." Gary put his head close to Nelda's and whispered confidentially.

"Flirting again, Gary? I'll tell Rhetta."

"You would, you . . . Judas. See you tomorrow."

Nelda didn't speak until they were on the highway.

"Will he know where to find me?"

Lute looked at her then. It was cozy and intimate inside the car.

"I like the way this car handles," he said, instead of answering her question. "Is it a '54?"

"Yes. It's my first car. I paid down on it with my very first paycheck."

His reply was a noncommittal, "Yeah?" He didn't trust himself to say more. Memories of his teaching her to drive—his hand over hers on the shift, his arm brushing her breast, the scent of her hair—flooded back.

"I like your hair short that way," he managed to say after a few minutes of silence. "It suits you better than long."

He turned his head to look at her, then quickly tore his eyes from her to focus on the road, allowing her a view of his profile. His hair tumbled in disarray, his nose, seen from the side, was straight and finely chiseled, his mouth firm.

The thought seeped into her mind that it would be wonderful to kiss him again. A longing to touch him started in her lips and slowly enveloped her. She sucked in her stomach against the aching sensation and, trying for a distraction, turned to look over the back of the seat at Kelly.

"Everyone in five townships knows that Eli Hansen's granddaughter is back living in the home place," Lute said abruptly, reverting to her question as if nothing else had been said in the meanwhile. "Not much happens around here, you know. You being here is big news."

"How strange. I've only had one visitor. Ervin Olsen. What a nice man. He pulled into the yard the other morning and stopped to talk for a few minutes. I thought he'd appointed himself a welcome wagon of one—or else was a square-dance recruiter."

Nelda went on to say that the snowy-haired widower had asked if she'd like to join him and his "lady friend" at their square-dance group that met in the Ventura Community Hall. He explained, as if she didn't know, that Ventura was a village at the head of the lake. He was so formal in his speech and so "down-home" in striped overalls, that he had reminded her of her grandfather.

Lute chuckled. "Ervin's the best newspaper we have, once he gets his crops in. He makes his rounds every day or two. Usually drives up to the house and honks for someone to come out."

"That's what he did. He drove in and honked. I went out to see what he wanted. We talked for a while. I enjoyed our visit."

They rode along in a silence filled with unspoken and unanswered questions. Nelda didn't dare steer the conversation into the personal channel she longed to explore.

Lute, tell me about yourself. Tell me every little detail of what you've been doing. Tell me you grieved just a little for me and our baby.

"How long will you be . . . here?" His voice was quiet, hesitant, as he turned onto the gravel road leading to the farm.

"I had planned to spend the winter, but now . . . I don't know."

"Tired of country life already?" The edge in his voice hurt.

"Oh, no. I love it here. I always loved being at Gran's. You know that."

He glanced at her, and her eyes followed his down to the cleavage revealed by her partially unbuttoned shirt. Her hand moved to fasten the wayward button. It was an automatic gesture to fend off the sudden heat she felt as she recalled the sweetness of his lips on her breast. She looked straight ahead, conscious of the blond head that turned toward her often now that they were on the little-used road.

Once she turned and gazed back into his eyes, so astonishingly blue in his tanned face. *Why does he keep looking at me?* She began to feel uncomfortable. She knew that her face was dirty and that the humid warmth had made a curly mop of her hair. Dimly she registered that her shorts were soiled, her shirt limp.

"Nelda." The sound of her name coming from his lips made her heart lurch. "You never did say why you came back. I'd think that it would be pretty tame around here for you."

She pulled in her bottom lip several times and stared straight ahead, mulling over in her mind what to reply.

"I suppose you would think that," she said slowly. "But I can sum up my reasons in a few words. I got tired of the rushing, the noise, the backbiting, dog-eat-dog business of commercial decorating. I had a very successful year, so I could afford to come back to the farm to decide if I wanted to sell it or not. I also wanted to try my hand at a craft I haven't had time for before."

She waited for a reply, supportive or sarcastic; but Lute didn't speak until they reached the house. He drove into the backyard and parked the car near the back door.

"You'd better see about getting the garage cleaned out so you can get the car into it this winter."

❧ *Chapter Five* ❧

NELDA'S LEGS WERE TREMBLING WHEN SHE GOT out of the car. She started toward the house to open the door for Lute, then remembered that she had put the house key on the ring with her car keys. She turned back and ran full tilt into Lute, who had moved to open the back door of the car. His hands shot out to steady her. Her thighs and hips came into contact with his. She jumped back.

"Oh, sorry. I need the keys."

Still holding on to her arm with one hand, he reached into the car and pulled them from the ignition. She took the keys, and, when she moved away, his hand dropped from her arm.

"Are you going to put him on the porch or in the house?" His voice sounded perfectly natural, but her poise had vanished, and she croaked out her answer.

"The house."

"Fix a place for him. You'd better lay papers; he won't be able to go out for a while."

Nelda escaped into the house. Lute had the power

to completely disarm and frighten her, yet he thrilled her, too. Right now she fought to get a handle on her emotions before she made a fool of herself. Damn him! Why couldn't he have just turned into a balding, potbellied, beer-swilling redneck that she could have dismissed from her thoughts at first sight.

Lute carried the groggy dog into the kitchen and gently placed him on the bed Nelda brought down from her bedroom.

"It would be cooler if he lay on the tile. You should have an air conditioner. It's like an oven in here."

"Oven! Oh heavens! I forgot my roast." She hurried to the stove and pulled down the oven door. The light came on and she saw the small dark brown roast lying in a sea of juices. "It isn't ruined," she said with surprise. She looked over her shoulder at Lute. He was standing on spread legs, his hands wedged in the back pockets of his jeans. Something close to a smile on his face. Happiness suddenly filled her and she smiled too."

"Here, let me get the pan out and you can turn the oven off." He took a towel from the counter and lifted the roaster to the top of the stove. "It's no wonder it's hot in here. All the windows are closed.

"This type of storm window stays on, and the bottom slides up," he explained, as he twisted the hook on the top of one window sash, effortlessly lifted the window, and reached out to slide up the outer pane and pull down the screen. "This winter, if you're here, you'll slide the screen up again and lower the storm."

"I know how they operate, but I wondered how in the world I was going to get to them when I couldn't raise the inside window." She was talking to Lute's back, trying to ignore the fluttering of her heart. He was moving through the house raising the stuck windows. "It's cooler already. I had to prop open the front and back doors to get the smoke from my first cooking disaster out of the house. Oh, Lute! Smell that fresh country air." Nelda knew that she was babbling as she followed him from room to room, but she couldn't seem to stop.

"All I can smell is that roast." He strained to lift a tight window that had been closed for years. Fascinated, she watched the muscles rippling across his shoulders. "There's not much you can do about the porch, but during the day you can open the inside door and unfasten this glass panel on the storm door." He suited his words to action, and soon a nice breeze was cooling the house. "How about the upstairs?"

"Oh, yes, please. If you have time," she added after a moment's hesitation, following closely behind when he went up the stairs. "This is the only room I use up here," she said, as they approached an open door.

Lute's eyes swept her bedroom, and she was glad it was neat. Her robe, a gauzy cotton, was flung over the foot of the bed, but everything else was in order. A tightness gripped her throat when his eyes settled on the framed picture of Rebecca on the table beside her bed. He picked it up and looked at it for a long while. His back was to her, and she couldn't see the expression on his face.

Like one hypnotized, she watched him. When he replaced the picture, he turned and his eyes met hers. A startling thrill of desire coursed through her. Standing there, the sweat trickling down between her breasts, she felt more vulnerable than she had ever felt in her life.

It was heart-stopping to see this handsome man towering over her bed, the photo of the child they had created together between them. When his eyes dwelt for an inordinate amount of time on her mouth, she could almost taste his lips, feel his arms.

For what seemed an eternity they were held in suspended animation. Not daring to breathe, she drank him in with unquenchable eyes. Lute raised a hand—to touch her? she wondered fleetingly. She glimpsed the ring on his finger.

The spell was broken.

Reality returned like a kick in the teeth. She turned quickly and went down the stairs. The pain in her chest was almost more than she could endure, but she was not going to crumple in front of him. Damned if she would!

In the kitchen she turned on the light, suddenly realizing darkness was only a few minutes away. She bent over the sleeping dog, gently stroking his satiny head and hoping her bleak hurt was not visible in her eyes.

"He'll be all right." Lute was behind her. "Mind if I have a drink of water?"

Nelda stood quickly and moved to the sink. "I'm sorry. I'll wash my hands and get some ice." She turned on the tap, letting it run full force. The cold water on her wrists and palms calmed her a little.

"Do you want me to put the pan back in the oven to keep your supper warm?"

"No, I'll probably eat it cold." She dried her hands and took two glasses to the refrigerator to fill with ice. "I'd invite you to stay for supper, but I'm sure your wife is expecting you home." They were the most difficult words she'd ever had to say, and she tried fervently to keep her voice from betraying her desperation. Before she turned around, she asked, "Cola, ginger ale, or water?"

When he didn't answer, she turned, a glass of ice in each hand. He was leaning against the counter, his eyes on her face. She felt her pulse beating frantically at the base of her throat. She stood waiting, leaving the refrigerator door open. He stepped forward, reached around her, took out a large bottle of cola, and shut the door. She moved to the cabinet and put the glasses down. He came up behind her and, reaching around her again, set the bottle on the counter.

"I've never had but one wife."

Nelda didn't expect the whispered words or the tenderness in his voice. She swallowed hard and tried to control the trembling that traveled from her knees up to her chin. *Was he saying that he wasn't married?* She couldn't turn and face him. She was incapable of moving.

"But . . . the ring—" she whispered.

"I've worn it for almost nine years. I can't get it off now. I sat in my truck, not ten minutes after we were pronounced man and wife and put the ring on my finger. It's not been off since. I had brought one for you, too, but I never had a chance to give it to you."

A dam seemed to burst inside her. She could no more hold back the cry that tore from her throat than she could have stopped a steamroller. She bent over the counter, her face in her arms, her body convulsing as she began to sob. All the harrowing tension of the day—Kelly's accident, Lute's unnerving presence, and now the knowledge that he didn't belong to another woman after all—broke through all the barriers she'd been trying to erect.

A torrent of tears came roaring from deep within her, and she cried like a newborn, every vestige of self-control gone with the first sob.

Nelda knew that Lute's eyes were on her back as sobs wrenched her body. His arms reached for her, turned her around, and pulled her up against him. Cradling her head with one large hand, he wrapped his arms around her. She nestled against him, her wet face pressed into the curve of his neck. The haven of his arms was a wonderful, safe cocoon, and minutes passed while he held her.

"Shhhh . . . shhhh—" he crooned softly. "Don't cry, honey. Kelly will be all right." He pushed his fingers through the riotous curls on the back of her head.

He buried his face in her hair and breathed deeply the scent of her shampoo. He stroked her body from shoulder to behind, feeling each vertebra along her spine. She inhaled the male scent of him and tasted the salt of her own tears. It had been so long . . . so damned long.

Her sobs subsided, reason returned, and she tried to pull away, but his arms held her tightly. Embarrassment and shame at her loss of control almost started the tears again. She tried to turn her head so that he couldn't see her blotchy, wet face, but it wasn't to be. He cupped her chin in his hand and tilted her face toward him.

"Please don't look at me. I'm so ashamed." She felt a tear escape over her lower lid and roll down her cheek.

"Is it Kelly? Gary said he'd be all right." Lute's face was as concerned as his voice.

"I don't know what got into me. It was just . . . a lot of things coming all at once. I . . . was taking my clothes off the line . . . and then . . . Kelly—" Her throat hurt with the effort to control her voice.

"Is that all?" Lute laughed. She felt the movement of his chest against her breast. His voice was deep, humoring her.

His face was close, so terribly close that it was difficult to think of something to say. His blue eyes, half-shut, were within inches of her own, and his mouth, that firm-lipped mouth, was so near hers she could feel his breath on her lips. *Oh, Lord, I wish he'd kiss me . . . just once.* The thought raced repeatedly through her mind. His lips open, he seemed to hesitate, then he smiled.

"Go wash your face. You'd scare even Kelly if he woke up." There was a huskiness to his tone, and he dropped his arms and gave her a gentle push toward the bathroom. "When did you eat last?" His voice trailed her to the lavatory through the open door.

"This morning, I think." She was hurrying to wash her face, irrationally afraid he might vanish if she was gone too long.

"You think?" He was filling the glasses with soda when she came out of the bathroom. Her eyes clung to the ring on his finger . . . her ring. He handed her a glass, picked up his own, and took a long swallow, poured in more cola, then returned the bottle to the refrigerator. "Drink your soda. It'll help to get some sugar into you. Then we'll go bring in your clothes."

Nelda's heart lurched. Lute's face wavered in her vision. She felt precariously poised in a vacuum of weakness, lost in a fantasy that couldn't possibly be happening. She followed him to the back porch, where he reached up and flipped a switch. A light on a pole lit the yard from the house to the barn.

"I didn't know about that light."

"I put it in when I was filling the corncrib. It's darker than the bottom of a well out here at night." He turned to look down at her. "Did Hutchinson tell you that I rent the land?"

"Yes, he told me." She didn't say that the lawyer hadn't told her until she asked.

Nelda hurried to the end of the line that held her panties and bras.

"I'm starting at this end," Lute teased. "You get the sheets and towels."

"Oh, no you don't."

Nelda went down the line removing her intimate

garments as fast as she could and dropping them in the basket. Lute folded the two sets of sheets, neatly and swiftly and carried the basket to the porch while she carried the clothespin bag.

"Put away your wash. I'll make gravy to go with that roast. I'm starving."

"Gravy?" she repeated incredulously. "I haven't had roast gravy since Grandma used to make it."

"Well, you're back now, and you'll have some. I'm a darn good cook, even if I do say so. Get moving, or I'll eat without you." It was the teasing, scolding tone he'd used long ago when he'd said, "Come on, slowpoke, we'll be late for school."

Nelda took a few sips of soda and hurried up the stairs with the clothes basket. The breeze coming in her bedroom windows cooled her hot face. She put the sheets and pillowcases in the chest in the hall, her underwear in her bureau drawers. Happiness played in her heart like a concerto.

She went back downstairs and stood silently in the doorway of the kitchen, watching Lute. He had lifted the meat onto a platter and placed a carving knife beside it. Now with sure, economical movements he was vigorously stirring the bubbling liquid in the roasting pan. She admired his efficiency—and the way his slim hips swiveled slightly as he stirred.

"I couldn't find the cornstarch, so I used flour," he said without turning around. She jumped, feeling every inch a spy at her own door, but he continued speaking conversationally as she entered the room. "Sometimes I get lumpy gravy with flour, never with cornstarch. Find me a bowl to put this in, and stick some bread into the toaster, and set out the butter. I hate to spread hard butter."

Nelda went to check that Kelly was still sleeping before she sat down across the table from Lute. She was still amazed that he was really here. His hair was damp and combed. He must have done that while she was putting away the clothes. He pulled her plate toward him and filled it at the same time he filled his own; a potato, a slice of buttered toast, then an abundant layer of sliced beef topped with a ladle of streaming gravy.

"Try that. That's a Hanson special."

"Looks good." Nelda laughed. It was really more like a giggle. "Maybe you should open up your own place and run the cafe uptown out of business."

"Not a bad idea." He got up between forkfuls and slipped two more slices of bread into the toaster.

She wanted to know so much about him but was afraid to ask, afraid he would go all icy as he had at the cemetery.

"This is good," she complimented honestly. "I've never bought cornstarch. Is it just to make gravy?"

"You can use it for lots of things. White sauce, puddings, chafing—"

"Chafing?"

"In the place of talcum powder."

"Well, thank you, Betty Crocker. Where did you pick up all this valuable information?"

"4-H." When he grinned, her heart did a rapid flip-flop. "I was a leader for a couple of years. Even the boys learn to cook these days, so I learned right along with the kids and we picked up a few blue ribbons at the fair." The bread popped up, and he stood to pluck it from the toaster. Holding a slice out to her, he asked, "More?"

"I believe I will," she responded, surprised at her own appetite.

"Good. Hand me your plate and put more toast in for me. I've just gotten started."

"I saw Linda Sharp the other day. She's Linda Branson now. She was the best student in my home-making class."

"I can understand that. She did most of the cooking at home—plus taking care of her brother and sister."

"Do you know her husband?"

"He's a mechanic at the garage . . . when he isn't drinking in one of the joints."

"Poor Linda. I remember her going to the Town Pump after school to see if her mother was there."

"There isn't anything wrong with going to the Town Pump if you know when to leave. Linda's folks spent more money on booze than they did on groceries."

The conversation between them was impersonal and nonstop. Nelda finally got up the courage to risk a direct question.

"How many acres do you farm, Lute?" She quaked inwardly; it was her first inquiry about his personal life.

"A section, not counting yours. I also own the sale barn." He smiled an endearing smile that lifted the corners of his mouth and spread a warm light into his eyes.

"Do you have help?"

"I have a hired man who lives with his family in our tenant house—and other help. Wouldn't the captain be surprised to know that I didn't end up in the gutter after all?" Although he was smiling when he started to speak, by the time he finished, the warmth in his eyes was replaced by a steely cold gleam.

Nelda hesitated. If she answered his jibe she would have to say that, yes, her father would be surprised. She could remember with clarity his words regarding Lute: *You've not got a pot to piss in, nor has your old man. All he knows how to do is scratch in the dirt out on that hardscrabble farm his daddy left him.* How galling it must have been for Lute!

Lute gave her a sharp glance, and then lowered his eyes to his plate. *I never thought my daughter would stoop so low as to get herself knocked up by a rutting, wet-eared, hog-slopping hayseed.* The humiliating words her father uttered that day that would stay with him forever.

The atmosphere was suddenly cooler. Her heart sank as she realized that he was putting her on trial, too. She hoped her stomach would settle down and that she wouldn't burst into tears again.

She pushed back her chair. "Would you like some coffee?"

"No, thanks. I've got to be going. Mom's putting sweet corn in the freezer tomorrow, and I promised her that I'd pick and husk it tonight."

"In the dark?"

"I've got a light on the tractor. Mom wants to

get it done. She's going to California at the end of the week to visit her sister." He squatted down beside Kelly and fondled the dog's ears. "He'll be out for a while yet. When he comes to, he'll be thirsty. Don't let him fill up on water—it'll make him sick."

The telephone rang and Nelda answered it.

"How's my babe?" The voice of Aldus Falerri boomed in her ear.

"Fine, thank you." Her eyes went to Lute, pleading with him not to leave.

"When are ya comin' home, puss?"

Oh, Lord, I hope Lute can't hear this.

"I'm not sure, Mr. . . . ah, Aldus. I've got a lot to do here."

"Hurry up, puss, or I might come out and carry ya back."

"No, don't do that. I'll call you."

"I'll be waitin', puss. Aldus Falerri ain't used to waitin'."

"I know. Good-bye."

Nelda hung up the phone before the man at the other end could reply.

"Boyfriend?"

"No! I decorated his nightclub. Thanks for taking us to the vet's. I don't know how I'd have managed otherwise."

"You'd have managed," he responded matter-of-factly. "Thanks for the supper. Or, I guess the upper crust in Chicago say 'dinner.' " At the door he turned and looked at her.

She stood at the table, her hands clutching the top of the ladder-backed chair.

"I saw your picture in a magazine after you'd decorated the club rooms in some fancy hotel. You looked like one of those high-society dames. I never thought to see you here, living in an old farmhouse, hanging clothes on the line. What are you trying to prove, Nelda?"

She felt as if he had kicked her in the stomach. She could only stare blankly. Inside, she was hollow, unable to think. Then rising anger helped her find her voice.

"Why should I be trying to prove anything? I told you once my reasons for coming here and I don't need to explain them futher." *He thinks I have some ulterior motive for coming here,* she reflected. *He believes that I'll pack up and leave if the going gets rough.* Mentally straightening her spine, she reminded herself that the only person she needed to prove anything to was herself.

If he noticed the anger in her reply, Lute showed no evidence of it. His lack of response infuriated her even more.

"I'll get my bike and be off," he said tersely as he crossed the porch to the screened door.

Nelda went to the porch and watched him. The yard light was still on. He turned back and looked at her, lifted his arm briefly in salute, and disappeared around the corner of the house. She stood at the door until distance ate up the sound of the motorcycle.

Lute's sudden antagonism had banished some of her hopes for a reconciliation, but not all; for, as she quickly reminded herself, he had not remarried, and he was still wearing his wedding ring.

When the phone rang the next morning as Nelda was drinking coffee and listening to the news on the radio, she groaned thinking that it might be Aldus Falerri. The call was from Rhetta, the veterinarian's wife. She wanted to know if it would be convenient for her to stop by that morning.

Nelda was pleased she was going to have a real visitor. Though Ervin Olsen came by often, he seldom stayed more than five minutes, and she had to admit that she longed for a little chitchat.

Right on time, a small yellow Volkswagen came up the lane and a tall, large-boned woman got out. She had thick, wheat-colored hair tied at the nape of her neck, a suntanned face, and friendly brown eyes. Nelda met her at the back door.

"Hello. I'm Rhetta." The smiling woman extended a hand in greeting.

"I'm Nelda, obviously. Do come in."

"Gary told me to get myself over here and welcome you to our metropolis. How's your dog doing?"

In ten minutes they were chatting as if they had known each other for years.

"I swear to goodness, Nelda, if I take on any more projects, Gary will raffle me off at the next veterinary convention. I had decided that I was absolutely not going to be the next president of the Women's Club even if they got down on their knees and begged me, and what did I do? I sat there like I was dead from the neck up, and they elected me!

Now I've got the membership drive, the charity ball, the drive to expand the library, et cetera, et cetera."

"It sounds to me as if you have your hands full. What about your children? Did you say they were twelve and fourteen?"

"Our boys are so self-sufficient they scare me! The only thing they'll ever need a woman for is sex. They cook, do their own laundry, clean their rooms, manage their own money. They both think the sun rises and sets with their father. The other hero in their lives is Lute. He's taught them gun safety, how to drive a tractor—he even took them to the north woods in Minnesota and taught them what to do if they should ever be stranded up there on one of the many fishing trips they make with Lute and Gary."

In order to hide her elation on hearing these things about Lute, Nelda got up and refilled their coffee cups.

"Have you known Lute long?" she asked as casually as possible.

"Four . . . no, maybe five years now. We've been here six years and met Lute as soon as he came home from the Navy. He's sure come a long way since then. He farms the place left to him and his mother, and he bought some adjoining land. That boy works like a son of a gun. I understand he leases another section. He's got equipment you wouldn't believe— four-row planters, two-row pickers, and even his own corn sheller. After he shells his own, he shells for others."

Rhetta's large capable hands turned her glass around and around. Nelda sensed the woman's eyes glued to her while she talked about Lute. A question about her and Lute was coming, and before Nelda could head it off, it was asked.

"You're Nelda, the mother of Lute's little girl?"

"Yes."

"I thought so. Nelda isn't a common name around here."

After a slightly awkward silence Nelda was compelled to offer a reason for her being here.

"My grandparents left me this farm. Earl Hutchinson is the executor of the estate, and he leased the land to Lute." She laughed nervously. "I didn't know that until I got here."

Nelda's eyes were bright and her fingers tightly gripped her cup. She knew that Rhetta noticed.

"Yeah, our Lute has done well for himself. He deserves it; he puts in long hours. Gary and I have wondered what drives him. Did he tell you that he owns the sale barn? I suspect that the bank owns a share of it, but not for long. Lute knows farming and cattle like the back of his hand. He'll make a go of it."

"I'm sure," Nelda mumbled.

"Well, I've got to scoot. I'm on the committee to explore the idea of an indoor community swimming pool; and if I don't want to be put in charge of raising the money for it, I'd better be there to say no."

When Rhetta stood, Nelda was surprised to realize how tall and sturdy her new friend was.

"Why build a pool when you're so close to a lovely lake?" Nelda asked.

"The swimming season here is short for one thing, and there are so many cottages around the lake that it's beginning to get dirty. Years ago, they tell me, the lake was so clear you could see to the bottom—so the name Clear Lake. It's not that clear anymore, but we're working on it."

"Stop, stop!" Nelda laughed. "I'm convinced."

"Good! I'll get you onto the committee."

"I'm not *that* convinced!" Nelda protested.

"Will you come to supper some night? It might be hot dogs."

"I love hot dogs."

"Ahhh . . ." Rhetta sighed with relief. "I thought that coming from the big city you'd expect Chicken Kiev, or something equally impossible for me to make."

"Just because I lived in a big city doesn't mean I have gourmet tastes. I don't cook much for myself. Alongside one of my usual meals, a tuna sandwich looks like a feast."

"That's comforting to hear. I hate people who think everything worth doing is worth doing well. Thanks for the coffee and the chat." Rhetta talked nonstop until she folded herself into the small Volkswagen, yelled " 'Bye," and slammed the door.

❧ *Chapter Six* ❧

AS THE DAYS PASSED NELDA BEGAN TO FEEL THAT the brief hint of a reconciliation with Lute had never happened. He was putting up hay, she knew. A tractor pulling a wagon piled high with bales had gone by while she was out with Kelly.

A sense of belonging had settled over her, and she looked around the farmhouse with pride at what she had accomplished. She had worked all one day cleaning out the garage, carrying some things to the barn and piling junk in a heap to be hauled away. In a far corner on the floor among cardboard boxes, she discovered a fairly new clean blanket, an empty brown paper bag, and a Baby Ruth wrapper. Who had left them there? As she shook the blanket out and put it on the back porch, she felt a small tingle of fear course down her spine.

By the end of the day, the Ford was crowded into the building that had never before housed a car; her grandpa's pickup had been too long to fit.

When Ervin Olsen pulled into the lane for one of his brief visits the following morning, he found

Nelda tinkering with an old power mower she had pulled out of the garage. She asked him how to start the machine. He took one look and shook his head.

"That machine is old as the hills and has been sittin' there longer'n that. It ain't never goin' to start."

"Oh, shoot. The yard needs mowing. Grandpa never let it get this high."

"Tell ya what. Cliff Peterson, down at the farm store, has mowers. Hop in and we'll go take a look."

Before noon, Nelda, wearing an old pair of pedal pushers and a scarf around her head, was happily walking behind a new power mower with Ervin looking on and grinning broadly.

"Don't that beat all—old Eli's city granddaughter out mowing like an old hand. 'Course I'll have to take some of the credit." He chuckled. After loading her old mower to take back to Cliff to use for parts, he climbed into his pickup and announced that he was off to spread the news.

Gary stopped by several times to check on Kelly. The Irish setter was still stiff and sore and moved cautiously from the house to his favorite spot under a lilac bush. Nelda fretted and tried to cater to his every whim, constantly reminding herself of Gary's brisk announcement that in a few weeks Kelly would be "right as a London rain."

"I think you've decided that city life isn't so bad after all, haven't you?" Nelda patiently held the screen door open so the dog could painfully climb the three steps necessary to reach the porch. "Just as soon as you're able, we'll go for a long walk, and you'll begin to like it here again."

The veterinarian's visits had cheered up several mornings. He dropped by to check Kelly when he was in the area. The Englishman had a genuine interest in her work. Nelda enjoyed explaining to him about the specimens she was pressing and the groups of wildflowers she had hanging upside down on the porch.

"Did Rhetta see this? She'll ring you in to teach an arts and crafts class for one of her clubs."

"Oh, no. That's out of my line. I'm not a teacher."

When the phone rang the next morning, Nelda expected it to be the vet's wife.

"Nelda, this is Linda."

"Linda. How are you?"

"Fine. I have the car today. If you're not busy, I thought I would come out this afternoon while Eric's in school."

"I'm not that busy. Come for lunch."

"You don't have to feed me."

"I want to. It'll not be anything fancy."

"Then I'll be there about twelve-thirty."

She was glad Linda was coming out. She opened a can of chicken and made salad for sandwiches, then a can of peaches to eat with cottage cheese. After making a pitcher of tea, she put a cloth on the round kitchen table and set it with her grandma's colorful Fiesta pottery.

Lute came by shortly before Linda was due to arrive. Nelda heard the rumble of a pickup approaching the house. Ervin Olsen had already made one of his "driveway visits," as Nelda had dubbed them, early that morning. She went to the porch and saw the pickup parked at the gate leading to the corn-crib. Her heart hammered in anticipation when Lute swung down from the pickup and strode toward her.

"Hi there," she sang out cheerfully.

"How's the patient?" Lute asked, his blue eyes looking not at her but at the level of her knees.

"Fine. He's out to lunch right now. I'm sure he'd like for you to join him. This way," she concluded, trying to keep the conversation light as she led the way through the porch to the kitchen.

Lute looked at her with a curious mix of amusement and exasperation before he knelt beside the dog.

"Hey there, fella." Kelly's ears pricked up, and he turned from his dish with a half wag of his tail. He limped over to Lute and nuzzled the hand that descended to pat his head, then he slowly circled around and returned to his chow.

"His appetite's certainly none the worse for his injuries," Lute commented. "And he seems to be getting around pretty well. What does Gary have to say about him?"

When Lute didn't lift his gaze to her, for a moment Nelda found herself wishing she were an Irish setter—then at least she would get some attention from him.

"He expects him to be back chasing motorcycles in a few weeks."

"Good."

He finally looked up at her, and, over the sound of her galloping heart, she said,

"Linda is coming for lunch. I've made sandwiches. Would you like to stay?"

"Thanks, but no. I've got to get back to work."

She listened for regret in his voice, but heard only what sounded like a subtle accusation.

"Okay. I just thought you'd like to take a break and have some lunch."

"You may be used to long lunch breaks in Chicago, but here we're sometimes forced to skip the martinis and grab a sandwich while we work," he said tightly.

With the emphasis falling heavily on his last word, Nelda had not a doubt that she'd interpreted the accusatory tone correctly. Miffed, all she could think of to fling at his retreating back was,

"I don't even like martinis!"

The phone rang, and she jerked the receiver off the hook.

"Hello."

"How's my babe?"

"Oh, hello, Aldus—"

Nelda heard the screen door slam. *Lute had stayed hoping to find out who was calling*. She hoped he got an earful!

"Babe, I'm havin' a problem with the lights over the bar—"

"Aldus, you'll have to call Elite Decorators, and someone will be out right away."

"Dammit to hell. I don't want them. I want you!" he shouted into the phone.

"I'm sorry, Aldus, I'm scheduled to go into the hospital tomorrow for an exploratory operation. I can't help you." *Here I am lying again, God.*

"What's the matter with ya?"

"They won't know until they operate."

"Well, that's a hell of a note."

"Isn't it?"

" 'Bye, puss. Let me know when ya know somethin'."

" 'Bye." Nelda hung up.

Maybe that'll take care of Aldus Falerri for a while.

She went to the door to see if Lute's truck was still there. It was, and the barn door was open. She looked at her watch. Linda would be here in fifteen minutes. Deciding not to let his boorish actions intimidate her, she marched out the door and crossed the yard to the barn. After all it was *her* barn!

She paused in the doorway to allow her eyes to become accustomed to the gloom.

"I see you bought a new mower." Lute's voice came from the back of the barn.

"Yeah, I did."

"I've been mowing the yard and the ditches."

"Well you don't need to do that anymore."

"Suit yourself. You going to take care of the snow, too?"

"If I can't, I'll hire someone."

"I want to rent your barn." *That was a dumb thing to say. When he rented the land he rented the outbuildings.*

"It's your corn in the silo, isn't it? Weren't the barn and the silo included when you rented the land?"

"The silo was. I'll have to check with Hutchinson about the barn."

"You can use it."

"I'll bring over a couple of my horses. I'll have to do some work on those stalls."

Nelda shrugged. "Be my guest."

"I'll also fill the hay mow."

"Be my guest," she said again, then changed the subject suddenly. "I think someone has been in the garage. Does anyone come around here besides you?"

"My hired man. Why do you think someone's been in the garage?"

"I found a blanket and candy-bar wrappers when I cleaned it out."

"They could have been there a long time."

Nelda went to the door and looked out when she heard a car coming down the lane.

"Linda's here. Excuse me."

"Yes, ma'am. Your boyfriend coming out?" he said to her back as she walked away.

"I don't know yet," she answered without looking around. *Take that and chew on it, Mr. Lute Hanson. Damn him. He can make me so mad! If he hates me so much, why hasn't he cut the wedding ring off his finger?*

Nelda would have enjoyed Linda's visit more if Lute hadn't been hammering out in the barn.

"Are you and Lute getting back together?" Linda asked.

"No. He's renting my barn and fixing the stalls for his horses. Have another sandwich?"

"No, thanks. But I will have some more tea. I love iced tea, but I seldom make it. Kurt doesn't like it."

"You could make it just for yourself."

"Yeah, I guess I could." Linda's shoulders slumped.

"Tell me about your little boy."

"He's smart as a whip. Of course, that's a mother talking. But he really is. He can already read a little and write his name." She dug into her purse and brought out a picture of a smiling dark-haired child with two front teeth missing. "He was so cute when he lost his front teeth. I just had to have a picture." Her eyes were sad when she looked up. "He's the joy of my life."

"I can see that he would be."

"You're so lucky, Nelda. You've got a home here, a career. I wanted to take nurses' training, but . . . well . . . things happen. I was so anxious to get away from my family that I said yes to the first man who asked me to marry him."

"You still could go back to school. Lots of women do after they have children."

"Ah . . . Kurt would have a fit if I even suggested it."

"Explain to him that someday you may need to support yourself and Eric and—"

"—Kurt believes that the man is the head of the family, and the woman stays home and does what he tells her to do." There was bitterness in her voice. "He hasn't had much luck holding jobs. I guess that's why he has to prove he's the boss in his own house."

"You were the smartest girl in our class, Linda. I think you'd make a terrific nurse."

"Oh, I'd love to do it."

"Then make a start. The hospital gives scholarships. Find out how to go about getting one."

"I'll do it." Linda stood, her face beaming. "I've got to get Eric. Nelda, I'm so glad you're back. You've been to so many places, done so many things. You give me courage."

"Promise you'll come back and bring Eric."

"I promise."

Lute, followed by Kelly, came out of the barn when Nelda went to the car with Linda. Linda waved to him and stooped to pat Kelly's head when the dog came to her.

"He'll let me pet him now."

"Out of the car, he's friendly. The car is his territory."

"Good boy."

Nelda watched Linda drive away, then, ignoring Lute, went back into the house. If he wanted to talk to her, he knew where to find her.

He evidently didn't want to talk to her. He got into his pickup and drove out of the yard. Several hours later, the lumber-company truck came with a load of lumber. The man opened the barn doors and piled it inside.

The next morning, before Nelda was out of bed, Kelly barked. She got up, slipped on a robe, and went downstairs expecting to see Lute's truck. Two men were taking tools from a panel truck to the barn. Nelda let Kelly out. He hurried to them, his tail wagging.

"Heck of a guard dog, you are," Nelda fumed. "You can just stay out there until I take my bath."

Several days passed. The panel truck came every morning at eight o'clock sharp. It left at twelve noon and returned at one o'clock. During the time the workmen were there, she heard constant hammering or the buzzing of a power saw. There was no sign of Lute.

One evening after the men left, she went to the barn to see what they were doing. After all, she reasoned, it was still her barn even if she had rented it to Lute.

Three horse stalls had been built in the back of the barn: one large one and two smaller. A window had been installed in each stall. A grain manger had been built into one corner of each stall and, in the opposite corner, a watering bowl.

What's going on here? she thought as she surveyed the extensive remodeling. *He's spending quite a bit of money on someone else's barn. What if I decide to sell the farm. The man must be out of his mind. I'll tell him so the next time I see him.*

Telling him about the barn didn't even enter her mind when next she saw him.

The days slipped by. One morning Nelda discovered the trees were bare of leaves and among the dead vines, yellow pumpkins dotted the patches. When she and Kelly took their daily walks, the dog liked to frolic in the piles of dry leaves. Fall was in the air. She loved being in the country and had no desire to return to the city.

Saturday night she went to town for groceries. With a week's supply in the trunk of her car, she walked up to the Corner Drug and bought a new lipstick. She was surprised at how long her hair had grown when she saw herself in the mirror at the cosmetic counter. She'd had it cut just before she left Chicago. Could that be three months ago? Of course, it was the middle of October.

After leaving the drugstore she walked past the Oluf T. Hanson department store. It looked just as it had when she and her grandma went there to buy fabric for her prom dress.

On an impulse she turned in at Halford's Cafe to treat herself to dinner instead of going back to the farm and eating a sandwich. The brightly lit cafe was half-filled with diners and a delicious aroma filled the air.

Walking down the row of booths to a vacant one halfway along the side, Nelda's eyes collided with those of Lute sitting in a booth with a dark-haired girl. He nodded. She continued on, not sure if her steps had faltered. Sliding into an empty booth, she found herself looking across at the woman Lute was with.

She was pretty, with brown hair shaded with red and beautiful dark eyes. It was easy to see that she was giving Lute all her attention. Nelda felt sick. She had known that a man as virile as Lute would have female friends, but knowing and seeing were two different things. She picked up the menu that was propped behind the paper-napkin dispenser. When the waitress came for her order, she chose the first item that caught her eye—a hamburger with everything on it.

There was one booth between where she was sitting and where Lute sat with the dark-haired girl who was laughing and talking nonstop. Nelda had never felt lonelier in her life.

It seemed to Nelda that she sat there years before the waitress returned, but it could only have been a few minutes. She longed with all her heart to be home, but she didn't dare leave with Lute sitting there. She had cut her hamburger in two and taken a bite when she saw a familiar face coming toward her.

"Hello." Earl Hutchinson stopped beside the booth. "I see you've discovered Halford's. This cafe is an institution here in Clear Lake."

"I can understand why, if all their food is as good as this hamburger." It was lip service, of course. She was too numb to taste a thing.

"I usually come here on Saturday night. Are you alone? Do you mind if I sit down?"

"By all means. Happy for your company."

He shrugged out of a light coat, folded it, and placed it on the seat before he slid into the booth.

"When I first came here to open my practice, my wife and I came here on Saturday night for our special treat. The habit has continued." His gray eyes appraised her. "You're looking good. Country life must agree with you."

"It's all the peace and quiet. I've not heard a horn blast from one impatient taxi since I've been here."

"Hello, Earl." The waitress set a glass of water on the table.

"How you doing, Mavis?"

"Fine. You want the usual?"

"Is there anything else for me on Saturday night?" He smiled at the woman.

"Guess not. We've got pumpkin pie tonight."

"I'll have some. How about it, Mrs. Hanson? The pie here is about this thick." He held his forefinger and thumb about three inches apart.

"You're fibbin', Earl. You'll get me in trouble if she expects pie that thick."

"You're safe, because by the time I finish this hamburger, I'll be full."

"Nice woman," Earl said when the waitress left. "I handled her divorce. Now she's working two jobs to put her daughter through nursing school."

"I have a friend who would like to go to nursing school, but she doesn't think her husband will allow it and she doesn't have enough confidence in herself to confront him."

"That's something that would have to be worked out between them. Mavis's husband was a woman-chaser. Thank goodness he left the state after the divorce; it saved her a lot of embarrassment."

"If my friend was accepted for nurses' training, how would I go about contributing to a scholarship for her without her knowing it?"

"Through me. I'm your lawyer."

"Could the farm account stand a five-hundred-dollar gift?"

"Easily."

"Would you be opposed to advising my friend Linda Branson, should she ask for advice, that is? I will pay for your time . . . again without her knowing."

"I would be glad to advise Linda. And without cost to you. I do a certain amount of pro bono work."

"That's good of you. Linda was my one true girlfriend when I was in school here. I'd like to see her achieve her ambition."

Nelda could see that Lute and his friend were leaving. He turned as he got out of the booth, and their eyes caught for an instant. She looked away and smiled at Earl. When she looked up again, Lute was paying at the cash register, and his date was waiting beside the door. She was attractive and well dressed, and Nelda didn't care if she was a saint; she hated her.

The waitress brought Earl his meal: a hot beef sandwich, a pile of mashed potatoes, and a lot of hot brown gravy. By the time she left the booth, Lute and his date were long gone.

Nelda decided that she liked Earl Hutchinson. She learned that his wife had died two years before. They had married right out of high school. She had worked while he went first to college, then to law school at night. They had not been lucky enough, Earl said, to have children.

He told her some things about the farm that she had not concerned herself with before.

"The propane-gas company will automatically keep your tank filled. They send the bills to me. If you'd rather see them, along with the electric and telephone, I can have copies sent to you."

"That's all right. It's a luxury not to have to fool with them."

"We have kept heat in the house even though it wasn't occupied."

"That's why things are in such good shape. I remember hearing that extreme cold would cause good furniture to crack and tile flooring to buckle."

"The well," he said, "is about 380 feet deep. I had it looked at when we evaluated the farm. It'll not cause trouble for years. The septic tank, however, should be cleaned next spring."

"If I'm still here, you'll have to remind me."

"I'm surprised Lute didn't say something. He knows about it."

"Did you know that he's putting stalls in the barn for his horses? If I sell the farm, he's going to lose a lot of money."

"He's taking the chance that if you sell, it will be to him."

"He wants to buy it?"

"Hasn't he told you?"

"No. He's expecting me to run back to Chicago at any time. He'd probably rather deal with you than me."

Nelda and Earl left the cafe together, she to go one way, he another. On the way to her car, Nelda met Linda and her husband.

"Linda. Imagine seeing you again so soon."

"Hello." Linda glanced up at the man beside her. "This is my husband, Kurt. Nelda and I went to school together."

"Hi." The man burrowed his bare head into the

collar of his coat, but his eyes never left Nelda's face. "So this is your big-shot friend?"

Linda looked as if she would like to sink into the sidewalk.

"Big shot? Hey, I always did want to be one," Nelda said laughingly. "I guess I've made the grade."

"You're the one that put the bright idea in Linda's head to go to nurses' school, ain't ya?"

"No. It's my idea," Linda said quickly.

"Ha! Don't give me that bull . . . shit. You ain't never had a bright idea in your life."

The man was drunk. Nelda was embarrassed for Linda. She looked ready to cry. Anger made Nelda's voice sharp.

"Linda asked me what I thought of the idea. I think it would be great. She was the smartest girl in our class. She'd make an excellent nurse. Someday she may need to make a living for herself."

"Bull . . . sshee . . . it." He drew the word out as if knowing it was embarrassing to his wife. "Ya think I can't support my wife and kid? Is that it?"

"I didn't say that. It's a blessing if the wife has the brains and skills to get a job and support the family if her husband gets sick or has an accident."

"Big-city gal's got all the answers. Huh?"

"I'd better be going, Linda. I've Kelly and groceries in the car. Give me a call, and we'll go to lunch sometime. I want to keep in touch."

Nelda walked on down the street without looking back. What an awful, awful man! He surely couldn't have been that bad when Linda married him. She deserved better than that.

On the way back to the farm, Nelda mulled over the meeting with Linda and her husband and hoped that Linda would have the courage to stand up to him, to enroll in school, and make a better life for herself and her son.

Nelda was glad when she turned down the lane that she had left the yard light on. Reluctant to go into the garage, she parked beside the porch, let Kelly out, and watched for his reaction. If anyone was around, the dog would know it. Nelda stayed in the car until Kelly smelled around, and headed for the door.

❧ *Chapter Seven* ❧

NELDA DIDN'T BELIEVE IN THE SUPERNATURAL until one cold morning when she thought to put a blanket on the tiled floor in the kitchen for Kelly. She went to the porch to get the one she had taken out of the garage, and it wasn't there. She looked blankly at the spot on the bench where she had put it. It had been there a couple of days earlier, she was sure.

Back in the kitchen she closed the door and stood for a minute looking out the glass pane. There was no lock on the screen door opening onto the back porch. Anyone could have come in. But who had? Lute never came to the house anymore. He avoided it as if there were a smallpox quarantine sign on the door. His hired man came to do chores, sometimes with a young girl. They never even looked toward the house as far as Nelda knew.

Tuesday she had gone to the garage to get a road map out of her car. When she opened the car door and bent over to open the glove compartment, she had caught a whiff of a strange odor.

Someone had been in her car!

No, it couldn't be. Her car had been in the garage for a couple of days. On the floor on the driver's side she had noticed a tiny piece of foil. She had picked it up, grabbed the maps, and hurried back to the house.

By the time she got into the safety of the house, she had almost forgotten the reason she wanted the map. Of course, it was to see how far it was to Minneapolis, where she could shop at an arts and crafts store.

She had carefully unfolded the tiny piece of foil and pressed it out. It appeared to be the wrapping from a "candy kiss," a small cone-shaped chocolate. Now where had that come from? She never ate chocolate. She'd never had much desire for sweets.

Nelda moved away from the window, remembering the picture album which had seemed out of place on the coffee table and the unlocked porch door. None of these little "oddities" was in the least threatening, but as a pattern, they were disturbing to a woman alone.

After several killing frosts, the rush was on to get the corn out of the field.

One morning Nelda awakened to hear the sounds of farm machinery in the fields surrounding the house. She went to the window and watched the two-row corn picker make a sweep around the edge of the field before beginning on the evenly spaced rows.

A cold wind was blowing from the north when

Nelda went out for her daily walk with Kelly. She put on her grandpa's old shearling coat and tied a wool scarf about her head. Fastening the leash to Kelly's collar because she didn't trust him to stay close along the road, she set out with him on a brisk walk.

They reached the end of the lane and paused beside the fence to watch a machine pulling a wagon across the field. The machine's large spout was spitting ears of corn into the wagon. When it was filled, a second wagon was hitched to the corn picker and the process began again.

Nelda stood leaning on the fence, fascinated by the mechanical rhythm of the corn coming from the spout. When the machine reached the end of the row near the fence she saw that it was Lute driving the picker. It had been several weeks since she had seen him and a fierce joy suddenly pounded in her blood. The picker swung around to start back down the rows, then stopped. Lute jumped down.

In worn jeans and heavy sheepskin jacket, he was so handsome that Nelda could hardly take her eyes off him. She had seen the blue knit caps like the one he wore many times on the military bases and knew that it was a leftover from his Navy days. When he came toward her, Kelly whined and wiggled a welcome. Lute stooped to poke his fingers through the fence and scratch behind the dog's ears.

"Cold day." Nelda thought she had to say something.

"Not too bad. No wind," he yelled over the sound of the machine. "I should get this field picked by evening. We're getting a darn good crop this year. It's pretty dry, too."

She scarcely heard his words, but she recognized that he was being friendly. Her heart danced happily in her breast.

Lute leaned toward her and shouted. "Would you like to make a trip across the field and back?"

"I'd love to, but what about Kelly?"

"Tie him to the fence. He'll be okay."

Lute grabbed hold of a fence post, stuck his booted toe in one of the wire squares, and jumped over. He took Kelly's leash from her hand and tied it to the post then jumped back over the fence and waited for Nelda.

"I don't know if I can do it."

"Sure you can." Lute grinned. "Put your foot on the wire and grab the post."

Determined to try, Nelda did as she was told, but the fence was too high for her and she ended up helplessly suspended, a leg dangling on either side.

"Heavens! Now what'll I do? The barb at the top has caught my jeans."

"You're in a hell of a mess." Lute laughed. "Maybe I should leave you there. You'd make a damned good-looking scarecrow."

"Lute! You buzzard! Help me! Get me off," she wailed.

Still laughing, he circled her waist while she held on to his shoulders. He lifted her until she leaned against him, then reached around her to unhook her jeans from the strand of barbed wire.

"It was fun while it lasted—the chic Mrs. Hanson classing up a cornfield."

Try not to clutch at him, she commanded herself. *Act as though it's no earthshaking event to be so close to him.* She slid down the solid length of him until her feet touched the ground. Her arms were still about his neck when she looked up. Surprised by the emotion on his face, she tried to turn away, but his fingers beneath her chin lifted her face toward his, and he kissed her lips gently.

Abruptly he pulled away, turned and strode to the picker. Panic and confusion tore at her heart. *He acts as if he's angry because he kissed me. One minute of sweet sharing, the next moment rebuff.*

From the picker he beckoned to her. He wasn't smiling. His brows were knit together, and she desperately wished she had refused to come. Lute sprang lightly up onto the spring seat, then reached a hand down for her. She stretched to put her foot on the high step and he hauled her up to sit on his lap, her back snug against his chest.

His gloved hands worked the controls of the machine and it began to move. The engine didn't sound so loud up here, or maybe she had become used to it. Lute steered between the rows of tall dried cornstalks. Nelda watched as the machine seemed to swallow them. She saw Lute glance from time to time in the mirror to check the ears of corn spewing out of the funnel and into the wagon behind.

She turned so that she could speak close to his ear.

"How do you take the corn off the cob?"

"I have a corn sheller up at the house. It takes off the corn and discards the cob," he explained almost grudgingly, she thought.

At the end of the field, a man was waiting with an empty wagon. While they waited for the full wagon to be taken away and the empty one connected, Lute was silent. The arms around her held her loosely. The hard thighs she was sitting on could just as well have been a bench.

Why is he acting like this? Nelda fretted silently. *He's sorry he asked me to come. Lute, please don't shut me out. I can share your life. I know I can.*

"I've started making my block prints," she volunteered. She had to make him talk to her. In a few short minutes they would be back at the fence where they'd left Kelly. She probably wouldn't see him again for weeks. "I had my screens burned in Mason City," she continued, her lips close to his ear. "I think you'd like them. They're earthy—corn, milkweed pods, wild tiger lilies, and even thistle."

"Thistle? Strange you find something pretty about thistle. We have to spray constantly to keep it out of the fields."

His words were cynical, and they hurt. Uneasy silence hung between them. Uncertain how to deal with his mood, she tried to keep a tremor out of her voice as she acknowledged, "I didn't know that."

"I'm sure you didn't." This time there was no mistaking the sarcasm in his voice.

Nelda drew in a deep breath, deciding to say no more. They reached the end of the field; Lute swung the machine in a wide arc, stopping beside the fence.

Kelly barked and wiggled and tried to get through the small wire squares to reach them.

Lute held on to her hand and lowered her to the ground, then jumped down.

"It's not as exciting as a taxi ride, but it's all we've got to offer."

"It was wonderful. I loved it. Don't you get awfully cold out here all day?" Nelda was determined not to react to Lute's sarcasm.

"This isn't cold. I've picked when it was twenty below."

"Thank you." She started to move away, but he grabbed her arm and pulled her back to him.

"You forgot to pay the driver. Nothing in this life is free, not even here in the middle of a cornfield."

He crushed her to him so hard the air exploded from her lungs. His mouth found hers. His lips were cold, but warmed against hers. His hands gripped her arms ruthlessly, almost as though he wanted to hurt her, but then gradually they gentled. His lips softened, and he kissed her again.

Nelda forced herself to stand quietly in his embrace, straining to conceal the wild, tremulous sensations that swamped her. Presently he loosened his arms and held her away from him to look down into her face. His expression was grim and hard.

"You seeing Hutchinson now?"

"When I need to know something about the farm." She forced herself to answer calmly.

"Business is usually taken care of in his office. He's a good catch, you know. The day after he buried his wife, half the single women in town were taking him food and offering to clean his house."

"That was nice of them," she said quietly.

"He's more your type than a farmer, huh?"

Nelda's temper began to rise. She jerked away from him. "What do you care, Lute? You don't want me."

She left him without a backward glance, but she knew that he watched her climb back over the fence. Thank goodness, she managed to get to the other side without getting her jeans caught again. She untied Kelly, and they continued their walk down the road. Behind her she heard the tractor pulling the corn picker roar into action.

During the next couple of weeks the landscape around the farm changed dramatically. Gone were the fields of yellow cornstalks. When Nelda went to town, she no longer needed to slow down at the "corn" intersections; she was able to see for a quarter of a mile in either direction.

This morning she had called Linda and suggested they meet for lunch.

"I'd rather meet you at the library, Nelda."

"The library will be fine with me. There are a couple of books I'd like to pick up anyway."

The public library was across from the Congregational Church. The librarian was friendly and helpful. Nelda found the books she wanted and took them to a far table to wait for Linda.

Linda hurried in right on time. Her face was rosy from the cold.

"I didn't think about your having to walk. I could have picked you up."

"It wasn't bad walking. I don't even mind the snow, but I hate it when it's all icy." Linda took off her coat and put it on the back of a chair.

"I was hoping you'd call or come out."

Linda sat down and put her hands over her face. "I was too ashamed."

"Ashamed? Why?"

"The way Kurt was . . . that night. He'd had a little too much to drink."

"I knew that. Forget it. I asked Mr. Hutchinson about scholarships, and he said that he thought one could be arranged."

"Really?"

"Yes, really. You made all A's in high school. I'm sure that's what will get you one . . . if you decide to go."

"Oh, Lord. I do want to go. Eric's in school a half a day. My neighbor would watch him the other half. Next year he'll go all day."

"Call the hospital and find out how to go about getting into a class, then go see Mr. Hutchinson. He's really a nice man. He'll help you." Nelda reached out and put her hand on Linda's.

"Yes, he is nice. If you don't get back with Lute, he would be . . . right for you."

"Hey, now. What are you, the town matchmaker?" Nelda laughed, trying to lighten Linda's mood.

"I'm being selfish. I want to keep you here. I've not had a friend of my own for a long time."

They spent the rest of their time together looking for books on nursing. The librarian helped and by the time they were ready to leave, Linda had picked out three books on nursing and two children's books for Eric.

Nelda offered to take her home.

"No, but thanks. I passed the garage where Kurt works. He'll be looking to see what time I go back home."

"Linda?" Nelda tilted her head quizzically.

Linda laughed nervously, and her cheeks reddened.

"I'm used to him. Don't worry about it."

On the way back to the farm, Nelda noticed that she was low on gas and stopped at the service station on the edge of town. She saw several boys inside the building, and she waited for one to come out. When one did, he strolled leisurely, calling to his friends back over his shoulder. Nelda rolled down the window.

"Fill it please."

He took off the gas cap, put the nozzle in tank, leaned close to the window.

"Does that dog bite?"

"Put your hand inside, and you'll find out."

"He'd get a load of buckshot if he bit me."

"He'd not bite you unless you were trespassing."

"You still out there on Lute's farm?"

"I'm out there on *my* farm." Surprised by the question, Nelda turned and met his eyes head-on. His traveled over her, then returned to her face. Nelda wanted to laugh. The kid was flirting with her. "Why do you ask?"

"I keep track of all the good-looking women who come to town. Need any company out there?"

"How come you're not in school?" She felt a need to put him in his place.

"School?" He laughed cockily. "You mean college."

"I mean high school. You can't be old enough for college." Nelda turned up the volume on the car radio. The Everly Brothers were singing, "Wake up, Little Susie."

When the tank was full, the boy removed the nozzle and hung it back on the pump. While he fiddled with the gas-tank cap, Nelda took a bill from her purse and held it out the window. When he snatched it from her hand, a grin twitched her lips. He returned with her change and shoved it into her outstretched hand without looking at her. Nelda laughed out loud as she drove away.

That night she received her first obscene phone call.

It was cold.

She watched the ten o'clock news and waited for the weather report. The weatherman in the uniform of the Shell Oil Company, pretended to climb the mythical Shell Weather Tower inside the studio to give the forecast.

"The rain that started an hour ago is turning to sleet. The temperature is falling here at the Shell

Tower," he said. "Expect icy conditions by morning."

"Now isn't that great?" Nelda said to Kelly. "We're going to be housebound. I don't intend to venture out on the ice."

She was at the top of the stairs when the phone rang. It was ten-thirty.

"You go on up to bed, Kelly. If that's Aldus Falerri, I'm going to tell him that I'm the maid and 'puss' has gone to China. Hello."

"Hello, yourself." It was a muffled male voice.

"Who is this?"

"Someone who'd like to be there with you."

"What are you talking about? Who is this?"

"It's a cold night. You sleepin' alone?"

"What's it to you?"

"You need a man in your bed, sweet thing."

"What . . . what did you say?" Nelda wasn't sure she had heard correctly.

"You got on your nightgown, ain't ya? Reach up under it and poke your finger—"

Nelda slammed down the receiver. She placed her hands against her hot cheeks and started up the stairs. The phone rang again as she reached the top. She stood waiting for it to stop. After fifteen rings she went back downstairs and jerked up the receiver. The man spoke without waiting for her to say anything.

"You know what I'm playin' with? Guess. It's big and hard and—"

"You pervert! If you call here again, I'll call the police."

"No, ya won't." He laughed. "Are ya curly down there like ya are on top?"

Nelda slammed down the receiver, then lifted it and laid it on the counter. After checking the doors to make sure they were locked, she went up to bed only to lie awake wondering about the calls. It wasn't anyone she knew or had met, she was almost sure of that. The voice didn't sound like the boy at the filling station. She would like to think that the caller had dialed her number at random, but the second call ruled that out. Her name wasn't even in the phone book. She mulled over the possibilities until finally sleep came.

Kelly's excited bark awakened her. He raced from the room and down the stairs. Then she heard the pounding on the kitchen door. Nelda reached for the light and turned the switch. Nothing. The electricity was off, and someone was at the door. Could it be that awful person who had called her? Frightened, she got out of bed, felt her way to the closet, and put on her heavy robe. Why hadn't she thought to take the flashlight out of the car?

The pounding on the door continued, now accompanied by Kelly's barks. With her heart racing, she groped her way down the stairs. The dog was at the kitchen door, whining a welcome to someone. The beam from a flashlight shone through the window.

"Nelda!" Lute's voice. "Nelda—"

Weak with relief, she reached the door and unlocked it. Lute stomped into the kitchen. The first thing he said was, "Get some shoes on."

"What's happened?" she asked, so frightened that she hadn't noticed the cold floor.

"Hell of an ice storm. The electricity is out. Phones are dead. I tried to call you earlier and the damn line was busy. Boyfriend again?"

"No. I left it . . . I forgot to hang it up. What time is it?"

"Four-thirty. Don't flush the toilet until you just have to. Once the tank is empty it won't fill. Without electricity the pump doesn't run, nor the forced-air furnace. Cripes, I forgot about this electric range. It's going to be really cold in here in a little while. Get upstairs and put some clothes on."

Nelda went to the living room and brought a scented candle in a glass jar from the coffee table. Lute took a book of matches from his pocket, struck one, and lit it. With a little more light, Nelda would see that his face was red from the cold.

"How cold is it?"

"Ten below. Are there any oil lamps around here?"

"There's one in a bedroom upstairs."

"After you dress, bring it down. I'm going to check on my horses, and I'll bring in the can of kerosene from the barn. I need some light to check the chimney on that cookstove before I build a fire in it." He went to the door and Kelly followed him out.

Nelda picked up her candle and headed for the stairs. Would she ever understand this man? They hadn't exchanged a word for weeks, and here he was in her house in the early-morning hours taking charge as if he lived here.

❧ *Chapter Eight* ❧

LUTE CAME IN CARRYING A LOAD OF SCRAP WOOD from the barn and a big red can. From the can he filled the lamp that Nelda had brought down from the upstairs bedroom. The light bathed the kitchen in a warm glow.

Working swiftly, he stuffed paper and kindling in the firebox of the cookstove and put a match to it. When it began to blaze, he added pieces of the scrap lumber, and soon the fire was popping and crackling and giving off heat. He closed the door of the firebox and adjusted the damper on the tin stovepipe.

"I threw firewood in the back of the pickup before I left home. I'll bring it in."

Lute's eyes flashed over her before he went out the door, noting her wool slacks and heavy wool sweater. Her face was pale, and she had dark circles under her eyes as if she'd been up all night, as he had been.

He had called her over a period of an hour when he realized that there was the possibility the power would go off. Getting the busy signal at that time of night meant that she must be talking to someone very important to her, more than likely the nightclub owner in Chicago. What the hell kind of man would have a name like Aldus?

Damn her! Why did she have to come back? I was on the verge of falling in love with Meredith and asking her to marry me. She would be the ideal wife for a farmer.

Lute made three trips to the pickup to bring in wood for the cook stove.

"My wood is cut for the fireplace. I had to scrounge around to find some smaller stuff." He took off his gloves and his heavy sheepskin coat and hung it on the back of the chair. "We've got to keep heat in here or the pipes will freeze, and you'll have a real mess. We can't drain them completely just by opening the taps. If I could have got through to you . . . on the phone"—his tone was accusing—"I would have told you to draw some water to have on hand."

Nelda stood beside the stove saying nothing. Lute looked at her with a tilt to his head.

"You sick or something?"

"No. This came on so suddenly that I'm . . . that I just don't know what to do."

"I figured you wouldn't. That's why I'm here."

"Shouldn't you be with your mother?"

"She's in California for the winter. A friend who's there will keep the fireplaces going."

"A . . . friend?"

"Yes. He came up from Des Moines to hunt

pheasants. Did you think I had a girlfriend over there? If I had, I'd certainly not have left her to come over here and freeze my rear off trying to keep your pipes from freezing."

"I wouldn't have expected you to." She turned her back and held her hands over the warm stove. If he hated her so much, why was he still wearing the wedding ring?

She wanted to cry.

"The wind is coming up; and with the wires and branches covered with a coat of ice, there'll be more outages." Lute took a bottle of water from the refrigerator and poured it into a pan and set it on the stove. "Get some pans and we'll drain the water out of the pipes. Where's the coffee?"

"On the shelf above the range. There's a drip coffeepot there, too." She took a large kettle from a lower cupboard and placed it on the counter. "Is this big enough?"

Nelda sat down on a chair and watched him. Kelly came close and sat beside her. Automatically her hand began to stroke his head. Lute was perfectly at ease in her house. She had never even been in his. Thinking about it, she became so depressed, she shivered.

"Are you cold?"

Did he have eyes in the back of his head?

"I've been warmer."

"If you don't have any long johns, you should put on several layers of clothing. A couple pair of slacks, and a light sweater or two under the heavy one."

In the silence that followed Nelda heard the ice-covered branches scraping the house. It was eerie in the kitchen with Lute. The furniture in the flickering lamplight cast strange shadows, making her feel that they were living in another time. This was how a bitterly cold night had been for pioneer women, for her grandmother when she was young, dependent on her man, needing him to take care of her.

She looked to see Lute gazing at her. What was going on in that blond head under the knit cap?

"Coffee in a minute. It'll warm you up." He lifted his coat from the back of the chair and draped it around her shoulders. "When daylight comes, I'll have to go back over to the farm and see that my livestock have feed and water."

"Will your horses be all right?"

"The barn is good and tight, and there are a couple of barrels of water that'll last for a while." He lifted two cups down from the cabinet and set them on the back of the stove to warm. He chucked another piece of split log into the firebox, then opened the door of the oven and pulled a kitchen chair over to it. "Come sit over here. Feel the heat coming from the oven? I wish Mom had kept our old cookstove. I just may have to buy one."

When Lute put the cup of hot coffee in her hands, she looked up at him with bleak eyes.

"You don't have to stay, Lute. I can keep the fire going. I appreciate your coming and bringing the wood."

"You want me to go?" he asked quietly, his eyes holding hers.

"No. I didn't mean that. Just because I'm here alone, I don't want you to feel obligated to come over here to help me when you're needed at home."

"Don't worry about that. I look after my own first." He turned back to pick up his coffee mug, cupping it in his two hands. He moved over to the far side of the room to look out the window. Dawn had lit the eastern sky. "Wires will be whipping and breaking in this wind. Already a couple of limbs are down. The danger is that someone may come in contact with a hot wire and be electrocuted."

Why in the hell did he continue to say cruel things to her? he asked himself. The words just seemed to seep out of the depth of his bitterness. He had been hurt so damn bad! He hadn't wanted her to come back. He hadn't wanted ever to see her again. She didn't intend to stay here. She was worming her way into his heart and would break it again.

Hell. She'd never left a small corner of it, even when he was sure that he hated her.

When he heard about the ice storm coming, he'd worked most of the night taking care of his own place so he could come here. The thought of her being alone, cold and scared, would have brought him here if he'd had to crawl. He didn't dare let her know that. She already had a tight enough hold on him.

He turned wearily from the window and looked at her. She sat huddled beside the open oven door of the cookstove, her hand buried in the fur around Kelly's neck.

"Are all the storm windows down good and tight?"

"I did that some time ago. I couldn't budge a couple of them. Mr. Olsen helped me. He squirted something on the tracks that made them slide more easily."

Lute snorted. "And probably told everyone in the township about it."

Nelda glanced at him and then looked away. He had something sarcastic to say about everything she said or did. She swallowed hard and concentrated on not letting him see the deep ache within her, even though her eyes misted over at the anger he showed in his caustic comments.

"Are you hungry?"

"No. Fix something for yourself if you want. There's bacon and eggs."

"I'll eat when I go home to do chores." He straddled a chair and rested his arms on the back. "When you put wood in the firebox, put in one chunk at a time. You don't want to build up too big a blaze."

"I'll remember." *Go. Please go. I don't want you to see me cry.*

Finally, Lute stood and reached for his coat. "It's getting light. I'll go on home. When I come back I'll bring more wood and a battery-powered radio."

"You don't need to do that."

"Don't you want to hear the news?"

"I can go out to the car—"

"Don't go out. You could fall on the ice, lie there, and freeze to death in a couple of hours. It's slicker than greased lightning out there. I'll bring you a radio."

"All right," she said.

What was the matter with her? She was as docile as a lamb all of a sudden. It's as if the fight had been taken out of her. He studied her face. It was devoid of expression.

"Are you sure you're not sick?"

"I'm not sick. I'm tired."

"Well, don't go to sleep and let the fire go out." He was putting on his gloves.

This final order was the last straw! Nelda looked up at him. "You think because I've lived in a city for most of my life that I'm not smart enough to keep a fire going when it's ten below outside. My survival instincts are just as strong as yours. As long as there is anything in this house made of wood, the fire will not go out."

"I'm glad to hear it." He went to the door, turned to look at the back of her head. "I'll be back."

Nelda sat rigidly in the chair until she heard his pickup start. She went to the window and watched his truck creep along the icy lane to the road.

Tears rolled slowly down her cheeks.

When the light of day entered the kitchen, Nelda blew out the oil lamp and left the warmth of the cookstove to go up to her bedroom. Hurriedly, she gathered up a couple of sweaters, two pairs of pajama pants to put on under the slacks, a couple pairs of socks, and Kelly's bed.

Back in the kitchen she placed the cold pajama

pants on the oven door to warm them before stripping and pulling them on. After re-dressing, she heated a small amount of water and made a cup of tea. Carrying the cup with her, she went from window to window looking out on the winter wonderland.

Everything was covered with a thick layer of ice. The tree branches drooped with the weight of it. The electric and telephone wires coming from the road to the house were heavy with ice and swaying in the wind.

Nelda felt terribly alone and isolated in her icy prison. She was grateful that Lute had come, even if he had felt obligated because she was a neighbor. *If I'd had a lady friend, do you think I'd have left her to come over here and freeze my rear—*

His words had cut her to the quick.

Kelly whined at the door.

"Do you need to go out?" Nelda opened the kitchen door, then closed it behind her while she crossed the porch to let the dog out. "Hurry, Kelly."

The dog reached the bottom of the steps, fell, and started sliding. He slid on his rear, yelping in surprise. He tried to stand several times before he could stay on his feet. Nelda watched him through the door pane. When he made his way carefully back to the steps, Nelda opened the door, grabbed his collar, and helped him up onto the porch.

"Are you ready to go back to a warm apartment, Kelly? We had bad weather in Chicago, but nothing like this."

After feeling the bite of the cold wind they both

returned to huddle beside the stove. The dog whined a response and curled up on his bed. Nelda wandered into the living room and looked longingly at the big, three-cushioned sofa. If only it wasn't so far from the stove. Well, it didn't have to be, that is if she could budge it, she could move it into the kitchen.

First she would have to slide the kitchen table away so that she could position the sofa near the stove. Then the table could back up to it to allow the back door to open. Strengthened by a purpose, she went back to the living room, and removed the cushions and carried them to the kitchen table, then she went back to push the sofa, inches at a time, across the carpet. When it reached the tiled kitchen floor, it slid and was much easier to move into place in front of the cookstove. She replaced the cushions and sat down to catch her breath. Her heart was beating so fast it seemed to fill her ears.

"I did it, Kelly. Aren't you proud of me? I just wonder if my back will ever be the same."

She brought down from upstairs three big wool blankets and a wool comforter and piled them on the table behind the sofa. She spread one blanket over the cushions, then raced back up the stairs to grab the pillow from her bed.

"If we run out of wood, we'll not freeze right away, Kelly."

After she fed the dog, she opened a can of soup for herself and set the can on the stove to heat, then ate the soup from the can.

The hours dragged by. When the fire burned down she added another stick of wood. After warming a small amount of water, she washed her face and hands and applied a thin film of cold cream. She felt refreshed.

On the sofa with a blanket around her shoulders and another across her legs, Nelda looked at her watch for the hundredth time. Two o'clock. The long afternoon and evening loomed ahead. She laid her head back and was just about to fall asleep when Kelly stirred and lifted his head to listen. He got up and went to the door. Nelda followed.

Backing up to the porch door was Lute's pickup, loaded with sand and cut stove wood. The truck was sliding on the ice and unable to get close, so Lute got out and threw several shovels of sand under the back wheels and one on the steps. When the back of the truck was over the steps, he stopped, propped the door open and began unloading the wood, stacking it neatly on the porch.

Nelda watched from the kitchen door window, wondering if he was going to come into the house. When he finished, he went to the cab of the truck and brought out a radio. When she opened the door, he shoved it in her hands and went back to the truck. By the time she had set the radio on the table, Lute was back with a large jug of water and a brown grocery bag.

Nelda felt a flicker of panic when he entered the kitchen. He seemed to fill it. He was so big, so virile, and so capable of crushing her spirit with just a few short words. She moved around to the front of the sofa and stood with her back to the stove. When she looked at him, his eyes were dancing, and his face wore a warm smile. The charm of that smile invaded every corner of her mind.

"That was a good idea," he said, indicating the sofa. He snatched the cap off his head and shrugged out of his coat. "I worked up a sweat out there."

He still wore his ring! Each time she saw him Nelda was compelled to look at his hand.

Lute came over to the stove where she stood. His plaid wool shirt, open at the neck, showed a heavy undershirt beneath it.

"How did a little thing like you get the sofa in here?"

"It . . . wasn't easy."

"You should have waited for me." He reached out with the back of his hand and stroked her cheek. "Are you feeling better?"

"I'm fine."

"I was worried about you when I left this morning."

"I was tired. I've been just fine . . . thanks to your bringing the wood and starting the fire. I wouldn't have known how to get it going in the cookstove."

"You're tougher than you think." He continued to smile down at her, rubbing her cheek with his knuckles.

"How cold is it?" She had to say something sensible.

"It's still ten below. It's supposed to be between twenty-five and thirty tonight."

"Oh, my."

"You'll be all right."

"I was thinking of the poor animals and the peo-

ple who have to be out in the cold fixing the wires
and . . . things."

"If the animals have food and water, they can
make it." Something like a smile crossed his wind-
reddened face as he continued to study her thoughtfully. His fingers moved down to her chin. "I'm
inviting myself to supper."

"I can give you a can of soup." She hoped to
God he was unaware of the turbulent feelings he was
stirring in her.

"You'll be able to do better than that. I brought
a jar of canned beef, a few potatoes, carrots, and
onions."

"For a stew."

"Think you can handle it?"

"Did you bring a cookbook?" Her eyes glowed.
She was suddenly crazily, mindlessly happy.

He laughed and moved to the table to bring the
radio to the counter at the end of the sofa.

"You may get only the Mason City station. Even
if the power goes off over there, they've got a couple of generators that will keep them on the air." He
turned the dial until he had tuned out the static. A
voice came on.

"A year after nine black teenagers, backed by
Federal troops integrated Central High School in Little Rock, Arkansas, a small group of white protest-
ers—"

Lute turned the dial. "I'll see if I can get some
weather news." On one station Elvis was singing
"Love Me Tender." Lute grinned at Nelda. "I wonder how Elvis is liking the army."

"I doubt that he'll have it as tough as a regular GI."

He flipped off the radio. "We'll save the batteries for tonight. I'm not sure how old they are."

Lute checked the firebox on the stove and added a stick of wood. He reached up and turned down the damper on the stovepipe.

"Closing the damper a little keeps the wood from burning so fast. Have you been warm enough?"

"I took your advice and put on more clothes."

"You did, huh?"

"Two sweaters under this one and a pair of pajama pants under my slacks. I was going to put on two pair, but my slacks were so tight I couldn't bend over."

He laughed. "I'd like to have seen that."

"I left my ski suit in Chicago. I never thought I'd need it in north Iowa."

"You planned to go back." It was a statement.

"My job is there. I have to support myself."

"The income from this farm wouldn't keep you in the style that you're accustomed to, is that it?"

"I don't know."

This was dangerous ground, Nelda knew by the tightening of Lute's mouth. The thick-lashed eyes that seemed endowed with the ability to look a hole right though her, wandered over her face.

"Do you plan to go back to that man ... the nightclub owner?"

Nelda laughed nervously. "*Back* to him? You should see him. He's Al Capone reincarnated."

"Did you go out with him?"

"Not out. I had supper with him a few times at his club. We discussed the decorating."

"Then why does he keep calling you?"

"I don't know. Men like him always want something they can't have."

"You've known a lot of men like him?"

"A few. Chicago is full of them. Why the questions, Lute?"

A curious stillness followed, an uneasy silence that deepened and pushed them apart. A faint color spread across her cheeks, betraying the fact that she was shaken by their exchange.

Lute turned away first. "I'll bring in some of that wood from the porch before I go." He proceeded to do that; and after he had a good supply stacked beside the stove, he put on his coat. "I'll need to get my chores done before dark."

"Are there any wires down around your place?"

"Not yet, but there will be if the wind keeps up. There are quite a few branches down. Trees split under a heavy load of ice."

"Be careful."

"Nelda Elaine Hanson with an *o*. Are you worried about me?" He teased, but there was no laughter in his eyes.

"Why sure. No telling how long I'll be . . . icebound here. Without you, I might . . . might—" Her voice trailed.

Lute suddenly hooked a hand behind her neck and pulled her to him.

"Don't be afraid. You'll not be left here alone. I'll be back."

He was out the door before she could gather her wits about her. She followed to watch him through the door pane. He moved the truck down to the barn and went inside.

❧ Chapter Nine ❧

NELDA FELT AS IF SHE OWNED THE WORLD. SHE was fixing supper for Lute. It might be the one and only time, but she refused to think about that.

Her hands stilled as she stirred the bubbling stew. She had to put a lid on her thoughts and stop analyzing each look and each word he said and enjoy the time she had with him. She had just about convinced herself that there was a chance that he was fond of her because of what they had been to each other when they were young and that he might even still love her . . . a little.

She sat down on the couch and stared at the stove. She was letting her imagination run away with her. Lute's emotions ran deep; she had known that when they were young. Whatever feelings he had for her, if any were left, were more than likely related to her being the mother of his dead child, sentimental remnants of a first love gone astray. She must not get her hopes up, and she must not make the mistake of talking about her life in Chicago.

She left the warmth of the kitchen and went into

the bathroom, where she looked at herself in the mirror.

Sheesh! I look like death warmed over.

She repaired the ravages of a sleepless night as best she could by applying light makeup. She didn't want Lute to think she'd made up her face for him. There wasn't much she could do with her hair. It needed to be cut. She brushed it and looped the strands behind her ears.

Lifting the lid on the toilet, she grimaced. She couldn't use it again. A sudden thought flashed through her mind and she headed up the stairs to see if the chamber pot was still in her grandmother's room. She found it in the closet. Grandma called it a toilet bowl. Grandpa called it a slop jar.

Nelda smiled at the memory as she pulled down her various garments and sat down on the ice-cold rim. When she finished she covered it with the china lid and hurried back down to the warm kitchen.

During the long afternoon, she paced the floor and tried to get interested in the daring new novel, *Peyton Place*. She had brought the Grace Metalious book with her from Chicago, but this was the first time she had opened it. Lastly, she brought her grandmother's picture album in, thumbed through it, and laid it aside. It brought back too many memories, happy and sad.

It was after seven o'clock when Nelda, standing beside the window, saw car lights coming up the lane. A feeling of excitement quickened her heartbeat. Regardless of what happened in the future, she would be with Lute for an hour or two tonight.

Lute went first to the barn. When he came out, he moved his pickup up closer to the house, out from under the ice-loaded branches of the oak tree. Nelda was waiting for him when he came in, bringing with him the biting cold of the outdoors.

"It's getting colder." He wiped his boots on the rug just inside the door and took off his gloves and cap. "I smell the stew. Smells good."

"Let's hope it tastes as good as it smells." She took his coat and hung it on the back of the chair.

Kelly was there wiggling and waiting for attention. Lute scratched him behind the ears.

"How'er you doin', fella? Cold enough for you?"

"He's stayed on his bed all day. He doesn't like the cold floor."

"Can you spare water for me to wash?" He looked tired, she thought.

"Right this way." Nelda dipped water into the wash dish from the pan on the counter and added hot water to it from the teakettle. "There are soap and towels in the bathroom. Also a candle."

"All the modern conveniences." He grinned at her, lifted the pan, and disappeared into the bathroom.

Doing this small thing for him made her almost stupidly giddy. Unable to keep the smile off her face, she moved the oil lamp to the table and set places for two. She brought out bread, butter, peanut butter, and jam. After moving the coffeepot to a hot spot on the stove, she lifted the lid and stirred the stew.

Lute came out of the bathroom and stood for a moment watching her. He was struck with the thought that he was asking for a million heartaches. She turned, smiled, and he forgot about everything except that he was here with her now. He said the first thing that came to his mind.

"I flushed the toilet with the water from the wash dish."

She averted her eyes and turned away quickly. He went to her and his hands gripped her shoulders.

"I'm sorry I embarrassed you. I forgot that you're not used to the earthy ways of a farmer." His mouth was close to her ear.

"I'm not . . . embarrassed."

"Liar," he whispered and moved away. "I hope you've cooked plenty. I'm starved."

"I have, and I've made strong coffee."

"Strong enough to float a horseshoe?" he teased.

"I don't know if it's that strong."

"Why don't we set the stewpot on the table?"

"Good idea. I don't think the Queen of England is coming to dinner tonight. I'll get something to set it on. I wish I'd thought of making corn bread. I could have baked it in the oven."

As they ate, they talked about the events of the day. She realized that there was a great deal more to this grown-up Lute than good looks. He was a kind, strong, hardworking man who loved the land, his animals, and even the challenge of the weather.

"Do you suppose Ervin made his rounds today?" Nelda asked with a smile.

"Believe it or not, I did see his truck on the road."

"I wouldn't have gone out if he had stopped here.

Both times I let Kelly out he fell on the ice. I tried not to laugh, but each of his four legs went in a different direction. Before you put the sand on the steps I had to grab his collar and help him up onto the porch. He didn't like it out there one bit. He came in and curled up on his bed."

Nelda hoped that she wasn't talking too much. But it was so wonderful having him here, relaxed and hungrily eating the meal she had prepared. She wanted to prolong this wonderful time with him for as long as possible because he might leave as soon he finished.

But when they were done eating, he surprised her by adding a large stick of wood to the firebox, then sitting down on the end of the couch. He pulled off his boots, propped his feet up on the oven door, and lit the pipe he had taken from his coat pocket.

"This couch is like one of those old settle chairs the pioneers used to use. The high back keeps the heat from spreading out."

"That pipe smells good." Nelda cleared the table and stacked the dinner dishes in the sink. She couldn't spare the water to wash them. "Grandpa used to put his feet on the oven door and smoke his pipe while Grandma did the dishes."

"Did you listen to the radio today?"

"I turned it on a couple of times. One time I heard President Eisenhower talking about the formal declaration of statehood for Alaska. I tried to get the weather report, but all I heard was about school closings. No school anywhere in north Iowa tomorrow."

"We'll wait and listen to the ten o'clock."

He was staying until then? She kept her face turned away from him for fear that he would see the elation she was feeling.

"I did hear the news that the trial of Caril Ann Fugate is over. She was the girl traveling with Charles Starkweather when he went on the killing spree through Nebraska last year and killed eleven people. The jury gave her life in prison."

"I guess that's fair. She was with him, but she didn't pull the trigger." Lute picked up the heavy picture album she had left on the end of the counter. "What's this?"

"It's Grandma's. I was thumbing through it this afternoon."

When Lute opened it to look at the pictures, Nelda moved the oil lamp over to the counter.

"This is the house when it was first built in 1879. It didn't have the porches. My great-grandfather built it. Grandma and Grandpa were married in 1894 and lived here with his parents. They did that in those days."

"Come sit down and tell me who these people are."

Nelda sat down on the sofa and leaned over, trying to see where his finger was pointing.

"That's . . . that's—"

"Move over. I'm not going to bite you. Put your feet on the oven door."

"They don't reach that far."

Lute set the album aside, picked up her feet and pulled off her shoes. He rubbed her feet, then turned to frown at her.

"They're like two chunks of ice. Don't you have wool socks?" She shook her head. "I'll bring you some tomorrow." He pulled her close to him and propped her feet on his legs near the open oven. "Can you feel the heat?" he asked when he felt her shiver.

"Uh-huh." The chill that had shaken her was only partly due to the cold. She gave him a shaky, but happy smile.

Her shoulder was tucked behind his, her hip and thigh tight against his. He reached for her hand and pulled it through his arm, then opened the album again.

"Now, who are they?"

"Grandma's mother and father."

"They both look mad enough to bite a nail in two."

"People didn't smile in pictures in those days."

Nelda tried to keep her mind on the photographs, but the feel of him overwhelmed all thought. The smell of him was so totally male with its overtones of tobacco smoke. She wanted desperately to lay her head against his shoulder and press her lips to his neck.

When they came to a picture of a man in overalls and a woman in a cotton dress with a small boy between them, Nelda said, "That's my dad, with Grandma and Grandpa."

Lute turned the page without commenting. The next dozen pages showed Donald Hansen at country school, then school in town. There were pictures of him in his first suit, and one of him standing beside his first car. There was only one college picture. In that one he was wearing a straw skimmer and smoking a cigarette in a long holder.

"Regular jelly bean," Lute murmured, then turned the page.

Next came photos of a very young Nelda with her mother, after that several pages of Nelda as she grew up.

"You had that mop of curly hair even then," Lute teased. "When I first saw you, I thought you'd had one of those frizzy permanent waves."

"Was it that bad?"

His answer was a chuckle.

Nelda knew what was coming next because she had looked at the picture for a long time today. Lute turned the page and found the photo of the two of them. It had been taken with a regular camera and enlarged. It was the only picture on the page. They were standing beside Lute's old truck. Lute had one leg bent back, his heel hooked on the fender. His arm was around Nelda.

Nelda held her breath while waiting to see what he would say. He chuckled . . . a little.

"I remember that day. You were wearing the new skirt your grandma had made. She wanted a picture. You fooled around fixing your hair, and I was late getting out to Kennedy's, where I had a job topping sugar beets after school."

"I don't remember that part of it. Did you get fired?"

"No, I lost a couple hours' work." Still looking at the picture, he said, "Gee, we were young."

He reluctantly turned the page to find a few more

photos of them together. The first picture of Rebecca was one of the ones taken at the hospital the day after she was born. Frances, Nelda's stepmother, had taken it. The next one was of the baby lying in the crook of Nelda's arm. Tears came to her eyes and, without realizing it, she sniffed back tears.

Lute looked down at her and looped his arm over her head and pulled her close to him. Nelda laid her cheek against his shoulder and, through misty eyes, watched as he slowly turned the pages that followed. The final photos were of Rebecca when Nelda brought her back to the farm, where she had lived for one short month. She was sitting up alone then. Nelda had pulled up a sprig of her hair and tied it with a little bow.

"This is the only picture I have of her," Lute said. "Your grandma gave the negative to Mom."

Nelda leaned back and looked into his face. "I'm sorry. I'll share with you what I have."

Lute closed the album and lowered it to the floor beside the couch. He leaned back and, holding Nelda tightly to his side, reached and pulled her knees up onto his thigh.

"It seems a long time ago, doesn't it, mop-head?" he said tiredly.

Mop-head. It's what he had called her in high school.

"A lifetime ago," she murmured.

They were silent for a while. He continued to hold her against him, his hand on her knees. He leaned his head against the high back of the couch.

"You didn't get any sleep last night. I know

you're tired. If you want to lie down here and sleep a while, I'll keep the fire going."

He wrapped his arms around her. "It's tempting. But first I should tack one of those blankets over the door going into the other part of the house and hold the heat here in the kitchen. It's going to be twenty-five below tonight."

"I'll help you. Let's see what we can find in Grandpa's 'hell' drawer. It's got everything in it from nails to wire to hammer, pliers, pencils, and twine."

A few minutes later the job was done, and Lute had brought in another armload of logs from the porch.

"I don't think I can stay awake another hour to listen to the weather report." He stretched out on the couch, and Nelda covered him with the blanket and the wool comforter. He took her hand before she could move away. "Blow out the lamp and lie down with me for a while." His voice was barely above a whisper.

Her eyes met his. "There isn't enough room."

"Wanna bet?" He squeezed her hand.

Mindlessly she moved to the lamp and blew it out. The room was dark except for the light of the fire coming through the vents on the front of the firebox. Lute had folded back the blankets and turned on his side. She lay down beside him. His arms went around her and he pulled her hard against his chest until they lay spoon-fashion. He arranged the covers over them.

Her head was on his arm, her bottom pressed firmly against his crotch. Her senses took over, and she refused to think about anything but the feel of him. She desperately wanted to turn and accept the touch of his lips on her face. She could feel them in the hair above her ear.

"There's plenty of room. Are you warm?"

"Heavenly warm."

"Go to sleep."

"I'd better stay awake and watch the fire."

"Go to sleep. We won't have to add more wood for a while."

His breathing was steady. She was almost breathless.

Nelda wondered if he could feel the thumping of her heart through two light sweaters and one thick one. *I'm really here with Lute*, she thought incredulously. Lute, the boy who had kissed her so awkwardly at first, until they learned together the joy of soft, tender, merging kisses, the boy who had trembled so violently when his fingers found their way into her blouse. She hadn't pushed him away.

Together they had discovered the joy of uniting their bodies. Together they had made a child. Her father's intervention had torn them apart. Lute's desire to be his own man had led him to join the Navy. She had focused all her attention on Becky, then herself, unthinking, not realizing *his* need.

Lute, darling. I can make it up to you. I know I can.

She hadn't wanted to sleep and miss one minute of being with him like this. She was so deliciously warm and comfortable and . . . happy, that she dozed.

"Honey," Lute's lips were against her ear. "I hate

to wake you, but I need to put more wood in the stove."

"I wasn't asleep," she murmured, and sat up.

He laughed softly. "If you say so." Lute swiftly filled the firebox and returned to the couch. "Come on. I need you to get me warm again."

"What time is it?" She slid beneath the covers.

"Don't know. Don't care. Turn over, honey."

Nelda turned to face him, her face in the curve of his neck, her arm around him. With his hand on her bottom, he pulled her close and tucked her leg between his thighs.

"I always regretted that we didn't get to sleep together like this."

"I regretted it, too."

His hand moved up under her sweater and fanned out over her bare back. He turned his face, and she could feel the soft scrape of the whiskers on his chin. Then his mouth was against her cheek. It was more than she could bear. Her mouth blindly, desperately sought the warm comfort of his. Their instinctive, undeniable need for each other was a force suddenly unmitigated by reason. They clung to each other compelled by fear that the naked hunger they sought to appease would be unfulfilled.

Nelda's arms clutched him to her in agony over thoughts that he might pull away. But the arms that gripped her and the hand that moved to cup her firm bottom and press her against what deemed him man, were an unmistakable indicator that his desire was as strong as hers. Desperate with hunger, they deepened the kiss.

"Oh, Lord, honey—I want more—" The words came out of his throat in a growl of agony. He was trembling and holding her tightly. "I've been hard as a stone since you came back. Just knowing you are here—is driving me crazy."

His mouth fastened to hers again, molding it, sculpting the soft flesh breathing life into it. The fierce possession lasted several minutes.

"Lute, darling . . . you don't have to be—"

His hand burrowed into the waistband of her slacks under the pajama pants, into her panties to cup her bare buttock.

"I want more than memories." His ragged voice tore at her heart.

"I want more, too. Lute, please . . ." It was a whispered plea, and she wasn't sure if she heard it.

He nibbled at her lips with his, stroked them with his tongue, pulled her lower lip into his mouth. Small sounds came from her throat.

"Sweetheart . . . I don't have protection—"

"It's . . . all right. Please . . ."

"I wish we didn't have on all these clothes. I want to feel all of you." The world had stopped. There was only the holding, touching, tasting of each other. "Help me," he whispered, and pulled down on the slacks that were keeping him from her.

Her answer was to loosen herself from his arms, and quickly slip out of the clothing. His arms reached for her and crushed her to him. Hungry mouths searched, found each other, and held with fierce possession. Her hands, beneath his shirt couldn't stop caressing him.

He broke away gasping. His urgent hands found the snap of his jeans, fumbled with the zipper, pushed them down. The next moment they were joined, and he was raining kisses on her face.

"Nelda . . . my . . . sweetheart," he whispered hoarsely.

A deep longing compelled her to meet his passion equally. She kept her eyes tightly shut, not wanting to come out of the dreamlike state she was in. The driving force of her feeling was taking her beyond herself into a mindless void where there was only Lute's hard demanding body.

She heard sounds of his smothered groans, as if they came from a long way to reach her ears. Incredibly, their pleasure rose to almost intolerable heights before they merged in a long, unbelievable release. She clung to him as if she were about to slip off the edge of the world.

"So quick—" He brushed the hair back from her face. "I wanted it to last . . . forever."

She placed her palms against his cheeks, her thumbs caressing his lips.

"I did, too."

"Remember that first time. I came almost the instant I touched you."

"You were embarrassed—"

"You were sweet. We didn't have protection then either."

"It's all right," she said again.

"I didn't know enough to get rubbers until it was too late."

"I don't regret it."

She could feel his body demanding more, now that the initial frustration had been appeased. His heart was pounding against her chest, and she was surprised that she could feel it through their clothes and the hammering of her own. He was quivering with the effort to love her leisurely, but tenderness was not what she needed. When she felt that she would explode with longing, he was there, moving, driving, as wonderful as before.

Awed into silence by what had happened between them, Lute held her gently to him, cradling her head against his chest. He stroked her bare bottom with his rough palm.

"I didn't intend this to happen," he whispered. "I was so hungry for you I couldn't help myself."

"It's what you said . . . that other time. Then you got up and ran out into the water."

"You remembered that?"

"Oh . . . Lute, I remember so much!" A little whimper escaped her lips.

"You can't turn back the clock, sweetheart. That was a happy time of our lives, but it ended in pain. I wouldn't like to relive it."

The tone of his voice ravaged her, sending a shiver of dread down her spine. She turned her face into the curve of his neck. Lute's hands continued to stroke her buttock, her thigh, his breathing slowed, his heart beneath the palm she had slipped under his shirt was quieter.

They fell into a warm, languid silence not unlike the peace of that summer day at the beach so long ago. She pushed aside thoughts of morning, blocking out everything but this moment, this night. He stirred, and his lips touched her forehead.

"What are you thinking?" she asked, and tilted her head so she could rub her nose against this chin.

"This . . ." The hand that hugged her buttocks pulled her tightly against him.

"Well . . ."

"How long has it been for you?" The words seemed torn out of him. "How long? Don't tell me that bed-hopping isn't an accepted thing with the crowd you've been with."

"It is accepted in some circles," she whispered, trying to staunch her pain. "Please don't spoil this, Lute. Don't put it on that level."

"I didn't mean that."

"Then what did you mean?" Her voice trembled. "I'm surprised you don't carry something with you like you used to do . . . after it was too late."

"Stop it, and go to sleep."

None of this means any more to him than any other diversion for the night. He's remembering, but not feeling any of the things I'm feeling. Her eyes were tightly closed, though tears pricked beneath the lids.

Exhaustion finally sent him into a deep sleep and Nelda into that limbo between unconsciousness and awareness. She lay molded to his body, her cheek nestled in the warm hollow of his shoulder. She had not been this happy in a long, long time. Lute had been a gentle, considerate lover, but in a small corner of her mind lurked the feeling of impending doom.

∾ *Chapter Ten* ∾

MORNING CAME TOO QUICKLY.

Nelda instantly awakened to full awareness. She was cradled in Lute's arms. She moved her mouth against his neck.

Suddenly he stiffened.

"What is it? What's wrong?"

"It's daylight. I've got to go."

He moved her away from him, swung his legs off the couch, and reached for his boots. He slipped into them, stood and shoved his shirt down into his jeans. His hair was disheveled, his face hard and angry.

"I must have been out of my mind!" he rasped. His eyes were cold, glittering strangely as they looked at her.

The shock of seeing him in this mood was like a dash of cold water after a warm bath.

While putting on his coat, he looked back at her with narrowed eyes and spoke in a sharp, cruel voice.

"I don't need you in my life, Nelda. You don't fit into my lifefstyle any more than I'd fit into yours back in Chicago. I'm a farmer. I'll always have dirt under my nails."

Nelda sat still, the blanket wrapped around her bare limbs, unable for a minute to utter a sound. Shaken, she tried to think of something to say in her defense, but . . . what was she defending?

"I didn't drag you in here, Lute." By main force she was able to keep her voice surprisingly calm. Inside she was screaming.

"That's true." His harsh laugh was sudden and jarring. "But what do you expect if you put a stallion in a stall with a mare in heat?"

She gasped but took care not to allow him to see that his crudeness cut into her heart like a knife.

"That's unworthy of you, Lute," she said sadly.

He glared at her for a minute before he said, "I'm sorry for saying that." Then he was gone.

When the echoes of the back door slamming died away, Nelda sagged. She was alone, she could let down her guard and cry if she chose. But she didn't cry.

"You really asked for it, didn't you, you poor, dumb, stupid fool." It was weird to be talking to herself this way, to feel as if she didn't belong to herself, but somehow she needed sound. "Since the second day you were here, it was in the back of your stupid little mind to try and win him back."

Kelly got off his bed and looked at her with his head cocked to one side.

She wanted to laugh, but laughter wouldn't come. Depression did. It settled over her like a shroud. She felt utterly lonely, lost, and then frantic. She began to shiver. The look in Lute's eyes when he walked away would stay in her mind forever. She wanted to hate him, but all she could hate was her own weakness for him. He had not forced her. She had gone into his arms willingly.

Kelly stood in the doorway, his tail swishing. He looked at her expectantly. His obvious need to go out moved Nelda to get up off the couch, put on her slacks, slip her feet into her shoes, and open the door.

She stood at the porch door and looked at the ice-storm damage with dulled eyes. Branches were lying all over the yard. When the phone lines were repaired, she'd call Mr. Hutchinson and have him send someone out. She'd take nothing more from Lute.

While drinking coffee she listened to the weather report. The temperature hadn't dropped as low as had been expected during the night, and today a warming trend was predicted. The sun came out in the middle of the morning and thawing began. By noon water was dripping from the ice-covered wires and tree branches.

Nelda moved automatically, as if she'd had a death in the family. She fed the cookstove with the wood from the porch and removed the blanket from the doorway leading to the hall. She ate the leftover stew just because she knew that it was necessary to eat.

In the middle of the afternoon, as she stood in the sunshine coming though the window, she saw Lute's truck coming down the lane to the house. She backed away from the window as he passed. While he was in the barn, she went up to her bedroom, not that she expected him to come to the house; but in case he did, she didn't want to see him. What was left of her pride would be cut to ribbons if she burst into tears in front of him.

She heard Kelly barking a welcome, then the back door opened. A minute passed. She imagined he was giving his attention to the dog.

"Nelda." His voice came up the stairwell and into the cold bedroom. "Nelda, are you all right?"

Nelda swallowed hard, then answer. "I'm fine. I'm changing clothes. Take your radio when you leave. And . . . thanks for lending it to me."

"Are you coming down?"

"Not for a while."

There was a silence. Nelda held her breath for fear he'd come up the stairs.

"Then stay up there and freeze your butt!" There was accusation in his voice, and it almost made her lash out at him, but she forcibly restrained herself.

She heard the back door slam and moved to the other bedroom to peek out the window. Lute was going across the yard to his truck. She waited until he had driven out of the farmyard before she went back down to the warm kitchen.

The radio was still there.

Nelda slept that night on the couch. In the isolated farmhouse she felt as if she were the only person in the world. She pulled Kelly's bed up next to her, stroked the dog's head, and talked to him.

"It's just the two of us again, Kelly. It was dumb of me to think that there was a chance he would want me again. He wanted me, all right, but only for one reason. He meant it when he said, 'put a stallion in a stall with a mare in heat.' That's why he stayed, Kelly. He considered me a mare in heat eager to service a stallion.

"It was partly my fault. I wanted him to make love to me. He thinks I'm one of those bed-hoppers. Wouldn't he be surprised to know that I've never been with another man?"

During the long day she had decided that it had been a mistake to come here. She would tough it out and not let Lute think she had run back to the city with her tail between her legs. She couldn't go back to Chicago right now anyway. Elite Decorators didn't expect her until spring. One thing was sure—from now on she would avoid Lute at all costs.

She cried for a little while before she went to sleep.

When morning came, the hum of the refrigerator told her the electricity had come on. She picked up the phone and heard the dial tone. She was connected to the world again.

At nine o'clock she called Earl Hutchinson and asked him to send someone out to clear the yard of fallen branches. The ice was disappearing, and the fallen tree limbs would prevent her from getting her car out. He was glad to oblige. He called back to say that someone would be out either late that afternoon or early in the morning.

By noon the house was comfortably warm, and Nelda began to put it in order. Moving the couch back into the living room was backbreaking work.

She did it in stages, then flopped down on it to get her breath.

Shortly after noon, Nelda heard Lute's truck. He was coming to tend to his horses. If he should come to the house, she wanted to be prepared. She quickly put his radio out on the porch bench, locked the kitchen door, and went up the stairs to her bedroom. She lay down on the bed and covered herself with a blanket. Why she did this, she did not know, when she thought about it later.

Lute's rap was loud on the door. Kelly, traitor that he was, barked a welcome, happy to see him. Lute banged on the door several more times; then she heard the porch door slam, and, later, the sound of the truck going down the lane.

When next Nelda went to the porch to let Kelly out, she saw the radio still on the bench where she had left it. Damn him! Why hadn't he taken it? She wanted nothing of his. Nothing.

Early the next morning, Nelda heard a buzzing sound and Kelly making a fuss in the kitchen. She dressed hurriedly and went downstairs. A truck with high sideboards was parked in the yard and two men were loading the fallen branches. Those too large to lift were being cut with a chain saw.

Nelda put her coffee on to perk, then donned her coat and took Kelly outside. She wasn't sure what he would do about the chain saw. City dog that he was, he might try to bite it. She needn't have worried. Kelly was totally intimidated by the shrill sound of the saw that cut into the thick branches as easily as a knife going through butter.

"Morning," she said when the saw was finally still.

"Do you want any of this wood, ma'am?" The man who spoke was the one wielding the power saw.

"Would it be suitable for the cookstove in case we have another power failure?"

"Sure. I can cut some of this small stuff in short lengths."

"I'd appreciate it. And please stack it at the end of the porch. Was there a lot of damage from the storm?"

"Quite a bit, but mostly power and telephone lines. Power and phones are still out south of the lake."

Nelda was drinking her coffee at the kitchen table when Kelly let her know another vehicle was coming down the lane. It was also a truck with high sideboard. When it stopped, Lute got out. Nelda's heart began to thump nervously. He talked for a moment to the men cleaning her yard, then went to the barn.

On a sudden impulse, Nelda grabbed up his radio and went out onto the porch.

"Mister," she called to the man nearest her. "This is Mr. Hanson's radio. Would you mind putting it on the seat of his truck?"

"Be glad to."

"Thank you."

Nelda went back into the house and locked the kitchen door. She didn't think Lute would risk the embarrassment in front of the men of coming to the door and not being admitted, but she didn't want to take the chance.

She needn't have taken the precaution. Lute didn't knock at the door. He came out of the barn, got in his truck, and left.

The telephone rang. It was Rhetta calling to see how she had fared during the ice storm and to invite her to dinner on Saturday night.

"I'd love to come." Nelda had to force an eager tone into her voice.

"Don't dress up, for heaven's sake! We'll probably cook something on the grill."

"Isn't it too cold to cook outside?"

"It never gets too cold for Gary to grill. He cooks on the glassed-in porch. Oh, yes, one of our friends is building a house on the lakeshore, one of those big fancy places that will cost more in real-estate tax than some people make in a year. He could hardly contain himself when I told him we had a real live decorator from Chicago living in our midst. He'll be at the party, so you may find yourself with a job."

"Oh, Rhetta, I'm not a home decorator. I specialize in decorating commercial properties. You know, offices, cocktail lounges, stores, and the like."

"That's okay. He lives all over the place, but mostly in Minneapolis." Rhetta talked on and Nelda half listened. "We're dying to get you on the arts council. We need some new blood."

"Don't count on me, Rhetta. I may not be here that long. I'm getting pressured to return to Chicago. I've not decided yet when I'm going."

"Nelda, no!" Rhetta wailed. "Promise you'll give

us a chance to grow on you. We're really quite nice people out here. Gary got used to us, and he had lived in London all his life."

"I'll certainly be here until Saturday night anyway." Nelda laughed. "I'll see you then."

When she hung up the phone, she sat beside it for a long moment. It had been pleasant talking to Rhetta. Maybe what she needed was more women friends. She'd never had girlfriends in school . . . except Linda, and even that had never been a close friendship. She was two years younger than the kids in her class, a baby to the other girls. But she'd had Lute, he had been enough.

Lute. Nearly everywhere her thoughts wandered, she found him. How had she managed to carry on all those years in Chicago, she wondered. Chicago—being there was how she managed it—far enough away and totally occupied in a kind of work that had no relationship with Lute. Maybe she should sell the farm, go away, and never return. Even if she did that, she doubted that she could ever purge her thoughts of him now, after . . .

She pulled herself up short and concluded that at least somewhere else there wouldn't be as many reminders. But what had become of the Nelda who had resolved to provide proof of her maturity, her talent, her stamina—to Lute, to herself? Damn! How was she ever going to straighten out her life?

Thankfully, her inner struggles were called to a halt right after she had eaten a tuna salad she'd thrown together while jousting with her mental giants. Ervin Olsen arrived, pulled up close to the door and honked. Nelda pulled on her coat and went out to the truck. He rolled down the window.

"I see ya got things cleaned up already."

"Mr. Hutchinson sent the men out. It didn't take long."

"I figured Lute would be over here, Johnny on the spot."

"Why would he? Just because he rents the land and the barn doesn't mean he's responsible for the yard."

"I stopped at his place the other day, and he was loading up wood to bring over here."

"It was neighborly of him. Was there a lot of damage?" she asked to change the subject.

"Fair amount. Was far worse back in '36. A month went by, and it didn't get above zero. Had to dig graves with a pickax. A body came in from back East someplace, and there was so much snow they couldn't find where to bury it."

"Kelly, come back here," Nelda called when the dog strayed out into the old cow lot.

"Got to be getting along. I'm glad it's warmed up some. We'll be getting snow soon now. What we just had wasn't snow weather. It was too cold. We've not had a Thanksgiving without snow since I was knee-high to a pup."

"Come again, Mr. Olsen." Nelda backed away from the truck and held on to Kelly's collar.

Nelda waved and watched the truck go back down the lane. It seemed like it took forever for it to reach the road. Ervin could never be accused of being a speed demon. He was off to spread the news that Earl Hutchinson had sent someone out to take care of her yard. Thank goodness he didn't know that Lute had spent the night here.

Just before she went to bed the phone rang for the second time that day. When Nelda picked it up, she heard a low laugh on the other end of the line.

"I got somethin' for ya. It's bigger and harder than old Earl's. Bigger'n Lute's too . . ."

Nelda slammed down the receiver and began to shake. This pervert was someone who had seen her with Mr. Hutchinson and who knew of her connection with Lute. As she waited to see if he would call back she concentrated on keeping her fear at bay. He knew where she lived, she was sure of that. Was he getting into her house some way? Leaving things, moving things—just to scare her? She checked the doors, called Kelly, and went upstairs.

From a shoe box, high on a closet shelf, she took out the small pistol that one of her coworkers had insisted she bring on her trip from Chicago. She had laughed at first, then they began telling the stories of the killer Starkweather. Nelda had been around guns all her life. In Germany, with her father when he was stationed there, she had learned, at his insistence, how to load and fire several types of guns. She never thought that she would ever thank him for anything, but she did that now.

With the loaded pistol in a drawer beside the bed she lay in, she opened her mind to the events of the past week. The obscene phone caller was only one of her worries.

Lute thought that she had come back to the farm

as a lark—something of a change of pace from her
job in Chicago—and when the newness wore off that
she would leave again. She considered long and hard
the reason she had come here. It truly was because
she had reached a crossroads in her life, and that
here at Grandma's house she could figure out what
mattered and what didn't—and even maybe what to
do about her future. She hadn't counted on Lute's
being here. Now everything was jumbled in her head.

She closed her eyes and prayed for sleep.

On Saturday morning she went into town to buy groceries and see Mr. Hutchinson. She had called first
to make sure that he would be in.

After a greeting, the receptionist waved her back
to Mr. Hutchinson's office. He stood and held out
his hand.

"Hello. Did you have any trouble getting into
town?"

"Not a bit. We drive in snow and ice in Chicago,
too."

"I suppose so. Have a seat." He picked up a pen-
cil and slid it back and forth between his fingers.
"What do you think about our north Iowa ice
storms?"

"I can think of several things that I like better
than having the power go off. I managed fine."

"Lute said that he'd look after you."

Lute again. "It was neighborly of him to bring
wood for the cookstove. Thanks for checking with
him. I've come to you with another problem, Mr.
Hutchinson. I've received several disturbing tele-

phone calls. Do you know if there is a way to trace the calls?"

"There are in some areas. I don't know about here. I can talk with Bob Halford at the phone company for you. Are the calls threatening?"

"They are obscene."

"Good Lord! Have you reported the calls to Chief Larsen?"

"No, the farm is outside his jurisdiction. I'm going to buy a whistle today. A friend in Chicago had annoying calls. Every time the person called, she blew a loud whistle into the phone, and after a while he stopped."

"I don't like to think of you alone out there—"

"Don't worry about me. I have a pistol, and I know how to use it. I don't have many things to thank my father for, but I have that."

"Speaking of your father. I've had another letter from him. It seems he tried to get in touch with you at your job in Chicago, and they told him that you were here."

Nelda frowned. "What does he want?"

"He's still interested in buying the farm. He's prepared to pay cash."

"His new wife must be in the money."

"She is, and she's the one who wants the farm."

"Why? They'll never live there."

"She raises Arabians and thinks it would be great to have a stable on her husband's family farm."

"I'll never sell to him. Never."

"Even if you can get an outlandish price?"

"Not even at a thousand dollars an acre."

Earl laughed. "That's the offer. I'm thinking they've been pricing land in Manhattan. There's one more thing," he said when she rose to leave. "He said that he would be here sometime between Christmas and the New Year. He said to tell you to be here."

"He did, did he?" Nelda buttoned her coat up to her neck and pulled on her mittens. "If he thinks that he's dealing with a sixteen-year-old who quakes each time he looks at her, he's got a surprise coming. I had planned to be here, but now I'm not sure. I don't want him coming to the farm. I don't want to see him."

"That's up to you."

"You may think that I'm unnecessarily hard where my father is concerned. He doesn't care about me. He cares for himself first, the Marine Corps second, money and social standing third. He ruined my life. His actions caused my grandparents untold grief. I'll never forgive him."

Earl took her arm before she passed through the door.

"Don't let hate eat you up, Nelda. It could destroy you, and he would win. Stand against him and show him that you are a better person than he is. If he sees how much you hate him, he will gloat over it."

"I know you're right. Thanks for the advice."

"I'll talk to Chief Larsen; he may have a suggestion. And I'll talk to Halford at the telephone company about the calls. I'll be in touch with you. By the way, does Lute know about this?"

"No, and I don't want him to know. It's none of his business."

After leaving the lawyer's office she went directly to Oluf T. Hanson's store and bought wool socks, heavy underwear, and a pair of heavy wool slacks. She was determined not to be caught unprepared should the power go off again.

At Moeller's shoe store she bought boots, large enough to accommodate the heavy wool socks, and a pair of fur-lined mittens. Pleased with her purchases, she headed back to the farm.

❧ *Chapter Eleven* ❧

NELDA LOOKED FORWARD TO THE DINNER AT Rhetta's.

Kelly was obviously unhappy to be left behind when she closed the door firmly and got into the car at seven o'clock. He must have known something was up when his mistress had taken a leisurely bath, washed her hair, and used big rollers to take out some of the curl. She had held several different outfits up for inspection before finally choosing the blue suit and the peach silk blouse.

Nelda had needed to feel she looked her best—not that she expected Lute to be there, but because this was her first social outing since the end of August, when she had come to north Iowa.

She knew the suit accentuated her small waist, and the luscious peach blouse gave her pale, delicate skin a warm, rosy blush, bringing out the flecks of green in her dark eyes. She carried blue shoes with slender heels to replace the flats she wore to cross the yard to the car. The shoes were shamefully expensive, but whenever she wore them she felt especially feminine and graceful. Over the suit, she wore a matching blue box coat with a small fur collar.

Nelda arrived at Gary and Rhetta's just on time. She parked in the driveway alongside a long, low, dark blue Lincoln, put on her heels, and walked up to the door. Rhetta opened it immediately, smiling her greeting, but once Nelda was inside, her mouth turned down at the corners, her expressively mobile face wry.

"Oh, dear! I swear the next friend I pick is going to be fat and so ugly her mama had to tie a pork chop around her neck to get the dog to play with her."

Nelda found herself relaxed and laughing. "You don't exactly look like a ragamuffin yourself."

Rhetta slid a hand through Nelda's arm. "Come, have a drink and meet our crazy friend. He's divorced, and has kids, but he's eligible—and fun."

The man who came toward them with a drink in his hand was slightly taller than Nelda and had dark red hair. Here in the corn country he displayed all the accouterments of New York and Chicago. The shoes on his feet were Italian, and the watch on his wrist had two diamonds on each side of the dial. Experience that went with his forty-odd years showed in his face.

The bright blue eyes unabashedly assessed her and obviously approved of the quality they found in her apparel, as she had found in his. Before Rhetta could make the introductions, he held out his left hand and clasped hers. He raised his glass and toasted her.

"To Nelda," he saluted. "Will you permit me to ask a stupid question?"

"Why sure. If you don't expect a clever answer." Nelda laughed, surprised at how at ease she felt with him.

"What's a nice girl like you doing in a place like this?"

Nelda joined in the clichéd words of the question as soon as he was halfway though asking it.

"A place like what?" Rhetta bristled with indignation. "I'll call Gary and have you thrown out, you city slicker! Are you going to let me make proper introductions, or not?"

"No, darling. We are not. This is Nelda, and I'm Norris, dashing, sophisticated and, by far, the best-looking man here tonight."

"You're impossible!" The doorbell rang and Rhetta grinned. "The war is on. I hate to desert you, Nelda, but from now on it's every woman for herself."

Norris led Nelda to the bar and made a wry face when she asked for a white wine. After Rhetta introduced the arrivals as Bill and Jean, Norris guided her to the couch and sat down beside her.

"Now my proud beauty, as long as I'm labeled wolf I may as well act the part. What big eyes you have—"

"That's my line!"

The friendly eyes sparkled. "Tell me about yourself."

"I was born in a log cabin beside a clear stream.

My pa was a poor woodsman and my ma took in washing."

His laugh rang out. Nelda decided that she liked him, and during the next few minutes she framed a brief résumé of her life over the past eight years— omitting all mention of her marriage and divorce— making her life sound carefree and happy.

Twenty minutes later the room was awash with voices. Gary had returned from an emergency call and was telling Bill about the Arabian foal he'd delivered.

"I didn't think the old girl would make it," he said in a voice that mixed pride and relief.

Another couple arrived—Julie and Tom. She was on the plump side and he had a flattop haircut. The conversation jumped from Arabian horses to firm-bodied pigs versus fat ones for sausage. Nelda was lost in the conversation. She noticed that Norris, who had been focused on her, joined the discussion when a mention was made about the huge, self-propelled machines that foraged up and down the corn rows, turning dry, tattered plants into cash.

"My business," he whispered to Nelda. "I sell farm machinery."

"What kind?"

"All kinds." His eyes twinkled. "That's why I'm here buttering up the farmers."

"Makes sense to me."

Tom and Bill, she learned, were cash grain farmers, who sold beans and saved corn for feed. At present they were working long hours getting in as much fall plowing as possible before snow and the ground freezes. They pushed hard; and when the equipment failed, they were cross, according to their wives, who added their bit to the conversation.

Nelda listened with envy to the two wives talking as knowledgeably as their husbands about farm activities. She was the outsider here. Norris, for all his sophistication, was at least in at the fringe, since his business was farm-related. Still, she was pleased that the only time he left her side was to fix himself another drink.

She was just about to relax and enjoy herself when Lute appeared in the doorway. A tall dark-haired girl wearing a full skirt and high-heeled shoes was clinging to his arm, the same girl who had been with him at the cafe.

"Hello, everybody. Sorry we're late. Lute's been plowing and forgot to quit," she explained with easy familiarity.

"No harm done." Rhetta made a strange face. "I was about to pry Gary loose to put the steaks on the grill. Come meet Nelda. I think you know everyone else."

"'Course I know everyone. Hi, Julie. Hi, Jean," she said, then nodded to the men, her heavily mascaraed eyes focusing on each one in turn. "How are you, Mr. Smithfield?" she purred.

Although the blood was pounding in her ears, Nelda registered the name. This friendly man couldn't be the *Smithfield* who manufactured farm equipment? Impossible! Even Chicagoans knew that *Smithfield* was by far the leading name in the industry.

"Nelda, this is Meredith McDaniel, the home economics teacher at the high school." Rhetta spoke from beside her. "Nelda Hanson, interior decorator, late of Chicago, and now a permanent resident of our fair city, if we can convince her to stay."

"Hear! Hear!" Norris raised his glass, the others followed his lead.

"Hello, Nelda." the tall girl looked at her coolly. "You have an unusual name."

"Maybe so, but I've become used to it." Nelda smiled one of her sweetest smiles.

The girl laughed. "Hanson. Do you spell yours with an *e* or an *o*? People around here are touchy about that."

"My ancestors were the Hansens with an *e*. But now my name is Hanson with an *o*."

The girl laughed again, but Nelda knew the battle lines were drawn. *She knows who I am, and she sees me as a threat.* The thought was quickly replaced by another when her eyes shifted to Lute and found his on her, his brows drawn together in a frown. Thank heavens for Norris! How would she get through this evening without him?

The men continued to chat in spurts about the weather, crops, farm subsidies. Lute offered his opinion, too. Twenty minutes passed and Nelda hadn't added a word to the conversation, while Meredith chimed in constantly, usually to back up some comment of Lute's.

As her morale deteriorated, Nelda began to plan an escape. Because she was nervous, she had to force herself to get to her feet and walk into the kitchen in search of Rhetta. At the door she turned and saw that Lute was watching her over the rim of his glass.

"Is there anything I can do?" Nelda spotted Rhetta standing at the oven.

"No, but thanks. I'm trying to thaw out another steak. I didn't know the all-American girl was coming. Damn that Lute! He could have called me."

"You mean they're not a steady twosome?" Nelda kicked herself mentally for asking the question.

"Meredith would like them to be. She's been after him for a couple of years now." Rhetta opened the oven door. "Thank goodness. I think this thing is thawed enough now." The steak she took from the oven was enormous.

"My goodness. You don't expect each of us to eat something the size of that?"

"Some will, some won't. What's left, the boys will eat cold tomorrow. They're a couple of human garbage cans! Okay, back to the party with you. Gary will have these charred in no time."

Nelda found herself sitting beside Norris during the meal. It was all very casual: picking up a steak, filling a plate from the buffet, and finding a place to eat. She and Norris shared a small, old-fashioned, marble-topped ice cream table, a relic from a drugstore of long ago. She remarked on the excellent condition of the table.

"Do you like antiques?" he queried.

"Some of them. The ones that work well in contemporary settings."

"My sentiments exactly. How about helping me decorate my house?"

She laughed. "Just like that?"

"Why not? I'm an up-front guy." He grinned at her, his handsome face wreathed in smiles. It was a memorable face, the bones large and angular, the dark red hair disheveled in an appealing fashion, the eyes as bright as blue crystals.

Her gaze lifted past his head to where Lute stood, plate in hand, looking for a place to sit. A maverick thought crossed her mind before she could capture it and wrestle it away. *He thinks Norris may be interested in me. Good!* She tore her eyes away from Lute.

"Thanks, but if you're not planning a supper club or a suite of offices, I'm lost," she explained, looking into Norris's face. He met her look with smiling eyes.

"I always wanted a suite of offices on the lakeshore," he quickly replied.

"You're about as obvious as a tank," she said, glancing at him sideways. She had read of Norris Smithfield's rumored sexual exploits in the gossip columns. That is, if this was really the Smithfield who was heir to the farm-machinery fortune. From the facts she had picked up, she was almost sure he was.

"I try never to miss an opportunity." He grinned wickedly.

"Foul creature."

The repartee was easy for Nelda. In her line of work, such light banter was something that went along with the job. It was in no way threatening.

Norris's tone grew more serious. "What do you

find to do out at the farm all day? Don't you find it dull?"

"Dull?" She glanced away, veiling her expression and carefully avoiding looking at Lute. "Dull?" she repeated, and laughed. "I should say not. I love it. I miss the traffic, the noise, the tight schedules, and the pickpockets like I'd miss a toothache. Besides, I do get out now and then. And then there are exciting moments like being propositioned by the boy putting gas in my car."

"What did you say?" The words traveled across the quiet room.

Nelda's eyes flew to Lute. His lips were still parted from speaking. He was looking at her as if she'd just exploded a land mine. She felt herself flush. Later, when she had time to sort things out, she would be angry with him for forcing her to take center stage, but at the moment all she felt was embarrassment.

"I said that I don't miss noise and traffic—"

"—You said that you had a flirtation with a gas station attendant," he interrupted.

"Boys will flirt, that's all there was to it." Nelda replied with a forced smile.

"Boys don't usually flirt with an older woman unless they are led to believe she welcomes that kind of attention."

Nelda checked a gasp. She wanted to laugh, or scream, but she did neither. The room was deadly quiet, everyone locked into silence by the vehemence of the exchange.

"If I did lead him on, it wouldn't be any business of yours. I told you it was no big deal, so back off!" She spoke quietly and with dignity.

Burning with humiliation, Nelda turned and faced Norris's twinkling eyes.

"She's right, Lute." It was Meredith's lilting voice. "I imagine things like that are an everyday occurrence in the city. I'm sure Nelda is old enough to handle them."

Her emphasis was decidedly on the word *old*. Nelda saw that Norris could barely contain his laughter. She chuckled, too. This whole argument was so ridiculous.

Meredith was speaking again. "I've been to every gas station in town, and the boys who wait on me are always pleasant, and never say anything out of line."

"I guess you're not as lucky as I am," Nelda responded coolly; she let her gaze include Lute. He was still glaring at her.

Later, while the men were playing pool, Nelda had the opportunity to apologize to Rhetta.

"I'm sorry for losing my temper with Lute and embarrassing your guest."

"Lute's the one who should apologize," Rhetta said with raised brows. "I've never known him to be so boorish. He acted like a tomcat with a sore tail." When she continued it was with mischief in her eyes. "It sure didn't take Miss Home Ec long to figure out you're the Nelda from Lute's past."

Past, is right. She's his future.

"I didn't come here to interfere in Lute's life. I

didn't know he was here. I thought he was still in the Navy."

"I don't know why he got so riled up all of a sudden. Our Lute has been acting strange lately."

Nelda waited patiently for one of the couples to leave, not wanting to be the one to break up the party. After Bill and Jean left, Nelda announced her intentions and went with Rhetta to the closet where her coat had been hung.

"I'll follow you home, love." Norris took his overcoat off the hanger.

"You don't need to do that," Nelda protested.

Rhetta lifted a brow. "Don't argue, Nelda. He'll do as he pleases."

Lute and Meredith were standing in front of the house with Gary and Rhetta when she pulled out of the drive. Seeing him with the girl clinging to him had pierced Nelda like a knife to her heart. She just wanted to go home, get in her bed, and cry. She hoped that Lute noticed that Norris was following her home. It was comforting, she admitted, to see the headlights of his car in the rearview mirror as she approached the farm.

Norris was pulling into the yard behind the house when Nelda got out of the car to raise the garage door. He waited for her after she parked it inside.

"Thank you for seeing me home."

"My pleasure." He pulled down the garage door. "Shall we have dinner together some evening?"

"I'd love it. Give me a call."

"Let's make the date for tomorrow night, so I'll not have to remember your phone number."

"I wouldn't want to put a strain on your memory, so tomorrow night it is."

He looked around, before remarking, "It's pretty isolated out here for a woman living alone. What kind of protection do you have?"

"I have a good yard light, as you can see. I have a dog who barks at every rabbit or squirrel who crosses the yard, and I have a small handgun. I'm well equipped to take care of myself."

"Good girl. Do you know how to use the gun?"

"You betcha."

His next question surprised her. "What's between you and Lute?"

"I was married to him once," she admitted without missing a beat.

"Uh—oh. I should have known. It's no wonder Miss Home Ec was in such a twist."

Nelda forced a laugh. "She's got nothing to worry about. Lute can't stand me."

"Thank heavens for that!" he teased. "I'd hate to think all this hard courting I'm doing is for naught."

"Good night, Norris. I've got to let my dog out, and he just loves to gnaw on the legs of men with red hair and glib tongues."

"I'm glad you came to town, Nelda Hanson . . . with an *o*," he called, and waited until she had unlocked the door and had walked into the house before he got into his car. Then, with a short toot of the horn, he was gone.

"Did you miss me, Kelly?" Nelda fondled the dog's ears. "I'll let you out, but you stay close, hear?"

She stood on the steps and watched Kelly roam the yard. He had decided of late that it was fun to wander in the grove beside the house and venture off down the road, blatantly ignoring Nelda's call to return. The coddling he'd received during his convalescence had had an adverse effect on his behavior. If Nelda was out of his sight, he conveniently put her out of his mind as well, returning to the house whenever he pleased.

After Kelly had revisited the various places where he had left his scent and had rewatered some of them, Nelda called to him.

"Kelly, come." The dog looked at her and then away. There was something very important out of the circle of light that needed his attention, so he paid no attention to her summons and disappeared around the corner of the house. "Kelly! Dammit, Kelly!" she called, then shivering, she stepped inside the house to wait. Minutes passed, but the dog didn't come back.

"Dumb dog," she muttered. "Tomorrow I'm going to get a rope and tie you to a tree. Your gallivanting days will be over, and you've brought it on yourself."

When headlights lit up the lane she frowned, thinking Norris was returning, but the vehicle that came into the yard was unfamiliar to her. When Lute got out with his hand firmly attached to Kelly's collar, Nelda flung open the door. Dog and man came inside.

"I found him down the road. You'd better keep him at home, or he'll get to running with a pack and someone will shoot him."

"He's just started running away." Nelda's voice trembled as she explained. Her frantic thought raced even as she spoke. *Go away, Lute. I don't want you here*.

Lute stood there, looking down at her.

"You'd better get on back to Miss Home Ec," she reminded him.

"There's plenty of time."

"I'm surprised you'd leave her to come over here and freeze your rear off to bring my dog home."

"You don't forget anything do you?"

"Not when someone tries to make me look foolish."

"If you must know, I took her home."

"It isn't important to me what you do with her."

"Norris will have you in bed before you know it. Is that what you want?" he asked angrily.

"You had me in bed before I knew it. What do you expect from a mare in heat?"

Nelda lifted her face and glared at him defiantly.

The ringing of the telephone broke the tension between them. Nelda took the necessary steps to reach it.

"Hello," she said crossly.

She heard heavy breathing on the line, then— "Are ya in bed? If I was there, I'd be rammin' it in ya—"

"Pervert!" she yelled, and slammed down the receiver.

"Who was that?" Lute's voice came from behind her.

"A personal call."

"Why did you say 'pervert'?"

"Did I say that?"

"What's going on, Nelda?"

"Butt out of my business!"

The phone rang again. Lute's hand darted out and beat hers to the receiver. He held the phone to his ear. An expression of surprise flickered across his face, then anger.

"Listen to me, you lowdown piece of shit," he bellowed into the receiver. "When I find out who you are, I'll break off that thing you're playing with and stuff it down your throat." Lute slammed down the phone and glared at Nelda.

"How long has this been going on?"

She looked away, tilted her chin, and looked down her nose in a dignified manner.

"It's not your concern. I'm asking you to leave."

"How many times?" he insisted.

"I haven't counted them. The door is right behind you."

"Have you reported these calls?"

"I'm perfectly capable of handling this by myself without any advice from you."

"Like you were capable of handling the cookstove."

"It's decent of you to throw that up to me." She moved around him, went to the door, and opened it.

"You little fool! The man could be dangerous!"

"I'm from the big city, remember? I can take care of myself."

He looked down at her for a long while before he said, "Be careful of Smithfield. He's rich, and he's got more women on the string than a dog's got fleas. He'll sleep with you, but he'll not marry you."

"Well, look who's talking!" Nelda countered, her voice heavy with sarcasm. She was so angry she failed to notice the stricken look that flickered for an instant across his face.

Suddenly and violently, his arms came around her, and he jerked her against him and jammed his mouth down on hers and held it there for a long, hard kiss.

"Think about that, you stubborn little mule!"

He pushed her from him and was out the door, slamming it behind him.

❧ Chapter Twelve ❧

NORRIS TOOK HER TO DINNER AT WITKE'S Lakeshore Cafe. They sat beside the window and looked out over the frozen lake.

"Have you ever gone out in an iceboat?" he asked after they had ordered *filet mignons*, baked potatoes, and salad.

"Iceboat? That's a sled with sails. Right?"

"It's a little more than a sled, it's a boat with runners and a sail. It's a fast ride."

"And a cold one, I'm sure. I've seen them out on the lake, but I've never been in one."

"Want to try it?"

"No, thanks! My idea of boating is drifting among the lily pads in a rowboat on a shallow lake."

"Sissy," he scoffed. "I don't suppose you've been ice fishing either. The ice isn't thick enough now to move the icehouses out, but in another few weeks, dozens of icehouses of all sizes and all shapes will be out on the ice."

"I can't see that it would be much fun to sit out there on the ice looking down a hole."

"Some of the icehouses have heaters, and some have battery-powered lights for night fishing. I've seen lights out on the lake at two and three o'clock in the morning."

Nelda laughed. "Only a dedicated fisherman would spend the night on a cold frozen lake."

Their meal was served. Norris joked with the waitress in an impersonal way, and she clearly loved it. Nelda enjoyed his company. He wasn't the *wolf* he pretended to be at Rhetta's party. He was a warm, considerate companion who, Nelda suspected, was very lonely.

"What are you doing Thanksgiving?" he asked.

"I've not given it any thought."

"I've a business meeting in Minneapolis on Friday after Thanksgiving. I'll go up there on Wednesday. Will you be alone?"

"Probably, but I'm used to it."

She looked around Witke's restaurant with a professional eye and decided the decorators hadn't done badly, considering what they had to work with. She said as much to Norris, then told him about decorating the nightclub for Aldus Falerri and smiled when he gave a snort of disgust.

"I take it you're not a bosom pal of Mr. Falerri."

"You take it right. He's bad news. I hope you got paid for your work."

"Elite Decorators was responsible for collecting for the job. They must have collected because I got my commission. Hey, look. It's snowing."

"So it is. How about doing some cross-country

skiing before I go north? That is, if there's enough snow."

"Sounds like fun, but I don't have skis."

"That's no problem."

Large fluffy flakes were coming down when Norris turned up the lane to the farmhouse. He parked close to the house, and Nelda could hear Kelly barking inside.

"Would that dog jump someone breaking into your house?"

"I don't know. He's never been tried. He'd certainly bite someone trying to get in the car."

"He's territorial. My guess is that if you indicated you were frightened, he'd protect you. That relieves my mind some. I don't like to think of you out here alone."

"It's good of you to be concerned," she said, and meant it. "Kelly lets me know if a rabbit runs across the yard."

When she put her hand on the door handle, he got out of the car, came around, and opened the door. Holding tightly to her arm so that she would not slip on the snow, he walked her to the door.

"Shall we do this again?" he asked.

"I'd love to."

"If this snow keeps up, we should have enough to cross-country ski. I'll give you a call."

"Thank you for a lovely evening."

"It was my pleasure."

On Monday morning there were three inches of snow on the ground, and at noon it started snowing again.

Nelda attached Kelly to the fifty-foot rope she had tied to the tree trunk and watched him frolic in the snow. When he was ready to come in she let him onto the porch and unhooked him from the rope. He shook himself vigorously.

In the afternoon she had a call from Mr. Hutchinson telling her that he had spoken to Chief Larsen about the obscene calls. Since the farm was out of his jurisdiction, Chief Larsen had suggested that she inform the county sheriff.

"Write the sheriff's number down and leave it beside the telephone," Earl suggested. "I spoke with Bob Halford at the telephone company, and he says there isn't much they can do about tracing the calls."

"I was afraid of that."

"Lute was in here this morning—" Earl began.

"—Oh, no! He found my dog on the road and brought him back. While he was here, I got one of those calls. Two in fact. He heard the second one."

"He's ready to tear someone apart."

"He's overreacting. It's really none of his business. Mr. Huchinson, have you seen anything of Linda Branson? I tried to call her and was told her phone had been disconnected."

"You're on a private line?"

"Oh, yes. I requested one and was lucky enough to get it."

"Linda came to see me this morning. She wants to take nurses' training. Her husband is dead set against it. She's not ready quite yet to break with him; she fears what he will do, and she's afraid of what it will do to her boy."

"Coming to you was the first step. It took courage."

"I told her to come see me when she decided what she wanted to do, that help was available."

It was evening when the phone rang again. Nelda was almost afraid to answer it, but curiosity outweighed her fear.

"Hello, ladybug."

"Norris!"

"You sound like you're glad to hear from me."

"Well, of course I am."

"Ready to go cross-country tomorrow?"

"If I had skis."

"I'll bring a pair. How about two o'clock?"

"Fine, if you'll stay and have chili with me when we get back."

"Best offer I've had all day. See you tomorrow."

Nelda was smiling when she went to the small freezer in the refrigerator, took out a package of hamburger, and placed it the sink to thaw.

When Nelda woke and looked out her window, the landscape was pristine white and still. She heard the sound of a tractor, then Kelly whining to go out. She put on her slippers and robe and went down stairs, clipped Kelly's collar to the end of the rope, and opened the porch door. The space between the barn and the house had been cleared of snow and the tractor driven by Lute's hired man was chugging down the lane to the road.

While her coffee perked, she ran back up to her bedroom and dressed in a pair of slacks and a

pullover sweater. When she went to the door to let
Kelly in, she was surprised to see Lute playing in
the snow with her dog. He was tossing a stick in the
air, and Kelly was making a halfhearted attempt to
catch it.

Where had he come from? He was wearing his
sheepskin coat and that blasted blue knit cap. She
hadn't heard his truck drive in. Nelda backed away
from the door, determined to ignore him.

When her coffee was ready, she poured a cup
and went upstairs. After making her bed, she laid out
the clothes for her afternoon with Norris, killing time
until Lute left the farm.

Standing at the window drinking her coffee, she
saw Lute on horseback riding down the lane. He
hadn't come to the house. She was both relieved and
disappointed as she went down to let Kelly back in.

The temperature was only ten above, but Nelda found
herself sweating from the exertion of shuffling the
light skis over the loose snow. She pulled off her
muffler, and then, still too warm, partially unzipped
her down jacket. The feel of cold air rushing against
her throat and chest was exhilarating.

She followed along behind Norris, who slowed
his pace to accommodate hers, until they reached the
crest of a hill and surveyed the countryside below.
Spread before them was a panorama of farmhouses
surrounded by windbreaks—tightly branched black
pine trees all lined up in orderly rows along the property squares.

Nelda's eyes quickly singled out Lute's house

and dwelled there for a long moment. To the southeast they could see the tall, rounded, concrete silos of the grain elevator. The scene was like a Christmas card in shades of green-on-white and white-on-white, interrupted only by an occasional red barn.

Norris was silent while they rested, and Nelda was consumed by a feeling of belonging, a rarity for her. She loved this place, this life, this view. *Dear God*, she thought, *I'll be going back to Chicago in the spring. But I'll return to it often in my mind.*

"You okay?" Norris had moved up beside her and was searching her face.

"Sure." She lifted a hand and pointed. "There's my farm. My barn needs painting. I hadn't noticed it before."

"You like it here, don't you?"

"I love it here, but I don't belong. I realized that the other night at Rhetta's. I had not one thing to add to the conversation."

"Do you think that's important?" His serious blue eyes were on a level with hers.

"It is if you want to fit into a community."

"Listen, little girl, you don't need to take a backseat to anyone. You'd fit into this community. There are people here who talk about things other than hogs and cows."

"You're good for a girl's morale, Norris."

"Something else is bothering you. No, don't tell me. I'll figure it out." He reached out and zipped up her jacket, winding the muffler about her neck. "Let's go home and eat that chili."

Home. There was that word again. Not too long

ago she'd thought that Iowa and her grandparents' farmhouse might become her home. Now she didn't know just where her home might be. The word had rolled so easily off Norris's tongue, but its meaning was still to be resolved.

Guiltily bringing her attention back to Norris, she inwardly acknowledged how grateful she was for his friendship at this particular time in her life. She unhappily faced the fact that her heart would forever belong to Lute, even if he didn't want it. Sometimes in the dark of night she was so lonely for him, and the thought of the years ahead without him so painful, that she wondered if it might almost be better to die than to feel this way. She could begin to plan for her future again only when morning shed its light on the subject.

She plunged her ski poles into the snow and pushed off. The vigorous exercise felt good. As they moved lightly over the snow, the silence complete, they seemed to be in another world.

Nelda laughed aloud when she scared up a jack-rabbit, who went bounding helter-skelter over the white landscape. Losing her balance, she fell and lay sprawled in the light, fluffy, whipped-cream snow laughing until Norris returned to help her back onto her skis.

Kelly was delighted to see them when they returned, and Norris frolicked with him in the snow. When Nelda went to the porch to call the two playmates in for dinner, Lute's truck was coming down the lane. He stopped at the barn and got out. Norris yelled a greeting. Lute responded and disappeared inside the barn.

After the meal Nelda beat Norris soundly at a game of Chinese checkers, then accused him of being a poor loser when he refused a rematch.

"How about blackjack?" he asked hopefully.

"Sure. That's my game. I remember cards. You wouldn't stand a chance."

"I detest smart women," he teased, getting up to take his coat from the hall tree. "You're still in love with Lute, aren't you?"

Nelda was stunned into silence.

"Why do you say that?" she asked tightly.

"It was obvious to me the night I met you." He smiled at her anger, and his hand came out to clasp hers.

"Oh . . ." she wailed.

"Don't worry. You hid it well. But I'm Norris, the womanizer, remember? It's my predatory nature to know if a woman will go to bed with me, or if she's pining for another man, or if she'll go to bed with me in spite of the fact that she's in love with another man and wants to try and get him out of her system."

Nelda put her fingers over his lips. "Norris Smithfield, never in a million years will you make me believe you're a predatory man. You're a fraud!"

His hand cupped the back of her head and drew it to his shoulder in a brief hug.

"I'm going to Minneapolis tomorrow. I won't be back until next week. I'll give you a call."

"I enjoyed the outing. Thank you for taking me."

"Thanks for the chili . . . and the heartburn that will follow."

"Next time I'll make meat loaf."

"You mean I was such a gentleman that you'll invite me again? My, won't Rhetta be surprised?"

"Go on with you. Have a safe trip to Minneapolis."

Nelda stood in the kitchen window until Norris passed the house headed up the lane. He honked, and she waved.

Nelda woke early on Thanksgiving morning with a sore throat and a headache. She got up, let Kelly out, took a few aspirins, and made a cup of tea while she waited to let Kelly back in.

She brought down a blanket and a pillow and lay on the living-room couch. She hadn't felt this rotten in a long time. The next time she got up to let Kelly out she would take her temperature, she promised herself.

She dozed, woke, and dozed again.

The phone rang, and she roused herself to answer it, walking into the kitchen with bare feet.

"Hel . . . lo," she croaked.

"Nelda? Is that you? This is Rhetta."

"It's me. I've got a cold."

"I'm calling to ask you to come to dinner, if you haven't made plans."

"Thanks, but I'm afraid I'd not be fit company." Nelda's throat was so sore she could hardly get out the words.

"Do you have a temperature?"

"Probably."

"Take aspirin and drink juice. It may be just a one-day thing."

"I'd not be so lucky. Thanks, Rhetta—"

After she hung up the phone she made a peanut butter and jelly sandwich and carried it to the couch. She crawled wearily under the covers and nibbled on the sandwich.

When the harsh ringing of the telephone broke the stillness, she sat upright, holding her hands to her head as if to keep it from bursting. Maybe it was Rhetta again. She wasn't aware she was counting the rings, but on the fourth one she got off the couch, went to the kitchen to pick up the phone.

"Hello," she whispered.

"Nelda, are you all right?" It was Lute's voice, and there was exasperation in his tone.

"Yes. I'm . . . all right."

"What took you so long to answer the phone?"

"It only rang four times."

"Are you alone."

"No."

"Who's there?"

"None . . . of your . . . business."

"Rhetta said that you're sick. Why in the hell didn't you call someone?"

"You? And have you come over, freeze your butt—"

"I'm not in the mood for your smart answers, Nelda."

"If I have to stand here much longer," she croaked, "I'll be dead! Good-bye—"

"—Don't hang up, Nelda. Do you need a doctor?"

"No. Don't bother me again!"

She leaned weakly against the counter after she hung up the phone. Her head was pounding as if it was caught in a vise, and her stomach was convulsing with dry heaves, protesting the peanut butter sandwich. She hurried to the bathroom and leaned over the commode. When she thought she could make it, she stumbled back through the kitchen to the living-room couch.

When next she roused, Kelly was running through the house barking. It was a nightmare, of course. No, it was reality. Someone was pounding on the door. Nelda struggled to awaken like a swimmer fighting to surface. When she stood and walked to the kitchen, her limbs were like lead. Through a daze she saw Lute's face through the window of the door. For a few seconds she stood as though turned to stone. Seeing her, he pounded on the door. Then, holding her flannel gown up so she could walk barefoot across the kitchen floor, she unlocked the door, immediately reeling back to the couch in the living room.

"What do you want?" she called back over her shoulder.

"Has Kelly been out?"

"Yes . . . no—"

Lute let Kelly out and then made several trips from outside to the kitchen. Nelda couldn't see what he was doing from where she lay shaking on the couch.

"Have you taken your temperature?" He came only as far as the living-room door.

"No."

He shook his head and turned. She could hear his steps going toward the bathroom. He returned with the thermometer in his hand.

"Open up," he said, and slid it beneath her tongue. He stood looking down at her. His lean brown face was freshly shaven and his hair was neatly combed. When he spoke, his voice held teasing laughter.

"You look anything but the self-sufficient, sophisticated city girl now. You look like a poor little pussy cat dragged in out of the rain."

She reached to take the thermometer from her mouth so she could retort, but he grabbed her hand.

"Now, now. You'll have equal time later."

He crouched down on his heels beside the couch, his palm cupping her chin so she couldn't open her mouth, and grinned at her. His face was so close she could see the small lines fan out from his eyes, the gold tips on the ends of his lashes, and her own reflection.

"It bothers you, doesn't it? For once I have the advantage. You've got to lie there and listen to what I've got to say. No, keep quiet," he ordered when she made a croaking noise. "Mom made Thanksgiving dinner and put it in the freezer before she went to California for the winter. When Rhetta called—

"Hush," he said gently when she made protesting noises. "I brought it and put it in the oven." He picked up her wrist and circled it with his thumb and forefinger. He didn't say a word, but his eyes told her he was aware of her recent weight loss.

"There's giblet gravy, sweet potatoes, and pumpkin pie. Doesn't that whet your appetite?" He took the thermometer from her mouth and walked to the window. "Hummmm, you do have a fever."

"How much?"

"Enough that you'll spend the day right there."

"How much?" A fit of coughing followed the words.

"Three degrees. I'll get a couple of aspirin, and we'll take it again later." One brow arched. "Aren't you glad I came over?"

"I'd have managed," she said ungraciously.

"That's gratitude for you!" He crossed the room to her and flipped the blanket off her feet. One large hand grasped a foot. "Your feet are cold. I'll go up and get a pair of socks." He tucked her feet back under the warm gown and covered her with the blanket.

"Go away," she whispered hoarsely.

"Don't be a pickle-puss. You're angry because I'm here, but you'll get over it when you smell the turkey and dressing." He tossed the words pleasantly over his shoulder as he took the stairs two at a time.

❧ Chapter Thirteen ❧

I'VE GOT TO GET MYSELF TOGETHER!

The thought traveled repeatedly through Nelda's mind. She couldn't let him see how much she loved him and how glad she was that he was here. Oh, Lord, she felt so rotten, and he was being so . . . sweet. In this mood he was almost irresistible! Why had he come? Had Rhetta laid a guilt trip on him, or was he lonely? That was it. He hadn't wanted to spend Thanksgiving alone. Where was Miss Home Ec? Maybe she had gone out of town to be with her folks.

She closed her eyes. *Oh, Lord, I wish my head would stop throbbing.*

"Don't go to sleep before you take these." Lute's arm slipped beneath her shoulders and lifted her. She put the tablets in her mouth, and he held the glass of water to her lips. "Don't you think I'd make a good nurse? I've been practicing on the cows and pigs. I've even delivered a litter of pups."

Nelda gulped the water. "Thanks! I'm flattered by the attention of one so gifted."

"I'm just trying to assure you that you're in experienced hands."

"That will be a comfort when the hearse comes to take me away."

"You won't shake my confidence with remarks like that." He tucked the blanket around her shoulders. "Do you want to watch Macy's Thanksgiving Day parade?"

"No. I'm not much for television."

"You mean to tell me that you don't watch *Life of Love* or *The Revolving World*?"

"I think you mean *Love of Life* and *As the World Turns*. But no, I'm not hooked on them. Believe it or not, I watch news and an occasional ball game."

"Then you should enjoy the football game this afternoon."

Lute's manner was easy, and a roguish light entered his eyes when he teased her. But on close inspection he looked tired. The smooth skin over his cheeks and jaw was tight and drawn, and the jeans that had fit him like a second skin in the late summer no longer did so. There was something different about him that frightened her a little.

"I do like football," she whispered.

"I remember. You came to all the Lions' games when I played." A slow smile curled his lips. "Now go to sleep. I've got to let that pesky dog in."

Nelda had to admit that she was glad that she wasn't alone. She enjoyed being pampered, especially by Lute. She stopped trying to understand his strange behavior and gave herself up to listening to him moving about the kitchen and talking to Kelly, who was wiggling around and making a fool of himself over him. How could she possibly go to sleep with him here, she wondered, and it was her last coherent thought before she dozed off.

The smell of food woke her. She lay with her eyes closed for a long moment, then opened them slowly. Lute was sitting in the big chair, his legs stretched out in front of him and his blond head resting on the back cushion. Kelly was standing with his head resting on Lute's thigh, and Lute's fingers were lost in the tangle of long red hair about the dog's ears.

It was a picture she would carry in her heart forever. Lute turned his head. His magnetic eyes met hers and seemed to swallow her. A slow smile softened his face.

"It's about time you woke up. Do you feel better? I think I should take your temperature again before we eat."

Kelly followed along behind him when he left the room and was still trailing him when he returned.

"I may sue you for alienation of affection. I thought I had a one-person dog." That was all she had time to say before the cold thermometer was popped into her mouth.

"He likes me. He's one smart dog."

Unable to talk, Nelda rolled her eyes to the ceiling in mock disgust. Lute laughed softly and went back to the kitchen. She watched him leave. He'd removed his boots and was in his socks, heavy gray-wool ones with blue toes and heels. He'd also taken off the heavy sweater, and the tan knit shirt he wore hugged his broad shoulders. He was making himself at home, she thought with a pang. It was almost as if they lived together.

She was trying to find the reading on the thermometer when he came up beside her and took it from her hand. He moved to the window.

"Are you sure you didn't shake it down?" he asked, as he squinted to make sure of the reading. "It's down a degree and a half."

"I didn't shake it down."

"Okay. I'll take it again later. Dinner is ready. Do you want to go to the bathroom before we eat?" he asked with easy familiarity. "I brought down your robe and your slippers. I also brought down a cup of cold chocolate and a sandwich that looked like a mouse had nibbled on it. Your supper last night?" he asked accusingly.

Nelda swung her legs off the couch and reached for her slippers, but Lute evaded her hand, bent down, and slipped them onto her feet. Her eyes lingered on the top of his blond head. It was hard to believe that just a few days ago they had been shouting angry words at each other. He pulled her to her feet and helped her into her robe while she stood like an obedient child, thanking God she had bought the bulky, loose-fitting Mother Hubbard gown and robe.

"You're such a little thing." His eyes slid over her slowly. He raised a finger to her cheek, gently caressing. "Little, but mighty." His voice was deep and raspy.

Taken completely by surprise by this gentleness when she remembered the hostility in their last encounter, she moved abruptly away from him. He took her arm and walked with her to the bathroom door, gave her a kindly shove into the room, and pulled the door closed firmly behind her.

Inside the door Nelda put her hands against the sides of her head. *I must be crazy*, she thought. *I shouldn't have let him in. You're a fool, Nelda Hanson. You love his touch. You'd give your soul to melt in his arms!*

"You could get him to marry you again," a little imp whispered to her. "Get him to sleep with you again, get pregnant, and he'll haul you off to the minister like a shot."

"But what then?" her common sense responded. "He'd resent you for forcing him into an 'unsuitable match.' Lute isn't a man to be pushed. How would he feel about having an unwanted child? Enjoy being with him today," she told herself. "Soon you can vanish from his life."

Nelda looked at her reflection in the mirror. Hardly a woman a man could feel romantic about, she thought dryly. Her face was pinched, her eyes dull, and her hair tumbled and ragged. She washed her face and hands and ran a comb through her hair. She considered adding a touch of lipstick but decided against it; he'd guess she had tried to look good for him.

Lute was taking a pan from the oven when she came out of the bathroom. One-half of a small turkey lay in a nest of moist dressing.

"Get back on the couch. We're eating on trays."

"I can help," she offered weakly.

"And spoil my fun. Go get settled, and I'll bring you a plate."

"Not too much," she cautioned, before going back to the couch.

The tray he brought her was set with a napkin, silverware, and a plate of food that looked delicious. He had arranged thin slices of white meat on a mound of dressing and topped it with giblet gravy. Sweet potatoes and celery stalks stuffed with cream cheese lay alongside the entrée. He put the tray on her lap and stood back.

"Well? What do you think?"

"It looks divine." She smiled up at him. "But there's so much of it."

"Eat what you can. Kelly will love the leftovers. I'll get mine and join you."

Nelda ate more of the food than she thought she could. Her throat was sore, but she finished most of the dressing and gravy because it slid down easily. Lute chatted through two plates of food, telling her about Thanksgivings he had spent while in the Navy. Both of them carefully steered away from the only other Thanksgiving they had shared.

She learned that he had been asked to run for county supervisor but had declined, and because of his interest in 4-H, he was on the county fair board. She learned of his political inclinations and prejudices, and freely volunteered information about her own. The meal stretched over an hour and ended with pumpkin pie and coffee for Lute and hot tea for her.

Lute finally carried their trays to the kitchen.

"Leave the dishes in the sink. I'll do them later," Nelda called.

"I'll let them soak. We'll have the leftovers for supper."

Nelda lay back on the couch. *He's going to spend the day. Why is he doing this?*

Lute sprawled out in the chair to watch the football game, and Nelda watched him. A thousand memories somersaulted through her mind at the sight of him there, legs stretched out in front of him, eyes half-closed. He was a handsome man, charming when he chose to be with a sensual masculinity that her coworkers at Elite Decorators would adore. She couldn't blame Miss Home Ec for being wild about him.

During the eight years she had been away from him, she hadn't forgotten one thing about him. Without her acknowledging it, he had lived in her dreams, in her mind, and in her heart. She had looked for his face on every man she had met, gazed into so many laughing eyes, passionate eyes, indifferent eyes, but none of them were Lute's eyes. Something had drawn her back here even when she had thought he would be miles away on the high seas. She knew now that he would forever be in her heart. Tears glistened in her eyes, and she closed them tightly lest he turn and see them.

The afternoon seemed to pass in the wink of an eye. When darkness came, Lute turned on the lamp and let Kelly out to run on the end of his rope. He returned and sat down on the edge of the couch, holding his palm to Nelda's forehead.

"Hungry yet?"

"Are you kidding? I may never eat again."

"I make a mean turkey sandwich." His eyes dared her to argue.

"Okay. A half." Her eyes devoured his face.

"I'll take your temperature again, and if it's not down, you'll see the doctor tomorrow, my girl." His voice threatened, but his hand was gentle on her cheek.

Nelda's temperature was down another degree, and Lute was quick to take credit for it.

"It was the tender loving care I've given you today."

"It was the aspirin and good food."

She sat on the couch, the blanket across her knees, while her mind strove to sort out Lute's strange behavior. It would be wishful thinking on her part to assume that he felt any more for her than an obligation and the desire a male feels for a female. He had said it all when he referred to himself as a stallion and to her as a mare in heat. Thinking about that humiliating episode was enough to shrivel her soul.

Once he had given her his love, and she had carelessly let it slip away. Now all that he felt for her was pity for a girl alone and sick. They were two lonely people held together by a slender thread of memory: youth, young love, and Becky.

They shared the supper tray, Nelda nibbling at her sandwich half. She drank the hot tea, and it helped to soothe her sore throat.

Despite her protest, he insisted on doing the

dishes and leaving them in the rack on the counter. When he returned to his chair, they watched *Gunsmoke*, then *Wagon Train* on the television. Nelda could barely keep her eyes open, and finally she fell asleep.

Lute switched off the television and turned on the radio. Weather news was important to a farmer. He twisted the dial to the local station. Patti Page was singing, "Tennessee Waltz."

Lute, sprawled in the chair, watched Nelda and remembered when they had danced together at the Surf when they were young. They had gone to the ballroom only on special occasions. They were so close in those days that they discussed the cost of an outing because he didn't have much money.

She's much prettier now than she was at sixteen, he thought, with his eyes dwelling on her face. Some women improve with age, others lose their looks. Nelda was one of those who would look more and more beautiful as she got older.

The women he had known during the past few years had meant little to him. He could hardly remember some of them. There was always something missing, however nice they were. They'd walk out of the room and right out of his head. Only one woman stayed with him and he couldn't force her out of his mind and his head.

He had tried at first.

The lines of his jaw softened, and his blue eyes filled with tenderness as they focused on her parted lips. Godalmighty! What had caused him to act such a fool and spout such cruel, stupid words after they had slept together on that couch.

Embedded in the woman whom he had loved all his adult life, he had thought he was in heaven. Then he had awakened with the realization that she was a career woman who would go back to the city, leaving him as miserable as before. Thinking of the lonely years ahead, he had grown so angry that he had lashed out at her.

Nelda coughed and flung off the blanket. Lute covered her arms and shoulders again. She moaned softly when he held his palm against her forehead. Her fever had risen.

Not one to hesitate once a decision was reached, Lute took a glass of water and the bottle of aspirin up to her bedroom. After turning low the lamp beside her bed, he flipped back the covers and fluffed up her pillow.

Kelly was whining at the door when he went back downstairs. He let him out on his rope, then went to the couch and lifted Nelda up in his arms. He had not expected her to be so light. She awakened and looked at him with dazed eyes.

"Lute . . . ?"

"I'm putting you in your bed."

"Thank you—"

Her head fell to his shoulder, her arm moved up and around his neck. Lute carried her up the stairs to her room and lowered her to the bed.

"Here are a couple more aspirin." He put the tablets in her mouth and held the glass of water to her lips. "Now, go back to sleep. I'll be here." He lowered her to the pillow, removed her robe, and covered her with the flannel sheet and down comforter. After placing a gentle kiss on the side of her face, he stood looking down at her.

Lute Hanson, you're the biggest fool in Cerro Gordo County. After living in Chicago, having a career, hobnobbing with people like that nightclub owner who called her, she'd never be content to live on a farm where the most exciting thing that happened was a new litter of pigs or the birth of a foal.

Lute admitted to himself that he hadn't realized how dull it was here until after Norris Smithfield became interested in Nelda. Norris hadn't shown any interest in any of the local women that he knew of and some, including Meredith, had given him plenty of encouragement.

Well, to hell with Norris Smithfield, his money, and his damn smooth talk, Lute thought as he went down to let Kelly back into the house. Tonight was his.

He locked up the house and turned off the lights just as if he lived there, then went up the stairs to Nelda's bedroom. Her forehead was hot and dry when he touched it, with the back of his hand. Lute moved around to the other side of the bed, took off his clothes, folded them, and placed them on a chair. Kelly watched him, then curled up on his bed beneath the window.

After turning off the lamp, Lute slid into bed wearing only his shorts, and pulled Nelda close to his side, pillowing her head on his shoulder. Awakening, she pushed against him.

"It's me," he whispered. "Go back to sleep—"

"Lute . . . ?"

"Yes, honey, it's Lute. Are you feeling any better?"

"I want a drink of water."

"Sit up. I've got some right here on the nightstand."

With his arm around her, Lute held the glass to her mouth. She drank thirstily. When they sank back down on the bed, she snuggled against him and went back to sleep. He had thrown caution to the winds when he undressed, got into bed with her, and pulled her into the crook of his arm. This was far more than he had expected to do when he came here this morning.

Her palm lay flat against his chest, her cheek against his bare shoulder, her soft breasts against him. Lute wondered suddenly if she had nursed their child. He hoped that someday they would be close enough that he could ask her. Tonight he had to be satisfied being here in the dark with her, holding her, looking after her.

Lute was unaware that he slept until he awakened suddenly and glanced at the window. Dawn streaked the sky. Soft fingers were stroking the back of his hand. They were touching the ring on his finger. It was so tight it wouldn't turn. He captured her hand and held it against his chest.

"You could have cut it off." A tear had seeped from the corner of her eye. He felt the wetness on his shoulder.

"No," he said.

"Why are you here?"

"To take care of you. Your fever has broken. Do you feel better?"

"Much better. But it's crazy being here like this," she whispered.

"I know." The words were a sigh, but his arms tightened, and he drew her legs more intimately between his.

"Do you ever think of that other life—when we were young and in love?"

There was a long silence. The hand holding hers to his chest moved to slide up and down her arm in a slow rhythm.

"I try not to think about that other life," he murmured into the darkness. "It's over. What's important is what's ahead."

"I like to think about it because what I was and what I am now will be the total of what I will be."

"That's heavy thinking. I try to concentrate on whether or not to pick the beans, or if I have enough hail insurance, or if I'll get the crops out and still have time for fall plowing." The hand on her arm continued to stroke.

"You've always loved farming."

"Yes, I knew what I wanted to do after that first summer when we moved to my grandpa's farm. I like working the land, watching the crops grow, caring for my animals."

"I always wanted to be a decorator."

"Well"—he sighed—"you got what you wanted."

"I wanted it then. Now I'm not sure what I want."

She held her breath as soon as the lie left her

lips. She knew what she wanted: She'd walk over hot coals to be with him; he had only to beckon.

"I don't know what to do about the farm." She rushed into speech before he could comment on the remark. "I can't decide if I should sell it or hold on to it for an investment."

"You can always lease out the land, but if the house isn't lived in, it'll deteriorate."

"My father wants to buy it."

Lute heaved a deep sigh. "Hutchinson said he had a buyer. I never thought *he'd* want it."

"I'll never sell it to him."

There was a long silence. She turned her lips to the warm skin of his chest and choked down the disappointment she felt when he let the subject of selling the farm drop so blandly.

"Why haven't you remarried, Lute?"

"Why haven't you?"

"Too busy, I guess. And I've not met anyone—" She took a quivering breath. "Meredith, the Home Ec teacher seems perfect for you."

"She'd make a good farmer's wife," he acknowledged.

"And I wouldn't." The words were out before she could stop them.

"No. I can't see you as the Florence Nightingale of the calf barn, or being concerned with anything as unglamorous as corn or soybeans. I realized that more clearly the night I saw you with Smithfield. You fit into his world much better than you do mine." The hand holding hers gripped it tightly.

"Then why did you come here and . . . stay the night?" Hurt made her speak sharply.

"You know why."

"What does that make me, Lute? A whore?" she challenged in a choked voice.

"No! Whores are paid."

"You want pay for taking care of me today?"

"Hush up that talk!" he shook her gently.

"Why are you here . . . in bed with me?" There was a sob in her voice.

"I'm here because you're the most beautiful, desirable woman I've ever known. I want to grab you whenever I see you and lose myself in you. No woman feels like you feel, smells like you smell, tastes like you taste," he said gruffly and pulled her on top of him. "Love me again. Take me to heaven one more time." His words were a husky plea.

She put her arms around his neck and searched for his mouth. The feel of him was so good! Pride and logic fled her mind. Lute was here. This was now. She wanted to shout and scream for him to get the hell out of her bed, to stop torturing her. Instead, she kissed him, holding his mouth with hers for a long moment, trying to memorize the feel of firm lips. She caressed him, made sweet, slow motions over his body, trying not to rush, trying to make him hear her heart's song.

Is this all you want of me? She almost asked the question aloud, but she choked it back knowing it was just a fantasy to hope that he would respond with a passionate declaration of undying love.

It was over too soon. She nestled in his arms and listened to the rapid beat of his heart.

"I didn't mean for this to happen," he said, and kissed her tear-wet eyes. "If I had, I would have brought protection. I don't want to get you pregnant."

"Of course you don't." *I'd not be that lucky.*

Later Lute gently untangled his limbs from hers and without a word slipped out of the warm bed and picked up his clothes. Nelda watched him dress as the light of day invaded the bedroom.

"Lute." He paused in the doorway when she called his name, then walked back to stand beside the bed, where her next words confused him. "Will you be back?"

He looked at her for a full minute, then walked out without answering. Kelly followed him downstairs, then returned to his rug after Lute let him back in the house following his morning relief.

Nelda moved her head over to where his had lain and let the tears roll down her cheeks. He had wanted her for only one thing, and she had accommodated him.

❧ *Chapter Fourteen* ❧

THE NEXT TWO WEEKS PASSED SO QUICKLY THAT
Nelda wondered later how she had filled them. Her
unknown tormentor had called twice. After the first
call, she remembered to place the whistle she had
purchased beside the telephone, and as soon as she
heard the hated voice, had blown it as close and as
loud as she could before she hung up the phone.

The work of getting screens ready for block-
printing the patterns on the scarves she wanted to make
occupied her time. After she had made several buying
trips to Mason City, the dining-room table, where she
had moved her supplies for the winter, was littered
with cans of textile dye and screens set around a table
equipped with the frame and clamps for holding the
cloth. Her artwork had been completed, and now she
was down to the next part of the project.

She'd also had several dates with Norris and found
him to be an enjoyable companion. Outside of a few
chaste kisses when he brought her home, he had made
no move to plunge their friendship into an affair. Nelda
strongly suspected that the image he projected was a

cover-up for a man who was lonely—who missed the children who remained with their mother after his divorce and who knew their father mostly as the man who sent support money.

Norris had taken her to Shady Beach, a local nightspot on the lakeshore. They had danced to the tunes on the jukebox and had drunk tap beer with an inch of foam on the top. One afternoon they had driven to Pilot Knob, the highest spot in north Iowa, where they saw a large number of pheasants and a small herd of deer.

On the way back, they had passed Lute's farm. The house was large, fronting on a wide lawn that sloped down to the road. His mailbox was set atop a freshly painted post surrounded by dried hollyhock stalks. A wide glassed-in porch spread across the front of the house, and behind it was a cluster of well-kept outbuildings. Nelda had avoided passing the house lest she see Meredith McDaniel there.

Nelda had been queasy every morning for a week when she sat down with the calendar and tried to figure out when last she'd had her monthly period. She had always been regular, about every twenty-eight days, and never suffered anything but inconvenience at that time of month. The box of tampons she had bought the day she met Linda and her husband on the street was unopened. Then she remembered that the last time she'd had a period was the day she had ridden on the tractor with Lute. She'd had none since.

She began to get excited. Was it possible that Lute had made her pregnant the night they spent on the couch beside the cookstove? His sperm had poured into her twice in the night and once during the early-morning hours. When they were young they had been together more than a dozen times before she became pregnant. They had been so crazy about each other in those days, they'd made love at every opportunity.

Nelda counted the days since the ice storm. Six weeks. *Oh, God, don't raise my hopes to heaven and then dash them to pieces.* Nearly every hour on the hour for several days Nelda went to the bathroom, hoping against hope that she would not see color.

A mood of peace settled over her. She lay in bed at night and planned her future. She vowed that if she was pregnant, she'd not tell Lute. He would insist upon marrying her and then for the rest of his life consider himself trapped. Thanks to her grandparents, she could manage alone financially.

Oh, Lord. She had to stop thinking about it or she might, by her very wishing it to be true, reverse the situation.

Rhetta had proven to be a good friend. She nudged and pushed until Nelda volunteered a few hours work at the library, addressed envelopes for the swimming-pool committee when they sent out a mailing requesting donations, and went with Rhetta to deliver "meals on wheels" to shut-ins. But she absolutely drew the line when Rhetta tried to get her involved in politics.

Nelda stayed firm and resisted her friend's pleas to join the Republican Women. To make up for it, she agreed to a shopping trip to Minneapolis on Saturday, a week before Christmas.

Nelda had heard nothing from Linda and believed

that her husband's dislike of her probably was the reason.

Norris had been gone for almost ten days when he called one morning.

"You're back!" Nelda greeted him happily. "Did you turn the manufacturing world inside out with my idea to paint all your farm machinery robin's-egg blue?"

He laughed. "No. But they're still considering your idea of covering them with art deco tulip decals. Did you miss me?"

"Grieved every hour you were away."

"If only that were true," he groaned. "You sound awfully chipper."

"My work is going well."

"I'm glad. Want to take in a basketball game? The Lions are seven and 0."

"Sure. Will you buy me a hot dog?"

"Better than that, I'll pick you up at six-thirty and we'll go by the Lake Crest Cafe; and, if you're nice to me, I'll buy you a hamburger before the game."

"You drive a hard bargain, Mr. Smithfield."

"Wear your snow boots, it's snowing again."

Her coat was on the chair, and she was waiting for Norris when the phone rang.

"Yo're nothin', but a goddamn slut—" The phone clicked before she could reach for the whistle.

Shaking, her heart racing, she hung up the phone. Who hated her so much as to want to do this to her?

When she saw the lights from Norris's car come down the lane, she put on her coat. Leaving the light and the radio on, for Kelly, she waited for Norris to stop beside the porch.

"Ho, ho, ho!" he said cheerfully and helped her down the steps and into the car singing, "It's beginning to look a lot like Christmas."

Nelda's laugh rang out in the still, cold night. "I love you dearly, but you're no Perry Como."

"You wound me! How about, "Don't be cruel?""

"Give it up, Norris. I hate to give you this bad news. But you're no Elvis either."

Being with Norris pushed aside thoughts of everything but the pleasure of being with him. She asked him about his trip.

"Business, all business. All work and no play makes Norris a dull boy."

"Norris, you'll never be dull."

When they arrived at the restaurant, they had to wait while a black pickup backed out before they could park. It was Lute, and with him was Miss Home Ec. She waved. Nelda lifted a hand and let it fall to her lap. That was the first glimpse she'd had of Lute since he walked out of her house the morning after Thanksgiving.

Determined not to allow herself to dwell on Lute or his relationship with Miss Home Ec, she turned and smiled at a silent Norris, who was looking at her with a slight frown.

"He'll not marry her. She's a balm to his ego."

"Dear friend." Nelda put her hand on his. "I'm not going to let the fact that he doesn't want me ruin my life." She smiled brightly.

"Attagirl. Let's go eat."

Later, sitting with Norris on the crowded bleachers in the high-school gym, the thought struck Nelda that here was small-town USA, the grass roots of America. Mothers and fathers sat alongside businessmen like Norris who had no children in school. The support for the team was a community effort.

I want my child to grow up in a community like this, not in a high-rise apartment in Chicago.

Good Lord, what was she thinking of? She wasn't even sure . . . yet, but almost. *Please God. Please, God, let me have this part of him. It looks as though it's all I'll ever have.*

From high up on the bleachers, Lute had seen Nelda come in with Norris. Meredith had seen them, too. She snuggled her hand into the crook of Lute's arm but didn't speak until the couple sat down several rows below them.

"They've become quite friendly. I heard they were at Shady Beach the other night."

"Does anything go on around here that you don't know about?" he said without looking at her.

"I'm with a bunch of high-school kids all day, Lute. They know things, and I can't help but overhear."

"High-school kids don't go to Shady Beach." He looked down at her with a frown.

"You're out of touch, Lute. You'd be surprised where high school kids go and what they do."

"I suppose I would."

The band began to play, and the teams ran out onto the floor. Lute was relieved that it was too noisy to continue the conversation.

The game was close until the last, but Lute

couldn't work up any enthusiasm. When it was over the Lions had won, and their standing was now eight wins and zero losses. Lute lingered to allow Norris and Nelda time to leave the bleachers before he stood.

Meredith had been quiet. Lute knew that it wasn't fair to her to continue keeping company with her. At times he could hardly stand to touch her. She wanted to go to bed with him and had become quite forward about letting him know it. He had been tempted before Nelda came back. Now the thought was utterly repulsive to him.

When he took her home, he didn't get out of the car immediately. Since leaving the school, he had tried to think of a kind way to break with her.

"Meredith, I want to be fair with you. We both know that our relationship is going nowhere. It isn't fair to you to spend time with me when you could be dating someone else."

She didn't say anything for a while. Then she said, "You didn't used to think that."

"I've always thought that," he said kindly. "I enjoy your company as a friend—"

"—That's about as insulting as you can get. Friends," she scoffed. "There's no such thing as a virile man and a passionate woman being *friends*. It's utterly ridiculous to say so."

"Well, I guess I'm ridiculous."

"You've been different since *she* came back." Meredith put her hand on the door handle. "You're foolish to think you have a chance of getting her back when she can have a man like Norris Smithfield. Wake up, Lute. She's sleeping with him. Why do you think he's spending his time with her? Good Lord, you are naive."

Lute opened his door, then turned to look at her when the light came on. She had a sneer on her lips, and her expression was one of suppressed anger.

"I'm sorry, Meredith."

"I'm not. I'm glad to find out you're not the man I thought you were before I wasted any more time on you."

Lute walked her to the door. She went inside without another word and slammed the door. On his way back to the farm, Lute wondered at his state of mind. When he asked Meredith out tonight, he had fully intended to explore the possibility of asking her to marry him. He had to do something to get his life back on the right track. Even before he saw Nelda with Norris, he knew that he couldn't do it.

After Norris brought her home, Nelda stood on the back steps and watched Kelly frolic in the fresh snow. She doubted that he would run away if she turned him loose—he seemed to prefer lying on the warm rug beside the hot-air register these days—but she didn't want to risk having to get the car out to go look for him should he get it in his head to leave the farm yard.

She hugged her arms to herself. It was a beautiful, still night. The moonlight and the snow made the yard light unnecessary. She called Kelly in and prepared to turn in for the night.

Later, standing before the bathroom mirror, applying cream to her face, her mind kept returning to Lute and the smug smile on the face of Miss Home

Ec when she waved from Lute's truck. Thank goodness she hadn't seen them during the ball game.

Oh, Baby, Baby, she thought desperately, resting her hand on her slightly rounded stomach, *if not for you I just might lose my mind.*

Nelda turned out the lights and went up to bed, Kelly at her heels. She tried to get interested in a novel but gave up and laid it aside.

The secret of her pregnancy was so sweet in Nelda's mind that it helped hold thoughts of Lute at bay. She was resigned to the fact that she couldn't have him—that he desired her body, but didn't, couldn't love her whole self. So she made her plans carefully, pacing herself, knowing it would be necessary for her to leave Clear Lake the first part of February. She would make a business trip and never return.

Lying in bed, she heard the sound of cars on the road. They had unusually loud mufflers. She switched off the bedside lamp so she could stand at the window and watch them pass. To her surprise, the lead car turned up the lane toward her house, and the other followed.

Who would be coming this time of night? It was near midnight. She grabbed her flannel robe and slid her feet into slippers. The night-light burning in the hall was all she needed to see her way down the stairs. Kelly barked, and she put her hand on his head to quiet him. He growled, and she shushed him. Moving over to the back door, she tested it to be sure it was locked, then looked out. Two trucks were in the yard, their lights turned off. Nelda flipped the yard light on.

"Come join the party, sweetie-pie!" The voice was young and male.

"Nelda babe, won't cha come out tonight? Come out tonight, come out tonight. To dance by the light of the moon!" Laughter and shouts followed off-key singing.

"Come on out, come on out, come on out—" The figures moving around the yard began to chant.

One of the revelers tipped a bottle to his lips and another jerked it out of his hand. The yard light shining on the snow made the area almost as bright as day. The party was made up of boys of high-school age and older.

Nelda was nervous, but not terribly so until one of the youths came up to the porch and perched on the steps. Another came up onto the porch and sat on the bench beside the door. Then her heart jumped in her throat and began a wild gallop. They acted as if they had been there before. Could one or more of them have been inside the house? Taken the blanket from the porch? Did they have a hidden way of getting in?

She backed away from the kitchen door and felt along the cabinets for the telephone. She lifted the receiver and dialed the operator.

"Operator, will you ring the county sheriff for me? There are intruders in my yard. I'd look up the number but I don't dare turn on the light."

"I understand. Hold on."

The phone was answered after one ring. "Sheriff."

"This is Nelda Hanson, and I live on the Eli Hansen farm, one mile north of Clear Lake on County Road

G. There's a gang of ten or twelve boys in my yard, and I think they're drunk."

"Have they tried to get in the house?"

"No, but they came up onto the porch."

"You don't need to be alarmed. It's just some kids having a party. The high-school basketball team won tonight. One more win, and they'll play in the state championships."

"I know all that, but they have no business on my property."

"Kids are having parties all around Clear Lake. I don't have a car in your vicinity. You'll be all right. Keep the door locked."

"Thanks a lot!" Nelda slammed down the phone.

"One, two, three . . . charge!" The voice came from the bench on the porch.

"You guys are nuts! Are you tryin' to scare that woman?"

"Shut up, chicken," someone yelled.

"Hey, pretty woman . . . come out and play—"

Now three of them were on the porch. Nelda became so frightened she was almost sick. She picked up the phone again and started to feel her way around the dial to call Norris, but couldn't remember the number.

There was a banging on the door. Kelly set up a frenzy of barking. What to do, whom could she call? One thing was sure, she couldn't depend on the sheriff. As drunk as these kids were they just might break in, hurt her, in turn hurt her baby! Fear as cold as ice traveled the length of her spine. She hurried up the stairs to her room and got the gun from the drawer beside the bed and slipped it into the pocket of her robe.

When she reached the kitchen again, Kelly was still barking. The boys were bunched in front of the back steps, talking in low voices. Suddenly the huddle broke up, and they began to pound each other on the back. Several more of them came up onto the porch. One of the boys seemed to be trying to talk the others into leaving. They laughed at him and finally took him down and rolled him in the snow.

Without hesitation, she went to the phone again.

"Operator, this is Nelda Hanson again. I'm so scared. The sheriff won't come. Please call Lute Hanson, on Route Two. He's my nearest neighbor."

The phone rang four times before Lute answered.

"This is Nelda. Two truckloads of boys are in my yard and on my porch. They're drunk and pounding on the door. The sheriff won't come, but I've got a gun, and I'll shoot the first one that tries to come into my house." By the time she finished her voice was shrill.

"My God! Don't do anything. If you think they're coming in, go to the basement and get into the bin where your grandpa kept coal. Before they find you, I'll be there. For God's sake be careful with that gun!"

She held the phone for a few seconds after it went dead. Tears ran down her cheeks. She hated calling Lute, but what else could she do? She stood with her back to the basement door, her knees trembling, her hand on the gun in her pocket. Kelly stood cowering against her legs. Loud laughter came from the porch!

"Pretty la ... dy, come on ... out and play!" Was

it the voice of the kid from the filling station, the one she'd put down when he flirted with her?

"Mama's baby boy's scared he's goin' get his ass in a pile of shit. Scared baby boy!" They were harassing one of the kids. "You can't go 'cause I got the keys—"

She edged toward the door, then backed away when she saw a face pressed against the glass on the door.

"Oh, Lute, please hurry.

"Here come some more kids. Godamighty! Look at that fool drive."

Was it Lute or more kids joining the party? Fearfully, she darted a glance out the door. A black truck skidded to a stop, and she heard a shout.

"Hey! Hey!" Lute's voice.

Her relief was quickly replaced with fear for him. He was one against a dozen or more! She gripped the small gun and peered through the glass pane on the door. Only two of the youths remained on the porch. One of them said, "Lute Hanson. How'd he—"

Lute had shot out of the truck.

"What the hell's goin' on here?" he roared.

"Hi, Lute. We was just havin' a little beer bust."

"We wasn't hurting' nothin', Lute, we—"

"We were just horsin' around."

"Horsing around on someone else's property is a good way to get your heads blown off," Lute said angrily. "Now get the hell out of here. If you've got to act like fools, do it somewhere else. This woman thinks you're a gang of hoodlums."

Two of the boys climbed into the back of a pickup. Others began to follow.

"Scatter!" Lute said forcefully. "We'll talk about this after you've sobered up."

"Shit, Lute! If the coach finds out about this, we'll get thrown off the team," one of them whined.

"You knew the rules when you got tanked up and came out here."

"Yeah, but—"

"We'll talk about it later."

Nelda turned on the kitchen light, then unlocked the door and stepped out onto the porch.

"Lute," she called. "I want to see who they are. I want to know if I've seen them before, and you can bet I'll remember if I see them again."

"Let it go, Nelda," Lute said briskly. Then to the boys, "Get out of here, and count yourselves lucky."

Nelda went back into the kitchen and sat down because she feared her legs wouldn't hold her any longer. She heard the trucks leaving. She felt sick. Reaction set in, and she began to shake.

❧ *Chapter Fifteen* ❧

LUTE OPENED THE DOOR AND KELLY WAS THERE to greet him, obviously delighted, wiggling appreciatively when Lute fondled his ears. It took several seconds for Nelda's eyes to focus on his face. He stood just inside the door, his hair tousled, a faint stubble of beard on his cheeks.

"Are you all right?"

She nodded. "Thanks for coming. I tried to get the sheriff to come out, but he didn't seem to think it was much of an emergency."

"I know those kids," Lute said slowly. "I can't believe they meant to break into the house. They'd been drinking a bit, raising a little hell, and I doubt if they gave a thought to scaring you. I'll admit it was a dumb idea, but good Lord, Nelda, what if you'd shot one of them?"

Nelda began to laugh, a little hysterical. "You and the sheriff! This is rich . . . really rich."

"Calm down—"

"Don't tell me to calm down you . . . you horse's ass! Can't you get it through your thick head that this is my property, and they had no right to come here in the middle of the night and scare me half to death!" she shouted.

"You don't need to shout."

"I'll shout if I want to. Your good old country boys were just horsin' around, huh? Let me tell you something, Mr. Lute Know-It-All Hanson, fifty percent of all crimes committed in the United States are by boys that age."

"They didn't commit a crime, Nelda, unless you think trespassing is a crime."

"If anyone tries breaking into my house, they're in for a surprise," she said as if he hadn't spoken. "At least I could call the police in Chicago, and they wouldn't treat me like an hysterical old maid!" she shouted. "Now get the hell out of my house."

Lute stood quietly and listened to the torrent of words spilling from her mouth.

"Calm down—"

"If you tell me to calm down again, I'm going to . . . going to hit you in the mouth!" she yelled so loudly that Kelly sank down, then cowered on the floor.

"There's a world of difference between city street gangs and a bunch of high-school kids out celebrating a basketball victory. I realize you didn't know that."

"You think I'm a fool, don't you?" She watched him move about the kitchen as if he lived there. He took a pan from the cabinet and milk from the refrigerator.

"You need something hot to drink, and so do I."

"Then go home and get it," she said in what she hoped was a nasty voice. "Miss Home Ec wouldn't approve of your being here."

"What's she got to do with it?" He spoke with his back to her.

"I don't want to disrupt your orderly life. If you're hanging around thinking you'll sleep with me again, Lute, you might as well go. I'll not sleep with you again . . . ever. Go find Miss Home Ec, she'll be glad to oblige you."

All the resentment that had been bottled up inside her was pouring out. She wanted to pierce his calm shell, somehow find a way to make him suffer.

"The way you oblige Norris Smithfield?" he turned abruptly, and her bitter gaze locked with his while her mouth tightened with anger.

"Yes, if you must know, and the way I obliged you!" she hissed, and the bleak look that crossed his face brought a pleased little flutter to her rapid heartbeat.

His eyes assessed her critically, moving, she knew, over her hair to her tear-wet eyes and the lips that were trying so hard not to tremble. She did her best to return his gaze coolly, but she was very near the breaking point.

"Where's the chocolate?"

She looked at him as if he had lost his mind. Her face was tight with emotion, and her eyes, though glazed with tears, looked defiantly into his.

"I don't want you here, Lute. This is my house,

and I don't want you here." Her voice was savage, raw.

He turned his back to her and began to open cabinet doors. He found the box of chocolate mix and set it on the counter alongside two mugs.

"Don't make me lose my temper, Nelda," he said softly.

"Then don't make me lose mine. I'd appreciate it if you'd go. You got rid of those kids. That's all I called you for. I can handle things from here on. I'm going to that lousy sheriff tomorrow to file a complaint. You know those hoodlums. You'll have to name them, or be in contempt of court." She knew that she was being unreasonable, but she couldn't seem to stop spewing her anger.

"Don't do that, Nelda."

"Don't do it?" she echoed. "This is my home. I own it. I've got a right to be here and not be bothered in the middle of the night." Her voice began to break. "You never had any respect for my feelings. You never even tried to understand how I had to get out and make a living for myself after Becky died," she blurted angrily.

"You never understood my feelings about anything, either. Now shut up and drink this." He set the cup of warm chocolate down in front of her, picked up his own, and stood with his back to the counter.

His intense gaze was focused on her face, but she refused to look at him. The smell of the chocolate was nauseating. She pressed one hand to her abdomen and willed her stomach to settle down. It would be the final humiliation if she had to throw up.

"If you're sure the boys were doing more than trespassing, if they threatened you or tried to break into the house, you should file a complaint. But you must be very sure before you make a charge that will stay on a boy's record for the rest of his life."

"Chauvinist!" she spit. "We must protect the boys! What about me? If you'd found them raping me, I suppose you'd have thought I lured them in here! That I was 'asking for it.' "

"There are times when I'd like to shake you!"

"Why don't you? Are you afraid of the gun? Here it is!" She took it from her pocket and slammed it down on the counter.

"Do you know how to handle this thing?" Lute reached over and picked it up.

"You're damn right I do. My darling daddy taught me. A woman alone has to look after herself."

"I imagine you could have found any number of men to look after you," he said dryly. Then before she could retort, he asked, "Do you have a permit for this?"

"An Illinois state permit. I suppose *here* they don't give gun permits to women." She said it as sarcastically as she could, drawing in her lower lip, her voice stiff with brittle cynicism.

"We're not as rednecked as all that." His voice was caustic, his lips tight in an obvious attempt at self-control.

Nelda tried to tense her body, to stop the trembling. Her eyes flicked restlessly, trying to avoid him, but his presence seemed to fill every corner of the room.

Damn you! Damn you! Get out of here!

She glanced at him. He was watching her with a taut expression.

"Why didn't you call your friend, Norris?"

"He lives on the other side of the lake. It would have taken a half hour for him to get here."

"Too bad. It would have been a good excuse for him to stay the night."

"He doesn't need an excuse," she said rashly, looking up to meet angry blue eyes. His face was harsh and powerful, the jaw jutting in his obvious effort to control his temper. Nelda sucked in her breath and bent her head over her cup, pretending to drink.

"Are you moving in with him?" The words sounded as if they'd been torn out of him.

"Why would I want to do that?" She enjoyed seeing him squirm for a change. But then, he probably didn't care with whom she slept, just so it wasn't Norris. For some reason, he didn't like him.

"Why not? He hasn't had a woman out there for a while."

"You don't know anything about him. Just because he's rich and free to do as he pleases, you and the rest of your narrow-minded friends would like to think him a cad, a debaucher of young women, the sexual sultan of north Iowa." Her anger was making her defense of Norris too vehement, but she couldn't make herself stop.

"So it's like that, huh?"

"Like what, Mr. Know-It-All?"

"You're in love with him!"

Hysterical laughter bubbled up in her throat. She had finally touched a raw spot! She turned her face up to meet his accusing stare.

"I can't believe you!" She started to deny that she was in love with Norris, then cut herself off. She was tired, and it was suddenly easier to let him think what he wanted to think.

"How long are you going to be here?" he asked quietly.

"I haven't decided. I may stay and take up farming. What kind of a lease do you hold on my land?" She paused, her mind racing. "Norris will furnish me with all the equipment I need."

He was silent for so long that she looked up, surprised to see a grin on his face. It infuriated her.

"I suppose you think I don't have brains enough to farm: can beans, freeze corn, slop hogs, feed chickens, et cetera, et cetera—" It was crazy. The words flowed out as if she had no control over them.

The eyes that blazed into hers were astonishingly bright with anger.

"If you think this is such a corny, stupid place, why do you stay? I'm getting a little bit tired of you running down my hometown. You haven't changed a bit. You're a snob, Nelda, just like your old man. I can still hear him say: *'I never thought my daughter would stoop so low as to get herself knocked up by a rutting wet-eared, hog-slopping hayseed.'* That's exactly what I am, what I'll always be, and what I'm proud of being."

"Hear! Hear!"

He looked as if he hated her. "Don't threaten me with taking up permanent residence here. You wouldn't last a season, with or without Smithfield's help."

"Get out!" she ordered, surprising herself that she could even speak.

"Hurts, doesn't it, to hear the truth about yourself," he jibed, and strode toward the door.

Rage and frustration such as she had never known boiled up inside Nelda. She stood up abruptly, knocking her chair to the floor in the process. When he turned and grinned at her anger, she lost control. Her hand found his empty mug on the table, and she threw it at him. He dodged and it went crashing though the pane on the kitchen door and thumped on the floor of the porch. The sound of shattering glass was faint in her ears that were filled with a thunderous pounding.

Lute looked at her with astonishment. "What the hell—"

She stood wide-eyed, with the back of her hand to her mouth, while the realization of what she had done penetrated her scrambled mind. Then with a cry she ran out of the room and up the stairs to her bedroom, shut the door, and threw herself down on the bed, pulling the pillow over her head.

She cried bitterly. She had made an utter, complete fool of herself. She cried until her mind was numb with grief, knowing that she had destroyed any respect Lute might have had for her. She sank deeply into the pit of her misery, letting it close in over her.

When the storm of weeping passed, she took off her robe and crawled under the covers. She was shaking almost uncontrollably. She lay flat on her back, staring at nothing, as if her eyelids had been rendered powerless to close.

She could hear the sound of hammering down in the kitchen. Lute was still here. He was boarding up the window she had broken out of the door. *Good of him,* she thought bitterly. *Why is he bothering? It won't mean anything to him if I freeze to death.*

A feeling of desperate loneliness flooded her heart. Even her dog had deserted her to stay downstairs with Lute. She wasn't wanted or needed by anyone in all the world except the tiny life that grew inside her.

At that moment she vowed never, never to tell him that she was pregnant with his child. He would be insufferable. If she didn't marry him, he might even try to declare her unfit and take the baby from her. Oh, God, no!

Lute thought her stupid and useless. He didn't consider the work she did as real work. He hadn't shown the slightest interest in it. He hadn't asked her about Aldus Falerri's nightclub or about the prints she was working on.

They had needed each other when they were young and thought the whole world was against them, but now—. Trying to keep the pain in her heart at bay, she decided that tomorrow she would ask Norris how to go about renting an apartment in Minneapolis. It was ridiculous to stay here any longer.

"Nelda, are you all right?" Lute pushed open the

bedroom door. Kelly trotted in and flopped down beside the bed.

"You're always asking me that. What do you care?" she responded dully.

"Don't be foolish. I asked if you were all right."

"I heard you. I may be a stupid, useless city woman, but I'm not deaf."

"Stop being childish. I didn't realize you were so shaken by what happened."

"I've had it, Lute. I've given it my best shot and it didn't work. You've won. The phone calls . . . the other thing, and now this. I'll remove my irritating presence from here as soon as I can."

"What other thing?"

"Nothing. A figure of speech." She wasn't about to tell him about the blanket disappearing from the porch.

"What other thing?" he repeated. When she didn't answer, he said, "Is that bastard still calling?"

"Yes. But don't worry about it. It's probably some high-school kid getting his kicks out of talking nasty to an older woman."

"What did he say?"

"Things unfit for your delicate ears, Lute."

Nelda knew that he was looking at her, but she continued to look at the ceiling. Beneath the covers her hand stroked back and forth over her belly. *It'll be just you and me, Baby.*

"I had a piece of plywood in the truck. I nailed it over the broken glass in the door. It'll keep the cold out until you can get it fixed. Call Miller Hardware. John Miller will come out and put in a glass."

He paused. "Nelda, did you hear me?" He came to the side of the bed. "Nelda, why is it always like this between us?"

"Like what?"

"We're like a cat and a dog when we're together."

"Don't you mean like a stallion and a mare in heat?"

"I didn't mean that, and you know it," he said heatedly.

"No, I don't know it. Go home. I'm sorry I called you. I'm not your concern. I won't bother you again."

"It was no bother." He sat down on the edge of the bed. "You don't look well. Have you had a setback from the flu?"

"No. I've not had a setback. I'm just not the robust type. You've got me confused with Miss Home Ec, the all-American girl. I'll never be able to lift hay bales and milk cans. I'm just not built that way."

Now it was his turn to be silent. She looked at him with calm resignation.

"Go home, Lute," she said softly. "I'm getting my act together, and I'll be out of your hair soon."

He got up and went to the door.

"I left the gun in the cabinet above the refrigerator." He waited; but when she didn't speak, he went out the door and down the stairs. She heard him close the back door. Soon she heard the sound of his pickup going down the lane toward the road.

He called at noon the next day.

"Hello, Nelda. This is Lute."

"I know who it is," she said tightly.

"Are you still upset?"

"I'm busy, Lute. What do you want?" she asked sharply, trying to erect a barrier around her feelings.

"I've talked to the boys who were at your place last night. They want you to accept their apology. They won't trespass on your property again."

"I'm relieved to hear that. It's good of them."

"Well?"

"Well . . . what?"

"Do you accept their apology? Is this the end of it?"

"What did you think I'd do? Carry on a vendetta, put out a contract, notify my Chicago gangster friends?"

"Knock off the sarcasm. I'm in no mood for it. Is someone else bothering you besides that pervert making the phone calls?"

"Why do you ask?"

"Last night you, said something about . . . that other thing."

"You're mistaken. Is that all, Lute?"

There was a silence, and she thought she heard him say, "Shit!" Then he asked in a calm controlled voice. "Did you get someone out there to fix that window?"

She couldn't take another moment of his solicitousness, knowing it had nothing to do with his heart and everything to do with his concern for some high-school boys' criminal records.

"Good-bye, Lute," she whispered hoarsely, and hung up the phone.

Soon thereafter the man from the hardware store came out to replace the broken windowpane.

"Are you John Miller?" she asked before she let him in the house.

"No, ma'am. John's putting in windows across the lake. I'm giving him a hand today." He handed her a bill on a Miller Hardware letterhead.

"I'd like you to put a heavy bolt on the inside of the door."

"John told me. Somebody try to break in, did they?"

"Uh-huh." She said nothing more, and the man remained silent.

Nelda took the bill and went to the other room to write a check, trying to stay busy there until he finished his work.

As soon as he left, she called Norris and asked his help in finding an apartment, explaining simply that she wanted to move to Minneapolis as soon as possible.

"Honey, I've been called back to Chicago to straighten out some business. I plan to fly into Minneapolis just for Christmas Day, but I'll be back there right after the first of the year. Can you wait that long? If not, go on up and stay in a hotel. I can make a reservation for you."

"I can wait, Norris, but thanks anyway."

"What will you do on Christmas?"

"I've not decided."

"I hate to think of you alone."

She laughed nervously. "I can assure you that I'll not be alone."

"I'm glad of that."

When she finished talking to Norris, she got out the calendar. Eight days until Christmas. She had promised Rhetta she would go shopping on Saturday. They would go only as far as a few miles south of Minneapolis. Rhetta had said that she would rather not get into the Christmas traffic in the downtown area. Nelda was glad now that she had said she would go. It would be one day fewer to fill until she could leave.

By noon she was in a better frame of mind. It's surprising, she said to herself, as she drove out of the farmyard on her way to Mason City, how a person's mind can adjust to change. Today she felt reconciled to what lay ahead. Her future would hold both joy and sadness.

After a few hours of shopping, she headed home to decorate the small tree she had bought to put on Becky's grave. Kelly greeted her with yips of joy. She put him on the end of his rope and brought her purchases into the house. Since she was going to the cemetery, she left the car in the yard.

An hour later she put the small tree, decorated with tiny angels tied securely to the branches and a silver star on the top, in the front seat of the car.

"Get in, Kelly. You can go this time." She opened the back door. The dog didn't need a second invitation.

During the months she had been here, Nelda had made many trips to the cemetery. It was always so peaceful, especially so this time of year, with the ground covered with snow. Green Christmas wreaths with red bows decorated the newer section. Devoid of adornment, the older gravestones on the hill surrounding the statue of Abraham Lincoln were a stark reminder that immediate relatives of the loved ones buried there also were gone.

Nelda drove to the far end, and even before she stopped the car, she could see that Lute had put a small wreath on their daughter's grave.

"Stay in the car, Kelly. The snow is too deep. You'd just get all wet," she said as she took the small tree from the car. Glad to be wearing boots, because the snow was a foot deep or more, she carried the tree to the grave.

"Merry Christmas, Becky," she said aloud, and backed away after she had made sure the tree was solidly set in the snow. The small silver angels fluttered in the slight breeze. Next Christmas she would have the baby, Becky's baby brother or sister, who would be almost the same age as Becky was when she died. She forcibly banished the thought from her mind.

Back in the car Nelda sat for a long while looking at the fluttering angels. Her heart felt like a rock in her chest. She had to stop grieving over Lute and take care of herself. The baby growing inside her deserved the best start in life she could give him.

❧ *Chapter Sixteen* ❧

NELDA LEFT THE CEMETERY AND WENT TO THE grain elevator, where she bought a large sack of dog food, then to the post office for stamps to put on the Christmas cards she must get in the mail within the next few days.

Noticing that she had less than a quarter tank of gas in her car, she drove to the Herb's Shell, a station a block off Main Street, and pulled up to the pumps. She had been trading here since the incident at the station on the highway. A small, fast-moving man named Eddie came out to wait on her.

"Howdy, Mrs. Hanson. Fill'er up?"

"Yes, please."

After he had filled the tank, he washed her windshield, then the back window.

"What else can we do for you? Need your oil checked?"

"You did that last time, Eddie."

"By golly, we did."

When he came back to the car with her change, he gave her a candy cane.

"Merry Christmas, Mrs. Hanson."

"Thank you, and Merry Christmas to you too, Eddie."

Nelda left the station feeling a little bit as if she belonged. Never had a service-station attendant in Chicago called her by name or given her a small Christmas treat. It would be as impersonal in Minneapolis when she moved there. After her baby was born, she would decide where she wanted to live permanently. She made a mental note to see Mr. Hutchinson in the next few days and decide if it would be wise to sell the farm or rent it and live off the income it provided.

Nelda was halfway down the lane to the house when she saw the flashy blue car parked beneath the oak tree and Lute's black pickup in front of the barn.

"Who in the world . . . ?" She slowed as she made the turn into the yard, then stopped the car.

Kelly had spied Lute and was jumping and barking to get out. Nelda stepped from the car and opened the door for the dog who bounded over the snow heading straight for Lute in a frenzy of delight.

Nelda was stunned for a moment after the realization hit her that the man standing in the middle of the yard with Lute was her father. Her whole thought process shut down. By the time her feet had taken her around the car she was thinking again.

Major Hansen still looked every bit the dignified officer of the United States Marines. He wore a long, blue-belted overcoat, and on his head was the officer's cap: blue with gold braid. Nelda had no doubt that beneath his coat was an immaculate Marine uniform with officer's braid and possibly several lines of service ribbons.

The hair beneath the hat on his head was silver . . . what she could see of it, and his face was as hard as a stone. She felt no gladness at seeing this man who never had one ounce of compassion for her or her child, who had been ashamed of his hardworking father and gentle mother, and who had never in all the eight years since she left his Virginia home made any effort to see to her welfare, even when she had been only seventeen.

Lute was coming toward her. He stopped with his back to her father and bent his head as if to kiss her cheek.

"I let him think that we're together again." He breathed the words, then turned and put his arm across her shoulders and walked with her across the yard to where her father stood beside his car.

"Hello, Nelda." The major made no attempt to touch her.

"What are doing here?" she asked bluntly.

"I wanted my wife to meet you."

"Why?"

"The two women in my life should know each other."

"Then you've come to the wrong place. I'm not in your life."

"I would like you to be."

"Who are you trying to fool? You don't like me, and I detest you."

"I expect you to be civil when you meet her."

He showed signs of anger in his tone and the tightening of his mouth.

"You've no right to expect anything from me." Nelda glanced at the car, where a blond woman sat watching them. "Is she number four or five?"

"Don't be crude," he snapped. "My wife would like to see the place where I grew up."

"It's not a log cabin, but close, by your standards. Is she impressed with how you pulled yourself up by your boot straps to become the important man you are?"

Major Donald Hansen turned frosty eyes on Lute, then back to Nelda, and looked at her in the way that used to shrivel her insides. This time she didn't feel a thing.

"Are you going to show my wife my home or not?"

"Not." Nelda said the one word and looked him straight in the eyes. Then, with a half smile, "It's not *your* home."

"Donald? Is something wrong?" The blonde had rolled down the window.

"Nothing, dear. I'll be there in a minute." When he turned back, he spoke bitingly. "I thought we could have a civil conversation. Did Hutchinson tell you that I'm interested in buying the farm?"

"He told me."

"I'm prepared to pay what you want . . . more than you could get from a local buyer." He looked at Lute. "Do you have any say in this?"

"Not a word. I back Nelda in whatever she decides to do."

"I decided a long time ago. I'll not sell to you. I'll give the farm to the Salvation Army first."

"I see." His mouth snapped shut. "You're paying me back for forcing you to marry, so that your offspring would have a legal name." He put his hand on the lapels of his coat and seemed to be adjusting it on his shoulders, his anger overriding his judgment. "I was right in my assessment of you—an ignorant little slut. From the time you first knew the difference between the sexes, you've been attracted to the lower classes." His cold eyes went to Lute. "And he came running back as soon as you got your hands on the farm, didn't he?"

Lute hit him. Nelda never saw the blow coming and neither did her father. Lute's fist landed solidly on the major's mouth. He backstepped several times before he sat down hard in the snow. His hat bounced off.

"I've been wanting to do that for nine years. Get up so I can do it again." Lute stood over him. Blood was flowing from the major's cut lips. "Call her another name like that, and I'll beat you to a pulp."

The woman flew out of the car and ran to her husband.

"Donald!"

"I'll have you arr . . . ested," Donald snarled up at Lute.

"Go ahead. You're in my territory now, and you're not dealing with a seventeen-year-old kid."

"Donald? What's going on?" His wife tried to help him get to his feet, but he shrugged her hands aside and stood. Holding a handkerchief to his mouth, he picked up his hat.

"Get back in the car, Celeste."

"Is that your daughter?"

"My daughter isn't here."

Nelda moved over toward the woman who looked to be not much older than she was.

"He's right. She isn't here," she said simply.

"I'm so sorry. I wanted to meet her."

"You're about nine years too late."

"Get in the car, Celeste." The major held open the door, then warned Lute, "You'll be hearing from me."

"I hope so," Lute said, and grinned.

Nelda didn't speak until the flashy car was far down the lane.

"Why are you here?"

"Hutchinson called. He tried to get in touch with you this morning. Then after Donald left his office he called again, couldn't get you, and called me to let you know he was coming."

"I didn't need any help from you."

"You got it anyway."

"Yeah, well, thank you for hitting him. Kelly, come."

Nelda walked into the house, the reluctant dog at her heels, and shot the bolt, locking the door.

During the next couple of days a kind of peace settled over Nelda. She had scored a victory of sorts, two victories. She had faced down her father and had come away unaffected. And she was slowly breaking the ties that held her to Lute.

She was pregnant. She was absolutely sure in her own mind, although not confirmed by a doctor, that next July she would have Lute's baby. She had missed two periods and had had a couple of weeks of morning sickness. This time there would be no fear of facing grandparents or her father, and money was no problem.

She didn't have to worry whether or not Lute would marry her. He would, if he knew that she was carrying his child—she was sure of that. But he need never know that the seed he had planted during the ice storm would blossom into life in the summer. The whole scenario of their life would be played over again if he knew. He would feel caught in the same bind! Never, she vowed. Even if he'd wanted her for a wife back then, he certainly didn't now.

Most of Nelda's waking hours were spent in planning a future for herself and her child. Many single women raised children alone, she reasoned, and she welcomed the responsibility. She would like to raise her child in a medium-sized town somewhere in the Southwest. She could try to make a go of textile designing; but if that didn't work out, she could fall back on interior decorating.

It crossed Nelda's mind several times that it was unfair of her not to tell Lute about his son or daughter, whichever it might be. But weighing that unfairness against the fact that Lute had told her outright that he didn't want to make her pregnant and that she was totally unsuitable to his lifestyle, she knew that she had made the right decision.

Lute would never believe that her career would come second to her life with him and their children. He'd never believe that she could adapt to country living. Worse, she sensed he didn't want to believe it. He wanted to shut her out of his life the way he must have thought she had shut him out.

He'd been stubborn as a boy—as a man he was obdurate, unforgiving. He didn't want to love her. It was her problem that she'd found him again and confirmed that she still loved him. Loved him—Lute, the man—not just her romantic memory of a sensitive boy.

She tried dreadfully hard to close out thoughts of years ahead without him, hoping that somehow it would be slightly easier now that his child would be with her.

The day she spent shopping at the mall with Rhetta was one of the most enjoyable she'd had in a long while.

Rhetta had picked her up early.

"Good to see you," Rhetta greeted cheerfully.

"Good to see you, too. I've been looking forward to this."

Rhetta's mouth ran constantly as she drove up the highway and into Minnesota, but it didn't interfere with her driving. Nelda was able to sit back, relax, and talk with her friend. Rhetta had heard about the boys coming to the farm and frightening her.

"People should have more control over their kids.

If my boys had pulled such a stunt as that, they would have heard from Gary and they would have heard from me . . . big-time."

"I was frightened out of my wits and deeply disappointed that the boys were not punished. It reinforces their belief that because they are the big sports stars at the school, they can get away with anything."

"I agree."

The talk turned to other things, and Nelda told Rhetta of her concern for her friend Linda Branson. "It's a case of a woman who married too young, before she'd really developed a sense of her own worth. Her husband wasn't as successful in school as she was, and he's always trying to prove his own importance by running her down. She'd make an excellent nurse. I hope she gets the chance."

"If she had a chance to go to school, how could she afford it?"

"Earl Hutchinson tells me that there is a way."

"Earl is a dear man. The clubs around town have been known to band together and support a worthy student with a scholarship. Maybe they could be approached. And speaking of Earl, he'd be a good catch if things don't work out between you and Lute."

"There's no *if* about that, Rhetta. Lute and I are not even in the same world. Which brings up another subject. I'll be leaving soon to work on a project for a favorite client." She had decided that while she was with Rhetta today, she would lay the groundwork for leaving.

"Oh, no!"

"It isn't forever," Nelda laughed. "I still have the

farm. I'm about to decide not to sell it if I can find someone reliable to live in the house."

"I was planning on you to help with the Valentine's Day dance. Will you be going before then?"

"I'm not sure."

"When will you know?"

"After the first of the year."

"Oh, good. You're invited to our New Year's Eve party."

"I'm sorry, Rhetta. I've already made plans."

"With Norris?"

"No, not with Norris."

Nelda knew that Rhetta disapproved of her friendship with Norris only because both she and Gary wanted her to get back with Lute. How could she make her understand without whining that Lute didn't want her and she had too much pride to hang around? Of course, hanging around was impossible now that she was pregnant.

That brought another thought to mind. She needed to see an obstetrician, but not in Clear Lake or Mason City. She would not be giving birth in Iowa. As soon as she moved to Minneapolis, she would select a doctor.

They shopped, they lunched, and shopped again.

Nelda bought a sturdy pair of walking shoes and heavy socks. She bought a pair of slacks a size too large for her at the present time. Rhetta was in a frenzy of buying Christmas gifts and didn't notice. Nelda really had no one to buy for, and wanted to cry. Crying jags came suddenly and often these days.

"Look at these sweaters, Nelda. What color

should I buy for Gary. He's such a slob. He'd wear orange if I bought him one."

"A brown one is a safe choice." *The blue would be my choice for Lute.*

While Rhetta was selecting games for her boys, Nelda visited the bookstore and came away with a shopping bag full of paperback novels. Hidden beneath the pile were books on prenatal care, how to raise a baby, and a book of ten thousand names for boys and girls. She even bought a pattern book for knitting baby garments.

Before leaving the mall, she found the needlework shop and bought a large amount of soft yarn, telling Rhetta that she planned to knit an afghan.

It was almost dark when they reached Nelda's house.

"Thank you, so much. I enjoyed the day," Nelda said as she lifted her purchases from the backseat of the car.

"I enjoyed it too. Shall we do it again sometime?"

"I'd love to, but it'll have to be soon."

"Oh, yes, I'm trying to forget about that. Merry Christmas, if I don't talk to you before then."

Nelda hurried into the house to let Kelly out. She dumped her packages on the table and saw a note lying there.

I let Kelly out. L.

Her mind froze. Lute had been in her house while she wasn't here. How dare he do that!

She put the dog out on the end of his rope. On her way back across the porch she had another shock. The blanket she had found in the garage and which had later disappeared was back there on the bench, where she had put it before. An icy tingle feathered over her skin. Taking deep, stabilizing breaths, she fought light-headedness.

Who was doing this to her? It had to be Lute. He was here today on her porch, in her house!

She went to the phone and dialed his number.

"This is Nelda," she said when he answered.

"I know."

"I don't appreciate your coming into my house when I'm not here. Why have you never used your key before?"

"I never had a need to use it before."

"And what need was that?"

"Kelly wanted out?"

"He barked because he heard your truck. He has stayed in the house for longer periods of time. I leave him food and water, and he is in no way being mistreated."

"Why are you so riled up? Seems to me it happens a lot lately."

"There is something else. If it's your intention to cause me to doubt my sanity by leaving that damn blanket on the porch, you're wasting your time. So bug out of my life . . . and you can bet that during the remaining time I'm here, short as it is, the locks on these doors will be changed."

"Don't hang up!" he said quickly. "What blanket?"

"Don't give me that horse . . . crap. You know what blanket, dammit."

"Nelda . . . what's going on? Tell me or I'm coming over there."

"Come on. You won't get in."

"I've got a key."

"And I've got a bolt on the inside of the door and a . . . gun."

Nelda hung up the phone. She was so mad she was shaking. Who did he think he was fooling? The damn, sneaking . . . horse's ass!

After letting Kelly back in, she went upstairs to get her gown and robe. Making sure the doors were securely locked, and going as far as to wedge a chair under the doorknob of the front door because she didn't have an inside bolt, she brought her small radio to the bathroom and tuned it to her favorite evening station. Then she drew a warm bath, sprinkled in a generous amount of fragrant bath oil, and sank down in it.

Lying back, letting the warm water work its miracle on her tired body, she listened to the music of the Lawrence Welk orchestra coming from Yankton, South Dakota. They were playing "White Christmas." Kelly was lying on the bathmat beside the tub, and when he rose up and tilted his head to listen, she knew that someone was coming.

Nelda twisted the knob to allow more hot water into the tub. She had a pretty good idea who would be at her door in a matter of minutes.

Kelly got up and went to the kitchen. Soon he was whining a welcome. Lute had accepted her challenge as she had suspected he would. *Heck of a lot of good it will do him*, she thought smugly.

He pounded on the door.

Kelly barked.

Nelda smiled.

Lute shouted her name.

Nelda got out of the tub, turned up the volume on the radio until the strains of the "Beer Barrel Polka" were bouncing off the walls. She returned to the tub and sank down into the warm water.

When Lute finally went away, Kelly came back to the bathroom and Nelda felt as if she had won a small victory.

❧ Chapter Seventeen ❧

THE MORNING AFTER HER SHOPPING TRIP WITH Rhetta, Earl Hutchinson called.

"How did it go with your father? He arrived several days early. I had hoped to be able to prepare you for his visit."

"I was shocked to see him, but he doesn't frighten me anymore."

"Was Lute there? I called him when I couldn't get in touch with you. I would have come out to give you support, but I had to be in court."

"He was here." She implied by her tone that she wished he hadn't been.

"I'm sorry if by calling Lute I overstepped—"

"—It was all right . . . this time. Lute is no longer in my life, Mr. Hutchinson, and I'd rather keep my relationship with him on a strictly business basis. He rents my land, and that's it."

"I see. I was under the impression that you . . . er . . . maybe were getting back together."

"I don't know where you could have heard that. It's the farthest thing from my mind."

"I made a mistake, and I'm sorry."

"By the way, I'll be leaving after the first of the year. Will you get some figures together for me? I need to know what income I could expect if I kept the farm versus the income the proceeds from the sale of the farm would earn in interest."

"I can give you some approximate figures."

"That will be good enough."

After her talk with the lawyer she felt relieved. She had started the ball rolling.

Later in the morning while she was sitting at the kitchen table looking over the pattern book and trying to visualize some of the small garments made with the yarn she had bought, the phone rang again. She picked it up thinking Mr. Hutchinson was calling back.

"Hello."

"Slut . . . whore . . . ya uppity, fuckin' bitch. I'll get you—"

The angry voice shouted in her ear before she could slam down the phone. Her heart began to race until she thought it would gallop out of her chest. She pressed her hands tightly together and brought them beneath her chin. For a long while she sat with her chin pressed to her interlaced fingers.

I'll get you— This time he had threatened. The calls were being made by someone who really hated her. Why? What had she done to cause someone around here to dislike her so much? The question charged through the confusion in Nelda's mind. She wandered around the house feeling alone and menaced, and wondering how she was going to fill her time during the holiday season.

It was three days until Christmas. She had mailed cards to acquaintances in Chicago and one to the stepmother who had helped her leave Virginia. Nelda would be giving no presents and didn't expect to get any. It didn't occur to her to feel sorry for herself. She was used to being alone on holidays. The only Christmases she had known amid a loving family, with a tree and presents on Christmas morning, were during the time she had spent here in this house with her grandparents.

Since she had lost Becky, Christmas had not meant much to her. She looked around her house, devoid of any decorations, and tried to keep the pain in her heart at bay. She would be by herself again this Christmas Eve with only Kelly to keep her company as she had been many times before.

But something was due to happen. Nelda would not have believed it if she had been told that this Christmas Eve there would be a child in the house. A child expecting a visit from Santa Claus.

The sky had turned cloudy, and in the late afternoon a few intermittent snowflakes began to fall. After taking note of the supplies in the cupboard, Nelda began making a batch of cookies for herself and Kelly. She liked to bake, but it wasn't much fun baking for one person. The cookies were cooling on the rack and she was trying to decide on what type of icing to use as decoration when the phone rang.

The ring was startling in the quiet kitchen. Nelda

looked at it fearfully. It wasn't Norris; he was in Chicago. She was sure it wasn't Lute, or Rhetta. Would Mr. Hutchinson be calling this late? After four rings she lifted the phone with one hand and the whistle in the other.

"Hello."

"Nelda . . . this is Linda. I'm so glad . . . you're home."

"Linda, what is it?"

"I hated to call you, but I don't know what to do. It's getting dark, and Eric is cold—"

"Where are you?"

"I'm at the Shell station. Kurt . . . Kurt is drunk and—I was afraid he'd hurt Eric." Linda began to sob.

"Linda, listen to me. Do you want me to come get you?"

"I don't want to cause you any trouble."

"I'll come, Linda, if you want me to."

"Eddie, he's the man here at the station, said that I can hide in the back room until you get here."

"Is your husband looking for you?"

"Eddie says he's been by here twice."

"Linda, stay right there. I'll come get you and bring you out here."

"Nelda, thank you, thank you. What?" Nelda could hear her talking to someone. "Eddie will raise the big door so you can drive in like you were having work done on your car."

"All right. I'll be there in ten or fifteen minutes."

Nelda hung up the phone, put on her boots and

coat, then went through the house and turned on a few more lights. Kelly was watching her.

"Want to go in the car?"

At the sound of the magic words, the dog raced to the door. Nelda flipped on the yard light, locked the door behind them, and put the key in her pocket. She was immeasurably glad to have her canine friend with her when Kelly, who had run the yard and sniffed around, waited for her at the garage door. Had there been one strange scent to follow, the dog would have been after it like a shot.

Nelda wasn't used to driving at night on a snow-covered road, especially with the flakes coming down. She drove slowly and carefully into town, conscious that homes, businesses, and streets were glowing with Christmas lights but not really seeing them. She crossed Main Street and turned into the drive of the Shell station. The big door came up, and she drove into the station bay. The door closed immediately and Nelda got out of the car.

"She's in the storage room. It's warmer in there," Eddie said, leading the way.

"Oh, Linda, honey—" Nelda exclaimed when she saw her friend's eyes swollen from crying. Linda had on a rather light coat, but the little boy who huddled close to her was warmly dressed in a one-piece suit with a hood.

"I didn't want to get you involved in this, but I didn't have anyone else to call who wouldn't turn right around and call Kurt."

"I'm glad you phoned. You can stay with me until you decide what to do. Hi, Eric. I bet you're tired. Do you want to come home with me? My dog would love to have a little boy to play with."

Nelda helped Linda into the front seat of the car. She held Eric on her lap. Kelly was wiggling all over the back seat and making whiney noises.

"Settle down, Kelly. When we get home you can get acquainted with Eric."

"Mrs. Hanson," Eddie warned, after Nelda closed the door and was walking around to the driver's side. "Be careful. Kurt Branson can be mean when he's drunk. I'll go out and take a look up and down the streets. When I open the door, back out and take the dark streets out of town. He'll be looking for her to be uptown here someplace."

"I will, and thank you, Eddie."

"Linda's a nice woman and hadn't ought to be treated that way."

When the small man went out into the snowy night, Nelda slid under the wheel and spoke confidently to Linda.

"Eddie is looking around. Don't worry we'll be all right. Hey, Eric. I've got some fresh cookies at my house. Are you hungry?"

The child stared at her with wide frightened eyes. *Poor little fellow*, Nelda thought. *What must be running through his mind?*

The big service-station door went up, and Nelda started the motor and backed out. She waved at Eddie, who stood ready to lower the door, and drove down past Easter Super Value to a street that would take her to the north part of town. Linda looked behind them several times to see if they were being followed.

The snow was coming down in big flakes, but the windshield wiper was doing its job. Linda didn't talk, aware that Nelda needed to concentrate on driving. Soon they were out of town and traveling north on the gravel road. Nelda peered into the night, fearing that she would miss the corner where she should turn.

"We're about there," she said with relief when she passed a familiar landmark.

Snow was beginning to pile up in the lane leading to the house when they reached it, and in an hour it would probably be impassable. With relief, she turned into the lighted yard.

"I'll let Kelly out. If there is anyone around, he'll know it." Kelly sniffed out the area and, after relieving himself in several familiar spots, was ready to get into the warm house.

"I'll take you and Eric inside, then put the car in the garage."

When Nelda and Kelly came back into the house, their heads and shoulders were sprinkled with snow. Linda was sitting on a kitchen chair with her child on her lap. They had not taken off their coats.

"Let me have your coats." Nelda hung hers on the hooks her grandpa had put beside the back door and reached for Linda's and Eric's. "Are you hungry?"

"Eric hasn't had anything since noon. He's tired, too. He had to walk a long way."

"The bathroom is here"—Nelda gestured toward

the door—"if you want to put a wet cloth on your face. I'm going to run upstairs and open the door and the heat register to the bedroom you will use. As soon as it warms up, you can put him to bed. Would you like a cup of soup and some cookies, honey?" she said to Eric. "I'll fix it as soon as I come back."

Linda and Eric ate, but very little. Afterward, Nelda made up the bed in her grandparents' room with flannel sheets and warm wool blankets. She found a sweatshirt for Eric to sleep in and laid out a pair of her pajamas for Linda.

It's nice having someone to take care of.

Linda stayed with her son until he was asleep, then came down to the kitchen, where Nelda had hot spiced tea ready. They sat at the kitchen table.

"Thank you for letting us come here."

Linda's bruised cheek would be discolored by morning. Nelda reached across the table and clasped her trembling hand.

"Is this the first time he's hit you?"

"He has never slapped me before. He was drunk when he went to work; his boss told him to leave. I think he was fired, although he didn't say so."

"Did you quarrel because of your wanting to go to nursing school?"

"Every time I mentioned it, he'd go into a rage. But this time it was something else. He was using the phone, and I wanted to know if he was going to meet someone to go ice fishing. I stood in the door and listened. He was calling someone a slut and a whore and said he was going to get her. I don't know who he was talking to, but he turned, saw me and slapped me." Linda avoided her eyes.

Nelda's breath stopped in her throat, and her tongue clung to the roof of her mouth as her mind absorbed the meaning of Linda's words. Suddenly it was a relief to know her unknown enemy.

"Linda, look at me." She shook Linda's hand to get her attention. "Your husband was talking to me."

Linda's eyes remained on Nelda's, her fingers tightened, and her unwilling lips formed words.

"No! Oh, no!"

"He has made at least a dozen calls, obscene calls, but today was the first time he threatened me."

"Oh, Nelda, I'm . . . sorry." Tears rolled down her cheeks.

"Honey, it wasn't your fault."

"I . . . started this thing about wantin' to be a nurse. He blamed you for putting ideas in my head."

"He had to blame someone. Did he hit you in front of Eric?" Nelda asked.

"Yes. Eric was scared and began to cry. Kurt yelled for him to shut up; and when he didn't, couldn't, he said he was going to whip him. Nelda, if he had hit that child, I'd have killed him. I grabbed the deer rifle and told him to leave. He laughed at first, but finally went out to the car and sat there."

"How did you get away?"

"I grabbed Eric's snowsuit and my coat and went out the back door to the neighbors'. She saw that he had hit me, but she didn't want to get involved. I went from place to place until I finally got to the Shell station."

"Will your folks help you?"

"Oh, Nelda, you know what they're like. My sister Janice would help, but she lives in Iowa City."

"Do you want to get in touch with Mr. Hutchinson? He can get a restraining order to keep Kurt away from you and Eric."

"That wouldn't do any good. When Kurt is drunk, he doesn't have any sense at all. I know that I can never go back to him now. It makes me sick to think that he's been calling you and talkin' nasty."

"I'm glad to know at last who has been calling. I couldn't figure out who hated me that much."

"He's ruined Christmas for Eric. Poor little guy has been so excited."

"We can make Christmas a happy time for him here if you want to stay. It's only two more days."

"Why are you being so good to us? You've been away for so long, and we were only casual friends . . . back then. I was planning to go to the Salvation Army."

"He would find you there. Not much can be done about legalizing your separation until after the holidays."

"If he finds out I'm here, he'll come out here."

"We can keep him from finding out. Is there anything, besides clothes, you need from your house?"

"If we're leaving for good, I want Eric's toys and his baby pictures."

"Mr. Hutchinson will talk to the police and see if they will go with you to get your things. Eric could stay here with me."

"Kurt will follow and find out where we are."

"Why don't we talk about it in the morning. You'll feel better after a good night's sleep."

The phone rang as Nelda got up to take their cups to the sink. Linda looked at her fearfully.

"What if it's him?" she whispered, as if the person calling could hear her.

"We won't know until we answer." Nelda picked up the phone and before she could answer, the shouting, cursing voice boomed in her ear.

"Ya shitty slut! Ya blow that whistle in my ear and I'll come out there and beat the shit outta ya." Nelda held the phone so Linda could hear the loud, angry voice coming from the other end.

"Ya put them big ideas in my wife's head. Now she's took my kid 'n' left. When I get my hands on ya, I'll screw yore goddamn eyeballs out—" Nelda laid the phone on the counter.

"Ya ain't nothin' but a uppity bitch. If Lute Hanson ain't screwin' ya, your dog is!"

Linda put her hand over her mouth, shocked at what her husband was saying.

"Ya hear me, bitch?"

"I hear you, Mr. Branson. I'm recording what you're saying so that it can be used as evidence when you're arrested." Nelda spoke calmly.

There was a silence, then, "She told ya? That bitch told ya!"

"I don't know who you mean by *she*, but think of what you just said, Mr. Branson. You gave yourself away. Now I have evidence that will put you in jail. Mr. Smithfield is here making the recording, would you like to speak to him?"

"Bitch—" He hung up the phone.

Nelda gently placed the phone back in the cradle and smiled at Linda.

"I've grown kind of used to being called a bitch. This call wasn't as nasty as some of the others."

"He might come out here!"

"That's the reason I put in the little bit about Mr. Smithfield being here. I don't think he'll come out, but if he does, I've got locks on the doors and a gun. I can count on Kelly; nobody comes on the place that he doesn't know about. No one will slip in on us."

"I've never heard him talk so nasty. Being my friend has gotten you into a lot of trouble." There was real sorrow in Linda's voice.

"I didn't enjoy the phone calls, but I'm awfully glad you're here. I didn't realize how lonely I was."

"Aren't you and Lute—?"

"—No."

"I thought sure."

"He doesn't want me, Linda. I'm reconciled to that. He'll probably marry that Home Ec teacher."

"Oh, I'm sorry—"

So am I, but there's nothing I can do about it.

❧ *Chapter Eighteen* ❧

"CALL ME BACK, MR. HUTCHINSON, AND LET ME know when to bring her in." Nelda hung up the phone and smiled at Linda.

"He'll talk to Chief Larsen and tell him that Kurt is the one who is making the obscene calls. He'll see if Kurt can be held at the police station long enough for you to get into the house and gather the things you need."

"Someone will tell him you took me there, and he'll come out here."

"I thought of that. When Mr. Hutchinson calls me back, I'll tell him that I'm bringing you to his office and ask him to take you to your house. I'll wait at the office with Eric."

"Kurt will be wild when he discovers I've taken our clothes." Linda's voice trembled slightly.

"Are you sure this is what you want to do?" Nelda asked gently.

"Oh, yes. I can't go back to him. I just can't. All he wants to do is drink. And when he drinks he's mean. He was angry yesterday because I didn't want him to take Eric out on the ice. He drives on the lake and does what he calls 'twirlies.' "

"What's that?"

"He drives fast, then puts on the brakes. The car spins around on the ice. He thinks it's great fun, but I think it's dangerous. I was afraid Eric would get hurt."

"Well . . . I should think so! Is that sort of thing permitted?"

"I don't know. It would be hard to keep cars from driving on the ice. You can go out on it at any public approach." Linda drew her bottom lip between her teeth. "It breaks my heart that this will be the Christmas Eric will always remember. It's the first without his father."

"We're going to make sure that he'll remember how much fun it was," Nelda promised, remembering disappointing Christmases when she was a child. "The only child I've been with at Christmas was Becky. She was only five months old and didn't know what was going on. Please let me help make this a merry one for Eric."

"I'll pay you back. I swear I will."

"It's my pleasure having you here. You're my guest. I'll hear nothing more about paying back. We'll give Eric a Christmas he'll look back on with fond memories. Okay?" Nelda got out her notebook and began making a list. "After we get back from town, I'll do some shopping, buy a tree and some presents. Santa Claus comes tomorrow night," Nelda ended with a bright smile.

Linda cried quietly, tears rolling down her cheeks.

"I don't know how I'll ever repay you."

"Don't even mention it. I'm being selfish. I was hating the thought of being alone at Christmas."

"I'm just so wound up, I cry at . . . the drop of a hat."

"We'll have turkey for Christmas dinner and pumpkin pie. Do you know how to cook a turkey? I've never cooked one in my life."

"I can cook turkey," Linda laughed nervously. "I've had to cook . . . since I was knee-high to a pup." Linda stood and headed for the door leading to the stairs. "I'd better see about Eric. He might wake up and be scared."

"After I got the clothes, Mr. Hutchinson said we should take Eric's toys," Linda said on the way back to the farm the next morning.

"He's really a nice man."

"Could you ever . . . like him?"

"I do like him, but not the way you're thinking."

"He isn't all that old."

"I'd say he's around forty. Why don't you set your cap for him?"

"Nelda! Are you out of your mind? When I get rid of Kurt, I'm never going to marry again."

"Ha! We'll see."

As they approached the lane leading to the house, Nelda slowed the car and scanned the area before she turned in.

"The coast is clear. Let's hurry and get you and

Eric in the house. Lute comes about this time of day and tends to his horses. I don't want him to know you're here."

Linda didn't ask the question until Eric was settled in the living room with his toys and they had carried the two laundry baskets of clothes upstairs.

"Why don't you want Lute to know we're here?"

"For one thing, it's none of his business. For another, the fewer people who know you're here, the better."

Linda was surprised by her friend's almost bitter tone of voice.

Kelly was in dog heaven having Eric to play with. The two of them romped around the house, Eric throwing a ball and Kelly chasing it.

"I hate to break up their fun, but I'd better take Kelly with me. If Lute's truck comes in, Kelly will bark, and Lute might come to the door."

"What'll I do, if he does?"

"Don't answer. Bolt the door as soon as I leave, and if his truck comes up the lane, go upstairs." Nelda put on her coat. Kelly, always alert to the possibility of riding in the car, stopped chasing the ball and came to her wagging his tail enthusiastically. "Where is the best place for me to shop for what you have on the list?"

"You can get it all at Sears."

"You have only three things listed."

"Two for Santa and one to unwrap on Christmas morning." Linda whispered.

"Gotcha," Nelda whispered back.

Shopping in the toy store at Christmas time was

a unique experience for Nelda, and she had fun doing it. Uncertain about the game she had chosen to give Eric, she checked with the clerk.

"Is this too advanced for a six-year-old boy?"

"Candy Land? No, he'll love it, and will pester you to play it with him."

After loading up with gifts in the toy department, Nelda had to make a trip to the car with her purchases. She returned to the store to buy a sweater and a bottle of perfume for Linda, wrapping paper and ribbon, paper bells and a lighted plastic Santa Claus to decorate the house, fragile glass balls and silver icicles for the tree.

On her way home she stopped and bought a five-foot Christmas tree. The man who sold it to her nailed a stand to the bottom, put it in the trunk of the car, and tied the lid down with a rope. Her last stop was at the grocery store. When she came out, she had to make Kelly sit in the front seat in order to make room for the sacks of groceries.

It was almost dark when she returned to the farm, and she failed to see the pickup parked in front of the barn until she pulled into the yard. She had a moment of panic until she realized it wasn't Lute's, but that it belonged to his hired man. She and Kelly went into the house and waited until the man left before she unloaded the car and put it into the garage.

"Something smells good," Nelda exclaimed coming into the kitchen.

"I made something called Ted-a-rena. I don't know where the name came from. It's an old recipe."

"What's in it?"

"Ground beef, potatoes, carrots, onions, spaghetti, and cheese. I'll write down the recipe if you want it."

"I do. I like casseroles."

Eric was so excited about putting up the tree that he hurriedly ate his supper, then tugged on his mother's arm and whispered for her to hurry. Nelda suggested that the dishes be done later. They went into the living room, where she opened the packages of decorations, and Linda helped Eric fasten them to the thick branches of the fragrant tree.

"We've got an angel to go on top," Nelda said after all the the colorful balls were on the tree. She held up a silver angel with wings and a halo.

"Oh, pretty. What's her name?" Eric asked.

"Becky," Nelda said without hesitation. She fastened it to the top of the tree and stood back to look at it. "What'a you think, Eric?"

"I like her."

"It's bedtime for you, my angel," Linda said.

"Boy's ain't angels." Eric gave his mother a disgusted look.

"They certainly are."

"I've not seen one. They all wear dresses."

"My angel wears pants." Linda grabbed him up and hugged him.

"We forgot the sugarplum tree," Nelda exclaimed, and opened another box and set the small, clear-plastic tree on the coffee table. "Eric can't go to bed until we put the sugarplums on the tree. Come help me, Eric. We've got red and green gumdrops to put on the branches."

"Is this for Santa Claus?" Eric asked, when each of the spikes on the tree held a gumdrop.

"We'll leave cookies for Santa. This is for us, but we'd better put it up on the library table or Kelly will help himself." Nelda moved the plastic tree to a higher table. "When I was in Mason City, Santa sent a present for me to give you before Christmas because you've been a super nice boy." She went to the closet and brought out a brown teddy bear dressed in a Santa Claus suit.

Eric's eyes opened wide. He looked at the teddy bear and then at his mother.

"For . . . me?"

"Your name is Eric Branson, isn't it?"

"Uh-huh."

"Then it's for you."

"Golly." When Nelda knelt down, the child threw his arms around her neck. "Can I take him up to bed?"

"He's yours."

"Gee, thanks—"

"You're very welcome." Nelda had tears in her eyes as she watched Linda and Eric go up the stairs.

Nelda had just started washing the dishes when the phone rang. Kurt Branson again? She looked at the time; it was nine o'clock. She was tempted not to answer it, but after seven rings, she picked up the receiver.

"Nelda?" It was Lute's voice. "Where in the hell were you?"

"It's none of your business. What do you want?"

"Don't get on your high horse. What are you doing tomorrow night?"

"Tomorrow night? I'm not sure. I'll have to speak with my social secretary."

"I'm inviting you to come over to my place tomorrow night."

"And spend the evening with Miss Home Ec? No, thanks."

"She won't be here."

"You want me to fill in for her."

"No, dammit. It's Christmas Eve. I didn't think you'd want to spend it alone."

"That's very thoughtful of you. But what makes you think I'll be alone? You're only a neighbor, Lute. I think you're taking too much on yourself."

"I'm more than a neighbor, and you know it."

"I guess you're right," she said slowly, thoughtfully. "I did service you a couple of times."

There was silence on the other end of the line. Nelda smiled, knowing that she had made him furious.

"Don't ever say that again!" His voice was choked with anger.

"And . . . if I do?"

"You'll be sorry—"

"—I'm not afraid of you, Lute. You can't do any worse to me than what you've already done."

Another prolonged silence before he spoke.

"I'd like to spend Christmas Eve with you."

"I'm flattered, Lute, that I've aced out Miss Home Ec."

"Why do you keep bringing her up?"

"Because she's perfect for you. She knows about corn, cows, beans, hay. She could probably butcher a hog. I bet she knows which end of the hog the bacon comes from."

Lute ignored her sarcasm. "If you don't want to come over here, I'll come there."

"It wouldn't do you any good. I'm not going to sleep with you. I'm having my period."

"Damn you! There are times when I'd like to break your neck." There was a high note of anger in his voice.

"Merry Christmas, Lute." *You've already broken my heart.*

"Nelda—"

"Good-bye, Lute." Nelda hung up the phone and stood for a minute staring down at her hands resting on the counter without seeing them. She had to burn all the bridges because once she left here, she couldn't come back.

Nelda spent the next afternoon baking cookies. She cut a gingerbread man out of a piece of cardboard, placed it on the rolled-out dough, and cut around it. Before the cookie men were baked, she let Eric poke a hole in the head of each to run a string though so that they could be hung on the tree.

"He's so happy," Linda said later when Eric was in the other room. "The first night we were here he asked if his dad was coming. I told him no, and he's not asked about him since."

"I've read that children can sense tension. He sees that you're more relaxed, so he can relax too."

"As soon as Christmas is over, I've got to find out what my options are and make plans," Linda said tiredly.

"I haven't mentioned this before, but within the next few weeks, I'm going up to Minneapolis to do some work for a client."

I hate lying to you, Linda.

Linda was quiet for a minute. "Will you come back?"

"No, but you're welcome to stay here. Consider it house-sitting until I decide what I'm going to do with the farm."

"You're not coming back, ever?"

"No. I have to be where I can get work. There are not many offices, restaurants, and nightclubs to decorate in Clear Lake and Mason City."

"I'm thinking about leaving here, too. Even after I divorce Kurt, he'll not let go. He'll use the excuse of seeing Eric, even though he hasn't paid much attention to him before. Kurt is his father, but he's not a good influence on him. I never know what to expect from him."

"Do you have an idea where you would go?"

"Somewhere where I can earn a living for Eric and me. Even if the court tells Kurt to pay child support, he won't do it. He'd quit work just to spite me."

Nelda lifted the pan from the oven.

"Eric," she called. "The cookies are done."

"Let me see. Can I tie the strings?"

"Sure you can. Humm . . . not too bad. Maybe

we should go into the bakery business. But then you'd eat all the profit," Nelda teased.

Nelda was in the kitchen, Linda and Eric hanging the gingerbread men on the tree when she saw a flash of light coming down the lane toward the house. She immediately turned off the kitchen light so that she could go to the window and see who was coming.

"It's Kurt," Linda whispered, coming to stand beside her.

"Take Eric upstairs."

"I can't leave you down here alone."

"I'll not let him in. Now go. You won't want Eric here when he pounds on the door."

"He's mean. He might hurt you."

"He'll not get in to hurt me. Now go."

As soon as Linda left the room, Nelda made sure the door was locked, then went to the cabinet above the stove where Lute had put the gun. By the small light in the bathroom, she checked to see if it was loaded. Returning to the kitchen door, she heard the car door slam. Kelly heard it, too, and began to bark.

"Hush." Nelda placed the palm of her hand against the dog's nose.

The pounding on the door was loud and constant.

"Linda! I know you're here. Linda! Open this door, or I'll break it down."

"He's drunk," Linda whispered. "I couldn't leave you to face him alone. Eric is in a closet. He knows to stay there when Kurt is drunk. We've been through this before."

"I'm not going to face him unless he breaks down the door. Then I'm going to shoot him."

"Oh, no!"

"Linda! What the hell stunt you pullin' now? Get yore ass out here 'n' bring my boy."

"Linda isn't here. Get away from my door," Nelda shouted.

"Ya bitch! Ya turned my wife against me! Linda! Open this door, or I'll break it down."

"I'm telling you to leave," Nelda yelled. "I've got a gun, and I know how to use it. You try to come in here, and I'll shoot you."

There was silence, then they heard him leave the porch.

"He's going around the house. Now he's looking in the window. Don't let him see you, Linda," Nelda whispered. "He's headed around to the front. I'll turn on the front light so he can see that I have a gun."

Nelda went to the front of the house and switched on the porch light. He was shaking the door leading to the glassed-in porch. Nelda stepped out onto the porch with the gun in her hand.

"I've called the sheriff and told him you're trying to break in. I also told him that I've got a gun, and I'll shoot if you don't leave." Nelda made sure he could hear what she said.

He looked at her through the glass door with pure hatred on his face.

"My wife and my boy are in there—"

"Leave, or I'll file charges against you not only for the phone calls but also for trespassing."

"This ain't the last of it. I'll get ya—" He moved away from the door and started back around the house.

Linda was crying quietly when Nelda reached the kitchen. Together, they watched the car go down the lane to the road.

"I'm sorry. I'm so sorry to put you through this."

Nelda put her arm around her friend. "I'm glad you came to me. The day after tomorrow we'll talk to Mr. Hutchinson. He'll know what to do. In the meantime we've got to make this a merry Christmas for Eric."

"Poor little fella. He's worried his daddy will make us go back, and Santa Claus won't be able to find him."

"Go on up and reassure him. Tell him his daddy just wanted to say Merry Christmas."

"I'll tell him, but he won't believe it."

❧ Chapter Nineteen ❧

AT THE END OF THE DAY, NELDA CONSIDERED IT the best Christmas she'd had in a long, long time. Eric awakened early, and Linda had called out to Nelda before she let Eric go downstairs. The two women stood back while he excitedly examined what Santa had left.

After breakfast they opened the wrapped gifts. Eric was fascinated with the miniature train set. Linda smiled at Nelda.

"Thank you, thank you," she mouthed, then said aloud, "A friend of his has one. He loves to play with it."

Nelda spent most of the morning with Eric, helping him to put the tracks together.

Just before dinner, Lute drove into the yard. Kelly was out on his rope. The dog was delighted to see him. After tending his horses, Lute played with the dog for a few minutes then, to Nelda's relief, got back in his truck and left.

Christmas night Nelda lay in bed and thought about the day. It had gone quickly and she was glad of that. She thanked God for bringing Linda and Eric to her. She didn't know how she could have endured the holiday season without them.

There was more diversion to come . . . and from an unexpected source.

The day after Christmas was a lazy one, spent eating the leftovers from the Christmas dinner, playing Candy Land with Eric, and washing a couple of loads of clothes.

It was evening when a police car came into the yard and stopped beside the back door. As soon as Chief Larsen reached the porch, Nelda opened the door.

"Mrs. Hanson? I'm Chief Larsen. I understand that Mrs. Branson is here."

"Yes. She's giving her son a bath."

"I need to speak to her, and what I have to say isn't for the boy to hear."

"Won't you come in?"

The chief took off his overshoes before he came into the kitchen.

Nelda went into the bathroom and delivered the message. When Linda came out, her eyes were wide with fear.

"What's happened?"

"There's no easy way to say this, Linda. It's Kurt. His car went through the ice late last night. We just got him out."

"He's dead?" she whispered the question.

The chief nodded. "He couldn't have lived in

that icy water even if he'd been able to get out of the car."

"Oh, my . . . Lord—"

"There's more, Linda. He had a woman with him. She's dead, too."

"Who?"

"Kathy Freeman."

"Kathy? She's got two little kids!"

"Both Kurt and Kathy were drunk when they left the Town Pump. Kurt was asked to leave."

"He was out here Christmas Eve. He was drunk then."

"This happened late last night. Car lights were seen out on the ice, then they disappeared. This morning the Lake Patrol found where the car had gone in. We had posted signs warning that the lake wasn't safe to drive on."

"How did you know it was . . . him?"

"Divers. They brought him and Kathy up just a little while ago."

"I . . . just don't know what to say." Linda was trembling almost uncontrollably. "What do . . . I do?"

"We took him to the Wilcox Funeral Home. If you want him to go someplace else, we'll move him."

"No . . . that's all right."

"Do you want to go back into town with me? You'll have to make arrangements, and the neighbors will be coming to the house."

"I guess I should. What'll I tell Eric?"

"I can't tell you that, Linda. But you might consider telling him the truth. He'll have to know sooner or later. Maybe he could spend the night here with Mrs. Hanson."

Eric was out of the tub and into his pajamas when Linda went back to the bathroom.

"Come upstairs with me, honey. I'm going to go back to the house." She looked at Nelda with glassy eyes. "Chief Larsen will explain."

The reality of what his mother told him hadn't yet penetrated Eric's mind when Linda prepared to leave with Chief Larsen. She had packed her clothes and most of Eric's in the two laundry baskets and the chief had taken them to the car. She knelt to hug her son.

"Nelda will bring you home tomorrow. I love you."

"Don't go." Eric suddenly began to cry. "Don't go, Mama. He'll hurt you."

"He isn't there, honey."

"Where is he?"

"Oh, Lord, how can I explain?" Linda's tear-filled eyes met Nelda's.

"Eric, your mom's got to go. You and I will talk about it. Okay?" Nelda sat down in a kitchen chair and pulled the boy up onto her lap. "I'll bring him to you tomorrow. It's going to take a while for us to pack up all his presents. Isn't that right, Eric?"

Nelda bolted the door after Linda and the chief left, then she and Eric went to sit in the big chair in the living room lighted only by the Christmas tree lights and the glowing plastic Santa Claus. She told him about her little girl, Becky, who would live in her heart forever and about her grandparents, who had lived in this house all their married lives, but now were together in another place. She carefully avoided using the word "heaven."

"Daddy is in this other place?" Eric asked.

"Yes, he's in that other place. Just you and your mom will be a family now."

"I want you to be in our family."

"Thank you, sweetheart. I can't be in your family, but I want to be your friend forever and ever."

In the morning Nelda was awakened by the ringing of the telephone. She pulled on her robe and hurried downstairs to answer it.

"Nelda, this is Lute."

"You woke me up. What do you want?" she asked bluntly.

"Linda said you'd be bringing Eric into town this morning."

"You do get around, don't you?"

"I was there when they brought Kurt up. Later, I went to the house to see Linda."

"Good of you."

"It's been snowing, still is, and the roads haven't been plowed. The plows on the country roads won't start until it stops snowing. I'll come and take you and Eric into town."

"I . . . don't think so."

"Are you so stubborn that you'd put a child's life in danger?"

"I don't want to talk to you. I've not had my coffee. Good-bye."

Nelda hung up the phone and went to the window to look out. A small hump of snow had drifted across the lane, but it didn't look very deep. After putting a tea bag in the pot and the kettle on to boil, she called Linda.

"Mornin', Linda. How are you doin'?"

"All right. How is Eric?"

"He's still sleeping. He's a very intelligent little boy. I envy you having him."

"Did he say anything about . . . ?"

"His dad. Not really. He's taking this very well, considering his age. I explained to him that his dad was in another place and wouldn't be coming back."

"I don't want him to remember Kurt as angry and . . . mean."

"As time goes by, the good times will become exaggerated in his mind and the bad times will fade."

Oh, Lord. What am I saying? The bad memories of my father will never fade.

"Nelda, everyone has been so wonderful. Two of my neighbors spent the night, and another one is here taking in the food that's being brought. But . . . I miss Eric."

"As soon as I get him up and feed him breakfast, we'll come in. I packed up his toys last night after he went to bed."

"How are the roads?"

"I haven't been out, but they don't look too bad from here."

"Nelda, don't be mad . . . but Lute was here, and I told him that Eric was with you."

"What else could you say?"

"He went over to Britt and brought Kathy's mother to stay with her little girls."

"That's our Lute. Super Lute to the rescue. This town couldn't survive without him."

After a small silence, Linda said, "I'm just numb. I can't believe this has happened."

"Is there anything I can do other than bring Eric in?"

"You've done so much already. Nelda . . . do you think this would have happened if I hadn't . . . left him?"

"You'll never know the answer to that. Look at it this way. It could have been you and Eric in the car with him."

"I've thought of that. I know now that he'd been seeing Kathy off and on for quite a while. Poor Kathy. She was on the road to destruction when she was in high school."

While drinking her tea, memories of her own father filtered into Nelda's mind. In not one of them was she sitting on his lap, or having him read her a story, or winning his praise for making the honor roll in the many schools she had attended.

She sighed and went to refill her cup. She was no longer able to drink coffee. That was almost a sure sign she was pregnant. Even the smell of it on the mornings she had made it for Linda was nauseating. She checked the calendar. Two months and ten days since her last flow. She must see an obstetrician soon.

*   *   *

It was still snowing when Nelda set the box of toys and the sack containing Eric's clothes by the door. It didn't appear that the drift over the lane was any larger than when she looked at it an hour ago. She put on her boots and heavy coat to go to the garage and get the car.

"Wait here, Eric, while I bring the car up to the back door. Put on your mittens, honey."

Kelly had been whining to go out for several minutes, and the minute Nelda opened the door she knew why. He was out and bounding over the snow . . . to Lute's truck.

When did he sneak in? Anger boiled up in Nelda.

Choosing to ignore him and her traitor dog, she trudged through the snow toward the garage.

Oh, Lord! There's a foot of new snow on top of the old. I may not be able to get the car out of the yard, and he'll sit there with an I-told-you-so look on his face.

This thought had just passed through Nelda's mind when her feet went out from under her and she fell flat on her back in the soft snow. She rolled over on her knees; and as she struggled to get to her feet, she slipped down again.

From behind her, hands grasped her beneath her arms and lifted her easily to her feet.

"Get away from me." She tried to jerk her arm from Lute's grasp. Humiliation choked her throat.

"Use your head. You can't make it to town in that car. It's too light. You'd not reach the road."

"And that tickles you to death, doesn't it? My being unable to cope just proves your point."

"Stop being childish." He looked so big in his heavy parka. His face was red from the cold; the blue eyes fastened to her face were just as frigid. "I thought you had more sense than to put yourself and the boy in danger."

"You never did think I had much sense, did you?"

"I don't know what's got into you lately, but I don't like it."

"That's too bad. I couldn't care less what you like or don't like. I just want you out of my life, out of my sight."

His brows drew together in a frown. "What's changed you?"

Nelda rolled her eyes. "You are so damn dumb it's pitiful. Now get out of my way."

"You're not taking that car out and that's that."

"All right. You take him. You're the all-knowing, all-seeing, always right Lute Hanson, the backbone of this miserable community."

She shook loose from his hands and plowed through the snow back to the house. The pulse in her throat throbbed, and suddenly it was hard to breathe. Stomping her feet on the porch to rid them of snow, she opened the door to see Eric waiting patiently beside his box of toys.

"Eric, honey," she said, kneeling down to tie the hood on his coat, "Mr. Hanson is going to take you to your mother." She jerked her head toward Lute, who was standing in the doorway behind her. "My car won't make it through the snow."

"I'll carry you out to the truck, Eric." Lute picked the boy up and headed for the car. "Come on, Nelda," he said over his shoulder. "I'll come back for these and put Kelly in the house."

Nelda didn't answer. She feared that if she spoke, she would cry. As soon as Lute left the porch, she hurriedly carried the clothes sack and the toy box to the back porch, went back into the kitchen, and closed the door. When she heard Lute return, she opened it again.

"Thank you for taking Eric. Get in here, Kelly," she said to the dog who had followed him.

"Aren't you coming?" He tilted his head and looked at her quizzically.

"No. I'll call Linda."

"Nelda—"

She closed the door. *Get away before I scream!*

Standing at the window, Nelda watched the truck plowing through the snowdrifts on the lane, then went to the couch, sank down and let her misery wash over her. Pulling the afghan over her, she gave way to her tears. She hated herself for crying so much, but she couldn't help it.

Why was it that she could hardly bear to look at Lute anymore? Was the love she had for him turning to hate? She didn't want to be a bitter old woman. He had made what she had thought so sweet and wonderful no more than the mating of a man who needed relief and a woman willing to give it. It had no more meaning for him than that.

His bitter words, after the act that had planted

his seed in her womb, came floating back into her mind.

I must have been out of my mind. You don't fit into my lifestyle.

She had felt his accusing eyes all the way down to her toes.

What do you expect when you put a stallion in the stall with a mare in heat?

That he would say such a thing was like a thorn in her heart.

Watch out for Smithfield. He'll sleep with you, but he won't marry you.

Nelda began to feel sick to her stomach and hurried to the bathroom. While she was throwing up the Toasties and milk she'd had for breakfast, the telephone rang. She let it ring, and her mind recorded eight rings before it stopped. She was bathing her face with a wet cloth when it rang again.

"Nelda, I was worried," Linda said when she picked up the phone. "Lute was here with Eric. He said snow is drifting on the roads."

"That's the reason I let him take Eric. He was getting homesick for you."

"I wish you had come in."

"It's better that I didn't in this weather. Was it you who called a few minutes ago, Linda? I was in the bathroom. How are you doing?"

"All right. We'll have the service day after to-morrow. I dread it."

"You'll do fine."

"Are you all right? You don't sound like yourself."

"I might be getting a little sore throat."

"There's so much food here. I don't know what to do with it. Kurt's mother is here. She never liked me much, but she's being nice."

"She should be. You're a nice person."

"So are you. I'll talk to you later."

Nelda busied herself around the house for the rest of the afternoon, packing away the Christmas decorations. There didn't seem to be a need for them anymore. She washed the sheets her guests had used, dried them in the dryer, and put them back on the bed.

She couldn't get interested in her prints, so she took out yarn and the pattern book she had bought in Minneapolis and began working on a pair of baby booties. Soon she could see the booty take shape. So small. Nelda caught her lower lip between her teeth to keep from bursting into tears.

I really have to stop these crying jags.

During the night the snowfall ended. The sun was up, sending streaks of brightness through the bare branches of the oak tree when Nelda let Kelly out on his rope. A redbird, swaying on a slender branch at the very top of the tree, trilled, and was scolded by a sassy blue jay from the lilac bushes along the edge of the yard.

Despite the sun, it was cold and still. The landscape was pristine white. The wind had worked the snow into rolling drifts. No tracks were visible anywhere. On the north side of the house the pines grew close, their interlaced boughs all heavy with snow.

Later, when she heard the sound of a tractor, Nelda went to the window to see a big green machine with a blade on the front clearing the lane leading to her house. She was not sure whether it was Lute or his hired man, but as it neared, she recognized Lute's dark blue parka.

Lute saw Nelda standing in the window as he cleared the lane. An uneasiness crept into his mind that had nothing to do with the heavy drifts of snow. It lingered there like a nagging toothache. There had been dark circles beneath her eyes when he lifted her out of the snow, and her cheeks were hollow, evidence that she had lost weight. When she thanked him for taking Eric to Linda and then shut the door in his face, she had looked as if she didn't have a friend in the world.

Linda had told him that Nelda had come out in the snow to pick her up at the Shell station the night she left Kurt and that she had given Eric the best Christmas he'd had in a long time. Linda couldn't praise her enough.

Embarrassed, Linda had admitted that it had been Kurt making the obscene calls to Nelda and that he had come out to the farm looking for her.

A harsh hand squeezed Lute's dry throat. He had been a damn fool. He had let his fear of being cast again into that old pit of misery, that had taken him so long to climb out of, make him say hurtful things to her.

He was hopelessly, desperately in love with her, and had been since he was seventeen and she was fifteen. He wondered if he had the strength to endure the time it would take to adjust once again to life without her after she went back to the city.

❧ Chapter Twenty ❧

NELDA HAD NO INTENTION OF GOING TO KURT Branson's funeral. She had called the florist shop across from the cemetery and ordered a houseplant in a ceramic container to be sent to Linda.

Later, on the day of the funeral, Norris Smithfield called.

"Oh, Norris, I'm so glad to hear from you. I didn't think you'd be back until after the first of the year."

"Now that's the kind of greeting a man likes to get. I'll be heading out again soon. How'er ya doin', pretty girl?"

"I'm getting cabin fever." Nelda laughed nervously.

"How would you like to spend New Year's Eve in Minneapolis?"

"Yes, yes, yes."

"Hey, now. I like a girl who knows what she wants to do. I have a friend I want you to meet."

"How long will you be there?"

"A few days, then back here for a few days, after that, on to Ohio."

"I'll have to find a place for Kelly. Does Gary board dogs?"

"He does. If you'll cook me some supper, I'll be out and drop Kelly off at Gary's on my way back. We should leave for Minneapolis early in the morning. I have a round of appointments."

"Do I need to make hotel reservations?"

"You can stay in my apartment. I'll not be there, so don't be getting all nervous-Nellie on me."

Nelda laughed for the first time in days. "What time will you be here?"

"Around seven. Is that okay?"

"Perfect. See you then."

Nelda greeted Norris with a too-bright smile. He noticed immediately the tenseness in her manner.

"Something smells good," he said after he gave her a peck on the cheek and scratched Kelly behind the ears. He shed his coat and hung it on a peg beside the back door.

"I hope you like pasta."

"I'm Italian, couldn't you tell?" He toed off his boots and came in his stockinged feet to peer into the pan on the stove.

"With that red hair?" Nelda rolled her eyes.

She liked being with him. He was fun, comfortable, and unthreatening. She made a nest of pasta on their plates and filled it with a generous amount of meat sauce. After taking garlic bread from the oven, she took her place at the table and Norris sat down opposite her.

"Did you learn how to cook while decorating Falerri's nightclub?"

"Heavens, no. He wouldn't serve anything as mundane as spaghetti. If he did, he'd call it something else."

"You're right. By the way, while I was in Chicago, I went to the club. You did a classy job."

"Thanks. I guess he's given up on me. He's not called lately."

"I'm afraid you lost out to a leggy blonde. He was all over her like a cheap blanket, and she was loving it."

"Oh, shoot! I just can't win for losing." Her smile didn't quite reach her eyes, and Norris noticed.

"You're not very happy these days, are you, honey?" He reached for her hand. She placed her fork on her plate and her hand crawled across the table to meet his.

"Not really. I've got to get away from here."

"Can't stand the isolation?"

"That's part of it. I need to look for a furnished apartment in Minneapolis. I can stay in a hotel for a few days."

"I've got a few things in mind. I'll tell you about them on the way up tomorrow."

"More spaghetti?"

"No, but it's awfully good. I get hungry for a home-cooked meal. Living high on the hog isn't all it's cracked up to be."

He was so easy to be with. When she was with Lute she was constantly on guard.

After Nelda stacked the dishes, they wandered into the living room and sat down on the couch.

"I always did want to know about prenatal care," he said scanning the selection of books stacked on the coffee table. *"The Care and Feeding of an Infant, How to Toilet Train a Child with a Minimum of Fuss."* Hummm . . ." His bright blue eyes focused on Nelda's flushed face. "You're pregnant."

"How . . . did you know?"

"It wasn't hard to figure out." He carefully restacked the books. "Is it something you wanted to happen?"

"Not wanted, but now that it did, I'm glad."

"It's Lute's, of course. Does he know?"

"No. And he mustn't know!"

"Why not? You love him, don't you?"

She felt a spark of annoyance that her secret was so easily uncovered. He put his arm around her and pulled her close to his side. She laid her head on his shoulder.

"When do you expect the baby?" he asked quietly.

"August." She hugged him briefly, then pulled away from him. "I'm going to have a baby. I'm so glad to finally be able to say it out loud."

"How about that? I've turned into a shrink!" He kissed the tip of her nose. "Now pay me fifty bucks. I'll get the hell out of here and take Kelly to Gary's."

"I think I love you, Norris."

"Yeah. Like a favorite uncle." He groaned.

"Something like that, you fraud. Norris, I need to see an obstetrician," Nelda said as he was putting on his coat.

"Know one?"

"No."

"Do you want me to call my friend in Minneapolis and ask her to make an appointment for you?"

"I'd appreciate it," she said softly.

"Consider it done. I'll pick you up in the morning about seven."

She stood in the door and watched him brush the snow from the windshield of his car. He started the motor and set the wipers moving, then came back to the porch and took Kelly's leash.

"See you in the morning, sugar."

"Thank you for taking Kelly. 'Bye, Kelly," Nelda called. "You'll have fun barking at the other dogs at Gary's."

Nelda tidied up the kitchen, then went upstairs to get her traveling bag out of the closet. She packed all she wanted to take for the few days she would be away, planning to ship some of her things when she made the permanent move.

She undressed and sat on the edge of the bed until her feet got cold. She reviewed her situation and came to the same sad conclusions. She loved Lute, but he didn't love her. Since that was the way things had turned out, she would build her life around their child. She lay back, rolled over on her stomach, buried her face in her pillow, and wished for sleep to wipe the troubled thoughts from her mind and the ache from her heart.

It was a little after seven when Norris stopped the car at the end of the lane to let the black pickup pass. He tooted the horn and waved. Lute lifted his hand from the wheel in a salute. The glimpse Nelda had of his set face lasted only a few seconds, but the image stayed in her mind all day.

Lute thought Norris had spent the night with her! He thought she was the kind of woman who would sleep around. That hurt. Really hurt.

"Your appointment is for twelve-thirty. I'll have you there in plenty of time," Norris assured her.

While he drove, Nelda told him about the happenings during the Christmas holidays and how much she had enjoyed shopping for Eric.

"Linda is lucky to have you for a friend."

"I was lucky to have a child in the house during Christmas. I was dreading the holidays."

"Didn't Rhetta invite you out?"

"Yes, but I didn't want to intrude on their family holiday. She invited me for New Year's Eve, too. Oh, I forgot to tell her that I'd be away."

"Don't worry about it. I told her." Norris's devilish grin told her that he had let Rhetta draw her own conclusions about this trip to Minneapolis.

"You . . . didn't."

"I told her that you and I would be ringing in the New Year in the big city. I'm sure word will get around."

"You're trying to ruin my reputation."

"Yeah. How does it feel to be a fallen woman?"

The car edged into a lane of traffic when they reached Minneapolis, swung off the highway, and made its way down a tree-lined street of ultramodern buildings. They pulled into a circular drive and parked.

The inside of Norris's building fairly screamed affluence. In the elevator, he inserted a key, and the cage moved. In seconds it slid to a gentle stop, and the door opened.

The apartment was elegant but comfortable. When Norris invited her to make herself at home, Nelda slipped out of her cashmere coat and removed her hat and gloves.

"I've some calls to make," he explained. "There should be snacks in the kitchen if you're hungry. Lots of dill pickles and peanut butter." He grinned at her and tweaked her nose.

"Oh, hush! Go make your calls. I'm not going to throw up all over your lovely carpet."

He disappeared into another part of the apartment, and she surveyed the tastefully decorated room. Norris probably employed a live-in housekeeper or one who came in daily. The many plants, which were set in just the right places, would need constant care. The pale green silk-covered sofa and matching pillows, the Louis XV chairs, the tables with delicately carved legs and the silk-shaded lamps were all perfect, just the right setting for a man like Norris Smithfield. But not for Lute . . . or her, the thought popped unbidden into her mind.

She wandered down the hall and found a bathroom. When she came out, she heard Norris's voice coming from another room.

"Thank you, darling. Won't you try to come over?" He paused. "Then meet us for dinner. All right, we'll meet you here at six. Is everything all right? Jenny too? I'm glad your cold is better, sweetheart. I'm anxious for you to meet Nelda. You two are quite a lot alike . . ."

Nelda slipped by the door and returned to the living room. Obviously Norris was talking with someone he cared very much about. He seldom mentioned anyone in his life away from Clear Lake. He had spoken of his two daughters, both college students, who attended school in California. He wasn't speaking to one of them, she was sure.

When Norris returned to the living room, he was in high spirits, and they left for the doctor's office.

Norris let Nelda out of the car in front of the medical building without mentioning the six o'clock appointment back at the apartment.

"I'll park the car and wait for you in the lobby. You have the appointment card? Okay. Don't be nervous. You'll like this doctor. Every pregnant woman I bring to him falls in love with him." She knew he was trying to tease the serious look from her face.

Nelda walked into the building smiling. She was already comfortable with the idea that she was going to have a baby—and confident she'd be able to handle rearing one as a single parent. Despite her small bone structure, she had borne one child and she could do so again.

An hour later, over a cup of hot tea at a small

cafe near the medical building, Nelda told Norris about the doctor.

"I like him. I had thought to go south somewhere, but I may stay here until after the baby comes."

"Not back to Chicago?"

"No. I had many acquaintances there but not any real friends. All the people I know there are deep in careers." She sank into thought. "I can work on my prints here as easily as anywhere else, once the baby comes. Right now the smell of the paint makes me sick."

Norris looked at his watch. "Do you have any prescriptions to be filled?"

"I'm afraid so," she said apologetically.

He covered her hand with his. "We'll stop at a pharmacy on the way back to the apartment. Meanwhile, I have a couple of stops to make. If you'll come along and wait for me, it'll save a trip across town to the apartment. I'd like to get there a little before six. There's someone coming over I'd like you to meet."

There seemed to be a special brightness in his blue eyes. *He's in love with this woman.* She was glad for him and hoped the woman returned his love.

Aloud she said, "I hope you're not trying to fix me up with one of your friends."

"Hardly, sweetheart." He laughed and helped her up from the booth, then whispered in her ear. "You've already been fixed up, or had you forgotten?"

"That was crude!" she complained while he was fumbling for money to pay the bill.

"Yeah. Come to think of it, it was." He laughed and flung his arm around her. "But I thought it was rather clever."

"You would," she retorted, pretending huffiness.

It was dark by the time they returned to the apartment. The lamps were lit, and the music was playing softly. Norris helped Nelda with her coat, hung it in the closet, then excused himself and headed toward the back of the apartment.

Nelda went to the window and looked down on the street. The thought of returning to Chicago or going somewhere totally unknown in the Southwest had never been a pleasant one, she finally admitted to herself. She would come to Minneapolis, start her new life here. As long as Lute didn't know where she was, she could be as removed from him as if she were two thousand miles away.

"Nelda."

She turned to face Norris and the woman at his side. She hoped that her surprise wasn't written on her face. This was hardly the sleek, sophisticated type the world would expect Norris Smithfield to be attracted to, but a lovely, mature woman with soft, dark hair. She was not yet middle-aged, but she was no longer a young girl. There were tiny lines at the corners of her green eyes and her full, generous mouth. She was slender, yet the soft silk of her dress revealed her gently rounded figure.

Norris was looking at the woman with a happy smile in his eyes, as if she were something infinitely precious. *If Lute ever looked at me like that, I'd melt away.*

"Nelda Hanson and Marlene Lindon, I'd like for you two ladies to know each other."

"Hello, Marlene." Nelda held out her hand.

"It's nice to meet you, Nelda." Marlene's handshake was firm.

"Now that we have that out of the way, let's have some supper." Norris was practically beaming with pride. He put his hand gently on Marlene's back and urged her toward the kitchen. "C'mon, Chicken Little," he said to Nelda. "We'll have our orgy in the kitchen."

"Norris!" Marlene chided gently, then stage-whispered to Nelda, "I suppose you're used to him by now and know that he's the one who's chicken."

"Oh, yes, and he knows that I know that he's a fraud."

"I'm not sure that I like having my two favorite women talking about me as if I were a naughty child." Norris tried to form a frown, but it turned into a happy grin. "What did you bring us to eat, sweetheart?" He reached out an arm and hooked it about Marlene, as if compelled to keep her close to him.

"Chicken and rice and later chocolate cheesecake. You must share it with Nelda. She needs the extra calories."

"And I don't?" Norris protested in a wounded tone.

They spent a pleasant hour over dinner. Norris made no effort to conceal the fact that he was very much in love with Marlene. She, in turn, seemed totally happy to be with him. Nelda watched and smiled and felt something a little bit like envy. Such reciprocated love was so beautiful, so rare. She realized their relationship was not a new thing when Norris mentioned Marlene's daughter, Jenny, who was starting her first year in college.

"She's going to be every bit as pretty as her mother, though I didn't think so when she was going through that gawky stage."

Marlene positively glowed when she looked at Norris. Her face had a soft, luminous beauty, and her eyes held a passionate tenderness. Nelda wondered if Marlene knew about her and why she was here. Her next words told Nelda that Norris had no secrets from his lady love.

"What did Dr. Wilkins have to say? Do you like him?"

"Very much. And I thank you for making the appointment for me."

They spent some time talking about her condition and how she felt about having the baby. No mention was made of the baby's father, but somehow Nelda knew that Norris had discussed that with Marlene, too. She felt no resentment—she instinctively knew that Marlene could be trusted.

"I've got a full day tomorrow, Nelda," Norris said, as he and Marlene were preparing to leave. "Marlene will come and show you an apartment we thought might be suitable."

"Oh, please . . . I can't afford something as expensive as this."

"We've taken that into consideration. The present occupant will be leaving the fifth of February. There's an acute shortage of apartments here, and you almost have to get your foot in the door before one becomes vacant."

"I appreciate it."

"You'll be just fine under Dr. Wilkins's care." Marlene gave her a hug. "When you get settled here and need a friend, I'd like to apply for the position."

Norris put his arm around the calm, beautiful woman and kissed her gently.

"That's one reason why I love her so much. I left a number by the phone if you need anything. Oh, yes, go ahead and sleep in. The maid will let herself in in the morning. She won't be surprised to find you here. She's used to finding beautiful women in my bed."

Marlene rolled her eyes. "Come on, Romeo. Nelda's tired."

"You're not jealous?"

"Of course, I am. I'm breathing fire. Can't you tell? I'll call before I come over, Nelda. Good night."

"She wants to get me alone so that she can have her way with me," Norris whispered to Nelda, as they got into the elevator.

Marlene came for her in midmorning. They had breakfast together, then went to look at the apartment. It proved to be perfect for her needs. It was small—one bedroom, a combined kitchen and dining area—but the living room was large and had floor-to-ceiling windows along one wall. It was completely and tastefully furnished, including linens and dishes, and within walking distance of a shopping center.

"A rather long walk," Marlene mused.

"I'll have my car, but I'm going to need exercise," Nelda reminded her.

The manager of the building who had showed them the apartment explained that the present renter would be out of the country for two years and wanted to sublease. Nelda told him that she might not want to stay the full two years. He said he required two months' notice should she decide to vacate.

"There's a catch," Marlene said. "It won't be available until February fifth. That's four weeks away. Can you hold out until then? If not, come stay with me. Or I'm sure you can use Norris's apartment if you want more privacy. He may not be back for a while, but if he does come to town, he won't mind staying someplace else."

"Norris mentioned it wouldn't be available until the fifth. I'll be fine where I am until then, but thank you. I'm so glad I met you and Norris."

"Me too. I'm looking forward to having you near me. If anything comes up, and you want to come sooner, let me know."

Before they left, Nelda wrote out a check for a deposit and the first month's rent. She was disappointed about the delay, but didn't want to complain to Marlene.

How was she going to manage to avoid Lute for another month?

❧ *Chapter Twenty-one* ❧

NEW YEAR'S EVE WAS SPENT IN NORRIS'S APART-
ment, a decision he left to Marlene and Nelda.

"Everything will be so crowded," Marlene said.

"I didn't bring anything fancy to wear."

"Will you be disappointed if we stay here?" Norris's eyes went from one woman to the other.

"I'm not much for night life," Nelda confessed.

"You know how I feel." Marlene moved close to him and laid her cheek on his upper arm.

"We don't go out much," he explained to Nelda after he placed a kiss on Marlene's nose. "I'll have dinner brought in."

The caterers arrived at seven-thirty. Marlene had set the table beside the windows overlooking the city with beautiful china and silver, tapered candles in crystal holders, and a ring of fresh flowers. Norris poured the wine, and they made the first of many toasts to the New Year. He served the Peking duck, wild rice, and fresh spinach salad.

"This is wonderful. The food is not only superb, we don't have a waiter swishing back and forth behind us or hovering." Nelda smiled and lifted her wineglass to Norris.

"Not so fast," Norris teased. "I'm getting ready to hover." The evening was relaxed and fun. Nelda forgot to be lonely until the last few minutes of 1958. Norris adjusted the elaborate sound system, then dimmed the lights. He pulled Marlene to her feet. She went into his arms and they began to dance to the music of the Platters.

Nelda went to the window to give them some privacy. The moon was riding high in the sky above the twinkling city lights. She tried not to think about Lute dancing with Meredith at Rhetta's party or if he would take her home and spend the rest of the night with her.

Next New Year's Eve I won't be alone, Baby. She placed her palm over her stomach, where her child had been growing for three months. *It'll be just you and me—*

In the window, she could see Norris and Marlene reflected as they danced, her head on his shoulder, his lips in her hair. Nelda's heart felt as heavy as a rock in her chest. Then she felt their presence beside her.

"Happy New Year," Norris and Marlene said together, each planting a kiss on her cheek.

"Oh, is it midnight?"

"A whole minute ago."

"All this running around in the big city has worn me out. Would you mind if I took my aching feet and my tired body off to a warm bath and then to bed?"

"If that's what you want. Honey, will you be all right here tomorrow?" Norris asked. "I'm going with Marlene to take Jenny back to St. Cloud, where she goes to school."

"She'll be spending the week skiing with friends before school starts," Marlene added.

"Of course, I'll be all right. I'll read, knit, and make lists of what I have to do when I get home. I've decided to sell the farm, and I'll need to talk to a financial adviser. Can you recommend one?"

"I sure can. We'll talk about it on the way back to Clear Lake."

Nelda spent a lazy day in Norris's apartment. She didn't get dressed until noon, and in the afternoon fixed herself a lunch of tomato soup and celery with peanut butter. When Norris returned the next morning, Marlene was with him. Looking refreshed after ten hours of sleep, Nelda had risen early, bathed, and was ready to leave.

On the way out of town they took Marlene home. She lived in a lovely Victorian house set on a large lot in an older, well-kept section of the city. The driveway circled to the back of the house, where a carriage house had been converted into a garage. Painted a pale yellow with white trim, the house had gables, fretwork, and a wraparound porch.

"It's beautiful," Nelda exclaimed. "This is just the kind of house I want to live in someday."

"I'm glad you like it." Marlene turned around in the seat to speak to Nelda. "If you feel the need to come back before your apartment is available, come stay with me."

"Thank you. I'm living from day to day right now."

Before Marlene got out of the car, Norris pulled the calm, beautiful woman close to him and kissed her tenderly.

"I'll call you tonight, sweetheart. Take care of yourself for me."

"You too," she whispered.

Nelda got into the front seat with Norris, and they moved slowly down the drive toward the street. In the rearview mirror he watched Marlene standing in the drive, and waved to her.

Norris seemed to be wrapped up in his own thoughts, as they drove out of the city, and Nelda was reluctant to break into them. They were well on their way south when he turned and smiled tightly at her.

"Thank you for letting me meet Marlene," Nelda said. "She's lovely."

"Yes, she's lovely, sweet, compassionate—she's all things to me. I love her more than life."

"I could tell. She loves you, too." Nelda sighed. "It must be wonderful to be loved like that."

"She's the reason I live part-time in Iowa. I couldn't bear to be with her all the time and not have her."

"I . . . sorry—"

"She's married," he said, keeping his eyes straight ahead. "They were in a plane crash. He threw himself over her, saving her life. He has extensive brain damage and is being kept alive in a care facility. He'll never recover, and she'll never divorce him."

"How long have you known her?"

"Eight years."

Eight years, the same length of time that she had been alone. But now, she reminded herself, with Lute's baby growing inside her, she was no longer alone.

"I'm building the house on the lakeshore for her. It's just the way she wants it," Norris said quietly. "I keep hoping."

Before taking Nelda home, Norris stopped at the kennels and went in to get Kelly. The dog wiggled and made little yelping noises in his excitement when he saw Nelda, and could hardly wait for the door to open so he could get into the car. Nelda was glad she didn't have to face Rhetta's disapproving eyes.

"I wonder what Rhetta and the others would think if they knew you aren't the lecher you pretend to be," Nelda remarked, as they turned down the lane to the farmhouse.

"Give away my secret, and I'll put a hex on you," Norris threatened. Then, "Uh-oh. Reckon he'll punch me in the nose?" he asked when he pulled into the yard and saw Lute's truck parked beside the barn.

"He comes to tend his horses. He couldn't care less what I do."

"That's a relief. I'd hate to tangle with him if he had his back up."

The minute the door opened, Kelly raced across

the yard to Lute's truck, then squeezed himself through the partly open barn door.

Norris carried Nelda's bag to the house, catching her arm when she slipped on the slick steps.

"You stay in the house, young lady, and off these steps until they are either sanded or salted," he ordered sternly.

"Yes, Uncle Norris." She kissed him on the cheek.

"Want me to stay until Lute leaves?"

"No. He won't come to the house. He can hardly stand the sight of me." She laughed nervously.

"He's a damn fool."

Norris pushed open the barn door and walked down the lane between the rows of stalls to where Lute was combing the mane of his horse. He looked up when Norris approached, but continued to curry.

"Good-looking horse. Tennessee Walker?"

"Yeah."

"Registered?"

"No. Not pure-blood."

"Looks like it to me."

"You know horses?"

"A little bit."

Lute continued to curry the horse and had hardly looked at Norris until he asked,

"Do you love Nelda?"

Lute's head came up, and his eyes bored into those of the shorter man. Not a flicker of an expression crossed Lute's face. When he spoke it was softly.

"What's it to you?"

Norris shrugged. "Just wondered."

"I don't pry into your personal life. I'll thank you not to pry into mine."

"You're right. Sorry. I just didn't want to be stepping on your toes. See you around, Lute. Come on, Kelly, I'll put you in the house before I go."

Lute watched him leave the barn, and, for the first time in his life, he hated the farm, hated himself, and hated being who he was.

The next week brought a warming trend that melted the ice and made it fairly easy to get around again. Nelda talked several times with Rhetta. Although she didn't come right out and say so, she clearly didn't understand Nelda's friendship with Norris.

She brought up Lute's name several times in the conversation: Lute and the boys had been pheasant hunting; Lute and Gary were talking about going to Wyoming to hunt deer. Lute had bought a block of tickets to the Valentine's Day Ball, which was a benefit for the swimming-pool project.

As a favor to Rhetta, Nelda consented to work three afternoons a week for the next three weeks at the library. Being busy made the time go by faster. On her way home from the library, she occasionally stopped at the Lake Crest or Halford's Cafe and ate dinner so that she'd not have to cook when she got home.

One night, when Nelda was meeting Linda and Eric at Halford's, she saw Meredith, the Home Ec teacher, sitting in a booth with another woman. Their eyes met briefly, then when Nelda passed, the teacher deliberately turned her head and refused to look at her. Some little imp in Nelda caused her to speak.

"Hello, Meredith."

The teacher grunted a reply, and Nelda moved on.

Shortly after Nelda sat down, Linda and Eric came in. Nelda waved and they came back to where she was sitting.

"Hi, Eric. How ya doin'?"

"Fine. Can I come play with Kelly?"

"Anytime you want, sweetheart. Let me help you with your coat."

While they waited for their order Linda told her the news.

"Eric and I are moving to Iowa City. We'll not be too far from my sister. Mr. Hutchinson is helping me with my application to nursing school and getting a job in the hospital as a nurses' aide."

"That's wonderful. I'll be leaving here myself the first part of February."

"We must keep in touch." Linda reached across the table and grasped Nelda's hand. "I don't know what I'd have done without you."

"We'll not talk about that. I had the best Christmas I've had in a long time . . . thanks to this guy." She hugged Eric until he wiggled away.

On the way home, Nelda thought how ironic it was that the death of one person would free another. Linda was a loving, giving person who had the cards stacked against her when she was young, then jumped into a hasty marriage with a man who mistreated her.

Linda's experience convinced Nelda that it was far better to remain single than marry a man who didn't love her.

The minute she walked into the house she knew that something was not right, even though Kelly had met her at the door as usual. She had put him out on his rope and taken off her coat, when she realized that it was cold in the house and went to check the thermostat. Funny—it was set at the usual seventy-two degrees. Then she noticed that the chair had been pulled away from the table, and there was a glass in the sink.

Had Lute come into her house after she had told him she did not want him here? She could keep him out with the bolt on the inside of the door, but the only way to keep him out when she wasn't at home was to have the locks changed.

Suddenly uneasy, she went to the porch and called Kelly in. The dog padded to the door leading to the basement and sniffed, then followed her into the bathroom, where she creamed her face, preparing to remove her makeup. When she reached for the tissue box, it wasn't there.

"Damn. If I believed in ghosts, I'd feel sure I was being haunted by one," she said to herself.

She looked around and found the box across the room on the corner of the small commode. Puzzled, she brought it back, plucked the tissues she needed, and wiped the cream from her face.

"Ghosts, my foot. You may be losing your mind," she told the reflection in the mirror as she ran the hairbrush through her short curls.

Sure that she had inserted the bolt when she came into the house, she checked it anyway before she called Kelly and they went up to bed. She yawned on her way up the stairs.

Something awakened her.

Nelda lay for a moment, then turned over to see her lighted clock. Two-thirty. She lifted her head so that she could listen with both ears. No sound at all. She lay back down. Kelly's ears were alert to every unusual sound. He would have sounded an alarm had he heard anything.

Kelly. Nelda lifted her head again. Because of the white snow and moonlight coming in the window, it was light enough for her to see that Kelly wasn't in his bed. She looked on the other side of her bed. He was not there either. It wasn't unusual for him to go downstairs in the night for a drink of water, but he never stayed down there.

Wide-awake now and with growing anxiety, Nelda got out of bed and switched on the bedside lamp. She pulled on her flannel robe and slid her feet into slippers. Before leaving the bedroom, she reached out into the hallway and switched on the light.

"Kelly," she called. Then again, "Kelly."

Her anxiety grew when the dog failed to come to her, and she wished she had not left the gun in the cabinet over the stove. She looked around for something with which to defend herself should it become necessary and remembered the brass-headed walking stick in her grandparents' room. She had noticed it when she cleaned the room after Linda and Eric used it.

She hurried quietly along the hall until she reached the room where the heavy, dark walnut stick stood against the wall. Grasping it as an improvised weapon, Nelda tiptoed down the carpeted stairway and stood on the last step, waiting and listening.

"Kelly," she called again. When they were in the house, he always came to her when she called. Where was he?

Her heart was pounding and her breath was short. She gripped the walking stick, reached around the corner, and switched on the living-room light. Her eyes swept the area, then focused on the kitchen door.

All was quiet.

Nelda moved across the dining room and stood at the side of the kitchen door, vowing never again to go upstairs and leave the gun in the cabinet. Had someone come into the house and hurt Kelly, rendered him unconscious or killed him?

She had to know! Reaching around the corner, she switched on the kitchen light, then with the walking stick drawn back, she peeked into the kitchen.

Kelly lay on his bed beneath the coat hooks. Curled up on the rug beside him was a small person, covered with a blanket. Black overshoes stuck out from under the blanket at one end and shaggy black hair at the other. Kelly's tail wagged in greeting.

"What in the world?"

The dog was obviously comfortable with whoever it was under the blanket. He looked at Nelda as if apologizing, and his tail continued to swish back and forth across the floor. The room was cold. Nelda noticed that the basement door was open.

The blanket covering the person, Nelda realized, was the same gray blanket with the red stripes on each end that she had found in the garage and left on the porch. When it disappeared she had put it out of her mind; but it had appeared again, and she had laid it on the steps going to the basement.

Kelly made no attempt to move even when Nelda went hesitantly into the room and lifted the edge of the blanket with the end of the walking stick.

"Oh, oh! Forever more. Where in the world did you come from?"

Coherent thought left her when she saw a rather large head resting on a small, folded arm. The face beneath the shaggy hair was so horribly ugly that she shuddered involuntarily at the sight. The head moved and the face turned toward Nelda. Extremely small, dark eyes opened to look up at her. She tried not to show her shock on seeing the flat face with the high, wide forehead, the small pug nose, and the mouth with the slash in the upper lip that looked like something from a horror movie. From his size, she judged this was a boy, but she could not tell how old he was.

"Hello."

Nelda forced herself to smile and stoop down beside the rug. The small person sat up, cringed away, wrapped his arms around Kelly's neck, and clung to the dog. Kelly whined as if begging Nelda to accept the child. A wet tongue came out to swipe across the flat, deformed face.

Nelda was astonished at Kelly's behavior. He had liked Eric, but had not reacted to him in such a protective way.

"Hello," Nelda said again. She held out her hand. "How did you get here? Are you cold?" The flat, black eyes continued to stare at her. Her heart melted with pity for the small defenseless creature. *Maybe he can't hear or speak.*

After a long silence, Nelda stood and went over to close the basement door, shutting off the cold draft flowing into the kitchen. How had this child managed to get into her house? She went back to where he sat on the mat with Kelly and smiled down at him.

"Would you like a cup of warm chocolate? I would. It's cold in here."

Nelda took the milk from the refrigerator and poured some of it into a saucepan. Out of the corner of her eyes she watched the boy. His arms slipped from around Kelly and wrapped around the blanket. His eyes stayed on her.

When the milk was warm, she carried the pan to the table and poured the milk into two cups so that the child could see what she was doing. She spooned Ovaltine from the can she had bought for Eric into the milk and stirred. Smiling, she motioned to the cup, then sat down across the table and sipped the warm drink.

"This is good. Come drink yours while it's warm. Kelly, do you want a cookie?"

Nelda reached into the bowl of dog biscuits and held out the treat. It was too much of a temptation for Kelly. He got up and came to take it from her fingers. She stroked the dog's head to keep him beside her while she watched the child sitting on the rug.

When he got up and stood uncertainly beside Kelly's pallet, she kept the smile on her face despite the shock of seeing the short arms and legs. She pushed the cup toward him in invitation when he took a few steps toward the table, dragging the blanket with him. Keeping his eyes on her, he climbed up onto the chair and reached for the cup with both hands. As he drank, the chocolate dripped down his chin.

Nelda brought bread, butter, and peanut butter to the table. Without looking at him, she spread a slice, cut it in two pieces, and placed it on a plate in front of him. Although she wasn't sure she could choke it down, she fixed a slice for herself.

"What's your name?" She spread another slice of bread because the one she had given him was almost gone. "My name is Nelda. His name is Kelly." She gave the dog a crust from the bread. "I bet your name is Johnny."

The child shook his head.

"Billy? George? Herbert? Andrew?" He continued to shake his head. At least he can hear, Nelda thought. "No? Let me see . . . oh, I know. Your name is Santa Claus!"

What could pass for a smile stretched the boy's mouth.

"A . . . l . . . n"

"Alan?" Nelda wished that she hadn't made it sound like a question.

He nodded and reached for the slice of bread. Pity for the small boy swamped her. She glanced at the clock. It was four o'clock in the morning.

Why aren't people out beating the bushes looking for this child?

✥ *Chapter Twenty-two* ✥

"CHIEF LARSEN? THIS IS NELDA HANSON. YOU came out to my farm to get Linda when her husband was killed. Your dispatcher said she would ring you at home when I told her it was urgent that I speak to you."

"What can I do for you, Mrs. Hanson?"

"I know that this is out of your jurisdiction, but I've got a child here who has been in my basement all night and I think all day yesterday."

"A child?"

"I *think* he's a child. It's hard to tell. He said his name is Alan. He's . . . ah . . . terribly handicapped."

"If he's who I think he is, his name is Alan Oliver, and his folks live over on Lute Hanson's farm."

"Why in the world do they let him wander around when it's ten degrees above zero? He's been in my house before. I've noticed things moved in the house, and he has a blanket that I found in my garage last September and left on my porch."

"You don't need to be afraid of him. I've never heard of him hurting even a fly."

"I'm not afraid of him. Right now he's sleeping on my couch. Poor little thing was hungry and cold. I'm just angry that his folks don't take better care of him."

"Do you want me to call his folks and tell them where he is?"

"I'd appreciate it, Chief Larsen. It's the strangest thing. I'm quite sure that Alan has been around here quite a few times when I was unaware of it. My dog, who is usually very protective, loves him and didn't make a sound when he came up out of the basement last night to sleep on the rug beside the door."

"Animals are sometimes more sensitive to physical frailties than people are. I'll give the Olivers a call."

"Thank you, Chief Larsen."

Nelda had made a bed on the couch for Alan. She had coaxed him to take off his coat and boots. When he lay down he still hugged the dirty gray blanket though she covered him with a soft clean one. Sitting beside him, she smoothed the hair back from his face and spoke softly to him.

"Go to sleep. Kelly and I will be here."

Responding to her kindness his hand came out and grasped hers. She took it between her palms and held it until he went to sleep.

Sometime later she saw car lights coming down the lane, and she rehearsed what she was going to say to a parent who let a child like this wander a mile or more away from home.

She heard the footsteps on the porch. When she looked through the door pane it was Lute's face she saw before she jerked open the door.

"You do get around."

"Nels called me because the Olivers are not at home. Do you have any coffee?" Lute came into the kitchen and closed the door.

"I'm not serving this morning. Does Alan's father work for you?"

"He does. You've seen him over here tending to the horses."

"This child should be taken away from people who don't take any better care of him than to let him wander over the countryside when it's ten degrees above zero."

"His folks take care of him. Their daughter was killed in a car-train crash yesterday morning up near Mankato. They left him here with his sister Vicky. She is sixteen and going over fool's hill. She didn't come home last night, so she didn't know that Alan had wandered away."

"This wasn't the first time he's been here. He's been here so many times that Kelly knows him. I want to know how he gets in. If he can get into my house with the doors locked, others can."

"I don't know how he got in. Why don't you ask him."

"So far all he's said was his name."

"It's seven o'clock. If you're not going to offer me coffee, I'll take Alan and go."

"Leave him where he is if his folks aren't home. He was tired and hungry and cold."

"He didn't scare you?"

"I was scared when I thought someone was in the house. When I saw him, I was shocked at first, but I was not scared of a poor little boy."

"He's eighteen years old."

"He's a little boy in his mind. I'll bet that on the inside he feels the same as any other little boy. It's on the outside that he's different." Nelda tilted her chin up and glared at him.

"His folks love him and take care of him."

"Yeah, sure." Her voice was heavy with sarcasm. "If you want to be the good Samaritan *again*,"—she emphasized the word—"go find his irresponsible sister and bring her over here. I'd like to give her a piece of my mind. And there's another thing—"

"—I thought there would be," Lute said dryly.

"I don't appreciate it that you didn't tell me about him. He's been in my garage, in my car, on my porch, in my basement. The least you could have done, as caretaker of the vicinity, was to have told me that there was someone in the area like Alan."

"I didn't know he had been over here, Nelda, so get down off your high horse."

"Good-bye, Lute. I'm going to take a nap while Alan is asleep. You can come back later."

"Have you been sick? You've lost weight."

"I'm not sick. I'm tired. Too much night life."

"Lived it up in Minneapolis. Huh?"

"Of course. Why do you think I went up there?"

Lute shook his head. "I thought you were smart

enough to see through Smithfield. He's a womanizer, for God's sake. It's what he's always been. A leopard can't change his spots even for you."

"Don't you dare say anything bad about Norris." Nelda's eyes blazed. "You don't know him at all. You want to think the worst of him because he's charming and he's rich. He's one of the nicest men I've ever met, and that includes you, Lute."

"He's not capable of anything . . . permanent."

"I'm not looking for anything permanent. I'll never marry again. Remember the old saying, 'A burnt child dreads the fire'?"

"So you'd live with him?"

"He hasn't asked me."

"But you would if he did?"

"Maybe."

"So that's the way the wheel turns."

"Take it any way you want. He's my friend. I can depend on him."

"And not on me. Is that it?"

"That's it, Lute. You have your priorities, and I have mine. Now please leave. Come back for Alan this afternoon."

"I don't know what's gotten into you. You've changed."

"You've said that before. I have changed." She turned to go into the living room, then turned back. "On second thought, come for Alan at noon. I promised to work at the library this afternoon."

"You've taken a job there?"

"Only for three weeks, then I'm out of here."

Lute went out to his truck wondering how things could have gotten into such a hell of a mess so fast.

Rhetta came into the library and asked Nelda to come to her house on Saturday and help make decorations for the Valentine's Day dance to be held in a couple of weeks.

"Oh, I don't think I'll be able to, Rhetta. I think I'm coming down with a cold." It wasn't a contrived excuse. She hadn't felt well for several days.

"You're off the hook, love. Get the sniffles behind you, because we're not going to let you miss out on the Winter Dance Party at the Surf. Buddy Holly and the Crickets will be there on February 2."

"I'm not much of a rock and roller, Rhetta."

"Honey, the Big Bopper will be there . . . and Richie Valens. You can't miss it."

"When did you say it was, Rhetta?"

"February 2. Mark it on your calendar."

"I'll mark it on the calendar, Rhetta, but I can't promise to go."

"You'll be going with the right honorable veterinarian and his spouse. I won't let you wiggle out of it."

"But, Rhetta, I don't want to go without an escort. If Norris gets back, I'm sure he'll take me, but—"

"—Horse hockey!" Rhetta interrupted. "There'll be dozens of men and women there without escorts. In our town a woman would sit home all the time if she had to depend on an escort. Think nothing of it, and plan on going. Okay?"

Reluctantly, Nelda agreed to go. Rhetta had been a good friend. She couldn't very well be rude and throw the invitation back at her. It would be her final farewell to Clear Lake society. The one nagging concern she had about going was having to see Lute with Miss Home Ec.

The night of the Winter Dance Party, Nelda was no more enthused about it than she had been when Rhetta invited her. Her friend had called and told her to be at their place at eight o'clock for a predance drink.

Nelda stood in front of the mirror and studied herself critically. The makeup she had applied to the dark circles beneath her eyes had done its job, but even knowing that she looked her best did nothing to put her in a party mood. She sprayed perfume from an atomizer and watched the fragrant mist settle on the soft curls surrounding her face.

She was wearing an emerald green skirt and a loose black jacket that reached to her hips. It was an outfit she could dress up or down. Tonight she wore an emerald green scarf about her neck. The color was a perfect foil for her light skin, dark hair and eyes, and the loose fit of the sweater would conceal her thickening waistline.

Involuntarily she both looked forward to and dreaded the thought of seeing Lute. Even if he asked her, she would refuse to dance with him. He would be sure to notice that she was no longer pencil-slim.

At a quarter to eight she pulled on her snow boots, put on her heavy coat, and carefully pulled the hood up over her hair. Nervous as a schoolgirl off to her first prom, she picked up the small purse and slender-heeled shoes and went out to the garage. The night was cold and still. The forecast was for snow before morning.

Nelda pumped the accelerator several times before she tried to start her car. When she finally turned the key, nothing happened. Absolutely nothing. She tried the lights. Again nothing. She breathed deeply, trying to calm her nerves so that she could think rationally.

The car's battery was dead. Good! The perfect excuse not to go the Winter Dance Party.

Back in the house she dialed Rhetta's number.

"Hi, there. Guess what? My car's battery is dead, so I won't be joining you tonight. Have a wonderful time, and I'll call you tomorrow to hear all about it—that is, if your head will allow you to talk on the phone." She even managed a small laugh.

"Hold it!" Rhetta's voice was insistent. "Just hold it! There'll be someone for you in ten minutes. I'll send Gary or someone."

"No, Rhetta. I've already undressed." It was a fib that came easily to her lips.

"Well, get dressed, love. Ten minutes. 'Bye." The phone went dead.

"Oh, damn, damn, damn!"

When she saw headlights coming up the lane, she pulled up the hood on her coat, picked up her shoes and purse, and stepped out into the crisp cold night. The car swung toward her and then away from her, momentarily blinding her with its high beams.

It backed up so that the passenger door was toward her.

The door opened, and the interior light came on. Lute sat behind the wheel. Nelda was so startled that she just stood and stared. Lute, in a dark suit and topcoat, leather gloves on his hands, which gripped the wheel, and a grim look on his face, turned to face her.

Oh no! What now?

"Get in. The car's warm, but it won't be if you stand there much longer with the door open."

Nelda got in and shut the door.

The closing of the door brought blessed darkness, but almost immediately the scent of peppery male cologne assaulted her nostrils, sending explosive quivers through her. She adjusted her coat, buying time and courage. Nothing could have been harder than being with Lute so unexpectedly. Her hands trembled until she clasped them together.

I'll miss him dreadfully for the rest of my life. I'll store up all these little last-minute images of him to carry in my mind and to tell our child someday.

The car left the gravel road and pulled out onto the highway. The silence was heavy. Not a word had passed between them since Lute told her so bluntly to get into the car. Nelda felt as if the two of them were involved in some last, elaborate game: her purpose being to behave normally and his to endure her presence.

"Sorry to put you to this bother. Rhetta said that Gary would come for me," she offered in the way of apology.

"No bother. I was coming past your place anyway. What's wrong with your car?"

She met his glance with a pretense of calm. "Battery. I'll have someone come out tomorrow."

There was another long tense silence. Nelda stared at the ribbon of highway unwinding before them, wondering how she was going to bear seeing him with Meredith.

"How is Alan?"

"All right. His mother asked me to thank you for looking after him."

"Does he go to school?"

"Of course not. Children are cruel to someone like Alan."

"Kelly didn't mind how he looked."

"Yeah, sometimes dogs have more sense than people. I found out how he got into your house. He went in through the coal chute. He's small enough to wiggle through the outside door and slide down the chute into the coal bin in the basement. I came over the other day and nailed it shut."

"I didn't even know there was a coal chute."

"All old houses had coal furnaces. The coal was shoveled in through an outside door and down the chute to the coal bin."

"I remember you told me to hide there when the schoolboys were banging on my door. Even the hoodlums could have come in that way," she said accusingly.

"Nope." He gave her a cocky grin. "They are way too big and would've got stuck in the chute."

"I wish they'd tried. I'd have picked them off one by one."

It was unreal to Nelda to be having a conversation with Lute without the two of them snarling at each other. The congeniality didn't last.

"Rhetta tells me that you're leaving soon. You stuck it out longer than I thought you would." He changed gears violently, and the car shuddered.

"What do you mean by that?" Nelda knew, but she still had to challenge him.

"You know what I mean." He glanced at her quickly and then looked back at the road.

"Yes, I guess I do," she murmured, watching his dark profile.

A car swept down the road toward them, the headlights flashing briefly over his face. His lips were pressed tightly together, and his brows were beetled into a frown. His silence made her tense, and she began to shiver.

"Cold?" he asked instantly.

"A little."

"Is this better?" He switched the heater control, sending a waft of warm air over her legs.

"Much," she said, cuddling down in pretended comfort. "This is a nice car. I'm so used to seeing you in a pickup that . . ." Her voice trailed away. She didn't know how to finish what she'd started to say.

"Farmers nowadays can afford a few luxuries. They send their kids to college, take winter trips to Hawaii or Las Vegas occasionally, and, in my case, have a decent car." He was keeping his voice firmly under control, allowing only a hint of sarcasm to surface.

"I know that," she said sharply. "I've enjoyed the income from Grandpa's farm for a couple of years now."

"That's right, you have. The money is good, but the lifestyle stinks, right?" He was no longer hiding his feelings of contempt.

Nelda felt her skin flushing, and she looked away from him. *Let him think what he wants to think,* she thought bitterly. Lute slowed the car as he turned up the drive toward the veterinarian's house and circled to park so she wouldn't have to wade through snow to get to the door.

As soon as he braked to a stop, she fumbled for the door handle and pressed it, but it failed to give. Lute cut the motor and lights, then turned in the seat to look at her.

After a brief silence he said flatly, "You're not coming back."

"No." She decided to make an honest break.

"When are you leaving?" He asked the question without emotion.

The day after tomorrow, but I'm not telling you that. She tried for lightness when she answered.

"I haven't decided, but soon. I've got a wonderful opportunity to decorate an advertising studio. If I can come up with something spectacular, I'll truly be set in my career. The clients will be breaking down the door to get to me."

"And that's important to you?"

"Sure. It's what I went to school for, ate cheese

sandwiches for, wore runny hose for, lived in a third-story room for," she said, not meeting his eyes.

"Smithfield would fit into your life perfectly, wouldn't he?" The question was brutally sharp.

"Well . . . I guess so."

"No guess about it. You two zeroed in on each other like homing pigeons!" The vehemence in his voice was frightening.

She tried the door handle again. It was still locked.

"Thank you for picking me up. I'm sure you want to get going and pick up your date." Nelda felt her composure slipping through her fingers.

"You're my date."

Nelda's head turned slowly toward him and found that he had leaned closer to her, his eyes finding hers and holding them.

"What do you mean?"

"That's the second time you've asked that tonight."

"What do you mean, dammit?"

"Just what I said." The words left his mouth as if they were nasty. "We're a twosome, a couple, a duet . . . a pair for the evening, anyway."

Nelda drew back. He was too close! She could see the color of his eyes and smell the freshness of his breath. Irrational anger bubbled up inside her.

"I don't recall making a date with you. Now, let me out of this damn car."

"Why are you so riled?"

"I'm not riled, dammit! Well, yes, I am. You make me so mad I don't know what I'm thinking, much less what I'm saying. You take too much for granted, Lute. Didn't it occur to you to call and ask me to go out with you?" She took a deep breath. "Or did you think you were doing me a big favor to take me?"

"You wouldn't have gone with me if I had asked you."

"You've got it right there."

"Do you know what I want?" He was grinning.

"I'm sure you'll tell me . . . in time."

"There is one line of communication we had right up to the very last—"

"—You're being obnoxious!"

"And still have," he continued as if he hadn't been interrupted. "I'm going to kiss you, Nelda Elaine. What are you going to do about it?"

She knew that she wasn't going to do a thing. She wanted him to kiss her, hold her, make her blood rush around her body, make a thousand little memories to tuck away and bring out again in her lonely future. She turned her eyes away, afraid that he would read her thoughts.

Lute reached out to cradle the nape of her neck and pull her head toward him. His face was grave, and his eyes held a tenderness she didn't expect. Nelda felt the strength drain out of her, leaving her limp in his grasp.

"You'll smear my makeup," she said feebly.

"You don't need makeup. Never did."

"Rhetta will be wondering—"

"To hell with Rhetta."

"I don't want you to kiss me."

"Yes, you do."

"I'm not lying."

"I could always tell when you were lying. Now hush."

His eyes were astonishingly bright and luminous in the dim light. She clamped her mouth shut and tried to look away from him, but in the closeness of the car, and with his hand holding her still, there was nowhere else to look. He not only filled her eyes, but her senses, her mind.

His face came closer to hers.

"That mouth of yours always tells me what you're thinking. Right now your lips are pressed together—you're being stubborn. When I kiss you they'll soften, because you like me to kiss you. You draw your bottom lip between your teeth when you're puzzled and uncertain, and the corners of your mouth lift when you want to laugh but are trying not to. You get mad fast, but you get over it fast, too. Remember when you bit me?" He sighed deeply. "As soon as your teeth let go of my lip you were crying and kissing it. You were awfully sweet in those days."

"Those days are over," she whispered. That reminder of the past tore at her heart.

"Yes." He said it softly and took her chin tightly in his hand. She attempted to twist away from him, but he held her firmly and kissed her gently on the mouth. She tried to close her heart against the sweetness of it and the tender look in his eyes.

"The first time I kissed you was on a cold night after the last football game of the season. We were sitting in the pickup with a blanket over our legs because I didn't have enough gas to keep the engine running."

"Why are you bringing that up now?" Her heart was haunted and dark with despair. She tried to push him away.

"I don't know. I guess you never really forget your first love." With her head in the powerful grip of his two hands, he slowly lowered his lips to hers and kissed her with slow deliberation, his lips playing softly, coaxing.

Never had she had to fight so hard not to surrender completely, to cling to him and beg him to stay with her forever, tell him that a part of him would be with her always.

With blinding clarity the truth hit. He was amusing himself with her.

"Lute, no!" She pulled back, and he let her go. "Rhetta will be wondering what's taking us so long."

"Okay. I certainly wouldn't want Rhetta to get the idea that I'm out here kissing my ex-wife. It could damage my image of most eligible bachelor." His words were tinged with sarcasm.

"What you're really afraid of is that Miss Home Ec will find out." Her tone matched his.

"You're right. I've got to have someone to fill in when you leave."

She balled her fist, wishing that she had the nerve to hit him.

He reached across her and released the door. The interior light came on, and Nelda collected her shoes and purse. Without looking at him, she got out of the car. By the time she reached the porch he was beside her, his hand on her elbow. She wanted to jerk away, but the thoughts rushed in like an ocean wave—last kiss, last touch—

❧ *Chapter Twenty-three* ❧

RHETTA THREW OPEN THE DOOR.

"Well, you two. I was about to call out the emergency squad. I thought you'd slid into a ditch somewhere."

"It was nothing as exciting as that." Nelda forced a lightness into her voice. She glanced at Lute. He was handsome standing there, his dark suit dramatically setting off his blond hair.

"Come have a drink. Gary was late as usual. Give me your coat. Better yet, you take it, Lute. Oh, dear, isn't it awful to have to wear snow boots with a dress-up dress?" Rhetta's eyes ping-ponged continuously between Nelda and Lute. "Emerald green is a wonderful color on you. Don't you think so, Lute?"

"Great," Lute said softly.

Nelda rushed into speech. "If we're going to be here a while, I'll take off my boots."

"Leave them on. Gary's getting dressed, and if he knows that we're having a drink he'll hurry." Rhetta seemed nervous.

"Hurry," Lute scoffed. "Gary doesn't know the meaning of the word."

"Fix something for yourself and Nelda, Lute, and I'll dash upstairs and make sure Gary doesn't put his pants on backward. I'll be surprised if he even finds them, even though I've laid them out on the bed for him. We've been married eighteen years, and that man hasn't found the dirty clothes hamper yet."

Nelda tried to shake off the suspicion that had begun to grow on her little by little. Rhetta was contriving to throw her and Lute together. She was leaving them alone, and there had been a vivid sparkle in her eyes, as though she were feeling triumphant.

The intense silence that followed Rhetta's departure seemed to press in on her. Her face felt stiff, her body devoid of the strength necessary to turn and face Lute, so she pretended to study a landscape hanging on the wall over the couch.

"What will you have? Gary keeps a well-stocked liquor cabinet." Lute's voice floated across the room, and she turned to look at his back.

"Nothing, thank you."

"You drank the night you were here with Smithfield," he reminded her sharply.

"I wasn't here with Norris. I met him here." She looked at the amount of whiskey he'd poured into a glass and closed her eyes in misery. When she opened them, he had started across the room toward her.

"You look as though you could use a drink. Are you sure you're well?" He had added soda to the whiskey.

"Thanks a lot. Every woman loves to hear that

she looks like death warmed over when she's dressed for a party." She held the drink, knowing she couldn't possibly get a swallow down her throat, and if she did, she would throw it up.

"Fishing for a compliment? You know you're a beautiful woman. You don't need to be told."

"I'm beginning to wish that I'd stayed home with a good book."

"Don't worry. The party will liven you up. You just might be the prettiest girl there."

"Here we are!" Rhetta announced. "Isn't he gorgeous?"

"Yes, gorgeous," Lute said dryly.

Rhetta beamed at Gary, who on cue tucked his thumbs into the lapels of his jacket and pivoted like a model.

"He looks like a gigolo. Maybe you should go to the city, Gary, and get a job as a male escort for a rich old lady."

"Jealous, m'lad? That's what's wrong with you. You're jealous of my good looks and my charm, but I forgive you. Let's be off." He grabbed Rhetta and whirled her around and sang terribly off key. "I'm goin' to rock around the clock tonight with my beautiful wife."

"It's a darn good thing you're a vet and not trying to make a living as a singer," Lute remarked.

Nelda felt a stab of envy, and before she could stop them her eyes flew to Lute. She could hear some strange sounds from the past . . . a band at a prom and Lute saying over the music, *If anyone asks you to dance, I'll punch him in the nose.*

How had their love slipped away? Could she have held it if she had come back sooner or had it died the moment she had allowed her father take her from him?

By the time they reached the Surf Ballroom, it was crowded with dancers, all eager to see Buddy Holly and the Crickets. The evening was a total disaster as far as Nelda was concerned. Her strained nerves were near the breaking point by the time they reached the booth Gary had reserved for them.

Buddy Holly, a tall thin kid with black-rimmed glasses was belting out his latest hit tune "Peggy Sue."

It was mostly a young crowd in saddle shoes and full skirts. They were performing all sorts of gymnastic movements to the beat of the music.

Nelda looked around, recognized a few people she had met through her work at the library, smiled her greetings, and clutched her small purse as if it were a talisman. Rhetta beckoned, and the two of them went to the ladies' room.

"You're nervous about being here with Lute," Rhetta said as if reading her thoughts.

"Well, yes, I am," Nelda said unsteadily. "I wish you hadn't sent him for me. I'm sure he had a date and didn't want to be bothered."

"He didn't have a date. He was coming with Gary and me. I don't think he's seeing anyone right now."

"I'll be leaving soon, and I don't want any entanglements. Miss Home Ec is welcome to him."

Nelda added a touch of lipstick with a calmness she didn't feel.

Rhetta looked at her steadily. Nelda knew she was observing her quivering lower lip, the eyes that looked away, the hands that shook when she returned the lipstick to her purse.

"I don't believe that for a minute. But never mind. Let's get back to our men."

Lute was talking to a group of men near the front of the dance floor. Nelda and Rhetta slipped past and edged their way back to the booth. Nelda was chilled with nerves and wished fervently that the evening were already over.

Gary, singing "Chantilly Lace" along with the Big Bopper, stood and held out his hand to his wife. He pulled Rhetta out onto the dance floor.

Nelda watched Gary and Rhetta dance and realized that they were quite good. It must be wonderful to be able to let yourself go like that and enjoy the music.

A sudden fear almost bowled her over. *I've got to get out of here*, Nelda thought frantically. *What if I have to dance with Lute? He'll know I'm pregnant! My waist is thicker, my breasts fuller. He'll notice. I know he will. I didn't think there would be the remote possibility we'd be in the same party. I thought he'd be off somewhere with Meredith.*

As if on cue, he was beside her holding out his hand. "Nelda."

She froze, her heart turning to ice. She didn't need to see his face to know he was looking down at her. The sound of the music, the revelry in the background all receded to a distant murmur in her ears. There was only the tall form beside her, the blond head bending to hers.

"Nelda, dance with me."

Before she could protest, he had pulled her to her feet. Her hand went to his shoulder, his to her waist. He would have pulled her closer, but she stiffened her arm to hold him away. The band was playing "16 Candles." As far as Nelda was concerned they could have been playing "Stars and Stripes Forever." The roaring in her ears prevented her from hearing anything except Lute's voice.

"Nelda?" he breathed. His fingers held hers tightly. He was looking down at her with naked hunger on his face. She met his eyes briefly, then looked away. "Can't you look at me?"

She turned her head, but out of the corner of her eye she saw that his eyes, intensely serious, were riveted on her.

"The last time we danced together was at the high-school prom. The school gym was decorated with crepe-paper streamers that fell onto the floor and got tangled around our legs." His voice was hoarse.

"I remember."

"When Arlen Martin tried to cut in and dance with you, I threatened to strangle him with some of the streamers. You were so pretty that night," he said, then added in a strained voice, "You're pretty tonight, too." When he attempted to pull her close to him, she stiffened her arm again and he didn't persist.

"Thank you. Do . . . you come here to the Surf

often?" She was so breathless she could hardly speak, but felt she had to say something.

"Only on special occasions . . . like this. Do you remember what happened that night?"

"Bobby Jenkins got sick and threw up on Kathy Jacobs's dress."

He chuckled. "I remember that, but I remember something else, too." He bent his head toward hers. "That night after the prom we promised to love each other forever. Nelda, Nelda . . . what happened to that young love?"

The pain in her heart weakened her knees, but the courage she needed to reply lightly came from somewhere deep within her.

"It was puppy love, Lute. A lot of high-school kids mistake it for the real thing." She was even able to laugh a little.

They swayed to the music. Lute guided her into several turns. Into Nelda's clouded mind came the realization that she had to get out of here . . . away from him. His hand at her waist could move around and force her closer to him, where he would be sure to feel the baby that nestled inside her.

"I've got to sit down," she blurted. "I don't feel well."

Lute stopped immediately and with his arm around her, he led her to the booth.

"I thought something was wrong with you." Lute slid into the booth opposite her, his knees bumping hers. "You're sick! What's the matter? Do you have a temperature?" The concern in his voice brought a painful ache to her chest, and she had to force back tears.

"I may have a little fever, but I'll be all right."

"Do you want to go home?"

"No. I'm all right." Her voice stuck in her throat, and she dared not look at him. She kept her face averted. She couldn't let him take her home and run the risk of giving in to the temptation and letting him spend the night. That would be disastrous! *Oh, Lord . . . he can be so persuasive.*

"Do you want me to get you some aspirin?"

"No. I'll be all right." *That's the third time I've said that,* she thought crazily. "Go find someone and dance, Lute. You always liked to dance."

Richy Valens was on the stage singing his hit song, "Donna." Nelda turned from Lute and pretended to be interested in the song.

"Nelda. Look at me. What's the matter?" Lute asked quietly breaking into her thoughts.

She wanted to scream, *What do you think is the matter? I'm pregnant by a man who doesn't want me, I'm leaving the home I have come to love. I've got a perfect right to feel miserable.*

"You shouldn't have come."

"Try telling that to Rhetta once she's made up her mind."

"You could have told me." His soft, concerned voice threatened what remained of her self-control.

She clenched her hands so tightly the nails bit into the palms, but she felt no pain. Every particle of sensation was concentrated on keeping the tears from her eyes. She knew people were looking at her and Lute, and the few who knew that they were once married were wondering if they were getting back together.

Will this evening never end?

The music stopped. Rhetta and Gary, flushed from dancing, came back to the booth.

"Why aren't you two dancing?"

"Nelda doesn't feel well. She shouldn't have come." Lute stood and reached out a hand as if to pull Nelda to her feet.

"You can dance with my wife, Lute. I'll put it on your next bill. I'll sit with Nelda." Gary sat in the place Lute had vacated.

Rhetta took Lute's arm, and he reluctantly moved away. Nelda watched them until they were lost in the crowd of dancers.

"I hate to desert you, Gary, but I think I'll make a trip to the ladies' room." Nelda got unsteadily to her feet.

"It's a bloody shame you're under the weather, love. Is there anything I can do?"

"I'll be fine. Guard the booth. There's a packed crowd here tonight. I'll take a couple of aspirin."

Without any conscious notion of what she was going to do, Nelda hurried around the throng of dancers and headed toward the lobby. Did this town have a taxi? She couldn't remember seeing one. She'd get her coat and boots and at least get out the door while Lute was dancing with Rhetta.

"There you are." A cheery voice interrupted her flight. "I thought I might find you here when you weren't at home."

Nelda jerked to a stop. Norris stood grinning at her. Her relief was more than she could bear, and the tears started running down her cheeks. She clutched his arm.

"Help me get out of here!" Her voice cracked with the effort to say the words.

The smile abruptly left Norris's face. "Sure, honey. Where's your coat?"

"Checked."

"Come point it out."

Almost frantic in her haste, she found her coat and boots and stood by while Norris finagled their release without the check.

A few minutes later they were in Norris's car, and she was sobbing helplessly.

"I don't know what I would have done if you hadn't been there. I was going to get my coat and try to find someone to take me home. I had to get out of there. I was crazy to come in the first place, but Rhetta was so insistent. I thought it would be easier to come than to make excuses."

"I called the house; and when there was no answer, I figured Rhetta had dragged you to this thing." Norris pushed a handkerchief into her groping fingers. "I didn't dare call Marlene tonight without being able to give a report on how you're doing."

"Rhetta sent Lute to get me." Nelda was completely absorbed in her misery. "I was out of my mind to get myself into this situation."

"Does Rhetta know you're leaving?"

"No, she was dancing with Lute."

"We'll stop up here at the drugstore. I'll call and have her paged."

Nelda waited for Norris to make the call. He had left the motor running so she would keep warm.

"Rhetta was not pleased, to say the least." Norris slid in under the wheel and they moved away from the uptown area. "Lute will be furious. I know I would be if someone ran off with my date."

"He won't mind. He was a victim of Rhetta's manipulation, too. I'm sure he'll have a better time without me there."

"I hate to take you home and leave you alone." Norris eased the car off the highway and onto the snow-packed gravel road. "But I've got a plane waiting at the airport. I just stopped over to get some material I need for a meeting tomorrow."

"Will you see Marlene tomorrow?"

"Yes. Do you want to come along?"

"I can't. I'm driving up to the Cities the day after tomorrow. I've been sorting and packing up what I want sent to me. The battery in my car is down, I've got to do something about that first."

"Call the uptown Shell station. Herb will send Eddie out with a new battery."

Kelly was waiting for them beside the kitchen door. He stretched lazily, and Nelda felt a wave of relief to be back within the safety of the farmhouse. She smiled at Norris, not caring that her mascara and her lipstick were smeared from her bout of tears.

"You and Marlene are so lucky to have each other. Why do you hide the real you behind that playboy image?"

"It's easier to be what people expect you to be than what you are. If you're rich and unmarried and flit around the country—even if your trips are business related—you get the reputation of being a pleasure seeker. I know what I am, the woman I love knows what I am, so to hell with what everyone else thinks."

"Can I ask one more favor, Norris?"

"Of course you can, Chicken Little. Anything."

"After I leave here, will you arrange to have my things sent to me? Mr. Hutchinson has a key. I don't want anyone to know I'm in the Twin Cities. It's very important to me to lose myself for a while."

"Are you sure you want to do this, honey? Lute's a hell of a nice fellow, although he's had a personality change since you've been here. I'm sure he still loves you. Don't you think he's entitled to know you're having his child?"

"No. He mustn't know. It isn't a question of whether or not he's entitled to know. He has made it perfectly clear that I don't fit into his lifestyle. If I don't fit, our baby won't fit. It's that simple. After I'm gone, he'll marry one of his native lady friends and forget about me as I'll forget about him." Tears filled her eyes and she blinked rapidly.

"You love him desperately, don't you, Chicken Little?" Norris rubbed his knuckles across her cheek. "We'll play it the way you want it, but if you change your mind, he'll not be far away."

"I won't change my mind. He was forced to marry me once before because I was pregnant, and I'm sure he'd do it again. You're wrong, Norris, about his feelings for me. He never made any attempt to get in touch with me during the years we were apart. He thinks I'm dedicated to my career and completely unsuitable for his kind of life. He's old-fashioned where women are concerned. He'd never allow his wife an interest outside the farm, and I'm not sure I'd be able to handle that."

"He's a fool," Norris snorted. "But then, that's his problem."

"Tell Marlene that I'll call her as soon as I get there the day after tomorrow. I've talked to the building manager and explained about Kelly. He's allowing me to keep him at the apartment on a trial basis."

"If it doesn't work out, we'll find a kennel close by."

"Take Marlene this kiss." She planted a gentle kiss on Norris's cheek.

"That was prudish! Can't you do better than that?"

"Knock it off!" Nelda poked at his chest with her index finger. "You forget that I'm one of the privileged few who know the real you."

"Take care, honey. See you in a few days."

Nelda stood beside the kitchen window and waved as Norris drove out of the yard. He answered with a toot of the horn.

Nelda slipped out of her clothes, stood before the long mirror in her bedroom and studied her naked body. She was not happy with what she saw. Her arms and legs were thinner, and her collarbone protruded prominently. She had hard, dark shadows beneath her eyes, her cheekbones stood out as if she was half-starved. Grimacing in distaste she turned away. She reminded herself of pictures she had seen of hungry children with bloated stomachs and large, hopeless eyes. *You've got to eat more*, she chided herself sternly. *This can't be good for the baby.*

After a long warm bath, she fixed herself a cup of hot chocolate and a peanut butter and jelly sandwich and carried it upstairs to the bedroom. The aftermath of her ordeal had left her exhausted.

When the harsh ringing of the telephone broke the stillness, her heart skipped a beat. She glanced at the clock. It was a half hour after midnight. The dance would be over. Maybe it was Rhetta wanting to know if she was all right.

It was Rhetta. "Nelda? I'm worried about you."

"Don't be. I'll be all right. I must apologize for running off like that, but I didn't want to throw up in the booth and spoil the party. Did you have a good time?"

"Gary and I had a great time. I don't know what Lute did. He disappeared after you left. He wasn't too happy about you going off with Norris."

"I don't know why he should object. He wasn't my date. He merely gave me a ride to your place."

"I'll let you go. I had to know if you were still breathing. Gosh, but my feet hurt. I'm getting too old for this rock and roll business. See you later."

" 'Bye, Rhetta."

Wide-awake, Nelda took her knitting upstairs. She had completed one set of booties and was knitting what they called in the pattern book a "hug-me-tight." She would have called it a light sweater. She was using white yarn so it would be suitable for a boy or a girl.

She became so absorbed in her knitting that she didn't realize how late it was until a car came down the lane and Kelly raced downstairs to bark at the kitchen door. It was after two in the morning. When Norris left, it had been snowing. It was still snowing when Rhetta called.

Who would be coming at this time of night? By the time she had put on her robe and slipped her feet into her slippers, someone was banging on the door. It was someone Kelly knew. She could tell by the sounds he was making.

She switched on the kitchen light and saw Lute's face at the kitchen door. Now what did he want? Her eyes quickly scanned the room for signs of the baby. Thank heavens she'd packed the books, and the knitting was up in the bedroom; there was nothing visible to give away her secret.

"Are you all right?" he asked the second she opened the door. There was exasperation in his voice. "As I passed I saw your lights on." He moved into the kitchen and closed the door.

"Of course I'm all right. I've been . . . reading."

"Why did you leave like that? I offered to take you home. Did you know *he* was coming and wait for him?"

"I didn't know *he* was going to be there, but if I did, it's no business of yours. I wasn't your date. Rhetta shoved me off on you. You know it, and I know it. Now if you don't mind, I'm tired."

"Have you seen a doctor? You don't look well."

"It's kind of you to keep reminding me of that." Her voice had regained a crisp decisiveness. "We both know that I'm not a big, healthy, robust farm girl, Lute."

"Every time I see you, you get bitchier."

"Please notice that I haven't been seeking you out."

"You did one time."

"I needed your help and got insulted for it. What are you doing out so late? Rolling up the sidewalks of your perfect little town?"

"No. I went with the sheriff's deputy out to the site of a plane crash north of town." He spoke so matter-of-factly that at first the words failed to register.

Oh, my God. He's come to tell me that Norris—

"Three of the entertainers who were at the Surf tonight were killed, along with a good friend of mine who was the pilot of the plane."

"Oh, my. I'm sorry to hear that. Who was killed?"

"Holly, Valens, and Richardson, the guy they called the Big Bopper. I didn't know them, but I've known Roger Peterson all my life. He was a damn good pilot."

"That is so . . . awful. They seemed so young and . . . full of life. What happened?"

"They don't know yet. It was probably weather-related."

"I'm sorry about your friend."

"So am I. I'll go out and see his folks tomorrow. Would you like for me to let Kelly out? He's dancing around."

"Put him on his rope. I'll let him back in."

She waited to hear Lute's car start. But it didn't. She looked out the door pane to see him standing on the porch steps waiting to let Kelly back in.

When the door opened, both Kelly and Lute came in. He came directly to her and gripped her shoulders. The expression on his face was almost one of desperation. He pulled her to him and roughly kissed her lips.

"Nelda," he muttered savagely. His face pressed against her cheek, his lips trembling as he moved them down over her jaw.

"Don't," she whispered, her own lips quivering. Her fear intensified as his hand slide down her arms; she didn't dare let him pull her close. "No, Lute, don't." Desperation was making her angry. "No, no, no!"

"Dammit!" The word exploded from him. He shoved her away and she looked into blazing eyes. "You're blocking me out, because . . . I said we're not suited, aren't you? Well, I've changed my mind about that. We're suited for one thing, that's sure. And if you want me to marry you, then I'll do it to keep you here where I can keep an eye on you."

The sound of his voice, his words and his unbridled anger was destroying her.

"I . . . don't want anything from you, now or ever. I don't want to marry you. I want you to leave. Get out of my house and never come back."

"That's clear enough. I'm going. You've turned into a cold-blooded bitch!"

"It's what you've thought all along, isn't it?" Nelda asked quietly.

Lute closed the door firmly behind him, and moments later she heard his car driving down the lane.

This is the last time I'll see him, her mind screamed. *The very last time.* The tight rein she had kept on her emotions broke, her face crumbled, and she gave way to a storm of tears.

৵ Chapter Twenty-four ৵

FOR HOURS NELDA LAY AWAKE, HAUNTED BY Lute's accusations. No matter how often she told herself she was doing the right thing in leaving, she kept thinking of what it would be like to be married to him again. She ached with yearning to be with him.

All day as she prepared to leave her home she thought of the words he had snarled at her. *If you want me to marry you, I'll do it.* Nothing he'd ever said to her had hurt so much.

She flopped over on her back and looked at the clock. If she had swallowed her pride, he'd be with her now, and she wouldn't have to feel cold and lonely.

Somehow the night passed. She rose from her bed feeling haggard and with her spirits at a new low. She looked out the window on a cold, still dawn. *Oh, Lute, I'm leaving, and I can never come back!*

Nelda didn't allow herself the luxury of self-pity for long. She dressed quickly, ate a piece of toast, and drank a glass of milk, thankful she was spared morning sickness. In an hour she was ready to leave. With the new battery, her car started immediately and she backed it up to the back porch. Placing two suitcases flat in the trunk, she covered them with a sheet and, leaving her clothes on hangers, placed them in the trunk on the bed sheet. She piled boxes in the backseat of the car making it necessary for Kelly to ride up front with her.

Leaving the house was a traumatic experience. Boxes to be shipped were in the kitchen; the refrigerator was cleaned out, the shades drawn. Warmly dressed in wool slacks, a sweater, and a coat, Nelda looked around one last time.

"'Bye, Grandma. 'Bye, Grandpa," she whispered before she went out the door and locked it.

She called Kelly, urged him into the car, and drove down the lane to the road without looking back.

On her way through town she stopped at the grocery store and bought a bag of treats for Kelly, a couple of bananas for herself and a newspaper.

ROCK'N ROLLERS, PILOT DIE IN TRAGIC PLANE CRASH, read the headline on the *Clear Lake Mirror Reporter*. She tucked the paper in her carryall to look at later, thinking that the town would be talking about this for years to come.

At the Shell station she filled her car with gas and headed out of town. The drive to Minneapolis took about three hours. Nelda stopped a couple of times along the way to allow Kelly out of the car. The cold wind blasting from the north discouraged him from dallying.

In the city, she refilled the gas tank and asked directions to her new address.

The wind was whipping around the apartment building when she reached it. Nelda struggled against the powerful force on her way from the parking area to the door, leaving Kelly in the car barking his dismay at being left alone. She knocked on the manager's door.

After making arrangements to have the maintenance man unload her car and bring her things to the apartment, she went back to the car for Kelly. With every bone in her body aching, by midafternoon all she had managed to do was hang her clothes in the closet. She lay on the couch, knowing that she should take Kelly out, but was too tired to do it.

When the phone rang, it was Marlene.

"I'm checking on you. Norris said you were coming up today."

"I've been here a few hours."

"You sound as if you have a cold."

"Maybe a little one."

"There's a flu going around. If you have a fever, you probably should see a doctor."

"If I do have a fever, would it hurt the baby?" To her embarrassment, there was a sob in her voice.

"Honey, I'll be right over."

"Don't come, Marlene. If it's flu, you could catch it. I'll take an aspirin."

"I'm on my way." The phone went dead.

Several hours later she was tucked into bed. Marlene had taken her temperature and called the doctor, who prescribed an antibiotic, which was delivered.

The sound of the doorbell brought Marlene to her feet. A quick smile tilted her lips.

"That's Norris. I left word where I would be."

A few minutes later they came into the bedroom, arm in arm.

"Hi, Chicken Little. That old flu bug got you down?" He dropped a kiss on her head. "I suspected you were on the verge of it the other night."

"It's good to see you. I don't know how I was ever so fortunate as to meet you two."

"Sheer luck." Norris grinned and pulled Marlene close to him. "Isn't that right, sweetheart?"

"If you say so, love. Now sit down and talk to Nelda while I get you a cup of coffee. Even your nose is cold."

He placed a quick kiss near her ear. *The communication between them is so beautiful*, Nelda thought with a pang. *This is how love is supposed to be, not hurtful as it is between me and Lute.*

"Is there a kennel near here, Norris?"

"Not close by that I know of. Let me talk to the manager and see if we can pay the cleaning man a buck or two to take Kelly out a couple times a day when you can't."

"I can do it most of the time. Today, I just couldn't do it."

"Leave him to me, honey."

When Marlene and Norris were preparing to leave, Marlene made Nelda promise to stay in bed and take the medication every four hours during the night.

"I'll be back over in the morning."

"You don't need to, Marlene. You've done so much already."

"I'll be over in the morning," Marlene insisted. "You've got to have a healthy baby. Norris and I have part interest in him, you know. My house is only about a mile away. It won't take any time at all to get here."

"There's an instrument called the telephone right there by your bed," Norris said as patiently as if he were talking to a child. "Use it if you need us tonight."

During the days that followed, Marlene proved to be the mother-sister Nelda had never had. Her own mother had been a woman of strict self-discipline, who had loved her in her own way but had expected her to conform without question to what society expected of her.

Marlene, on the other hand, was warm, affectionate, and understanding, and Nelda thought it no wonder that Norris loved her so much. They had many interests in common. After Nelda recovered from the flu and Norris was away tending his various businesses, Marlene and Nelda spent hours together. They visited the Art Museum and the fabric and antique shops that were Marlene's primary interest. She was looking for pieces to furnish Norris's lakeside house.

Nelda had been in the apartment a couple of weeks when Norris arrived alone one night.

"I didn't know you were in town."

"I got here this morning." He set a bottle of whiskey on the table, then took off his topcoat. "I need a drink tonight."

"What's wrong, Norris?"

"Marlene's husband has taken a turn for the worse. They don't think he'll last out the night. I should be glad. She'll be free to marry me. I feel bad for her and Jenny."

"Are they with him?"

"Yes. It's his time to be with his wife and daughter. I'll keep my distance until Marlene is ready to think about us."

"How long ago was he injured?"

"Almost ten years. I met Marlene eight years ago and fell for her like a ton of bricks. She held me off for a while because of Ralph. His brain injury left him with the mental capacity of a three- or four-year-old child. He was confined to a wheelchair and had no control over his bodily functions. Marlene was loyal to the bone and went out there every week and every holiday, played with him, took him out when the weather permitted."

Once he started, Norris couldn't seem to stop talking. He told her that at first Marlene's daughter, Jenny, had resented him. Gradually he had won her over, knowing how important she was to Marlene. He missed being close to his own daughters and hoped someday they would see him as a father who loved them and not merely as the man who sent the check every month.

After several stiff drinks, Norris put the bottle away. Nelda had never seen him so solemn.

"I was in Clear Lake today," he said, changing the subject suddenly. "While I was at Hutchinson's getting the key to your house, Earl told me that he wanted to get in touch with you. He's got two people interested in the farm. One of them is Lute."

"The other is probably my father. I don't want him to have it."

"Hutchinson said the other buyer has offered a lot more money."

"That would be the major. I don't care how much he offers, he'll not get it because of the way he treated Grandpa and Grandma. He thought he was too good for them after he became a commissioned officer."

"I took a storage-company truck out to the house to load up your things. Lute came over while I was there. I've never seen a man so angry. He would have torn my head off if the storage men hadn't been there. There was no reasoning with him at first. He wouldn't believe that you're not coming back. Finally, he calmed down and left."

"Did he say anything to you about buying the farm?"

"Not a word. I'm going back down there in the morning. Don't you think I should give Hutchinson your phone number? You're going to have to talk to him about your income tax if nothing else. It'll be due pretty soon."

"That's right. I'd forgotten about it."

A week passed before Nelda saw Marlene again. Her husband's obituary was in the paper along with a picture. He had been an impressive-looking man and a successful stockbroker. Marlene called one day and asked if she would like to go to lunch. Of course she agreed, and they had an intimate conversation about life and love.

Marlene confided that her marriage had been a good one. She had married Ralph before she finished college. He had been older and already established in business. Her parents had been all for it, and she had been dazzled that an older successful man had wanted her. She knew that he loved her and she had thought that she loved him, but not in the way she loved Norris.

"There are different kinds of love between a man and a woman," Marlene said with a sad smile. "The love I had for Ralph was at first a love rooted in respect and admiration. Then I loved him because he had saved my life at this terrible cost to him. Later, I loved him as a mother loves a child. With Norris it is so different. I love him as a woman loves her mate. He's my lover, my friend. I'd crawl through hell on my knees to be with him."

"He feels the same about you. I never knew a man who loved a woman so much."

"Norris tells me that you love the father of your baby, that you were married at one time."

"It almost set a record for the shortest marriage in history. I've loved him since I was fifteen and he was seventeen. But people sometimes change after

358   Dorothy Garlock

they grow up. It was tough on Lute when my father sent him away. But it was tough on me, too. I've got to let go. I can't keep trying to hold on to the past."

It was the end of March. Nelda was alone much of the time now that Marlene occasionally went out of town with Norris. Dr. Wilkins assured her that her pregnancy was progressing normally. She forced herself to eat three small, well-balanced meals every day, and every afternoon she found new routes to walk the approximately two miles with Kelly.

The rest of her day was spent working on designs for her block prints. She set up a small table beside the living-room windows, and she sat for hours with a razor knife, cutting the film stencils to adhere to the silk screen she would use to make her prints. Even at that, time hung heavy, and certain days seemed a week long.

She had been in the apartment two months when she received the letter from Lute. Norris and Marlene had come over and before Norris took off his coat, he took an envelope from his pocket.

"Lute came out to my house," he said quietly. "He was quite civil and asked me to mail this to you after I refused to tell him where you were."

Suddenly heavy with apprehension, Nelda's heart plummeted as she reached with shaking fingers for the long white envelope. She was scarcely aware of saying,

"Will you excuse me for a minute?"

In the bedroom she looked at the envelope for a long while before she found the courage to open it.

This was the first piece of correspondence she'd received from him since he'd sent back the divorce papers eight years ago. With her bottom lip caught between her teeth to stop its trembling, she slipped a finger beneath the sealed flap and took out the single sheet of white paper.

The text of the letter jumped at her in a bold script. It was brief, formal, and agonizing.

Dear Nelda,

Hutchinson tells me that you've put the farm up for sale. As your land adjoins mine and I'm interested in acquiring more acreage, I've made him an offer to be relayed to you. I am not, however, interested in the house, only the land it sits on. If I acquire the property, I will probably demolish the house and till the ground. I'm aware that the house has sentimental value for you, but I can't afford sentimentality. It doesn't put dollars in the bank. I'm sure you can understand my position.

Lute

P.S. You and Smithfield should hitch well together.

Nelda sat for a long moment looking at the letter. She didn't cry—she was beyond tears—but she shivered uncontrollably. What was wrong with her that she still loved this cold, hard, unfeeling man? She wanted the tender, affectionate Lute of long ago and the warm love they had shared when they were young.

She didn't want to love this Lute . . . yet she was

realistic enough to realize that she had contributed to what her gentle boy-husband had become. Did the Lute she had loved still exist beneath this older, hostile Lute?

A couple of weeks went by. It was planting time. She could visualize Lute in the fields on his big tractor. She read, worked, walked with Kelly, and visited with Marlene, who was home less and less. Nelda grew tense and strained and was consumed with guilt over selling the farm. The thought of her Grandma's beloved house being torn down, the lumber being loaded into trucks and hauled away, was a constant ache in her heart. It would have been less painful, she thought, if a tornado had blown the house away.

At times she felt as if she were being pulled in a dozen different directions.

One day, on an impulse, she called Mr. Hutchinson and asked him if the deal to sell the farm to Lute was in the works.

"Not yet. I have Lute's offer, but I also have an offer from someone else other than your father. I was preparing a letter to give to Smithfield—"

"I don't want to consider another offer, Mr. Hutchinson. Sell to Lute for whatever he offers."

"If that's what you want. Where can I reach you? I'll call as soon as the papers are ready for you to sign."

Nelda gave him the number. "When you're ready, I'll meet you somewhere between here and Clear Lake. I want this over with as soon as possible."

She knew Mr. Hutchinson was puzzled by her unusual behavior, but she was past caring what anyone thought. Her only worry was the fear that she wouldn't be able to hide her pregnancy from him when she met him.

After that phone call there was nothing to do but wait. Wait for Mr. Hutchinson to call, wait for Norris and Marlene to come over, wait for appointments with Dr. Wilkins.

The weather was mostly good now. Spring had come to Minnesota. Nelda and Kelly had taken a long walk and returned to the apartment tired and hungry. She fed Kelly, then made herself a tuna salad and took it to the couch in the living room. When the telephone rang, she moved listlessly to answer it, hoping it was Norris and that he would volunteer some news about Rhetta and Gary and Lute because she would never ask.

"Hello?"

A few seconds of silence preceded the announcement,

"This is Lute."

Nelda felt her blood go cold. Her hand gripped the phone. She was too stunned to speak, and, in one moment, she experienced a great surge of both love and fright.

"How . . . did you get this number?" she whispered haltingly.

"It wasn't easy. Smithfield refused to tell me where you were. I was in Hutchinson's office when he pulled out a pile of papers from your file, and your number was written on the top. I jotted it down." Her heart throbbed painfully while she listened to the familiar voice. "I just want to talk to you for a minute. How are you doing?"

"Fine. Why wouldn't I be?" Her heart continued to thump painfully.

"I just want to talk to you," he repeated, "and make sure you're all right."

"I'm okay. Are you planting now?" she mumbled, trying to make conversation.

"We have some of the corn in. Some of the ground is too wet yet to plant. You're in the Twin Cities. I could tell by the area code," he said, switching the subject. "Are you working on the big decorating job you told me about?"

"I'm doing some of the preliminary work. I'll start the actual work . . . soon." Nelda dropped down in a chair, her legs suddenly weak.

After a silence on the other end of the line, he asked, "Are you going back to Chicago?"

"Yes."

"When are you going?" There seemed to be a note of pain in his voice, but Nelda was swallowing the sobs in her throat and couldn't be certain whether or not her own hopes were misleading her.

"I'm not sure."

"Did you get my letter?"

For a minute she couldn't speak, and when she did, her voice was pathetically weak.

"About . . . Grandma's house?"

"About my buying the farm. I've signed the papers and given Hutchinson a down payment. We're waiting for the loan to go through."

"Then . . . it's settled. I want to get Grandma's

furniture out before you tear down the house." She said the words with difficulty.

"I'm not going to tear it down, honey. I'm sorry I ever said that. I was hurt and wanted to hurt you. I know you love that old place." There was sincerity in his voice, as if he desperately wanted her to believe him.

She struggled to think of something to say.

"Did you hear me? I won't tear it down."

"I heard you," she whispered.

"I was at Rhetta and Gary's last night. They asked if I had heard from you." When she said nothing he went on. "Gary has gotten the bug to raise American quarter horses and wants me to go partners with him on a registered stallion."

"Are you going to?" It seemed unreal to be having this conversation with him.

"I'm thinking about it. It would mean going to horse shows and fairs. I'm not sure I have the time for it."

"I saw a horse show in Madison Square Garden once. The animals were beautiful, but I didn't know the difference between an Arabian and a Tennessee Walker without looking at the program."

"Do you like horses?"

She hesitated. "Yes, though they're awfully big. Dogs are more my size."

"How does Kelly like living in the city?"

"He likes the country better, but I take him for a walk every day."

"You could have left him with me." There was a long pause while he waited for her to respond.

Nelda was holding the phone in one hand, the other hand on her protruding abdomen where her baby was kicking. Thump, thump, thump.

"I want to call you again, Nelda." His voice came into her ear.

"No! Don't call. It's best that we make a clean break. It was nice of you to call and ask about me. I'm glad it was you who bought Grandpa's farm. 'Bye, Lute." She got up from the chair, holding the phone away from her ear as she went to lay it back in the cradle.

"Nelda—" His voice reached her before the connection was broken.

She went to the bathroom, closed the door, and turned the water on in the bathtub. If Lute called back, she didn't want to hear the phone ring.

That night she lay awake for hours, staring into the darkness, her thoughts in a riot of confusion. Why had he called? Did he want her because now he couldn't have her? Did he feel obligated to see to her welfare because of his fondness for her grandparents and the love they had shared when they were young?

It certainly wasn't for any love he had for her now. He'd made that perfectly clear months ago. He had probably called because he was grateful she had sold him the farm.

~ Chapter Twenty-five ~

NORRIS WAS SPENDING MORE AND MORE TIME IN
Minneapolis with Marlene. It was a joy to be with
them. Nothing had been said to Nelda about their
getting married, but she was sure that it would happen soon.

On Saturday night, Norris took Nelda and Marlene out to dinner. None of Nelda's regular clothes
fit anymore; tonight she wore her new maternity
slacks and a loose black top with the emerald green
scarf. She welcomed the outing. It was good to be
among people in a normal setting. She had spent too
much time alone.

Norris talked about the progress on his house on
Clear Lake's south shore now that it was spring and
work had been resumed.

"Won't you come down and see our new house
and ride in our new boat?" Norris coaxed.

"I'd love to see it, but . . ."

"She's not ready to go back." Marlene chided
Norris gently.

"I may never be, Marlene," Nelda said sadly.

The meal was delicious and the service superb, the conversation light and amusing. Nelda didn't mention Lute's call. The sound of his voice had affected her so deeply she tried not to think about it.

"Thank you so much," she said to Norris when he walked her to the door of her apartment building. She kissed him on the cheek. "Run on back to Marlene. You are so lucky to have each other."

"I'm almost afraid to let her out of my sight for fear she'll disappear," he confessed. "'Night, honey. I'll see you in about a week."

It was ten o'clock when she let herself back into the apartment. She looked accusingly at the telephone as she had done during the past week, as if it should tell her whether or not it had rung.

"Come on, Kelly, we'll go out for just a few minutes." She fastened the leash to Kelly's collar, and went out the back of the building into the lighted parking area.

After a few minutes they came back into the apartment and Nelda started preparing for bed. It had become a ritual to undress and look at herself in the long bedroom mirror before she put on her nightgown. She did this now, shook her head in disbelief, and rubbed her palms over her protruding abdomen.

"Baby, Baby! The way you're growing, you're going to be big enough for school when you get here. But I want you to be big and healthy . . . like your daddy."

As if in response, a small movement fluttered against her hand. She caught her breath. This wondrous thing was happening, and she had no one to share it with—no one to laugh because she waddled like a duck, or to rub her aching back, or to look forward to the day her son arrived.

Nelda looked down at her altered shape. She had wished for happier circumstances to surround the baby's arrival into the world; but, whatever happened, she wanted this baby too much to care. Only today Dr. Wilkins had said these months of her pregnancy should be carefree. Carefree? What in the world was that?

She was standing in front of the mirror when the phone rang. Her eyes darted to the instrument on the table beside the bed. It rang again before she moved, and that was to pick up her nightgown and slip it over her head, as if standing naked while the phone was ringing was somehow indecent.

Would Lute be calling this late on a Saturday night? It could be Norris or Marlene, and if she didn't answer, they would be worried. They might even make a trip back over to her building. If it was Lute, she didn't have to talk to him—she could hang up. After this momentary deliberation she reached for the phone.

"Hello?"

"Nelda, I've been calling all evening. I was afraid something had happened to you."

Lute. She didn't answer, couldn't answer.

"Don't hang up. Nelda . . . please—" His voice rasped strangely.

"What do you want? If it's something about the farm, call Earl Hutchinson." Her voice was more controlled than she expected it to be.

"It's not about the farm. I wanted to see how you're doing."

"It's good of you to be concerned, but—"

"Nelda, don't hang up!"

"We've nothing to talk about." She wrenched out the lie, forcing herself to remember her resolution to break the tie.

"I wish you didn't feel that way." There was a sadness in his voice.

"Why now, Lute?" she questioned, trying to sound annoyed, while her heart cried, *Why now, Lute, when I'm trying so hard to stay out of your life?*

"There will always be an emotional link between us. We had Becky. Remember?"

"I haven't forgotten my child," she said angrily.

"I didn't mean that."

"Then what did you mean? We had plenty of opportunity to talk when I was at the farm. The only times you called me then was to chew me out about something. What have I done wrong now?" she demanded.

"You did nothing wrong, and I did everything wrong. I loused up. My only defense is that it was a shock to see you, have you so near. I had my life in order, and had convinced myself that you would not be a part of it." His voice sounded haunted, tired, old.

"What do you want to talk about, Lute? I'm tired and want to go to bed." She sank down on the side of the bed.

Hang up, you crazy fool. You're asking for another sleepless night.

He hesitated. "Are you seeing a lot of Smithfield?"

A short explosion of breath escaped her lips. She wanted to slam the phone onto the hook in self-righteous outrage, but caught herself. After all, wouldn't it be easier if he thought that? Maybe then he'd stop torturing her with his confusing concern.

"Of course. I like sex. I sleep with a different man every night. Even you couldn't resist a mare in heat. Remember? Let's see . . . I've got you in Iowa, several men here in Minnesota, a couple in Chicago, one in Florida." She sniffed tears, ending with a sob. "What else do you want to know?"

"Nothing, sweetheart. I'm sorry I asked. But, dammit, it's been tearing me apart. Let me come see you."

"No. It's too late. I'm not the kind of woman you want. And I don't want it thrown up to me exactly how useless I am. I'd be no good trying to cook for a bunch of threshers or make apple butter or can dill pickles."

"Farmers' wives don't cook for threshers anymore. I do my own threshing, and if I have extra men to feed, I take them to town."

"Why are you telling me this? I have my career, just as you have yours, and they are miles apart."

"They don't have to be. Let me come see you. Just listen to me for a minute. Eight years is a long time. I thought I was over you, but there wasn't a time when I couldn't picture your face in my mind. Then you came back more beautiful than ever, sweeter to hold, a highly intelligent woman with a successful career to boot."

"I had to make my own living."

"I understand that. But how could an Iowa farmer hope to compete for a sophisticated woman like you?" His voice grew husky.

"I never thought I'd hear you putting yourself down."

"I'm not. I'm being realistic. After I lost you and, later, Becky, I made up my mind I'd never marry again, or have another child. It hurts too much to lose someone you love. When I met you at the cemetery, I guess I did resent your power to make me mindless when I was with you."

"If that's how you feel, why are you calling me?"

"Because I can't help myself, dammit! You're beautiful, intelligent, incredibly sexy—"

Incredibly sexy. That was all she meant to him. She didn't have to pretend anger and hurt anymore. A tight pain was squeezing her chest.

"If you're looking for a regular bed partner, Lute, I'm sure Miss Home Ec will oblige you. I'm not available!" she shouted wildly, and slammed the phone down, only to pick it up again when the connection was broken and let it lie on the table.

What a complete fool she was. She had dared to hope he was going to say he loved her. But he only wanted to go to bed with her. She flung herself down on the bed, struggling to swallow the wave of sickness that rose in her.

* * *

It had been a week since Lute's call and she could still hear the sound of his voice in the middle of the night. He had humbled himself and begged to see her. She was sure that his pride was wounded when she refused. He wouldn't call her again.

It had been a long, lonesome week. Norris and Marlene were in Clear Lake. April showers were living up to their reputation and had curtailed her long walks with Kelly. She had not been out of the apartment except to take him to the parking lot and to the grassy spot beyond.

After a long warm bath, she put on her gown and robe and sat down to watch *What's My Line?* on the television. She was going into her sixth month of pregnancy, and her swelling stomach tallied with the date. It was nicely rounded, and she patted it with a warm little smile.

The bell on the intercom sounded, startling her. The room was almost dark, and she fumbled for the lamp switch and pulled the drapes before she answered.

"Yes?"

"Mrs. Hanson, someone is here with a message from Mr. Smithfield," the manager said. "Shall I let him come up?"

"Yes, let him come up."

Had Norris and Marlene gotten married? Or had he arranged a surprise for her, knowing how long and boring the week had been? She turned on more lights, suddenly feeling less lonely.

The soft chimes of the doorbell sounded. Making sure her robe was closed, Nelda opened the door and froze, stunned.

Lute stood there!

The collar of his coat was turned up, his bare head and shoulders wet with rain. Nelda noticed this in a mere second before she closed her eyes. She opened them again to see if what she thought she saw was real.

It was. His face looked tired and thin, his eyes quiet and pleading. The last time he had looked at her, they had chilled her with their bitterness. He pushed the door open with one hand. By the time she came out of shock he was inside the room.

She turned and ran through the bedroom and into the bathroom.

"I'm sorry if I surprised you—"

She heard the words before she slammed the door and locked it. Her chin trembled. Why was he here? Had he come about the farm, or . . . had he heard about the baby and come to tell her he would fight her for it—Oh, God, don't let it be that!

Through the roar in her ears she could hear Kelly barking. He was glad to see Lute. Then a knock sounded on the bathroom door.

"Nelda. For God's sake! What's the matter with you? Open the door."

He pounded on the door and Kelly, thinking it was a game, barked in a frenzy of excitement. The manager would hear the commotion and ask her to move.

"Go away. I don't want to see you."

"Open the door. I drove all this way in the rain to see you, and I'm not going until I do."

"Please go. If Kelly keeps barking the manager will be up and ask me to move."

"I'm not going, honey. Not until we talk. I'll try to calm Kelly."

She heard him talking softly to the dog, and they left the bedroom. She waited. All was quiet. Had he left? She had to know and opened the door a crack just as he was coming back into the bedroom. Closing it again, she turned the lock.

"I gave him a small bowl of dry cereal. Come out and talk to me. Give me half an hour, and I'll go."

"We have nothing to say to each other that we haven't said on the phone."

"I think we do. I've got papers for you to sign. Papers concerning the farm."

"Leave them on the bed. I'll sign them and mail them back to Earl."

"I'd like to discuss them with you."

"How did you find me?"

"Smithfield or rather his lady friend told me. She said she hadn't promised not to tell me. It took a good hour on my part to convince her. They think the world of you, Nelda. I was wrong about Smithfield. He's crazy about the woman that was with him. Did you know they are planning to be married?"

Marlene, how could you do this to me? Did you tell him about the baby? Thoughts swirled round and round in her fogged brain.

"Nelda, you're scaring me. You know I'd never hurt you, so why are hiding from me?"

"I don't want to see you. I thought I'd made that clear."

"Why? Come out. You don't have to look at me if I'm so repulsive to you. Come out and sign the papers."

Nelda sat down on the stool and buried her face in her hands. What to do? He wasn't going to leave. She couldn't spend the night in the bathroom. Why hadn't she shut the bedroom door and stayed in there where there was a telephone?

Dammit, she was a prisoner in her own apartment. Damn him anyway. He had no right to do this to her. She would tell him to get the hell out and leave her alone. Before she could reconsider, she got up and flung open the door.

"All right!" she shouted. "Give me the damn papers, and get the hell out of here."

His eyes flicked over her. "My God, Nelda, you're—"

"Pregnant? Yes, it's obvious that I am." Her voice was defiant. "But it has nothing to do with you. Understand that right now."

He closed the gap between them in one long stride, and his hands on her upper arms pulled her toward him. She struggled in his grasp.

"That's why you've been sick . . . lost weight. Oh, honey, I remember how sick you were before—"

"Turn loose of me, you . . . horse's ass!"

"Why didn't you tell me?"

She closed her eyes tightly. "Why should I tell you? It isn't yours. It's a man's . . . from Chicago."

"You're lying," he said tightly.

"No!" She tried to twist away from him. "This is my baby. No part of it is yours."

"Ours!" he contradicted in a hoarse voice. "It's ours. Why are you trying to deny my child his father? Didn't you know that I'd be the happiest man in the world if you had my baby?"

"I knew nothing of the kind! You said just the other night that you never wanted another wife, or another child."

"It's what I thought when you were both taken away from me. You've got to know that I'd want our child."

"The child, but not the useless mother. We're a package deal. I don't want to marry you. I couldn't bear the same situation all over again. We'd be back to square one, with you caught in the same trap with the wrong woman."

"I never considered myself caught in a trap."

"I intend to raise my child alone, surrounded with love, not resentment. We ask nothing of you." She paused, summoning the courage to say the final words. "Please go," she whispered.

His hands dropped from her arms, and she turned her back to him and bowed her head. There was silence behind her. She held her breath, waiting to hear the door open and close.

"Nelda Elaine," he whispered raggedly, "you sweet little fool. Don't you know that you mean more than anything in the world to me and always have?

Why do you think I'm here? I didn't even know about the baby. Your friends were careful to keep that from me. It's you I want so desperately, I'm almost out of my mind."

"I can't believe that. I'm not suited for your kind of life. You told me that the night of the ice storm and several times since. No matter how hard I would try, you would be there just waiting for me to fail, waiting for me to give up. You'll never forgive me for letting my father throw you out after our wedding."

"We're not kids anymore, sweetheart," he said quietly.

"Please go," she whispered again.

"No. I'll not leave you to have our baby alone. You had Becky alone. I never got to see you big with our baby. I didn't even know when my little girl was born. This time it will be different."

He was behind her pulling her back against him. It was his warm hard chest, covered only by a shirt, that she felt. She could feel his lips in her hair.

"We don't have to live on the farm, honey. We'll live wherever you'll be happy. Even Chicago, if that's what you want. I love you so damn much!" There was desperation in his voice. "I can't remember a time when I didn't love you."

"You're just saying that because of the baby. How can you be sure it's yours?" she protested feebly, no longer certain what she was fighting.

He turned her in his arms. She could see the shadow of pain in his eyes. He had lost weight, and his leaner face was more forceful than ever.

"There's not a doubt in my mind that we made this baby the night of the ice storm. I was wild for you and thanked God over and over for the storm that gave me the excuse to be there with you. I'll always consider that one of the most wonderful nights of my life. I held you in my arms all night and you were as eager for me as I was for you."

"But you said—"

"About the stallion and the mare? Lord, I was so scared that you'd leave. It was a dumb thing to say. My only excuse is that I was trying to build up a shield to protect myself."

"It hurt . . . so bad—"

"I'm sorry, sweetheart. I'm sorry. Our baby needs two parents. You and me. I need my mop-head, and I hope you need me."

"I've . . . been so . . . scared." A dam broke inside her, and she began crying uncontrollably. She did need him, desperately, and yet she was frightened of the future.

His arms enfolded her slowly, as if he was afraid she would push him away. She turned her face into his shoulder and leaned against him wearily. His arms tightened and they stood there, pressed together, not speaking, merely drinking in the closeness of each other's bodies. She put her arms around him, her hands feeling his comforting strength. He buried his face in her hair, kissing it, murmuring her name softly.

"I'm so tired," she whispered, still unable to believe that he was here, that he still loved her and wanted her and the baby.

"Sweetheart, I've been through hell and back

these past few months. When you began to look so tired and had big circles under you eyes, I couldn't get it out of my head that you had some dreadful sickness, and I was losing you. I let you get away from me once. It'll never happen again," he told her huskily.

"I couldn't just come to you and say, 'Look, we've done it again.' I knew you'd want to marry me, and I couldn't have lived with knowing that the reason we'd married was because I was pregnant again."

"Silly woman! I want to marry you more than anything in the world. I wanted to before I knew that you were pregnant. I came here to bring you this." He eased her away enough to produce a small box from his pocket.

Then his mouth closed over hers gently and Nelda stopped smiling, but inside her the laughter spread out, dancing through her blood. The kiss was long and sweet and conveyed a meaning far too poignant for mere words. Still holding her in a kiss, he backed up and sat down in a big, easy chair, settled her on his lap, his hands roughly tender. He leaned back, cuddled her against him, and lifted her arm to encircle his neck.

"I love you, Nelda Hanson with an *o*. I've loved it that you've had my name all these years." He looked deeply into her eyes. His own were unexpectedly vulnerable, and they melted her heart.

"Aren't you going to open the box?" he prompted. "It's the wedding ring I didn't have a chance to give you nine years ago," he whispered, his voice deep with emotion.

Through misty eyes she saw nestled in a nest of cotton, the small gold band identical to the one Lute had worn all these years. She took it out of the box and Lute slipped it on her finger.

"When we get married I'll get you an engagement ring and another wedding ring if you want one."

"I don't want an engagement ring or any ring but this one. This is the ring the boy I fell in love with bought for me. He grew up to be a wonderful man."

"We can never replace the years we lost," he said sadly. "When I came home from the Navy, I thought about looking for you just to see what you were doing, but I was afraid that, like your dad, you might be ashamed of what I was . . . a farmer. So I worked my ass off to be the best farmer I could be. Then one day you came back, and my stupid pride made me act the fool."

"I'm proud of you. I wanted you to have Grandpa's farm."

"That reminds me, I've got papers for you to sign." He reached for his jacket and took a thick envelope from the pocket. Keeping her on his lap, he folded back a thick sheaf of papers. "Sign on the bottom where it says Nelda Hanson."

"Why . . . is it made out to Nelda Hanson and Lute Hanson?"

"Because, sweetheart, I knew how you loved that farm and I was not going to take it from you. Lute

Hanson and Nelda Hanson would be equal partners even if you didn't want me as your husband."

"But . . . what's mine is yours . . . now."

"And what's mine is yours. We'll incorporate. Hanson and Hanson Farms. How does that sound?"

"Better than Lute and Meredith Farms."

"There was never any danger of that. I never slept with her regardless of what she told around."

"I might cry again."

"No. Don't do that. The baby might think I'm hurting you. Can I touch him?"

She took his hand and pressed it to her abdomen.

"I want to do this—" he whispered, and moved his hand up under her nightdress and gently stroked the stretched skin of her swollen stomach. "Ah . . . what's that?"

"He's active. The doctor says he's healthy and doing just what he should be at this time."

Lute's smile lit up his face. "Little fella is strong. He's kicking me! Does it hurt?"

"No. It's a wonderful feeling."

"When is he due?"

"Last of July or the first of August." Laughter bubbled up within her, and, putting both arms around his neck, she pressed her parted lips to his. "I never thought that I would be this happy again."

"Me, either, sweetheart. When I saw your dad I wanted to tear him apart for what he did to us. Did I tell you how shocked he was that day when he came to the farm and I told him that my *wife* would be back soon? I couldn't resist, and I was hoping you'd not give me away."

"I'm glad you hit him. I wanted to do it my-self."

"We've got eight years to make up." He ran his fingers through her dark curls to the nape of her neck and gently massaged it.

"Are you staying all night?" she asked boldly.

"Tonight, tomorrow night, and every night for the rest of our lives. I'm taking you home. We'll be married as soon as I can arrange it."

"Do you mind if we stay in Grandma's house for a while?"

"We'll stay wherever you want. If you don't want to live on the farm, we'll live in town."

"You'd do that for me?"

"I'll do anything that will keep you with me."

"I love the farm . . . as inadequate as I am. I want to live there, if you'll put up with me."

"Sweetheart, we'll fix up a studio where you can work on your projects." His hand was massaging her aching spine.

"That feels so good," she murmured.

"Lie down, and I'll rub your back," he whispered in her ear. "I want to do everything I didn't get to do before."

Kelly came and laid his jowls on Nelda's thigh. She patted his head.

"We're going back to the farm, Kelly. You'll be able to run and chase . . . ra . . . bbits. What do you think about that?" Her voice was shaky.

"Arrr-woof—"

∾ *Epilogue* ∾

Thanksgiving 1959

LUTE, HAVING KICKED OFF HIS BOOTS AT THE KITCHEN door, came into the long living room with an armful of wood for the fireplace. After standing it upright in an old copper boiler beside the hearth, he knelt and added several more logs to the fire.

"It's really coming down now. We could be snowed in by morning."

"Will Norris and Marlene be able to get out here?"

"It isn't that bad yet." Lute removed his leather gloves and came to squat down beside the couch where Nelda was nursing their four-month-old son. "Greedy little fella, isn't he?" His eyes were smiling into Nelda's. She reached out and caressed his cheek.

"He's a growing boy and has a big appetite. You're so cold your nose is red." She placed the palm of her hand over his nose. He moved it down to his mouth and kissed it.

"I can smell the turkey. Remember last Thanksgiving?" Lute stood and removed his coat.

"How could I forget? I had morning sickness and the flu all at the same time."

"—And as independent as a hog on ice. You didn't need anyone to take care of you," he teased.

"I loved having you take care of me, but I wasn't going to let you know it. Your head was big enough as it was."

Lute rubbed his hands to warm them and then held them to the fire. He smiled down at his wife and son. He seemed to be always smiling these days.

"Want me to hold Chris while you see about the turkey?"

"Are your hands warm?"

He leered at her. "I know a place where I could get them warm in a hurry."

"I just bet you do!"

He sat down on the couch, put his arm around her, and pulled her and the baby close. His forefinger gently stroked the baby's head. Lute Christopher Hanson, Jr., looked up at his father and smiled, his mouth leaving his mother's nipple momentarily. Nelda shook him gently.

"Get busy, young man. I've got a Thanksgiving dinner to put on the table."

"Sometimes I have to pinch myself to see if I'm dreaming. I really do have you and this little bit of both of us," Lute said with wonderment in his voice. "Lord. This time last year I was so miserable." He hugged her to him and held her with a fierce possession that was tempered by gentleness.

"No more so than I," she said, and returned his kiss.

The first month after they'd remarried, they had lived in Nelda's grandparents' old farmhouse. Then Lute's mother wrote that she had met someone special and had decided to stay in California. She would bring him to Iowa to meet her family after her grandchild was born. Lute was delighted that his mother, widowed for so long, had found someone to share her life.

Lute and Nelda moved into Lute's big house and prepared a room for the baby. They exchanged some of the furniture in Lute's house for some of her grandmother's and converted a large attic room into a studio, where Nelda could work on her fabric designs.

The women in the neighborhood accepted Nelda as if she had been born on the farm and invited her to join both the Lake View Club and the Busy Bees. She declined both invitations until a later time.

When the baby finished nursing, Nelda slipped her breast inside her blouse, but not before Lute bent his head and kissed it.

"No time for monkey business, Mr. Hanson with an *o*," she chided. "I've got things to do before the company gets here. This is my first Thanksgiving in my new home, and it's going to be . . . perfect."

"Come to Daddy, Chris. You're mama is neglecting us. She'd rather fool around with a dumb old turkey than sit here and cuddle with us."

Nelda laughed happily. "You're a spoiled little boy, Lute Hanson. You get plenty of attention."

"Not enough, huh, Chris?" Lute took his son from Nelda's arms, slipped his hand up to the nape of her neck, and pulled her to him. He kissed her gently, then kissed her again as if in desperation. "I never get enough of you. How long will it be until I can keep you in bed all night long?" he said between kisses.

"You had me all night long last night. You're the one who brought Chris to bed with us."

"—And had to share your attention," he pouted.

"Oh, poor you." Her eyes bright with happiness, Nelda headed for the kitchen, confident of his love.

Lute followed and sat down on a stool to watch her. It was pure pleasure just looking at her . . . his mop-head, the sweetheart of his youth, his love, his only love. He had given his heart to her when he was seventeen and she would still hold it in her two hands if he lived to be 110.

Dear Lord, how was it that this small woman could make him feel like this with just her smile and a few soft words? The chilling emptiness that had accompanied him for the past nine years had completely vanished. Right here was what he'd dreamed of having when he was a callow youth working his butt off in the onion fields to earn money to take her to a picture show.

"Marlene called to say Norris wanted to buy Chris an antique rocking horse. She persuaded him that Chris was much too young."

"He's already bought him so much stuff I've had to put some of it in the attic. They take being godparents too seriously. I never thought I'd like the guy, but he's fond of my son, so I guess I can put up with him."

"Come on now. Admit that you like him a lot."

"He's lucky he survived those few months when I thought you were in love with him. I almost broke his neck a time or two."

His blue eyes danced over her face reddened from the heat of the oven. She removed the oven mitts, and came to wrap her arms around his neck. She placed kisses on his face until their son, sandwiched between them, began to wriggle in protest.

"My sweet, darlin', beautiful man, how could you have thought I'd love anyone but you?"

"There's only one way you can convince me," he replied haughtily.

"And I know what that is. I'll give you all the lovin' you can handle tonight," she purred with a wanton little smile, "if you'll lift that twenty-pound turkey you insisted on buying out of the oven for me."

"Hear that, Kelly? This is going to be the longest day of my life." He cupped her chin in the palm of his hand and captured her mouth with his in a deep kiss.

When he heard his name, Kelly lifted his head from his bed in the corner of the kitchen just long enough to say:

"Arrr-woof—" Then he stretched out and went back to sleep.

This is the recipe for the casserole dish Linda made on Christmas Eve. (I do not know the origin of its name.)

TED-A-RENA

(All ingredients can be adjusted to size of family.)

1 pound of lean ground beef
small onion
one-half of a green pepper
   Sauté onion and green pepper in butter, add ground beef, and cook until brown and crumbly.

Parboil for a few minutes the following:
1½ cups cubed raw potatoes
1 cup sliced carrots
1 cup broken uncooked spaghetti
   Drain and add to meat mixture.
Add a cup of shredded cheddar cheese.
1 can of cream of chicken soup—with a can of milk.
Salt and pepper to taste.
Sprinkle top with shredded cheese.
Bake 45 minutes in 350⁰ oven.

Dear Reader Friends,

For a long time, I've wanted to set a romantic novel in Clear Lake, Iowa in the 1950's, the time when my husband and I came here to make it our home. I had also wanted to memorialize, in my own way, the tragic event that is now called "the day music died," when Buddy Holly, Richie Valens, J.P. Richardson, and their pilot Roger Peterson died in a crash north of town on February 3, 1959. That is how this story of love and forgiveness, MORE THAN MEMORY, came to be. I hope you've enjoyed reading it. I intend it to be a single book which will have no sequels or prequels, unlike my series set in the Great Depression and its follow-up book, AFTER THE PARADE.

As you can see, if you turn the page to the excerpt that follows, I am starting another series, which begins with the novel, THE EDGE OF TOWN. It will chronicle the adventures of the Jones family in the 1920's, a dynamic time, when America began to come into its own. It will be published in hardcover in April 2001. I hope you will look for it then.

As always, I very much appreciate hearing from you and will answer your letters as time permits.

Dorothy Garlock

Clear Lake, Iowa

More
Dorothy Garlock!

Please turn this page
for a
bonus excerpt from

The Edge of Town

available from Warner Books
in hardcover in
April 2001

Fertile, Missouri
August 1922

"Lillian Russell's dead!" Jill made the dramatic announcement and waited for her sister to comment. When Julie continued to wash the dishes and drop them in the rinse pan, she said, "All the wonderful women in the world are dying. First Nellie Bly and now Lillian."

"Where did you hear that?"

"Ricky May told me last night. Lillian was so beautiful, so elegant. All the men loved her." Jill lifted her arms in a circling motion. "I'm going to be just like her."

"You'll have to grow some," Julie said dryly. "She had quite a bosom. They were out to here." Julie held her cupped, wet hands out six inches from her slender body.

"And a tiny waist."

"Helped by a tight corset."

"She was beautiful——"

"——And old enough to be your grandma. Dry the dishes while you're grieving for her."

Jill took a plate from the hot rinse water, dried it, and set it on the table.

"The men who gave her diamonds must have liked a woman with a big bust. Diamonds show up best lying on soft white flesh."

"Soft white flesh? Glory be! Well don't worry about it. You've got a good start for a fourteen-year-old." Julie slid a greasy skillet into the sudsy water.

"Jack said they were like half oranges stuck up there."

Julie looked at her sister and frowned. "Why would Jack be making a remark about his sister's breasts?"

"I asked him."

"Justine Jill Jones!"

Jill rolled her eyes on hearing her full name. "I hate it when you call me that."

"It's the name Mama gave you."

"I'll never know why she added Justine to it."

"She didn't. She added Jill."

"Kids at school laugh about our names. They say if Mama'd had more kids, she'd probably have named them Jericho and Jerusalem."

"And what did you say to that?"

"Nothing. Ricky May Jacobs said she should've named two of us Jenny and Jackass." Jill giggled.

Julie's shoulders shook with silent laughter. That all their names started with a J didn't bother her. She rather liked it.

"I never asked Jack about my bosom," Jill said after she placed a stack of clean plates on the shelf. "I asked him if the boys at school thought I was pretty."

"And what did he say?"

"He said . . . oh, he was so mean!" Jill flipped her long blond curls over her shoulder and tilted her freckled nose. "He said only the dumb ones thought I was pretty. He said my hair was like straw, my nose was so turned up he was surprised I didn't drown when it rained."

Julie laughed in spite of the serious look on her sister's face.

"Never ask your brothers if you're pretty. If you were a raving beauty, they'd not admit it."

"That's when he said my breasts were the size of half an orange."

"It's a pact made between brothers to tell their sisters that they are ugly as a mud fence even if they are as pretty as Mary Pickford."

"I hate brothers!"

"Mable Normand is pretty."

"She's in *Molly* O at the Palace. I want to see it, but Papa said picture shows cost almost as much as a pair of stockings, and I need stockings more." Jill sighed heavily.

"Julie, Julie, guess what?" Ten-year-old Jason always shouted if he was excited and even at times when he wasn't excited.

Since their mother's death four years earlier, Julie was the person her brothers and sisters came to with news, hurts, and needs.

Jason stumbled onto the back porch, yanked open the screen door, and bounded into the kitchen, shutting the door just in time to keep the shaggy brown dog, his constant companion, from following him. Besides being small for his age, Jason had been born with a deformed foot that made it necessary for him to wear a special shoe.

"Julie, guess what?" He was breathless.

"Well, let me think a minute. Oh, yes, I know! Bananas are growing out of the old stump out by the woodpile."

"Ah, Julie, you're so silly sometimes." Jason stood as tall as his slight frame allowed. His muddy shoes were firmly planted on the clean kitchen floor.

"Look at his shoes!" Jill sneered with sisterly disgust.

"Shut up." Jason turned on his sister. "Open your trap again, and I won't tell ya!"

"What's your news, Jason?" Julie poured water from the teakettle over the dishes in the pan.

"Joe . . . said that we're havin' a baseball game tonight. Both Birch families, the Humphreys, and the Taylors. Maybe the Jacobs and Evan Johnson. He helped the Humphreys today."

"Who cares about *him*?" Jill snorted.

Jason knew he would get the full attention of his younger sister when he mentioned the Taylors. She had been eyeing both Roy and Thad Taylor, who were a grade ahead of her in school.

"Joe told me to get out the stuffed bags we use for bases. I hope mice ain't chewed 'em up."

"Haven't," Julie corrected. Then, "When was this decided?" She stopped working on the greasy skillet to give her full attention to her brother.

"I dunno. They'll be done hayin' by midafternoon. Pa said to tell ya they'd noon at the Humphreys."

"Then I'll go to town this afternoon. We'll have a cold supper."

Julie put the kitchen in order. As she hung her apron on the back of a chair, Jill, with the youngest Jones child, Joy, in tow, came through the kitchen on the way to the front porch. Julie went upstairs to the room she shared with her sisters and changed out of her dress and into a white blouse with a drawstring neckline and a blue skirt. Julie knew herself for what she was: a strong, slim woman with clear skin and a wide mouth, and the responsibility of raising her siblings weighing heavily on her shoulders.

With a wide-brimmed straw hat set squarely on her head to shade her face as much as possible, she picked up the cloth bag she would use to carry home the few things she planned to buy at the store.

By the time Julie crossed the railroad tracks and headed back up the hill toward home, there were rings of perspiration under her arms, her forehead was beaded with sweat. She enjoyed her forays into town but was always glad to get back to the sanctuary of the farm. Each and every time she came to town she grew more certain that she would never want to live there.

She trudged up the hill, shifting the carrying bag from one arm to the other. The two books she had selected at the library for Jill were heavy. Deep in thought, deciding what she was going to give the family for supper, she was unaware of the wagon coming up behind her until it was just a few feet away. She moved over to the side of the road and glanced back over her shoulder. Panic crept up her spine, throbbed in her temples, choked off her breath. She was deathly afraid of the man on the wagon.

She had a right to be.

Walter Johnson was big, whiskered, and wore a straw hat smashed down on a head of gray-streaked hair. He spat a yellow stream of chewing tobacco out onto the dirt road. Julie choked down the panic that clogged her throat as he pulled the wagon up alongside her and stopped the team.

"Wal, looky thar!" He laughed as she continued to walk and passed the team. "If'n it ain't Miss Prissy-tail Jones. I ain't seen you for a right long spell." He walked the horses until he was even with her. "Climb on up here, and I'll give ya a ride home."

Julie tried to ignore him. There wasn't a house or a person in sight. Her heart pounded with fear. The man moved the team so that the wagon forced her to walk in the grass that edged the road.

"Seen ya in town a-switchin' that purty little ass around. Ya wearin' any drawers, gal? Be handier if ya ain't." He chuckled low in his throat. It was more like an animal growl that came from him. "Come on up here now. After a swig or two from my bottle, ya'll be more'n willin' fer me to plow ya deep and hard. Ya'll be beggin' for it." He rubbed his maleness with the palm of his hand and snickered.

Julie felt her face grow hot with humiliation and anger. Determined to defend herself, she switched the cloth bag to her right hand and prepared to swing it at him if he got down off the wagon.

"Ain't no need ya bein' so snooty. It ain't like ya ain't never had a man." He leered at her and lifted his brows. A short guffaw of laughter came from him.

Julie was so frightened she could hardly comprehend the man's hateful words. She feared he would force her off the road and into the woods ahead. She glanced behind her to see if anyone was coming. There was not a soul in sight!

Julie spun around and ran as fast as she could back toward town. She wasn't going near that woods as long as she was on her feet.

"It'll be you . . . or that gimpy kid. I ain't a bit choosy when it comes to gettin' my rocks off. Come back here, ya split-tailed bitch!" he yelled.

What does he mean? Oh, Lord. He means Jason!

She heard a yell and looked back, fearfully thinking he was coming after her. A rider on a buckskin horse had come out of the woods and was racing down the road toward the wagon. He reached it, whirled his horse, and lashed the team with the ends of his reins.

"You rotten son of a bitch! Get the hell away from her!"

Evan Johnson lashed the team again, and they shot off up the road. Walter Johnson was bouncing on the seat, roaring with rage and trying to hold the frantic mules.

Tears of relief rolled from Julie's eyes and down her cheeks. She hadn't realized how frightened she was. She stood in the middle of the dusty road and dug into her bag for a handkerchief to wipe her eyes. The square of cloth still had eluded her searching fingers when Evan Johnson rode up beside her.

"Did he hurt you?"

She shook her head and brought the handkerchief up to wipe her eyes. She turned her face away to keep him from seeing the tears and peered anxiously up the road to be sure her tormentor was gone.

"I'm sorry, Miss Jones. I'm real sorry."

Evan was a big man. He was tremendously tall and his eyes, shadowed with concern, were studying her with intensity.

How could this man possibly be the son of such a despicable character as Walter Johnson?

To read more, look for *The Edge of Town*.